Mary Gentle was born in ~~~~~~~~~~
Hawk in Silver, published ~~~~~~~~
worked in the civil service ~~~~~~~~~
and cleaner before going to ~~~~~~~~~
In 1985 she was awarded a first-class degree ~~~~~~~~~
and Politics and, in 1988, an MA with distinction in
English and History. She is also the highly acclaimed
author of *Golden Witchbreed*, *Ancient Light* and *Scholars
and Soldiers*. Her new novel, *The Architecture of Desire*, is
available in hardcover from Bantam Press.

Praise for RATS AND GARGOYLES:

'I was surprised not by Mary Gentle's talent – she has
always had that – but by the extraordinary individuality
of her vision . . . I'd cheerfully guarantee that it will bring
a sense of the marvellous back into the lives of the jaded
readers – while the unjaded had better prepare themselves
for something pretty special. From her wonderful opening
scene – surely one of the best ever done – Gentle draws
you into a bizarre and yet oddly familiar world of strange
reversals and unlimited surprises, paradoxes, puzzles, a
world dominated by the logic of alchemy, where a God
may live just around the next corner. Once you've entered
"the heart of the world" you will never, never want to
leave . . . ' —**Michael Moorcock**

'Her achievement is to take the reader to a time and place
where anything can happen – and often does' —*Today*

RATS AND GARGOYLES

Mary Gentle

CORGI BOOKS

RATS AND GARGOYLES
A CORGI BOOK 0 552 13627 1

Originally published in Great Britain by Bantam Press,
a division of Transworld Publishers Ltd

PRINTING HISTORY
Bantam Press edition published 1990
Corgi edition published 1991

This book is set in 10/11pt Plantin by
Chippendale Type Ltd., Otley, West Yorkshire.

Corgi Books are published by Transworld Publishers Ltd.,
61–63 Uxbridge Road, Ealing, London W5 5SA, in Australia by
Transworld Publishers (Australia) Pty. Ltd., 15–23 Helles Avenue,
Moorebank, NSW 2170, and in New Zealand by Transworld
Publishers (N.Z.) Ltd., Cnr. Moselle and Waipareira Avenues,
Henderson, Auckland.

Made and printed in Great Britain by
Cox & Wyman Ltd., Reading, Berks.

This book is dedicated to
G. K. CHESTERTON
and
JAMES BRANCH CABELL

Acknowledgements

I owe a debt to those investigators who have treated Renaissance Hermetic *magia* as a field for serious scholarly research. The fact that I have treated it as one vast adventure-playground is not intended to detract from this.

Those who helped include Goldsmiths' College, University of London; the albums *I'm Your Man* by Leonard Cohen and *Famous Blue Raincoat* by Jennifer Warnes; *Watkins Books* in Cecil Court; Rouen; and Alexandre Dumas. I also owe a debt to Sarah Watson for reading the manuscript, and for letting me read her (unpublished) 'The Jaguar King'.

1

In the raucous Cathedral Square the crowd prepared
to hang a pig.

A young man slowed his pace, staring.

The yellow wood of the gallows wept sap; hastily nailed
together; the scent of pine reached him. Stronger: the
stench of animal dung. Lucas reached for a kerchief to
wipe his sweating face. Finding none, he distastefully
used a corner of his sleeve. He thrust a way between the
spectators, head ringing with their noise.

A man and a woman stood up on the platform. Between
them, a great white sow snuffled, wrapped in a scarlet robe
that her split feet fouled, jaws frothing. She shook her
snout and head, troubled by the loose hemp rope around
her neck. It went up white against the sky, to the knot on
the gallows-tree.

Sun burned the moisture from the flagstones, leaving
dust that took the imprint of the young man's booted
feet. The steps and entrances and columns of the cathedral
towered over the square: a filigree of brown granite against
a blazing early sky; carved leaves and round towers still wet
with the night's dew.

'This beast has been duly tried in a court of law.' The
priest's voice carried from the platform to the small crowd.
'This she-pig belongs to Messire de Castries of Banning
Lane, and has been found guilty of infanticide, most
filthily and bestially consuming the child of the said
Messire de Castries' daughter. Sentence is passed. The
animal must be hanged, according to the law and justice.
Do your duty!'

The priest lumbered down the rickety steps from the

gallows-platform, her leaf-embroidered robe tangling at her ankles. She elbowed Lucas aside just as he realized he should move, and he bristled despite himself.

The man remaining on the platform knelt down beside the sow. Lucas heard him say: 'Forgive me that I am your executioner.'

'Hang the monster!' One fat woman in a velvet dress screeched beside his ear, and Lucas winced; a tall weather-beaten man cupped his hands and shouted through them: 'Child-killer!'

The executioner stood up and kicked back the bolt holding up the trap.

The trapdoor banged down, gunshot-loud. The sow plunged, a *crack!* cut off the squealing, screeching – the groan of stretched rope sang in the air. In the silence, Lucas heard bone splintering. The sow's legs kicked once, all four feet splayed. The scarlet robe ('I' for *infanticide* stitched roughly into the back) rode up as she struggled, baring rows of flopping dugs.

'Baby-killer!'

'May your soul rot!'

Lucas wrenched his way free of their rejoicing. He strode across the square, dizzy, sweating. The ammoniac stink of pig dung followed him. He stopped where a public fountain and basin stood against the cathedral wall, tugging at the buttons of his high collar, pulling his jacket open at the neck. Sweat slicked his skin. He bent and scooped a double handful of water to splash his face, uncertain at the novelty of it. Burning cold water soaked his hair, his neck; he shook it away.

Then he leaned both hands on the brown granite, head down. Sun burned the back of his neck. The water, feather-stirred by the fountain's trickle, mirrored a face up at him: half-man and half-boy, against a blue sky. Springy black hair, expensively cropped; eyes deep-set under meeting brows. For all that his skin was tanned, it was not the chapped skin of an apprentice.

He shifted his padded black jacket that strained across

his muscled shoulders; moved to go – and stopped.

The moon gleamed in the early morning sky. He saw it clearly reflected beside his face, bone-white; seas the same pale blue as the sky.

Across the moon's reflected face, a line of blood appeared, thin as a cat's scratch. Another scraped across it, curved; dotted and scored a third bloody weal across the almost-globe. A symbol, glistening red.

He spun round and jerked his head up to look at the western sky. The moon hung there, sinking over the city's roofs. Pale as powder, flour-dust white. No unknown symbols . . .

A pink flush suffused the gibbous moon, now almost at its full; and the seas flooded a rich crimson.

He turned, grabbed the edges of the basin, staring at the clear water. The reflected moon bore a different symbol now. As he watched, that faded, and a third set of blood-lines curved across that pitted surface.

Men and women passed him, dispersing now that the pig's execution was done. He searched their faces frantically for some sign they saw his bloody moon; they – in spruce city livery, open to the heat – talked one with another and didn't glance above the rooftops.

When he looked back, and again to the sky, the moon was clean.

''Prentice, where's your workshop?'

The man had obviously asked twice. Lucas came to himself and, seeing the man wearing the silk overalls of a carpenter, assumed the extreme politeness of one unfamiliar with such people.

'I have no workshop, messire,' he said. 'I'm a student, and new to your city. Can you tell me, please, where I might find the University of Crime?'

Not far away, a gashed palm bleeds. The hand is cupped. Blood collects, trickles away into life-line and heart-line and between fingers, but enough pools to be used.

The moon's face is reflected into a circular mirror, twelve hand-spans in width. This mirror, set on a spindle and in a half-hoop wooden frame, can be turned to face the room's ceiling, or its east, or (as now) its west window.

Through the open window comes the scent of dust, heat, fur, and boiled cabbage. Through the open window comes in the last fading image of the morning moon.

With the tip of a white bird's feather, dipped into the blood, she draws with rapid calligraphic strokes. She draws on the mirror glass: on the reflected image of the moon's sea-spotted face.

She draws, urgently, a message that will be understood by those others who watch the moon with knowledge.

White sun fell into the great court, on to sandstone walls as brown as old wax. Sweeping staircases went up at cater-corners of the yard to the university's interior, and Lucas thought of eyes behind the glazed, sharply pointed windows, and straightened. He stood with two dozen other cadets under the sun that would, by noon, be killing, and now was a test of endurance.

'*My* name', said the bearded man pacing slowly along the lines of young men and women, 'is *Candia.*'

He spoke normally, but his voice carried to bounce off the sandstone masonry walls. His hair was ragged blond, tied back with a strip of scarlet cloth; he wore boots and loose buff-coloured breeches, and a jerkin slashed with scarlet. Lucas put him at thirty; upped the estimate when the man passed him.

'Candia,' the man repeated. Under the lank hair, his face was pale and his eyes dark; he had an air of permanent injured surprise. 'I'm one of your tutors. You've each been invited to attend the University of Crime; I don't expect you to be stupid. Since you've been in the university buildings for an hour, I don't expect any one of you to have purses left.'

Candia paused, then pointed at three cadets in rapid succession. 'You, you and *you* – fall out. You've just told a pickpocket where you keep your purse.'

Lucas blinked.

'Right.' The man put his fists on his hips. 'How many of you now don't know whether you have your purses or not? Tell the truth . . . Right. You four go and stand with them. *You*—'

He pointed back without looking; Lucas found himself targeted.

'– Lucas.' Candia turned. 'You've got your purse? And you know that without feeling for it, and giving it away, like these sad cases? Tell me how.'

Surprised at how naturally he could answer the impertinent question, Lucas said: 'Muscle-tension. It's on a calf-strap.'

'Good. Good.' The blond man paused a calculated moment, and added: 'As long as, now, you change it.'

He barely waited for the ripple of laughter; flicked his head so that hair and rag-band flopped back, and spoke to them all.

'You'll learn how to take a purse from a calf-strap so that the owner *doesn't* know it's gone missing. You'll learn about marked cards, barred cater-trey dice, the mirror-trick, and the several ways of stopping someone without quite killing them.'

Candia's gaze travelled along the rows of faces. 'You'll learn to conjure with coins – get them, breed them, lend them out and steal them back. There are no rules in the university. If you have anything still your own at the end of the first term, then well done. *I* didn't.'

He allowed himself a brief, tailored grin; most of the cadets grinned back.

'You'll learn about scaling walls and breaking windows, about tunnels and fire-powder, and when to bribe a magistrate and when to stage a last-minute gallows-step confession. *If you live to learn, you'll learn it.* Now . . .'

Heat shimmered the air over the flagstones. Lucas felt it beat up on his cheeks, dazzle his water-rimmed eyes. His new cotton shirt was rubbing his neck raw, and when the shadow crossed him he was conscious only of relief. He glanced up casually.

13

The blond man raised his head. Then he took his hands from his hips, and went down on one knee on the hot stone, his head still raised.

Lucas gazed upwards into the dazzling sky.

He glimpsed the lichen-covered brick chimneys, wondered why a bole of black ivy was allowed to twine around one stack, followed it up as it thickened – no, it should grow thicker *downwards*, towards the root – and then saw the clawed feet gripping the chimney's cope, where that tail joined a body.

The sky ran like water, curdling a yellowish brown. Lucas felt flagstones crack against his knees as he fell forward, and a coldness that was somehow thick began to force its way down his throat. He gagged. The air rustled with dryness, potent and electric as the swarming of locusts.

Wings cracked like ship's sails, leathery brown against the shadowed noon.

It clung to the brickwork, bristle-tail wrapped firmly round the chimney-stack, wings half-unfolded and flicked out for balance. The great haunches rose up to its shoulders as it crouched, and it brought the peaks of great ribbed wings together at its flaking breast, and Lucas saw that the bat-wings had fingers and thumb at their central joint.

All this was in a split second, reconstructed in later memory. Lucas clung to the other cadets, they to him, no shame amongst them: each of them having looked up once into the great scaled and toothed face of the daemon poised above them.

A fair-haired girl of no more than fifteen stood up from the group. She began to walk towards the iron gates. Candia's gaze flicked from her to the roof-tops; when he saw no movement there, he relaxed. The girl paused, turned her thin face up to the sky and, as if she saw something in the gargoyle-face, slipped out of the side-gate and ran off into the city streets. Her footsteps echoed in the quiet.

The sky curdled.

That same gagging chill silenced Lucas's voice. He coughed, spat; and then the heat of the sun took him like a slap. He winced with the feeling that something too vast had just passed above him.

The blond man rose to his feet, dusting the knees of his buff breeches.

'Why did you let her go?' Lucas demanded.

Candia's chin went up. He looked down his nose at Lucas. 'She was commanded. The city proverb is: *We have strange masters*.'

His gaze lingered on the gate. Then, with a final flick at buff-coloured cloth, Candia said: 'You'll all attend lectures, you'll attend seminars; most of all you'll attend the practical classes. Punishments for absence vary from stocks to whipping. We're not here to waste your time. Don't waste mine.'

Lucas rubbed his bare arms, shuddering despite the morning heat.

'First class is at matins. That's now, so *move* . . . You four,' the blond man said, as an afterthought. 'Garin, Sophonisba, Rafi and Lucas. Accommodation can't fit you in. Here's addresses for lodgings.'

Lucas paused over his slip of paper. The other three cadets wandered away slowly, comparing notes.

As Candia was about to go, Lucas said amiably: 'I don't care to live out of the university. Fetch the Proctor.'

Candia shot a glance over Lucas's shoulder, Lucas turned his head, and the man cuffed him hard enough across the face to send him cannoning into the sandstone wall.

'You address tutors as "Reverend Master",' the man said loudly, bent to grab his arm and pull him up; winked at Lucas, and added: 'Do you want everyone to know who you are?'

Lucas watched him walk away, the cat-spring step of the man; opened his mouth to call – and thought better of it. He read the printed slip of paper:

Mstrss Evelian by the signe of the Clock vpon Carver

streete neare Clocke-mill. Students warned, never to leave the Nineteenth District between the University and the Cathedral. And then, after the print, in a scrawling hand: *Unless commanded by those greater than they.*

Candia pushed the cathedral door open and moved rapidly inside, shutting the heavy wood smoothly behind him. He stopped to quieten his breathing, and to adjust to the dimness. Light the colour of honey and new leaves fell on to the smooth flagstones, from the green-and-gold stained-glass windows.

The blond man's nostrils flared at the incense-smell: musky as leaf-mould and fungus. He padded slowly down between the pillars towards the altar, and his boots, practised, made no sound. He saw no-one in all that towering interior space. The pillars that were carved of a silver-grey stone to resemble tall beeches concealed no novices.

Once he froze, reached out to a pillar to catch his balance and remain utterly still. The stone was carved into a semblance of roots, with here and there a carved beetle or caterpillar, as above where the carved branches met together there were stone birds. The sound (if there had been a sound) was not repeated.

Coming to the altar, Candia settled one hip up on it, resting against the great polished and swirl-veined block of oak. He listened. Then he drew out his dagger, and began to clean casually and delicately under his fingernails.

He swore; stuck his finger in his mouth and sucked it.

'Master Candia?'

A man stood up in the shadow of a pillar. White hair caught a dapple of green-gold light. He dropped a scrubbing-brush back into a galvanized-iron bucket; the noise echoed through all the cathedral's arches.

Candia straightened up off the altar. 'My lord Bishop,' he acknowledged.

The Bishop of the Trees came forward, wringing water from one sleeve of his robe. The robe was full-length, dark green, embroidered with a golden tree whose roots circled

16

the hem and whose branches reached out along each arm. The embroidery showed threadbare; the cloth much worn and darned.

'The most recent intake – is there *anyone*?' He paused to touch the wooden altar with thin strong fingers, mutter a word.

'No. No-one. Four from Nineteenth District, nine from docklands and the factories; the rest from Third, Eighth and Thirty-First Districts. Three princes from the eastern continent incognito – two of whom have the nerve to assume I won't know that.'

'None disguised? Scholar-Soldiers travel disguised; one might be waiting to test you.'

Now Candia laughed. 'One of the acolytes came and took a girl. Just an acolyte terrified *all* of them. No, there's no Scholar-Soldier amongst them.'

'And this was our last hope of it. We can't wait for the Invisible College's help indefinitely.'

White hair curled down over the Bishop's collar. Seven decades left his face not so much lined as creased, folds of skin running from his beaked nose to the corners of his mouth. His eyes were clear as a younger man's, grey and mobile, catching the cathedral's dim light.

'Are you willing to risk waiting now, young Candia, with no assurance our messages have even reached them?'

Candia glanced at the washed flagstones (where the traces of scrawled graffiti were visible despite the Bishop's work) and then back at the man. 'So events force us.'

'To go to The Spagyrus.'

'Yes. I think we must.' Candia put the knife back into its sheath at his belt, fumbling it. He drew a breath, looked at his shaking hands, half-smiled. 'Go before me and I'll join you – if the faculty see me with a Tree-priest, that's my lectureship lost.'

He followed the Bishop back down the central aisle, through green light and stone. Dust drifted. The man picked up a broad-brimmed hat from a pew. Then he opened the great arched doors to the noon sun, which had been triple-locked before Candia chose to pass through.

'You and your students', he said, 'make a deal too free with us—'

'I send them here, Theo. It's good practice.'

'I was a fool ever to advise you to apprentice yourself to that place!'

'So my family say to this day.'

The Bishop snorted. He wiped a lock of white hair back with the sleeve of his robe, and clapped the hat onto his head. 'I had word from the Night Council.'

'And there was a waste of words and breath!'

'Oh, truly; but what would you?' The Bishop shrugged.

Candia smelt the dank cellar-smell of the cathedral's incense, all the fine hairs on his neck hackling. He shook himself, scratched, and moved to stand where he would not be visible when the door opened.

'You take underground ways. I'll follow above. We're late, if we're to get there by noon.'

Lucas put the address-slip in his pocket and strode across the yard, the side of his cuffed face burning.

A last student waited, leaning up against the flaking iron gate, hands thrust deep into the pockets of a brown greatcoat two sizes too large, and too heavy for the heat.

Either a young man or a young woman: the student had straight black hair falling to the coat's upturned collar and flopping into dark eyes. A Katayan, the student's thin wiry tail curved under the flap of the brown coat, tufted tip sketching circles in the dust.

'I can take you to Carver Street.' The voice was light and sharp.

'And take my purse on the way?' Lucas came up to the gate.

The student shifted herself upright with a push of one shoulder, and the coat fell open to show a bony young woman's body in a black dress. Patches of sweat darkened the underarms. Her thin fine-furred tail was mostly black, but dappled with white. Her feet were bare.

18

'I lodge there, too. By Clock-mill. The woman in charge – um.' The young woman kissed the tip of a dirty finger and sketched on the air. 'Beautiful! Forty if she's a day. Those little wrinkles at the corners of her eyes?'

The smell of boiled cabbage and newly laundered cloth permeated the narrow street; voices through open windows sounded from midday meals. Lucas fell into step beside the young woman. She had an erratic loping stride. He judged her seventeen or eighteen; a year or so younger than his calendar age.

'That's Mistress Evelian?'

'I've been there a week and I'm in *love*.' She kept her hands in her pockets as she walked, and threw her head back as she laughed, short fine hair flopping about her ears.

'And you're a student?'

At that she stopped, swung round, head cocked a little to one side as she looked him up and down.

'No, you don't. I'm not to be *collected* – not a specimen. You take your superior amusement and shove it up your anus sideways!'

'Watch who you're speaking to!' Lucas snarled.

'Now, that's a question: who *am* I speaking to?'

Lucas shrugged. 'You heard the Reverend Master read the roll. Lucas is the name.'

'Yes, and I heard him afterwards.'

'That's my business—'

'This is a short-cut,' the student said. She dived down a narrow passage, between high stone houses. Lucas put one boot in the kennel's filth as he followed. He called ahead. Her coat and tail were just visible, whipping round the far corner of the alley.

The light voice came back: 'Down here!'

As Lucas left the alley she stopped, halfway over a low brick wall, to beckon him, and then slid down the far side. Lucas heard her grunt. He leaned his arms on the wall. The young woman was sitting in the dust, legs sprawled, coat spread around her, wiry tail twitching.

'Damn coat.' She stood up, beating at the dust. 'It's the only thing that makes this filthy climate bearable, but it gets in my *way!*'

'You're cold?'

'Where I come from, this is midwinter.' She offered him her hand to shake, across the wall. 'Zar-bettu-zekigal, of South Katay. No-one here seems to manage a civilized language. I'll consent to Zaribet; not *Zari*. That's vomitable.'

Lucas grinned evilly. 'Honoured, Zari.'

Zar-bettu-zekigal gave a huff of exasperation that sent her fine hair flying. She crossed the small yard to a building and pushed open a studded iron door. It was cold inside, and dank. Wide steps wound down, illuminated by brass lamps. The gas-jets hissed in yellow glass casings, giving a warm light.

The side-walls were packed with bones.

Niches and galleries had been left in the masonry – and cut into natural stone, Lucas saw as they descended. The gas-jet light shone on walls spidered white with nitre, and on black-brown bones packed in close together: thigh and femur and rib-bones woven into a mass, and skulls set solidly into the gaps. Shadows danced in the ragged circles of their eyes.

When the steps opened out into a vast low-vaulted gallery, Lucas saw that all the walls were stacked with human bones; each partition wall had its own brick-built niche. The gas-lights hissed in the silence.

'Takes us under Nineteenth District's Aust quarter. Too far, going round.' Zar-bettu-zekigal's voice rang, no quieter than before. The tuft of her black tail whisked at her bare ankles. She pushed the fine hair out of her eyes. 'I like it here.'

Lucas reached out and brushed her black hair. It felt surprisingly coarse under his fingers. His knuckles rubbed her cheek, close to her long fine lashes. Her skin was warmly white. Practised, he let his hand slide along her jaw-line to cup the back of her neck and tilt her head up; his other hand slid into her coat and cupped one of her small breasts.

She linked both hands over his wrist, so that she was resting her chin on her hands and looking up at him. One side of her mouth quirked up. 'What I like, *you* haven't got.'

Lucas stood back, and ruffled the young woman's hair as if she had been a child. 'Really?'

'Really.' Her solemnity danced.

'This really *is* a short-cut?'

'Oh, *right*.' She stepped back, hands in pockets again, swirling the coat round herself, breath misting the cold air. 'Oh, right. You're a king's son. Used to stable-girls and servants; poor tykes!'

Lucas opened his mouth to put her in her place, remembered his chosen anonymity, and then jumped as the black-tipped tail curved up to tap his bare arm.

'I recognize it,' Zar-bettu-zekigal said ruefully. 'I'm a king's daughter. The King of South Katay. Last time we were counted, there were nine hundred and seventy-three of us. Mother is Autumn Wife Eighty-One. I don't believe I've ever seen Father close to. They sent me here', she added, 'to train as a Kings' Memory.'

Lucas took her chin between his thumb and finger, tipping her face up to his, and his facetious remark was never spoken, seeing those brown eyes turned sepia with an intensity of concentration. He took his hand away quickly.

'Damn,' Lucas said, ears burning, 'damn, so you are; you are a Memory. We brought one in, once, for the Great Treaty. Damn. Honour and respect to you, lady.'

'Ah, will you look at him! He's pissing his britches at the very thought. Do you wonder why I don't shout about it—?'

Her ringing voice cut off; the silence startled Lucas. Zar-bettu-zekigal's eyes widened.

Lucas, turning, saw a cloaked figure at one of the

21

wall-niches, and a beast's hand halted midway in reaching to pick up a femur.

Zar-bettu-zekigal's last words echoed, breaking the stranger's concentration. A hood was pushed back from a sharp black-furred muzzle. Gleaming black eyes summed up the young man and woman, and one of the delicate ears twitched.

The Rat was lean-bodied and sleek, standing taller than Lucas by several inches. He wore a plain sword-belt and rapier, and his free hand (bony, clawed; longer-fingered than a human's) rested on the hilt. In the other hand he carried a small sack.

'What are you doing here?' he demanded.

Steam and bitter coal-dust fouled the air. The slatted wooden floor of the carriage let in the chill as well as the stink, city air cold at this depth; and the Bishop of the Trees gathered the taste on his tongue and spat.

Spittle shot between his booted feet, hit the tunnel-floor that dazzled under the carriage's passing brilliance.

The wooden seat was hard, polished by years of use, and he slipped from side to side as the carriage jolted, rocking uphill after the engine, straining at the incline. The Bishop of the Trees stared out through the window. Up ahead, light from another carriage danced in the vaulted tunnel. Coal-sparks spat.

The window-glass shone black with the darkness of the tunnel beyond it; and silver-paint graffiti curlicued across the surface. Theodoret's gaze was sardonic, unsacramental.

A handful of young men banged their feet on the benches at the far end of the carriage. The Bishop of the Trees caught one youth's gaze. He heard another of them yell.

First two, then all of them clattered down the length of the empty carriage.

'Ahhh . . .' A long exhale of disgust. A short-haired boy in expensive linen overalls, the carpenters' Rule

22

embroidered in gold thread on the front. He grinned. Over his shoulder, to a boy enough like him to be his brother, he said: 'It's only a Tree-priest. Ei, priest, cleaned up the shit in your place yet?'

'No, fuck, won't do him no good,' the other boy put in. 'The other guilds'll come calling, do more of the same.'

Theodoret loosened the buckle of his thick leather belt, prepared to slide it free and whip the metal across the boy's hands; but neither youth drew their belt-knives – they just leaned heavily over the back of his seat to either side of him.

'Ei, you learned yet?'

'Tear your fuckin' place down round you!'

'*Tear it down!*' Spittle flew from the lips of the short-haired boy, spotting his silk overalls. 'You didn't build it. Fuck, when did any of you parasite Tree-priests *build*? You too good to work for our masters!'

'You make our quarter look *sick*,' a brown-skinned boy said. The last of the four, a gangling youth in overalls and silk shirt, grinned aimlessly, and hacked his heel against the wooden slats. The rocking car sent him flying against the dark boy; both sparred and collapsed in raucous laughter.

'Fuck, don't bother him. Ei! He's *praying*!'

The Bishop of the Trees looked steadily past each of the youths, focusing on a spot some indeterminate space away. Anger flicked him. Theodoret stretched hand and fingers in an automatic sign of the Branches.

'If you knew', he said, 'what I pray for—'

He tensed, having broken the cardinal rule, having admitted his existence; but the gangling youth laughed, with a hollow hooting that made the other three stagger.

'Aw, say you, he's not worth bothering – fuck, we're *here*, aren't we?'

The four of them scrambled for the carriage-door, shoving, deliberately blocking each other; the youngest and the gangling one leaping between the slowing car and the platform. The door slammed closed in Theodoret's face. He opened it and stepped down after them on to the cobbled platform.

He grunted, head down, bullish. Briefly, he centered the anger in himself: let it coalesce, and then flow out through the branching channels of vital energy . . . His breathing slowed and came under control. The colours of his inner vision returned to green and gold.

He walked through the great vaulted cavern. Sound thundered from stationary engines, pistons driving. The hiss of steam shattered the air. Vast walls went up to either side: millions of small bricks stained black with soot, and overgrown here and there with white lichen.

Water dripped from the walls, and the air was sweatily warm.

Somewhere at the end of the platform, voices yelped; and he quickened his steps, but saw nothing at the exit. He stomped up the stairs to ground-level. A vaulted roof arched, scaled and glittering, that might once have been steel and glass but now was too soot-darkened to let in light. Torches burned smokily in wall-cressets.

'Lord Bishop?'

Candia leaned indolently up against the iron stair-rail.

'I was delayed. The lower lines are closed off,' Theodoret said.

'*Already?*'

'I've always said that would be the first signal. Have you asked to see . . . ?'

Candia flashed him a knowingly insouciant grin. 'As we agreed. The Twelfth Decan – The Spagyrus. I've had dealings with him.'

Theodoret grunted.

As the Bishop of the Trees followed Candia out of the station hall, he passed the group of young men. Three crowded round the fourth, the youngest, whose nose streamed blood. The gangling youth swore at the blond man. Candia smiled serenely.

Outside the brick-and-glass cupola heat streamed down. Theodoret sweated. Pilings stood up out of the tepid sluggish water all along the canal-bank. The tide was far out, and the mud stank. Blue and grey, all hardly touched by the sun's rise to noon.

The Bishop knelt, resting his hand on the canal-path.

'It remembers the footprints of daemons.'

He reached, caught Candia's proffered hand, pulled himself upright.

'*They*' – Candia's head jerked towards the city – 'they're like children teasing a jaguar with a stick. When it claws their faces off, *then* they remember to be afraid.'

'Still, this will be a difficult medicine for them to swallow. For them and for us.'

The Bishop turned away from the canal, treading carefully across a long plank that crossed a ditch. Half-dug foundations pitted the earth, and the teams of diggers crouched in the meagre shadows in the ditches, eating the midday meal.

Broken obelisks towered on the skyline.

Candia picked his way fastidiously across the mud. His gaze went to the structures ahead. He thumbed hair back under his ragged scarlet headband. 'The Decans don't care. What's another millennium to them?'

Blocks of half-dressed masonry lay on the earth. Jutting up among them were narrow pyramids of black brick. Theodoret and Candia followed a well-trodden path. Half-built halls rose at either side, festooned with wooden scaffolding. The place was loud with shouts of builders, carpenters, bricklayers, carvers, site-foremen.

With every step the sunlight weakens, the sky turns ashen.

Theodoret favoured his weak leg as he strode, passing teams of men and women who (ropes taut across chests and shoulders, straining; silk and satin work-clothes filthy) heaved carts loaded with masonry towards the area of new building. All were dwarfed by what rose around them.

Staining the air, blocking every city horizon to east, west, north, south and aust; heart of the world: the temple-fortress called the Fane.

Sacrilege tasted bitter in Theodoret's mouth. The granite buildings, the marble, porphyry and black onyx; it grew as a tree grows, out in rings from the heart of divinity. Accumulating over centuries, this receding mountain of roofs, towers, battlements, domes and pyramids. The nearest and most massive outcrop drew his eyes skyward with perpendicular arches.

'Candia . . .'

Black as sepulchres, windowless as monuments. It flung storey upon storey, spire upon tower, straining towards the heavens. Walkways and balconies hung from slanting walls. Finials and carved pinnacles jutted dark against the noon sky.

The nearer they drew, the quieter it became. Silence sang in the dust that tanged on the Bishop's tongue. The paving that he trod on now was old. The flights of steps that went up to the entrances, wide enough to ride a horse up, were hoary with age and lichen.

Theodoret smoothed down his worn green robe. He and Candia stood out now, among the servants all in tightly buttoned black, lost in the silent crowds at the arched entrances.

Candia snapped his fingers at the nearest man.

'Tell The Spagyrus I am here.'

The Bishop glanced back once. The city sprawled out like a multi-coloured patchwork to the five quarters of the earth.

Noon is midnight: midnight noon.

The two pivots of the day meet and lock, and in that moment men are enabled to pass over this threshold. There is a tension in the filth-starred stone, receiving their footprints.

There are guides. They do not speak. They climb narrow

26

*flights of stairs that wind up and around. The stairways
are not lit. Their fingers against the slick stone guide
them.*

*Theodoret and Candia climb, ensnared in that mirrored
moment of midnight and midday.*

'What are you doing here?' the black Rat demanded.

'My lord.' Zar-bettu-zekigal bowed, the dignity of
this impaired by her hands being tucked up into her
armpits for warmth. 'We're students, passing through
to the other side of the Nineteenth's Aust quarter.'

Lucas noted the black Rat's plain cloak and sword-
belt, without distinguishing marks. A plain metal circlet
ringed above one ear and under the other; from it
depended a black feather plume. The black Rat, despite
being unattended, had an air that Lucas associated with
rank, if not necessarily military rank.

'You're out of your lawful quarter.'

The Rat swept the last fragments of bone from the
niche into the sack, and pulled the drawstrings tight.
His muzzle went up: that lean wolfish face regarding
Lucas first, and then the young Katayan.

'A trainee Kings' Memory?' he recalled her last words.
'How good are you, child?'

The young woman lifted her chin slightly, screwed
up her eyes, and paused with tail hooked onto empty
air. 'Me: *What I like, you haven't got*; Lucas: *Really?*
Me: *Really*; Lucas: *This really is a short-cut?* Me: *Oh,
right. Oh, right. You're a king's son. Used to stable-girls
and servants—*'

The Rat cut her off with a wave of one be-ringed
hand. 'Either you're new and excellent, or near the end
of your training.'

'New this summer.' Zar-bettu-zekigal shrugged. 'Got
three months in the university now, learning practical
self-protection.'

'I'll speak further with you. Come with me.'

'Messire—'

27

The Rat cut off Lucas's belated attempt at servility. 'Follow.'

They walked on into vaulted cellars, where the loudest noise was the hissing of the gas-lamps. Soft echoes ran back from Lucas's footsteps; Zar-bettu-zekigal and the Rat walked silently.

A distant thrumming grew to a rumble, which vibrated in the stone walls and floor. Bone-dust sifted down. The Rat carried his ringed tail higher, cleaning it with a fastidious flick. His hand fell to the small sack at his belt.

'Zari.' Lucas dropped back a step to whisper. 'Do they practise *necromancy* here?'

'I'm a stranger here myself!' The young woman's waspishness faded. 'The only good use for bones is fertilizer. Who cares about fringe heresies anyway?'

'But it's blasphemy!'

The Rat's almost-transparent ears moved. He stopped abruptly, and swung round. 'Necromancy?'

Lucas said: 'Not a fit subject for the location, messire, true. Does it disturb you?'

The black Rat's snout lifted, sniffing the air. Lucas saw it register the sweat of fear, and cursed himself.

'Even were it a fit subject for our discussion, necromancy – using the basest materials, as it does – is the least and most feeble of the disciplines of *magia*, and so no cause for concern at all.'

The Rat drew himself up, balanced on clawed hind feet, and the tip of his naked tail twitched thoughtfully. Metal clashed: sword-harness and rapier.

'Who sent you here to spy?'

'No-one,' Zar-bettu-zekigal said.

'And that is, one supposes, possible. However—'

'*Plessiez?*'

The black Rat's mouth twitched. He lifted his head and called: 'Down here, Charnay.'

Lucas and Zar-bettu-zekigal halted with the black Rat, where steps came down from street-level. The bone-packed vaults stretched away into the distance.

In far corners there was shadow, where the gas-lighting failed. Dry bone-dust caught in the back of Lucas's throat; and there was a scent, sweet and subtle, of decay.

Zar-bettu-zekigal huffed on her hands to warm them. The Katayan student appeared sanguine, but her tail coiled limply about her feet.

A heavily built Rat swept down the steps and ducked under the stone archway. Lucas stared. She was a brown Rat, easily six and a half feet tall; and the leather straps of her sword-harness stretched between furred dugs across a broad chest. She carried a rapier and dagger at her belt, both had jewelled hilts; her headband was gold, the feather-plume scarlet, and her cloak was azure.

'Messire Plessiez.' She sketched a bow to the black Rat. 'I became worried; you were so long. *Who are they?*'

She half-drew the long rapier; the black Rat put his hand over hers.

'Students, Charnay; but of a particular talent. The young woman is a Kings' Memory.'

The brown Rat looked Zar-bettu-zekigal up and down, and her blunt snout twitched. 'Plessiez, man, if you don't have all the luck, just when you need it!'

'The young man is also from' – the black Rat looked up from tucking the canvas bag more securely under his sword-belt – 'the University of Crime?'

'Yes,' Lucas muttered.

The Rat swung back, as he was about to mount the stairs, and looked for a long moment at Zar-bettu-zekigal.

'You're young,' he said, 'all but trained, as I take it, and without a patron? My name is Plessiez. In the next few hours I – we – will badly need a trusted record of events. Trusted by both parties. If I put that proposition to you?'

Zari's face lit up. Impulsive, joyous; cocky as the

flirt of her tail-tuft, brushing dust from her sleeves. She nodded. 'Oh, say you, yes!'

'Zari . . .' Lucas warned.

The black Rat sleeked down a whisker with one ruby-ringed hand. His left hand did not leave the hilt of his sword; and his black eyes were brightly alert.

'Messire,' Plessiez said, 'since when was youth cautious?'

Lucas saw the silver collar almost buried under the black Rat's neck-fur, and at last recognized the *ankh* dependant from it. A priest, then; not a soldier.

Unconsciously he straightened, looked the Rat in the face; speaking as to an equal. 'You have no right to make her do this – *yeep!*'

His legs clamped together, automatic and undignified, just too late to trap the Katayan's stinging tail. Zari grinned, flicking her tail back, and slid one hand inside her coat to cup her breast.

'I'll be your Kings' Memory. I've wanted a genuine chance to practise for *months* now,' she said. 'Lucas here could practise his university training for you!'

'*Me?*' Her humour sparked outrage in him.

'You heard Reverend Master Candia. There *are* no rules in the University of Crime. Think of it as research. Think of it as a thesis!'

Frustration broke Lucas's reserve. 'Girl, do you know who my father is? All the Candovers have been Masters of the Interior Temple. The Emperor of the East and the Emperor of the West come to meet in his court! I came here to learn, not to get involved in petty intrigues!'

'Thank you, messire.' Plessiez hid a smile. He murmured an aside to the brown Rat, and Charnay nodded her head seriously, scarlet plume bobbing against her brown-grey pelt.

'You'll guest at the palace for two or three days,' Plessiez went on. 'I regret that it could not be under better circumstances, heir of Candover. Oh – your uncle the Ambassador is an old acquaintance. Present my regards to him, when you see him.'

Zar-bettu-zekigal nodded to Lucas, thrust her hands deep in her greatcoat pockets and walked jauntily up the steps at the side of the black Rat.

'When you're ready, messire.'

Charnay's heavy hand fell on Lucas's shoulder.

As always, the height of the enclosed space jolted him. Candia reached to grip the brass rail as they were ushered out onto a balcony. The sheer walls curved away and around. Twilight rustled, shifted. The darkness behind his eyelids turned scarlet, gold, black. A stink of hot oil and rotten flesh caught in the back of his throat.

One of the servants clapped his hands together twice, slowly. Sharp echoes skittered across the distant walls.

A kind of unlight began to grow, shadowless, peripheral. Candia's eyes smarted. In a sight that was not sight, he began to see darkness: the midnight tracery of black marble, pillars and arches and domes. Vaulting hung like dark stalactites. A rustling and a movement haunted the interiors of the ceiling-vaults. The gazes of the acolytes that roosted there prickled across his skin.

Pain flushed and faded along nerve-endings as a greater gaze opened and took him in.

Hulking to engage all space between the down-distant floor and the arcing vaults, the god-daemon lay. Black basalt flanks and shoulders embodied darkness. Behind the Decan the halls opened to vaster spaces, themselves only the beginning of the way into the true heart of the Fane, and the basalt-feathered wings of the god-daemon soared up to shade mortal sight from any vision of that interior.

Between the Decan's outstretched paws, and on platforms and balconies and loggias, servants worked to His orders: sifting, firing, tending liquids in glass bains-marie, alembics and stills; hauling trolleys between the glowing mouths of ovens. Molten metal ran between vats.

'My honour to you, Divine One.' Candia's voice fell flatly into the air.

'Little Candia . . .' A sound from huge delicate lips:

31

deep enough to vibrate the tiled floor of the balcony, carried on carrion breath.

Lids of living rock slid up. Eyes molten-black with the unlight of the Fane shone, in chthonic humour, upon Candia and the Bishop. The grotesque head lifted slightly.

A bulging pointed muzzle overhung The Spagyrus' lower jaw. Pointed tusks jutted up, nestling against the muzzle beside nostrils that were crusted yellow and twitched continually. Jagged tusks hung down from the upper jaw, half-hidden by flowing bristles.

'Purification, sublimation, calcination, conjunction . . . and no nearer the *prima materia*, the First Matter.'

Down at cell-level, the voice vibrated in Candia's head. He stared up into the face of the god-daemon.

The narrow muzzle flared to a wide head. Cheek-bones glinted, scale-covered; and bristle-tendrils swept back, surrounding the eyes, to two small pointed and naked ears.

Theodoret leaned his head back. 'Decans practising the Great Art? Dangerous, my lord, dangerous. What if you should discover the true alchemical Elixir that, being perfect in itself, induces perfection in all it touches? Perhaps, being gods, it would transmute you to a perfect evil. Or perfect virtue.'

The great head lowered. Candia saw his image and the Bishop's as absences of unlight on the obsidian surfaces of those eyes.

'We are such incarnations of perfection already.' Amusement in the Decan's resonant tones. 'It is not that alchemical transformation that I seek, but something quite other. Candia, whom have you brought me?'

'Theodoret, my lord, Bishop of the Trees.'

'A Tree-priest?'

The unlight blazed, and imprinted like a magnesium flare on Candia's eyes the gargoyle-conclave of the Decan's acolytes: bristle-spined tails lashed around pillars and arches and fine stone tracery; claws gripping, great wings

32

*'Purification, sublimation, calcination, conjunction . . . and no
nearer the prima materia . . .'*

Reconstructed from an illustration in *Apocrypha Mundus
Subterranus* by Miriam Sophia, pub. Maximillian of Prague,
1589 (now lost)

beating. Their scaled and furred bodies crowded together, and their prick-eared and tendrilled heads rose to bay in a conclave of sound, and the unlight died to fireglow.

'I will see to you in a moment. This is a most crucial stage . . .'

On the filthy floor below, servants worked ceaselessly. The platform jutted out fifteen yards, overhanging a section of the floor (man-deep in filth) where abandoned furnaces and shattered glass lay. Here, the heat of the ovens built into the wall was pungent.

'Take that from the furnace,' the low voice rumbled.

One of the black-doubleted servants on the balcony called another, and both between them began to lift, with tongs, a glowing-hot metal casing from the furnace. Sweat ran down their faces.

'Set it there.'

Chittering echoed in the vaults. A darkness of firelight shaded the great head, limning with black the foothill-immensity of flanks and arching wings. One vast paw flexed.

'We reach the Head of the Crow, but not the Dragon. As for the Phoenix' – unlight-filled eyes dipped to stare into the alembic – 'nothing!'

Candia said: 'My lord, this business is important—'

'The projection continues,' the bass voice rumbled. 'Matter refined into spirit, spirit distilled into base matter, and yet . . . nothing. Why are you here?'

Candia planted his fists on his hips and craned his neck, looking through the vast spaces to The Spagyrus. The bruised darkness of his eyes was accentuated by the pallor of fear, but determination held him there, taut, before the god-daemon.

'It happens', he said, 'that we're traitors. The Bishop here, and I. We've come to betray our own kind to you.'

A shifting of movement, tenuous as the first tremors of earthquake, folded His wings of darkness. The body of the god-daemon moved, elbow-joints above shoulders, until

34

He threatened emergence from unlight-shadows. Lids slid up to narrow His eyes to slits.

'Master Candia, you always amuse me,' He rumbled. 'I welcome that. It's a relief from my failures here.'

Candia made a gesture of exasperation. He paced back and forth, a few strides each way, as if movement could keep him from seeing where he stood. He directed no more looks at The Spagyrus, his stamina for that exhausted.

The Bishop of the Trees reached to rest a hand on Candia's shoulder, stilling him. 'Even the worst shepherd looks to his flock. Doesn't the Lord Decan know what's happening in our part of the city?'

'Do the stock in the farmyard murmur?' A bifurcated tongue licked out and stroked a lower fang. The Spagyrus gazed down at Candia and Theodoret. 'What I do here leaves me no time for such petty concerns. The great work must be finished, and I am no nearer to completion. If it comes to rioting in the city, I shall put it down with severity – I, my Kin, or your lesser masters the Rat-Lords. You know this. Why bother me?'

Theodoret walked forward. His lined creased face, under the shock of dusty-white hair, showed sternness.

'Lord Spagyrus!'

'Harrhummm?'

'Our *lesser masters* are what you should look to.' Theodoret's grey eyes swam with light; mobile, blinking. 'The Rat-Lords are meeting now with the Guildmasters – the human Guildmasters, that is. Meeting in secrecy, as I thought.' Incredulity sharpened his voice. 'And I see we're right, Lord Spagyrus. *You don't know of it.*'

The Decan roared.

Candia slid to one knee, head bowed, ragged hair falling forward; and his white-knuckled fist gripped the Bishop's robe. A thin green-gold radiance limned him. He smelt the blossom of hawthorn and meadowsweet. The tiles beneath his knee gave slightly, as if with the texture of moss.

The Bishop of the Trees said softly: 'We were here before you ever were, Lord Spagyrus.'

The tendrilled muzzle rose, gaped, fangs shining in unlight and the furnace's red darkness, and a great cry echoed down through the chambers and galleries and crypts of the Fane.

Candia raised his head to see the acolytes already dropping from the ceiling vaults, soaring on black ribbed wings.

In a room that has more books than furniture, the magus stares out at a blinding blue sky.

Her mirror is shrouded with a patchwork cloth.

The day's air smells sleepy, smells sweet, and she sniffs for the scent of rain or thunder and there is nothing.

Suddenly there is a tickle that runs the length of her forearm. She holds up her hand. The gashed palm, half-healed by her arts, is aching now; and, as she watches, another bead of blood trickles down her arms. She frowns.

She waits.

Charnay paused on the landing, examining herself in the full-length mirror there. She took a small brush and sleeked down the fur on her jaw; tugged her head-band into place, and tweaked the crimson feather to a more jaunty angle.

'Messire Plessiez has a superlative mind,' she said. 'I conjecture that, by the time you leave us, in a day or two, he'll have found some advantage even in you.'

Lucas, aware of tension making him petty, needled her. '*Big* words. Been taking lessons from your priest friend?'

'In!'

She leaned over and pushed open a heavy iron-studded door. Lucas walked into the cell. Afternoon sunlight fell through the bars, striping the walls. Dirt and cobwebs starred the floor, and the remnants of previous occupations – tin dishes, a bucket, two ragged blankets – lay on a horsehair mattress in one corner.

'You have no right to put me here!'

36

Charnay laughed. 'And who are you going to complain to?'

She swung the door to effortlessly. It clanged. Lucas heard locks click, and then her departing footsteps, padding away down the corridor. In the distance men and Rats shouted, hoofs clattered: the palace garrison.

Lucas remained standing quite still. The sky beyond the bars shone brilliantly blue; and light reflected off the white walls and the four storeys of windows on the opposite side of the inner courtyard, mirror to his.

He slammed the flat of his hand against the door. '*Bitch!*'

Four floors below, the brown Rat Charnay had stopped in the courtyard to talk and to preen herself in the company of other Rats. Her ears moved, and she glanced up, grinning, as she left.

The shadows on the wall slid slowly eastwards.

'Rot you!'

Lucas moved decisively. He unbuttoned his shirt, folding it up into a neat pad. Goosepimples starred his chest, feeling the stone cell's chill. He rubbed his arms. With one eye on the door, he unbuttoned his knee-breeches, slid them down, and turned them so that the grey lining was outermost.

'If you're going to study at the university, start acting like it!'

His fingers worked at the stitching. A thin metal strip protruded from the knee-seam, and he tugged it free; and then stood up rapidly and hopped about on one foot, thrusting the other into his breeches-leg, listening to check if that *had* been a noise in the corridor . . . No. Nothing.

His dark-brown meeting brows dipped in concentration. The metal prong plumbed the depths of the lock, and then his mouth quirked: there was a click, and he tested the handle, and the heavy door swung open.

Clearer: the noise of the garrison below.

Lucas buttoned his breeches. He took a step towards

the open door. One hand made a fist, and there was a faint pink flush to his cheeks. Caught between reluctance and fear of recognition, he stood still for several minutes.

Coming in, they had passed no human above the rank of servant.

He bent to remove stockings and shoes, wrapping them in his shirt. Then he knelt, shivering, to rub his hands in the dirt; washing arms, face and chest in the cobwebs and dust.

A black Rat passed him on the second floor. She didn't spare a glance for this kitchen-servant. With the bundle under his arm, and an old leather bucket balanced on his shoulder, Lucas of Candover walked free of the palace.

Zar-bettu-zekigal leaned out of the carriage window, regardless of the dust and flying clots of dung the team's hoofs threw up.

'See you, we're out of Nineteenth District's Aust quarter already – oof!'

Plessiez's hand grabbed her coat between the shoulder-blades and yanked her back on to the carriage seat. 'Is it necessary to advertise your presence to the entire city?'

'Oh, we're not even out of a Mixed District, messire, what's to worry?'

She leaned her arms on the jolting sill, and her chin on her arms, and grinned out at the street. The carriage rattled through squares where washing hung like pale flags and fountains dripped. The sun beat down from a blazing afternoon sky. Humans and Rats crowded the cobbled streets – a dozen or so of the palace guard, in silks and satins and polished rapiers, drank raucously outside a tavern, and sketched salutes of varying sobriety as Plessiez's coach and horses passed them.

Zar-bettu-zekigal drew a deep breath, contentedly sniffing as they passed a may-hedge and a city garden.

'You have no Katayan accent,' the black Rat said. The dimness inside the coach hid all but the glitter of his black

38

eyes, and the jet embellishment of his rapier's pommel.

'Messire' – reproach in her tone, and humour – 'Kings' Memories remember inflections exactly – we have to. What would I be doing with an *accent*?'

'I beg your pardon, lady,' Plessiez said, sardonically humble, and the Katayan grinned companionably at him.

The coachman called from above, sparks showered as the brakes cut the metal wheel-rims, and the carriage rattled down a steep lane. Plessiez caught hold of the door-strap with a ring-fingered hand.

'Mistress Zekegial . . . Zare-bethu . . .' He stumbled over the syllables.

'Oh, "Zari" will do, messire, to you.' She waved an airy gesture. Then, leaning out of the window again as the carriage squealed to a halt, she said: 'You're holding this important meeting in a *builders' yard*?'

Plessiez hid what might have been a smile. The black Rat said smoothly: 'That is one of the Masons' Halls, little one. Show the proper respect.'

Zari pushed the carriage door open and sprang down into the yard. Two other coaches were already drawn up in the entrance, horses standing with creamed flanks and drooping heads. Plessiez stepped down into the sunlight. It became apparent that the black Rat had changed uniform: he now wore a sleeveless crimson jacket, with the neat silver neck-band of a priest. His crimson cloak was also edged with silver.

He paused to adjust rapier and belt, and Zari saw him straighten a richly gemmed pectoral *ankh*. A flurry of black and brown Rats from the other coaches rushed to meet him, those with priests' collars particularly obsequious.

'Mauriac, make sure the guards are placed unobtrusively; Brennan, you – and *you* – get these carriages taken away.' The black Rat's snout twitched.

A heavily-built brown Rat swaggered out from the back of the group. Pulling her aside by a corner of her cloak, Plessiez said sharply: '*My* idea of a secret meeting does not consist merely of arriving in a coach without a crest on it! Yours does, apparently. Get rid of this crowd. I'll take you only in with me.'

Charnay laughed and slapped Plessiez on the back. The black Rat staggered slightly.

'Don't worry, messire! They'll just think you've come for a plan for the new wing.'

'Perhaps. But do it.'

Zar-bettu-zekigal's bare feet printed the yellow yard-dust. The air shimmered in the heat. She wrapped her greatcoat firmly round her, and squinted up at the stacked clay bricks, timber put out to weather, and piles of wooden scaffolding that surrounded this Masons' Hall. Tiles and wooden crates blocked the view to the nearer houses.

She cocked her head, and her dappled black-and-white tail coiled around her ankles. With a nod at the weathered-plank structure – half hall, half warehouse – she said over the noise of departing coaches: 'Well, messire, have I begun yet?'

'As soon as we enter the hall.'

Leisurely, hands folded at his breast, the black Rat paced forward. Charnay fell in beside him. Two men pushed the hall doors open from the inside, and Zari gave a half-skip up the steps, catching up, as they went in.

'Messire Falke!' Plessiez called.

In a patch of sunlight from the clerestory windows, a man raised his bandaged face. His short silver-white hair caught the light, pressed down by the strips of cotton.

'Honour to you, priest.' The man faced Plessiez with a wry, somewhat perfunctory grin. His black silk overalls shone at collar, cuffs and seams; sewn with silver thread. A heavy silver pin in the shape of compasses fastened the black lace at his throat. Diamond and onyx rings shone on his left hand.

'Oh, what . . . ?'

The merest whisper. Charnay nudged the Katayan heavily in her ribs, and Zari bowed. She continued to stare at the fine linen bandaging the man's eyes.

The men and women with Falke drew back, bowing respectfully to the black Rat, and the sleek priest strode down the passage that opened in the crowd and seated himself on a chair at the head of a trestle table. This gave signs – like the eight or nine others in the room – of having been rapidly cleared of site- and ground-plans, measurements, calculations and scale models.

Charnay ostentatiously drew her long rapier and laid it down on the plank table before her.

'Zari,' the black Rat prompted.

The young woman was standing on tiptoe, and leaning over to stare into a tank-model of a sewer system. She straightened. Hands in pockets, she marched across the bright room and hitched herself up to sit on the trestle table.

'Kings' Memory,' she announced. 'You have an auditor, messires: you are heard: this is the warning.'

Some of the expensively dressed men and women began to speak. Falke held up a hand, and they ceased.

'What is your oath?'

She took her hands out of her greatcoat pockets. 'To speak what I hear, as I heard it, whenever asked; to add nothing, to omit nothing, to alter nothing.'

Falke passed her on his way to sit down, close enough for her to see dark brows and lashes behind the cloth shield. A lined face, and silver-fine hair: a man on the down side of thirty-five.

'And the penalty', he said, 'if otherwise?'

'Death, of course.' She slid down on to a collapsible chair, positioning herself exactly halfway between Falke's people and the Rats.

The light of late noon fell in through clerestory windows, shining on the plans, diagrams and calculations pinned around the walls. Falke, without apparent difficulty, indicated the half-dozen men and women who abandoned compasses, straight-edge and fine quill pens for the cleared trestle table, as they sat down. Silk and satins rustled; white lace blazed at cuffs and collars.

41

'The master stonemason. Master bricklayer. Foreman of the carriage teams. Master tiler.'

Plessiez, who sat with his lean black muzzle resting on his steepled fingers, said: 'You may give them their proper titles, Master Falke. If we're to talk honestly, we must have no secrecy.'

'"Honestly"? You forget I've dealt with Rat-Lords before.' Falke sat, pointing with economical gestures. 'Very well, have your way. Shanna is a Fellowcraft, so is Jenebret.' He indicated an older man. 'Thomas is an Apprentice. Awdrey is the Mistress Royal of the Children of the Widow. I'm Master of the Hall.'

Zar-bettu-zekigal leaned forward on the wooden table, brushing the black hair from her eyes.

'"Children of the Widow" . . . "Master of the Hall" . . .' she murmured happily. She caught Plessiez's warning stare and grinned, professional, her own eyes enthusiastic with Memory.

Falke began. 'We—'

The doors at the end of the hall slammed open. Plessiez stood up, his chair scraping back.

Two Rats and three or four men struggled to hold back a middle-aged man, himself in the forefront of a group. '*Falke!*'

Falke peered towards the bright end of the hall through his cloth bandage.

Charnay glanced to the black Rat for a cue, one hand reaching for her sword. Plessiez shook his head. 'I know the man, I think. East quarter. East quarter's Mayor?'

'Certainly I am!'

The man shook himself free of the brown Rats' restraining grip. He was in his fifties, and stout; raggedly cut yellow hair framing a moon-face. Confronting Falke, he tugged his greasy breeches up about his belly, and straightened a verdigris-stained chain of copper links that hung across his frayed jerkin.

'*Mayor* Tannakin Spatchet,' he rumbled, and pointed a beefy finger at Master Falke. 'What do you mean by holding this meeting without me? At the very least, some of the East quarter Council should be here!'

'Tan, get out of here.' Falke waved a dismissive hand. 'You'll bring the dregs in with you. A rabble of bureaucrats, shopkeepers, lawyers and teachers!'

The five or six men who had come in with Tannakin Spatchet shuffled and looked embarrassed.

'We have every right to be represented! If you're talking to the Rat-Lords, that concerns everyone in the quarter.'

Falke shook his head. 'No. You're not admitted to the mysteries here, not even to the outer hall. Thomas, take these people outside.'

'Damn your hall! Just because you won't admit us . . .'

Plessiez pushed Charnay in the direction of the hall door, and turned to Falke. 'Pardon me, messire, but it might not be amiss if other trades were represented here.'

A fair-haired woman leaned forward, looking down the table to the black Rat. 'Then we can't speak freely. Craft mysteries aren't to be disclosed to outsiders. You *know* that.'

Plessiez shrugged. 'Then, I must go. I don't belong to any Craft hall.'

'We can't have this scum here!' The Fellowcraft, Shanna, pointed at the Mayor, who bridled. 'You'll have us inviting *councillors* next.'

Falke's cupped palms slammed down on the table. The *crack!* echoed. In sudden silence, his bandaged head cocked to one side, he spoke.

'Our quarrels are meat and drink to our masters. Aren't they, messire priest?'

'I don't understand you, Master Falke.'

'You do. You think no more of using us than of saddling a horse to ride. You'd no more think of a man's name than a dog's name in the street if you kick it!'

His hand went up behind his head, pulling the knotted cloth bandage down. Prematurely white hair slid free. His fingers immediately clamped across his eyes, features blasted by the sudden light. Zari glimpsed wide eyes: no

43

injury, no scar; only immensely dilated black pupils.

He said: 'Because *my* name is on file, you can find and use me.'

As if prompted, the Fellowcraft Shanna spread her hands, turning to the other men and women around the table. 'The Rat-Lord's obliged to tell us nothing more than pleases him. We must tell him all. For all his alliance with us, he can sell us out any time that it should please him, and walk away unharmed. Remember that, when we come to trust him!'

Zar-bettu-zekigal's gaze darted from Falke to Plessiez. Her tail coiled up, lying across her arm, tense and twitching. Hearing and all senses acute – her smile widened suddenly.

Charnay marched back from the hall door, whisking her cloak past the seated Fellows, and leaned over to speak in the black Rat's ear. The Katayan heard: 'Desaguliers is coming!'

Falke froze.

The black Rat's whiskers quivered. His bright eyes fixed on Charnay, and the brown Rat stumbled back a pace.

'This was your idea of secrecy, was it, Charnay!'

Before she could do more than mumble, voices were raised, and the group of men at the door were pushed aside. Five sleek black Rats, with black-plumed headbands and drawn rapiers, shoved them aside; and a taller black Rat stepped in from the sunny yard to the white hall.

'Was it necessary', Plessiez murmured silkily, 'to bring the Cadets in such strength, Messire Desaguliers?'

The watermills turned slowly, dripping water catching the sun. Lucas gazed at the water running past the building's stone wall (some part of a concealed stream uncovered?), and then up at the watermills' tower.

A twelve-foot gold-and-blue dial gleamed in the sun. The clock's hands twitched once, to a metallic click inside the tower, and a bell chimed the quarter. Lucas stood watching as a silver knight, some two feet tall, slid out on rails from one side of the tower, to meet an approaching bronze knight on a similar curve. Their swords lifted jerkily; they struck a *clang!* that echoed the length of the cobbled street. A pause, and both began to retreat.

Lucas rubbed his sweating neck, took his hand away filthy, and glanced speculatively at the running water. He still carried shirt and stockings. His bare feet were chafing in his boots, and his filthy chest and arms were beginning to sting from the sun.

A first-floor window opened further down the street, and a woman shook out a quilt and laid it on the sill.

'Lady,' Lucas called, 'is this Clock-mill?'

She leaned one bare forearm on the sill, her other hand supporting her as she leaned out, so that her elbow jutted up and her thick yellow hair fell about her shoulders. She wore a blue-and-yellow satin dress slashed with white, with puffed sleeves and a low full bodice. Lucas moved a few steps down the street towards her.

'Clock-mill and Carver Street,' she called.

Lucas gazed up at the window. The quilt hung down, half-covering a frieze carved in the black wood: hour-glasses, scythes, spades and skulls. Seen closer, the woman's face was lined. Lucas judged her forty at least. Some twinge of memory caught him.

'Is there . . . are you Mistress Evelian?'

'You're not one of my lodgers?' The woman's china-blue eyes narrowed, studying the filthy ragged young man. 'Good God. What does Candia think he's sending me these days? Come in: don't *stand* there. Third door down will take you through into the courtyard. I'll let you in.'

Lucas had only taken a few steps before she stuck her head out of the window again.

'Have you met the other students yet? Have you seen anything of that Katayan child, Zaribeth?'

Zar-bettu-zekigal sat with her grubby hands in front of her on the table. Her dappled tail flicked sawdust on the hall

45

floor. A smell of cut wood, pitch, and long-boiled tea filled the heavy afternoon air.

Her eyes moved from the white-haired Falke, poised at rest in his chair, to Tannakin Spatchet (stiffly upright), and the well-dressed builders and ill-dressed councillors; to Plessiez and Charnay, and to the black Rat Desaguliers, standing and glaring at each other across the table.

'I think the King might be interested in this meeting,' Desaguliers challenged. He was a lean black Rat, tall, with the plain leather harness and silver cuirass of a soldier; the hairs on his thin snout grizzled.

'The Captain-General is aware, of course, that the King has full knowledge of—'

Desaguliers bluntly interrupted Plessiez: 'Horse-dung! I'm aware of nothing of the sort.'

'How very remiss of you.'

'Gentle lords. Please.' Falke spoke with a sardonic gravity. He sat with his hand shading his uncovered eyes against the hall's whitewashed brilliance. Tears ran down his cheeks; he rapidly blinked. 'You know how your honour suffers, to be seen quarrelling by we underlings.'

'Master Falke!' Plessiez snapped.

'I apologize. Most humbly. I hazard my guess, also, that this terminates our discussion. And that we shall be the ones to suffer for your plotting.' He smoothed the cloth bandage between his fingers, and bent his head to tie it back over his eyes.

Zari's gaze darted back to Plessiez and the black Rat Desaguliers.

'No.' Plessiez, sleek in scarlet. 'I put this hall under Guiry's protection. Let Messire Desaguliers hear our talk. Since I perceive his spies will have it sooner or later, let it be now. I have nothing to hide.'

Desaguliers snorted. 'A miracle, that!'

Welcome heat touched her with the room's shifting patches of sun. Zari coughed, and stuck her tail up above head-height, twitching it. 'If you talk through me, messires, it'll be easier for the record.'

Desaguliers peered down the table. 'What is *that*?'

Plessiez, seating himself, and draping his scarlet cloak over the back of the chair, murmured: 'Zari, of South Katay. A Kings' Memory.'

'A Kings' Memory.' The taller Rat shook his head in reluctant admiration, and slumped back into a chair on his side of the table. The sun glinted off his cuirass. He kicked his rapier-scabbard back with a bare heel. 'Plessiez, you miss few tricks. Let's hear what you have to say, then.'

Plessiez rested one slender clawed finger across his mouth for a few seconds, leaning back, thin whiskers still. His eyes narrowed to obsidian slits. The hand fell to caress his pectoral *ankh*.

'I don't think I need to do more than say what I said when we last met. Master Falke, we, your masters, confine humans to certain ghetto areas within the city—'

'As you are yourselves confined, by those Divine ones who are masters of us all.' The white-haired man sat back with his arms along the arms of the chair, cloth-blinded eyes accurately finding Plessiez's face. 'It may gall you, Messire Plessiez, but there are Human Districts forbidden even to you. The Decans decree it.'

'If I spoke sharply, Master Mason, you must pardon me. There is much at stake here.'

'You apologize to *this* scum?' Desaguliers guffawed loudly; broke off as Zari glared at him. He glanced around at black Rat cadets positioned on guard about the hall. She resumed the concentration of listening, head cocked bird-like to one side.

'We need your help, Falke,' the black Rat Plessiez said, in a tone of plain-dealing, 'and you, you say, need ours. Both of us for the same reason: that one can go where the other cannot.'

Falke inclined his head.

'If, therefore, we agree an exchange of mutual help—'

Tannakin Spatchet rose to his feet. He mopped his face, reddened by the airless heat. 'We don't enter into blank contracts. As local Mayor, I *must* know what you intend, messire priest.'

'You "must" nothing.' Plessiez's rapier-hilt knocked against the chair as he shifted position. 'However, I am prepared to discuss a little of the situation.'

The black Rat glanced towards Zari. She grinned and tapped her freckled ear-lobe with one finger.

Plessiez said: 'There are a number of locations within the city, at which, for purposes of our own, we intend to place certain . . . "articles". Packages. Three of them are within quarters humans may enter and we may not. Therefore—'

Desaguliers snorted. 'Purposes of your own, yes, messire, surely!'

'I see no need to discuss it with you.'

'It may endanger the King.'

'It will not. But if his Majesty is ever to be King in more than name only, then some of us must act; and you and your cadets will oblige me by keeping silent while we do!'

'Is this treason, messire!'

Zar-bettu-zekigal reached, sprawling halfway across the wooden table, and slapped her hand down over the hilt of Charnay's discarded sword as the Captain-General grabbed for it. Plessiez slowly relaxed his hands that gripped the arms of his chair.

Still sprawled across the sun-warmed wood, the Katayan said: 'You wouldn't be here if you didn't want to know what was going on, Messire Desaguliers, so why don't you shut up and listen?'

Plessiez threw his head back and laughed.

Zar-bettu-zekigal slid back into her chair. 'I don't have all day. If I miss this afternoon's lectures, I'm dead. So could we get on, please?'

The white-haired Mason, Falke, watched the armed Rat-Lords. 'Our part of the bargain is this. There are ancient buildings of this city that we may not enter, because of where they are situated. There are records and inscriptions in those buildings that we need. If Messire Plessiez and his people can gain us that, we'll run his errands.'

'No!' Tannakin Spatchet's fist hit the table. 'Who knows what retribution we'd bring into our quarter if we did? As Mayor—'

'Tan, be quiet,' Falke ordered.

Desaguliers leaned forward. 'The peasant's right. I want to know what and why, messire priest. Some scheme to open up every district to us, is it? That would be foolhardy, but of use. But, if you say to me certain "articles" needing to be put in certain places, that sounds like *magia*. Which one might expect from the damned Order of Guiry priests!'

Falke, head sunk to his chest, seemed by the turning of his chin to direct quick glances at both armed Rat-Lords. The corners of his mouth moved. 'Will you tell him, Messire Plessiez?'

The black Rat's eyes darted to Desaguliers and back to Falke. 'Would *you* speak of what it is you need, and why?'

Zar-bettu-zekigal held out her hand to Falke. Prompting.

'If I must. If it will make you speak, after.' Falke reached up with grazed and cut fingers. A few strands of black still ran from his temples into his curling white hair. He pulled the cloth bandage free of his eyes again.

'You and I', he said, 'are ruled by the Thirty-Six.'

His long fine lashes blinked over eyes without irises. Midnight-black pupils, vastly expanded, unnaturally dilated, swallowed all the colour that might have been.

He rubbed water from his left eye, blinking again, and shot a glance at Desaguliers.

'I don't want to make a display of this, but I will. I hide my eyes, because all light's too strong for me now, and because I don't want to think about them, being like this, what they are.'

'How . . . ?' Zari clapped her hand over her mouth.

Falke wound the cloth around his knuckles; his hand lifted to shade his eyes.

'You come to me, a Master Mason. I, and my hall brethren, all of us are builders for our strange masters. We build still, as we have built for generations uncounted. What we build – the Fane – is a cold stone shell. Nothing human has been into the heart of the Fane since building finished there.'

Sun and silence filled the hall.

'Except, once, myself. I *saw* . . .

'I was fool enough to find my way in. In to the centre. There's a cold cancer eating away, spreading out, stone by stone, year by year. We build it for them, and then they make it theirs. We build for God and They transform it. We only see shadows of what They seem. Inside, in the heart of the Fane, you see what They really are.'

His strong fingers began to smooth out the bandage; shifted to knuckle the sepia lids of his eyes.

'Only, having once seen that, you never truly cease to see it.'

The lean Rat, Desaguliers, grunted. 'All of which is no doubt true, and was true in our fathers' fathers' time, so why should we concern ourselves with it?'

Falke, very quietly, said: 'Because we are still building. We are compelled. Not even their servants – their slaves.'

'I can't see the importance of that. It's always been so. You . . .' The Captain-General's gesture took in the men and women who sat around the trestle table. Scepticism was plain on his wolfish face. 'You think you'll do what, exactly, against the Decans our masters?'

The fair-haired woman next to Zari sighed. 'Tell them, Falke.'

Falke stared at his hands.

'This hall is searching for the lost Word. The Word that the Builder died to conceal when this city was invaded, and the Temple of Salomon abandoned. The Word of Seshat – that has been lost for millennia. And for that long our own Temple has remained unfinished, while we're forced to build in slavery for strange masters.'

50

Tannakin Spatchet slowly sat down, pale blue eyes dazed.

'Yes, I'm speaking of Craft mysteries.' Falke's wide-set eyes met Zari's gaze, dark lashes blinking rapidly over pupils clear as polished black glass. 'We search for the lost Degree, and the lost Mark. And the lost Mystery: we know who built the South side of our Temple, and what their wages were; but until we know the secrets of the Aust side, and what the black-and-white pillars support, we remain as we are – slaves. When we know, when our New Temple can be begun—'

'We'll build it and make the heart of the world the New Jerusalem,' the fair-haired woman completed.

Falke lifted his shoulders in a weary shrug. 'We must have our own power, you see. Build for ourselves again, and not for our masters.'

The Captain-General stood, scaly tail lashing. 'And this is what you've got yourself mixed up in? Plessiez, you fool! Will you listen to him talk against the Thirty-Six and not protest? They'll eat him alive, man!'

Plessiez smiled. 'If I were afraid of the Decans our masters, I would not have begun this.'

Tannakin Spatchet stared at the *ankh* on the black Rat's breast. 'You're a priest, my lord! How can you talk against Them? They're the very breath and soul of your Church—'

Plessiez reached down and ran a thumb along the *ankh*'s heavy emeralds. Whimsical, he said: 'It is a little oppressive for any church, you must admit, to have God incarnate on earth; and not only on earth, but also, as it were, down the next street, and the next . . .'

Scandalized, the plump Mayor protested. 'Messire!'

'That They are god is true, that They are with us on this earth is true; and some say, also,' Plessiez added, 'that we would be better off were They to abandon Their incarnations here and resume their Celestial habitations.'

Desaguliers' tone of incredulity cut the hot white hall like acid: 'And *you* hope to affect the Thirty-Six?'

The black Rat smoothed down his scarlet jacket, a

slightly dazed expression on his face. 'Ah, perhaps my ambitions are not so high. Perhaps I only seek to move Them by affecting Their creations. I will say no more on this, messire; it is not part of our bargain.'

Desaguliers swore, and Zari motioned him to silence. She swung round in her chair, drawing one leg up under her, staring at Plessiez.

'Then, I'll speak for you.' Falke stood, both empty hands resting palm-down on the table. 'Knowledge was the price of my consent to the bargain. If our plans are betrayed to the King, then so will yours be!'

He faced Desaguliers. 'As to *magia* – yes. What Messire Plessiez will do might be called necromancy, being that sort of poor *magia* that can be done using the cast-off shells of souls, that is, mortal bodies.

'I know that Messire Plessiez plans the invoking of a plague-*magia*. A great plague indeed, but not a contamination that will kill my kind, or yours, Messire Desaguliers; instead a plague of such dimensions that it will touch the Decans Themselves.'

Desaguliers stroked the grizzled fur at his jaw-line. His slender fingers moved unsteadily. 'Plessiez, man, you are mad. The Fane knows all the pox-rotted arts of *magia*. This is lunacy.'

Plessiez rose from his chair. 'I will see his Majesty made a true King, Desaguliers, and that can't be done while there are masters ruling over us!'

Desaguliers snapped his fingers. Metal scraped as three more of the lithe black Rat Cadets drew their swords.

'Lunacy – and treason. I'm having you arrested—'

Zari felt the wood of the table shake under her spread palms.

The fat Mayor sprang back, swatting an armed cadet aside like a child; seized the arm of one of his companions and pulled her towards the door. 'What did I tell you? I told them so!'

A copper taste invaded her tongue, familiar from that morning in the university courtyard.

'Run!'

She got one foot on the chair, launched herself off it as dust and splintered wood thundered down across the table, blinded by sudden hot brilliance; missed her footing and sprawled into the warm brown fur of Charnay. She sat up, head ringing.

Falke stared up and flung an arm across his lined worn face.

The Katayan grabbed, missed, then got her hands to Plessiez's ankle where he gazed up, transfixed, and brought him crashing down on top of her; coiled her tail around Falke's leg and pulled. The man fell to his knees.

A searing chill passed overhead.

Zari gazed up at the open sky: brown now, and blackening, like paper in a fire.

Dust skirled up from the hall's collapsed roof. The far wall teetered, groaned, and with a wrench and scream of tearing wood fell into the yard.

Feet trampled her, human and Rat, running in all directions. She saw some men, fleeing, almost at the yard-gate, duck as they ran; and something chill and shadowed passed above her.

'Look—'

She caught Falke's arm, but the man was too busy scrabbling at the planks they sprawled on for his eye-bandage. Charnay grabbed her discarded rapier and pushed Plessiez down, half-crouching over him, snarling up at the sky.

A woman in red satin overalls threw up her arms and screamed. Coils of black bristle-tail lapped her body, biting deep into her stomach, blood dulling the satin. Ribbed wings beat, closing about her as tooth and beak dipped for her face.

Fire burst from the wooden hall walls in hollow concussive plops, burning blue and green in the noon-twilight. Rapidly spreading, consuming even the earth and the yard's timber outside, it formed a circling wall of flames. One of Desaguliers' Cadets thrust at it with his sword. A thin scream pierced the air: the Rat fell back on to the hall floor, fur blazing.

The sun burned with a searing storm-light.

Out of that sky, stinking of wildfire and blood, wings beating the stench of carrion earthwards, by dozens and hundreds, the Fane's acolytes fell down to feed.

2

Evelian bent over the washtub in the courtyard. The young man locked his apartment door and began walking towards the exit-passage. She looked up, red-faced, wiped her forehead with a soapy wrist, and called to him.

'Lucas, wait. Is Zaribeth there?'

The dark-haired young man shook his head. Despite the misty heat he was buttoned to the throat, in a black doublet with a small neck-ruff, and his breeches and stockings were spotless.

'Her bed hasn't been slept in.'

'*Her* bed!' Evelian snorted. Lucas paused.

A granular mist fogged the air, blurring the roofs of the two-storey timber-framed apartments overlooking the yard. Intermittent watery sun shone down on washing, limp on the cherry trees, and the scent of drying linen filled the air.

Evelian slapped a shirt against the washboard. She wore her yellow hair pinned up in a tangle, and an apron over the blue-and-yellow satin dress. 'Brass nerve, that child! Do you know, one night, I found her in *my* bed? Yesterday. No; night before last.'

She put a hand in the small of her back and stretched. 'I came up to my room and there she was, under the sheet in my bed, naked as an egg! Looked at me with those big brown eyes, and asked did I really want her to go, and didn't I need keeping warm of nights?'

Lucas coloured. Outside the yard, Clock-mill struck the half-hour.

'I told her we're in the middle of a heatwave as it is,' Evelian added, 'and up she got, all pale and freckled, little

55

tits and fanny, with that fool tail of hers whisking up the dust. I turned her round and smacked her one that'll have left a mark! Told her not to be an idiot; I don't sleep with my lodgers. Oh, now, see you; I've made you blush.'

'Not at all.' Lucas shifted awkwardly. 'It's just a warm morning.'

'I *wish*' – a vicious slap at wet cloth – 'that I knew where she *was*.'

Lucas felt the mist prickle warmly against his face. Looking at the cloud that clung to the roof-trees put the black timber frieze in his line of vision; bas-relief spades, crossed femurs, hour-glasses, money-sacks and skulls.

He snapped: 'I don't know where she is. I don't care! If you knew what I had to go through yesterday, to get out of what that little bitch got me into . . . '

Evelian flipped shirts into the soapy water, and plunged her arms in, scrubbing hard. The shadowless light eased lines from her face. She could have been twenty rather than forty.

'I'm not getting mixed up in whatever's biting you, boy. I swore last time that I'd have nothing to do with organizing against the Rat-Lords. The only good thing I ever got out of that was my Sharlevian. But, there, I live in the city; there isn't any escape from it.' Evelian stepped into the cherry tree, into cool green leaves and damp linen. 'The little Katayan's hardly older than Sharlevian. I like the girl. I worry about her.'

Another door opened across the yard, and a student scuttled towards the exit-passage, calling: 'Luke, see you there. Don't be late!' Evelian saw him bristle at *Luke*.

On the point of going, he turned back.

'Yesterday afternoon. I tasted . . . could taste blood. Coppery.' He went on quickly. 'Others, here, they did, too. Like yesterday morning, when one of the . . . one of them came to the university. As if something watched . . . '

She wiped her hands on her apron, and her blue eyes went vague for a long minute.

'Mistress Evelian?'

'Get someone to read the cards or dice for you,' she said.

'Yes! But is there anyone, here?'

Evelian nodded. A coil of fair hair escaped a clip and fell down across her full bodice.

'The White Crow. That's who you want. Do you dice, cards, palms – anything you can think of. The only practising Hermetic philosopher in this quarter, as far as I can make out.'

'I can't be late; it's my first day—' Lucas shut his mouth with a snap. 'Yes, I can. To quote Reverend Master Candia, there are no rules at the University of Crime. Where is this White Crow?'

'Right across the yard here. Those top apartments on the left-hand side.' Evelian pointed to the rickety wooden steps leading to the first floor. 'Just knock and go in. All my lodgers are . . . *unique* in some way.'

He took a few steps, and her voice came back from behind him: 'Ask about Zaribeth!'

The wooden hand-rail felt hot, damp in the swirling mist. Lucas glanced up at the windows and open skylight as he mounted the steps. The diamond-panes fractured thin sunlight into splinters. Children yelped in the street beyond the passage; somewhere there was a smell of boiled cabbage.

He rapped on the door, and it swung open, outwards. Calling loudly, 'Hello in there!' Lucas walked in.

The first room was light, airy, and piled high with volumes of leather-bound books. Books stood on chairs, shelves, leaned on the window-sill, slid off a couch. Only the round table, with its patchwork cloth, was clear.

'Mistress White Crow?'

'Here.' The far door opened. A woman in a white cotton shirt and cut-off brown knee-breeches came in. A white dog followed at her bare heels.

Her hair was a tumbling mass of dark red-brown, almost a cinnamon colour; and, where she had pinned the sides

57

back from her face, bright silver streaked her temples. She stood a few inches shorter than Lucas, wiry, with something languid in her movements. He thought her about thirty years old.

She nodded to him, and crossed to the window, leaning on the sill and sniffing at the heat of the morning. Her smile was melancholy. Lucas caught a flash of white; noticed that she wore a fingerless cotton glove on her left hand. The palm was dotted with red.

'Don't touch Lazarus,' she warned. 'He isn't a pet.'

Lucas turned his head. The dog was no dog. Large, with a shaggy white coat that faded into a silver ruff; the muzzle sharp and thinly pointed. It turned its head, staring at him with blue eyes. Sweat prickled between his shoulder-blades as the silver-grey timber wolf padded past him and lay down across the doorway.

The door swung back open, on creaking hinges. The White Crow raised red-brown eyebrows, and smiled at Lucas. 'Disconcerting, isn't it? Tell me about yourself.'

'Aren't *you* meant to do that?'

'You want me to read dice or cards,' the woman remarked, lifting several volumes of Paracelsus from an armchair, 'and you act like a damned aristo. You're studying at the university, but all of that I could have heard where I heard your name, Lucas. From gossip. I don't do party tricks. Sit down.'

Lucas stiffened. The cinnamon-haired woman dusted her hands together, and winced.

She pulled the patchwork cloth from the round table. Mirror-glass glimmered. Businesslike, she bent down, undid a catch, and spun the mirror on its spindle until the wooden backing was uppermost. A click of the catch and the table was firm.

Reaching up to a cupboard, the White Crow remarked, 'Dice, I think,' and pulled a brown silk scarf out and floated it down across the table.

Lucas picked the empty chair up and put it by the table. Something brushed his hair, buzzed sharply; he shook his head, and a honey-bee wavered off across the room. The woman put up a finger. The bee clung there for a moment while she brought it up close to eyes that, Lucas saw, glowed tawny amber; her lips pursed, and she blew gently. The bee hummed, flying drunkenly through the open window.

'Why "White Crow"?' Lucas sat, lounging back in the chair and crossing his legs.

She smiled. Under the white cotton shirt, her breasts were small and firm. Crow's-feet starred the corners of her eyes, and the slightest fat was beginning to blur the line of her jaw.

'Because it's not in the slightest like my own name— Quiet, Lazarus.'

The wolf snapped, snarled a quick high whine, as two more bees flew in at the door. The White Crow held out a hand absently. As the bees alighted there, she transferred them to her red-brown hair, where they crawled sluggishly, buzzing. Lucas's skin crawled.

'If you have a silver shilling,' she said, 'it would speed matters up considerably. Now where did I . . . ? Oh, yes.'

She pushed books off the window-sill left-handed, regardless of where they fell. The sill opened. From the compartment, she took a handful of dice. She looked about for a moment for somewhere to sit, and then pulled a tall stool out from a corner.

Lucas sat up. The White Crow threw the dice loosely onto the brown silk covering the table. There were eight or nine of them: cubes of bone. And laid into each die-face, in brilliant enamel, was a picture or image.

'Just handle those for a minute, will you, and then cast them?'

Mist cleared and clouded, visible through the open skylight, and the room seemed to swell or darken as the sun shone or diminished. The woman reached up to a high shelf. Her shirt pulled taut across her breasts and pulled out of her breeches waistband, so that he saw tanned flesh in the gap. Lucas shuffled the dice in both hands, leaning forward to the table to conceal his arousal.

She took down a stole and slung it about her neck. The white satin shone, embroidered with dozens of tiny black characters.

'Now,' she said, and Lucas cast the handful of dice on the table.

He drew in a sharp breath. Of the nine die-faces, four were showing a white enamelled skull with blue periwinkle eyes, the other five a tiny knotted cord – the knot with which a shroud is tied.

The White Crow leaned over, squinting, and her dark red eyebrows went up.

'Damn things are on the blink again. Here, we'll try the cards. How old are you?'

'Nineteen.' Lucas slid a hand down between himself and the table, and tugged surreptitiously at the seam of his breeches. His eyes followed the woman as she padded about the room, turning up books and piles of paper, obviously searching.

Something about her made him want to drop all pretence. 'Actually,' Lucas said, 'I'm the heir to the throne of Candover. Prince Lucas. Eldest son of King Ordono.'

She trod on the end of the satin stole, and swore.

'Incognito?'

'That was my idea.' He pushed his fingers through his thick springy hair. 'I thought it would be good. To not be a king's son. I suppose I thought people would treat me the same; that it would show through, naturally, somehow – what I really am.'

The White Crow said drily, 'Perhaps it does,' and straightened up with a much-thumbed pack of cards. She gave them to Lucas and slumped down on the stool, puffing.

'But there's no advantage to it, I can see that.' Lucas shuffled the cards. 'I'll give it up, I think.'

'Oh, to be nineteen and romantic!' The woman smiled, sardonic. She took the cards back and began to lay them out on the brown silk cover. When she had put twelve in a diamond-pattern, she stopped.

As she bent forward, squinting down at the table, Lucas saw that she had faint golden freckles on her cheek-bones. Her hair was coming down on one side, the silver flowing.

The White Crow fumbled in her shirt pocket for a pair of gold-rimmed spectacles, shoved them firmly on, and announced: '*Now* . . . '

Lucas saw a mess of deuces and knaves.

'What's a king's son doing studying at the University of Crime anyway?'

'My father said it would be the best-possible training for the crown. I already had an aptitude for it. What can you see?'

The spice-haired woman sat back and whipped off her glasses.

'Nothing. Oh, I can see pointers . . . You should go to the docks, soon.'

She peered at the cards again.

'Or the main station.'

She turned up another card: the Page of Sceptres.

'Or the airfield.' Disgusted, she swept the cards together. 'This is ridiculous! I've been doing this more years than you've been alive, and now I'm getting nothing here, nothing at all.'

Silence filled the room. The White Crow stood, moving to the window, replacing dice and cards in the sill-compartment. Mist frayed, admitting light, and the sun caught the silver in her hair; and Lucas stood up and walked to the window.

'It reminds me of the White Mountains,' he said, sniffing deeply.

The woman folded her satin stole. She put it down on the sill, rested her fists on it, and leaned out to look at the heat and droplets of fog. Sheets and linen draped the trees in the yard. There was a lingering scent of soap and drains.

'There comes a time', the White Crow said, 'when you can't smell the air of *any* kind of a day without it bringing some other past day to mind. When that happens, you're not old, but you're no longer young.'

Lucas leaned his arm across the window-frame behind her back, close enough that the hairs on his bare skin prickled.

'You're not old.'

The timber wolf whined, half-rose, and sank down again across the doorstep.

'Telling you you'll meet someone at an airfield, or a station, it's kitchen-teacup magic!' She picked up a heavy octavo volume from a chair. 'Birthdate?'

Lucas took his arm away, not certain it had even been noticed.

'Midwinter Eve, the seven hundred and fiftieth year from the founding of Candover.'

'That corresponds to . . . ' She flicked pages, resting the book on the sill, searching for the relevant page. A whisk of dust caught in Lucas's throat. Midway, she glanced up, thin shoulders sagging.

'Why lie? I can't do this. Yesterday – there was such a use of power in the city yesterday that it's deafened and blinded me. I could no more read for you than fly.'

'Evelian told me some people were injured, over in one of the other quarters.'

'Injured and killed. That's twice the acolytes have been sent out to feed since the spring.'

The White Crow held out a hand into open air, and another bee alighted, crawling across her unbandaged palm.

'Maybe I can do something for you, all the same.'

She nudged at her temple. One of the bees that crawled in her hair flew off. She abruptly closed her hand over the remaining one, blew a *ftt!* into her fist and opened it in front of Lucas's nose.

A solid gold bee lay on her palm.

'*Take* it. Think of it as a hair-grip.' The White Crow's

humour was exasperated. 'Go to your meeting, whoever it turns out to be. This may be some protection. You won't have heard of it, but a while back it was a recognized sign. If you need to convince anyone that you know a magus, then show them this.'

Lucas picked it up gingerly, between thumb and fore-finger. It was cold, heavy, hard metal.

'But I'd be obliged', the woman added, 'if you didn't show it to anyone unnecessarily.'

He opened his mouth to voice discontent, and the wolf raised its head and gazed at him with pale blue eyes. It did not look away. Lucas broke the contact first.

'One more thing,' he insisted. 'Evelian will be worried if I don't ask. The South Katayan student who lodges here. Zari. Can you find out where she is now?'

Desaguliers paused outside the audience chamber, remov-ing his plumed headband. A blowfly buzzed round his ears, and he swatted it irritably away. He pulled his cloak up about his lean shoulders, concealing the worst patches of charred fur, and took a deep breath.

'Enter!'

The Captain-General hesitated. His wolfish face was lost for a moment in calculation. Then he shrugged and pushed his way through the double doors.

Watery sunlight shafted from full-length windows into the audience chamber, glowing on the blue drapes and gold-starred canopy. Desaguliers approached the bed.

'Your Majesty,' he said.

Eight Rats lay on the great circular bed on the dais. Three were being fed and groomed by servants. Another lay asleep. One black Rat had a secretary seated on the carpeted dais steps, reading a report to him in a low voice, and two Rats (fur so pale it was almost silver) dictated letters. The eighth Rat beckoned Desaguliers.

The Captain-General climbed the steps to kneel before the bed. The Rats lay with their bodies pointing outwards, their tails in the centre of the bed's silks and pillows. Each scaly tail wound in and out of the others, tangled, tied, fixed in a fleshy knot; and Desaguliers could see (as a brown Rat page carefully cleaned) where the eight tails had inextricably grown together.

'A serious matter.' The Rats-King brushed crumbs from his gold-and-white jacket. He reclined on his side, facing Desaguliers: a bony black Rat in late middle age.

'One of my Cadets lost his life. Three others are so badly injured that it will be months before they return to military service.' Desaguliers paused. 'Has your Majesty received word from the Fane this morning?'

'No word—'

The bony Rat picked a sweetmeat from a dish, bit into it, and the half-sleeping black Rat on his left opened his mouth to murmur: ' – from the Fane at all,' while the first Rat chewed.

Desaguliers suppressed a shiver. He straightened his shoulders, wincing where his leather harness galled burned flesh.

'I discovered what I could, your Majesty. There were Rats present at this hall meeting, a priest called Plessiez, and one of your Majesty's guard, by name Charnay; both of whom were killed. There were also a number of humans that died in the attack, most but not all of hall rank.'

The first Rat bowed his head, while a page brushed the fur along his jaw and behind his translucent ears. His shining black eyes met Desaguliers'.

'And you have no idea of the purpose of the meeting?'

Desaguliers' gaze did not alter. 'None at all, your Majesty. I continue to investigate. The attack came very shortly after I entered the Masons' Hall, and I had no chance to question anyone.'

The bony Rat nodded. A fly buzzed thickly past. The sleeping Rat, eyes still half-shut, said: 'You were lucky, messire, to live.'

'The hall turned out to have a small cellar underneath. I and my Cadets took shelter there.' Desaguliers halted at the black Rat's glare, and qualified: 'Truthfully, your Majesty, we fell through when the floor collapsed, and emerged after the Fane's acolytes had gone. I had the cellar and the rubble searched for bodies – rather, remains of bodies.'

Another brown Rat secretary came to read reports; and Desaguliers overheard the twin silver Rats say, in perfect unison: 'Send in the ambassador first; then the Second District Aust quarter delegation—'

' – afterwards,' the bony black Rat finished, smiling. 'Very well, Desaguliers. We're pleased that we still have our Captain-General.'

'Luck,' Desaguliers said, relaxing, and with a genuine regret in his tone. 'We were lucky to come out of that. No-one else who was caught in the building survived.'

No through-draught moved in the room under the rafters. A fly skewed right-angles across the air, sounding distant in the heat, although it was only a few feet above his head. Lucas bent over the paper, imprinting neat cuneiform characters with an ink-stylus.

I like the University well enough, sister; you'd like it, too. Tell our father that I will stay here for the three years. It will please him.

Candover seems very far away now.

He put the stylus down on the table. His jacket already lay over the back of his chair; now he unbuttoned his shirt and pulled it out of his belt. Scratching in the dark curls of his chest, he wrote:

I consulted a philosopher (which is what they call a seer here) earlier this morning, but she could tell me nothing. She says she will draw a natal chart for one of the other students, but it will take her a few hours. I've said I'll go back at noon.

Footsteps crossed the courtyard below. Lucas leaped from his chair and leaned over the window-sill.

Mistress Evelian waved a greeting, gestured that she would speak but couldn't: mouth full of clothes-pegs. Last remnants of mist blurred the tiled roofs. A smell of boiled cabbage drifted in. On the street side of the room, the noise of a street-player's lazy horn wound up into the late-morning air.

Hugging himself, sweaty, Lucas crossed back to the table.

Gerima, perhaps I won't come back to Candover at all. I might not go to the university. I might just stay here in the city.

The skylight screeched, dropping rust-flakes into his eyes as he wedged it further open. The air up on the slanting roof hit him like warm water, and he drew his head back inside. A bird cried.

The seer is a woman who calls herself the White Crow. I said I would call back for the birthstar chart myself, although the person it concerns is no friend of mine. The White Crow—

The slow horn milked heat from the day, drowsing all the morning's actions away into dreams.

He scratched at the hair of his chest, fingers scrabbling down to the thin line of back-growing hair on his belly. Sweat slicked his fingers. The narrow room (only bed, table and cast-iron basin in it) stifled him. Dizzy, dazed, drunk on nothing at all, Lucas threw himself down on his back on the bed and stared up through the open window at the sky.

Imaging in his mind how her hair, that strange dark red, is streaked with a pure silver and white, flowing from her temples. How her eyes, when they smile, seem physically to radiate warmth: an impossibility of fiction, but striking home now to some raw new centre inside him.

Gerima, so much of her life has gone past and I don't know what it is. I would like to go back and make it turn out right for her. If she laughs at me, I'll kill myself.

The slow heat stroked his body as he stripped, lying back on the white linen. Imaging in his mind how sweat darkens her shirt under the arms, and in half-moons under each breast, and the contrast between her so-fine-textured skin and her rough cloth breeches. His fingers pushed through the curly hair of his genitals, cupped his balls for a moment; and then slid up to squeeze in slow strokes. His breathing quickened.

A faint breeze rose above the window-sill and blew the unfinished letter on to the floor.

On the far side of the courtyard Clock-mill struck eleven. An authoritative knocking came on the street-door. The White Crow swore, threw down her celestial charts and padded barefoot down the narrow stairway to the street.

'*Yes?*'

A man gazed nervously up and down the cobbled lane. A dirty grey cloak swathed him from head to heels, the hood pulled far forward to hide his face.

'Are you the White Crow?'

The White Crow leaned one elbow on the door-frame, and her head on her hand. She looked across at the hooded face (standing on the last step, she was just as tall as he) and raised an eyebrow.

'Aren't you a little warm in that?'

The air over the cobbles shimmered with heat, now that the early mist had burned away. The man pushed his hood far enough back for her to see a fleshy sweat-reddened face.

'My name is Tannakin Spatchet,' he announced. 'Mayor of the District's East quarter. Lady, I was afraid you wouldn't want to be seen receiving such an unrespectable visitor.'

The White Crow blinked.

'What do you want?'

'Talismans.' He leaned forward, whispering. 'Charms that warn you when the Decans' acolytes are coming.'

'No such thing. Go away. That's not possible.'

His fleshy arm halted the door as she slammed it. 'It *is* possible! A girl saved six people's lives yesterday with such a warning. She's dead now. For the safety of my quarter's citizens, I want some talisman or hieroglyph that will give us warning if it happens again!'

The White Crow gestured with spread palms, pushing

67

the air down, as if physically to lower the man's voice. She frowned. Lines at the corners of her eyes radiated faintly down on to her cheek-bones, visible in the sunlight.

He said: '*Is* it possible?'

'Mmm . . . Bruno the Nolan incontrovertibly proves how *magia* runs in a great chain from the smallest particle, the smallest stone, up to microbes, bacteria; roses, beasts and men; daemonic and angelic powers – and to those Thirty-Six Who create all in Their divinity. And how *magia*-power may be heard and used up and down the Great Chain of Being . . . '

The White Crow tapped her thumb against her teeth.

'I use the Celestial world. Yes . . . Master Mayor, you realize talismans can be traced to the people who made them? People who make them, here, they don't live long. Who sent you to me?' she temporized.

'A friend, an old friend of mine. Mistress Evelian. She mentioned a Hermetic philosopher lodging with her . . . '

The White Crow shoved a hand through her massy hair, and leaned out to look up and down the street. 'That woman is perilously close to becoming a philosopher's pimp. Oh, come in, come in. Mind the— Never mind.'

Tannakin Spatchet rubbed his forehead where the low doorway caught him, and followed her up the dark stairs.

She led him through a room with an iron stove to one side and a scarcely less rigid bed to the other, and through into an airy room smelling of paper and leather bindings. She held out a hand for his cloak.

'Can you help, lady?'

The White Crow folded the cloak, studying the bulky fair-haired man. He seemed in his fifties, too pallid for health. She dropped the cloak randomly across a stack of black-letter pamphlets.

'Mayor of the Nineteenth District,' she repeated.

'Of its East quarter. I regret coming to you in this unceremonious manner. I brought no clerks or recorders, thinking the whole matter best kept quiet.' He cleared his throat. 'Yesterday . . . '

68

Tannakin Spatchet touched a finger to the cleared chair, looked distastefully at the book-dust, and seated himself gingerly. Then he met the White Crow's gaze, his fussiness gone.

'Yesterday I saw Decans' acolytes', the Mayor said, 'closer than I ever hope to see them again. Five of my people are missing – dead, I should say. I need someone to advise me.'

A beast yipped. The White Crow's preoccupied gaze snapped back into focus. She crossed the room and squatted down, picking up from a padded box a young fox-cub and reaching for a glass bottle. As she seated herself on the window-sill, the reddish lump of fur in her lap stinking of vixen, and bent her head to feed it, she said: 'At a Masons' Hall, in the East quarter.'

'You know of it?'

'Evelian told me this morning. I think she knew some-one in the hall. I knew that *something* had been destroyed.' She held out a free hand, the bandages on the palm newly bloodstained. 'We respond, some of us, to such disturbances.'

The warm wind blew in at the window, easing the fox-stink.

'What I say must go no further.'

She jerked her head at the room: the books, charts, orreries and globes. 'I am what I am, messire. If you want my help, tell me why.'

'I . . . know so little,' Tannakin Spatchet confessed. 'We're not admitted to the mysteries of the halls. I heard of the meeting only at the last moment. I and my councillors thought fit to force an entrance. Would to god we never . . . Master Falke spoke there. Of ways to free us from those who rule the city.'

Pain ached in her palm. The fox-cub whined, nipping sleepily at her wrist.

'Stupid! *Stupid*. What were you going to fight Decans with, messire – your bare hands?'

'Lady, I have no proof, but I believed Master Falke

to be a secret officer in the Society of the House of Salomon – they having their secret officers infiltrated into almost every hall.'

He glanced over his shoulder at the open window.

'The House of Salomon say that since we build stone on stone to increase the Fane's power, then we could raze stone *from* stone, so raze the Fane and the power of the Thirty-Six with it. Could that be so, lady?'

'In all the greater and the lesser *magias*, patterns compel.'

The White Crow rubbed her knuckles along the fox-cub's rough coat. It opened tiny amber eyes. She yipped under her breath, very softly, and reached down to tap a heavily bound copy of Vitruvius' *The Ten Books on Architecture* resting on the sill.

'This House of Salomon seems to follow orthodox teaching. Vitruvius writes that the measurements of a truly constructed building mirror both the proportions of the human body and the shape of the universal Order. Microcosm mirrors macrocosm; the Fane mirrors the Divine within. Theoretically, break Their mirror and you remove Their channels of power. But we speak of the Thirty-Six.'

Tannakin Spatchet shivered. The White Crow shrugged. 'It's foolhardy. The Decans aren't so easily challenged.' She spoke with the contempt of long knowledge. 'They loosed the *least* of their servants on you, and—'

Tannakin Spatchet rose. 'Do I look so much of a fool? Falke called the meeting; I heard of it only by chance. Falke called in Fellowcrafts from half the halls in the quarter; *Falke* brought in the Rat-Lords, and a Kings' Memory!'

'This is the Master of the Hall? And you couldn't stop it, Master Mayor?'

'A builder listen to any one of us! Very likely.' Deep sarcasm sounded in the Mayor's voice. He looked down at the White Crow. 'Someone betrayed the meeting to those at the Fane. Falke's dead. So are those others who didn't get out in time. If they knew who betrayed them, I don't.'

He wiped his forehead. 'I'm sorry, lady. I've spent the morning with widows and children. It isn't easy explaining to them how I am still alive and the others dead.'

The White Crow put the fox-cub back into its box. She brushed orange hairs from her shirt and knee-breeches, sniffed her fingers, and wrinkled her nose. She raised her head and stared through the open window. No dark in her vision, no taste in her mouth but sour wine.

'Decans. As if', she said, 'you or I were to pour boiling water into an ant's nest. Does it matter if a few escape? With only a little more effort they could cauterize the city itself, humans and Rats together.'

Tannakin Spatchet sat down slowly. He absently began to straighten the edges of the stacked papers on the table. 'What are we? Their hands. Their *builders*. Of no more significance than a trowel, a hod, a pair of compasses. The least we need is warning, when they exercise their power. Lady, can you help me?'

'If I can, I will.'

The determination in that seemed to surprise even her. She stood and briskly began sorting through books on a low shelf.

'You tell me other halls were involved? And so there'll be more meetings . . . ?' The White Crow straightened, a hand in the small of her back.

Tannakin Spatchet said: 'Is a scrying spell possible?'

She looked questioningly at him.

'To discover who betrayed them to the Decans,' the Mayor amplified. 'And why.'

'More difficult. I can try. Tell me, first, who was there. Who was in the hall when it was destroyed.'

The White Crow looked out into the courtyard, and saw Mistress Evelian, golden hair shining in the sun, pegging out washing; and holding a shouted conversation with the dark-haired student, Lucas, at his attic window.

'The Master of the Hall, Falke; and his sister, Awdrey,

71

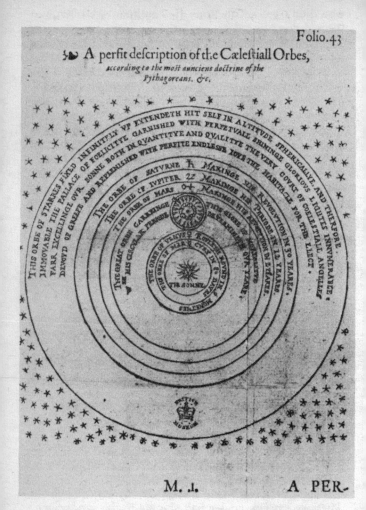

'In all the greater and the lesser *magias, patterns compel.*'

From *A Perfit Description of the Cælestiall Orbes*, Thomas
Digges, London, 1576

who was Mistress Royal to the Children of the Widow. Two Apprentices from out of the quarter. A man and two women I didn't recognize. The Captain-General of the King's Guard, Desaguliers.'

Tannakin Spatchet paused. The White Crow scratched at rough parchment with a quill pen, noting names.

' " . . . Captain-General." I'll have to ask questions carefully in *that* quarter. Who else?'

He watched her handwriting: stark and sloping across the page.

'A brown Rat. I believe she was a soldier. A priest: a black Rat that the Captain-General called by the name of Plessiez. And the girl who gave the warning, the Kings' Memory. Lady, she was very young. I don't know her name. She is the one who died – a Katayan.'

On the highest pinnacle yet built, among scaffolding lashed with hemp rope and net-cradled blocks of masonry, men are talking in whispers. Any sun is absorbed by the black stone. Acres of stone fall away below them, in crevasses and coigns.

Distance hides the ground below.

'They know!'

The hooks dangle from the derricks, empty, ropes creaking. All the cranes are abandoned.

'I tell you, they know what we're doing!'

They are in working clothes, silk and satin, each with the mark of his own particular Craft.

'We must act as if we were innocent. They need us to build for them.'

This ziggurat will rise between two pyramidical obelisks that are equal in thickness to the building itself. A mile away an identical pair of obelisks rises, completed two generations ago. Great hieroglyphs are burned into their stone sides. This burning of stone happened during an eclipse of the sun that lasted four days.

'No. We don't wait.' This speaker is the most assured. 'You're right: they need us to build, because they can't. So—'

'If we stop work, they'll kill enough of us that the rest will go back to work. We've tried that before.'

To north and east and aust of the ziggurat, more of the Fane's perpendicular frontages cut the sky. Here, the sky itself is the colour of ashes.

'They can force us to work,' the first speaker says, 'but who can force a man to eat or to sleep?'

The ceiling-fan's eight-foot blades circled a slow *wck . . . wck . . . wck . . .* The only other noise came from the clerk's quill pen. Afternoon heat slanted in through pale-green shutters, drawn closed on the large room's south-austern side.

A breath of air came in from the opposite full-length shutters, open to the terrace, and touched the forehead of the man sleeping in the chair behind the desk. His eyelashes flickered. The Candovard Ambassador saw through sleep-watered vision the whitewashed walls, the pale-green fretworked wood that decorated doors and shutters and terrace balustrade.

A fist rapped the shutters. The thin young clerk stood up.

'Mhrumhh?' Andaluz raised his head alertly.

A young man held one shutter open, slatted shadow barring his body: bare feet and knee-breeches, and a doublet carried slung over one shoulder. Chest and shoulders and arms were rounded with muscle. He looked at Andaluz from under meeting brows.

'My dear Lucas!' Andaluz sprang up, waved the clerk back and came round the desk. 'My dear boy! I've been waiting for you to call.'

The younger man dropped his doublet over a chair, and the smaller man embraced him, kissing him on both cheeks. He put Lucas back to arm's length, studying him.

'I hear that you came in on the *Viper* yesterday morning. You should have called. Do I take it from this dress that you're still determined on disguise? Your mother wrote

74

to me some months ago about that. Most censoriously, I might add.'

The young man laughed, holding up both hands. 'I'll tell you, Uncle, if you'll let me speak.'

'Tea.' Andaluz snapped his fingers. The clerk left silently. Andaluz tugged at the hem of his sleep-creased white jacket, not bothering to do up the neck buttons. He scratched at his curled, grizzled hair.

'And how is my dear Pereluz?'

'Mother's fine.'

The youth looked up at a portrait hanging above the mahogany filing-cabinets. A patch of light picked out the woman who sat beside a sun-haired man. She wore a coronet, as her husband did, on hair as dark as Lucas's; and her fine brows came within a hair of meeting.

Andaluz saw, reflected in the glass covering, his and the young man's same features: forty years between them. Andaluz's hair was grizzled sharply black and white, with little grey in it.

'She told me to tell you she misses her favourite brother at court.'

'Ah, Pereluz.' The Ambassador patted Lucas's shoulder as he bustled back behind his desk. He picked up gold-rimmed spectacles and put them on. 'What can I arrange for you, Prince?'

He saw the dark gaze glint out from under heavy brows. Lucas moved in the heat-shadowed room like a breath of the outside world: sweet-tempered, smelling of sweat and sunshine.

'Yes, I do want you to do something for me. I want it made clear to the university that I start there tomorrow, not today.' The young man paused, as the clerk returned with iced tea.

Andaluz scribbled a short note, handed it to the clerk and sent her off with whispered instructions.

'Done, I think. What else?'

Lucas smiled. 'Does it show so clearly?'

'My dear Lucas, if this were a social visit, you would

have called yesterday. Besides, I'm told that your stay here, short as it is, hasn't been uneventful.' Andaluz broke off, rubbing the bridge of his nose. 'Tell me about it. I can cease to be official for a few minutes.'

The young man shook his head decisively.

'I want you to investigate a death. A girl. She was a student, a Katayan; I can give you her full name.'

Andaluz's bushy eyebrows rose. 'A friend?'

'No. No . . . ' The young man looked away. 'I didn't like her, and I haven't changed my opinion because she died. I suppose I feel guilty about— *De mortuis nil nisi bonum.* But I want the full story. There are friends of hers who need to know. Her name was Zar-bettu-zekigal.'

Andaluz copied down the carefully enunciated syllables.

'Assume that I know something of this,' he said. 'The Embassy keeps an eye on you. What else?'

The young man paced across the faded carpet. He stopped for a time, looking out on to the wooden terrace, and across the stretch of yellow earth that, if not for the heat, would be a garden.

'I had another message for you, Uncle, but the person who sent it probably died when Zari did.' Lucas turned. 'A priest, a black Rat by the name of Plessiez. He said he knows . . . *knew* you. He sent his regards.'

Andaluz took off his spectacles, laying them on the papers on the desk. The ceiling-fan's *wck-wck* sounded loudly.

'The little priest is dead?'

'It's almost certain. Sorry.'

'I always *told* Plessiez that he'd go too far. Tell me all of it,' Andaluz directed and, when he had heard the boy out, shook his head slowly. 'The Embassy Compound's been quiet. I don't think we've had to deal with more than the Fane's intermediaries in five years. Now three secretaries and two ambassadors summoned by the Decans in half a day . . . '

Lucas said: 'I also need to know if you have a file on a woman. A natural philosopher: she calls herself the White

Crow. Most of what I've heard about the hall, I've heard through her. I want to know how reliable she is.'

Andaluz picked up a bell on his desk and rang it. After a few seconds, another clerk appeared; and the Candovard Ambassador handed him a slip of paper with two names on it. He sipped at his iced tea while he waited, studying the Prince's face.

'You're no longer incognito,' he said. 'Will you be moving in here? I've plenty of room.'

A chessboard occupied one corner of the large desk. Lucas leaned on his forearms, studying the game in progress, and reached to move a jet-carved pawn with dirty fingers. Andaluz all but saw images in the boy's mind: of the odd house off Carver Street to which the university had sent him. He restrained himself from comment.

'I'll stay where I am, Uncle, for the moment.'

The second clerk returned, putting a thick file of papers down in front of Andaluz. The Ambassador began to skim over the notes. When he spoke, it was without looking up.

'Your "White Crow" is easily identifiable. There aren't too many foreign natural philosophers in the city. Even though this one appears to change her name and move around – six months here, eight months there . . . '

Andaluz sat back. 'We have records for her going back five years. No reason in particular, except that, as a philosopher, she's kept under observation. She practises a little natural magic in order to make a living, it would seem.'

The boy had leaned forward. Now he bent his head, rubbing with both hands at the back of his neck. When he straightened, that might have been the reason for his heat-reddened cheeks.

Andaluz said gently: 'I hope you'll come here often, Lucas. I miss my countrymen, and family.'

The young man nodded, shifting awkwardly. 'Of course.'

'Sending you to the university was your father's idea. Of

course, the Ortiz have always had a strain of eccentricity in the blood—'

'And the Luz haven't?'

'My *dear* Lucas.'

A pair of blowflies buzzed around the tea-bowl, and Andaluz carefully fitted the weighted net cover over the ceramic. The flies settled on the cracked plaster ceiling, crawling there, beyond the fan-blades, with several dozen other insects.

'I intended to say, only, that this is not the summer I would choose to have the heir of Candover here.'

Lucas shrugged. 'I'm staying.'

'So I perceive.' Patience stayed Andaluz's tongue, long assumed and long practised. He looked up as the first clerk returned, handing him a written note in return for his message.

'Is there going to be trouble with the university?'

Andaluz read, and then looked up.

'I think not. All today's lectures were cancelled,' the Ambassador said. 'Term starts tomorrow. It seems that one of the lecturers has gone missing. A Reverend Master Candia?'

Lucas stared, startled. 'He was there yesterday with us. With the new intake.'

Andaluz shrugged. 'And now, apparently, drunk or dead or whatever the reason might be, completely vanished.'

Voices sound in the dark. The tones echo, as if from an immense space: bouncing back from hard surfaces. Mixed with those echoes is the sound of dripping water.

No light; no slightest peripheral gleam.

'Will you wait for me!' A scuffle and thud. 'You bastards can see in the dark and I can't!'

'Are you hurt, little one?'

An inaudible mumble.

Further off, another voice demands: 'What's she doing here?'

78

'She blundered in, Charnay, rather as you have a habit of doing. Don't complain. You have her to thank for your life.'

'Where the hell are we?'

'Not, I hope, in hell, although I confess to some doubt on the subject.'

Another voice speaks: 'Listen!'

The silence resumes. Far off, there is a noise that might be water, or wind, or some element of flux peculiar to darkness.

3

'The use', Reverend Mistress Heurodis announced, 'of the knife. You. Lucas. Come here.'

Light shone from perpendicular windows down into the university's training-hall. Lucas rubbed the sleep of his second night in the city from his eyes and walked out of the group of students.

'The knife can kill quickly, efficiently and, above all, *silently*.'

Heurodis's smoky blue eyes moved to Lucas. He hunched his shoulders unconsciously: her head only came up to the level of his collar-bone.

'Here.' She offered him the bone hilt of a knife, with a hand upon which the veins stood up, skin brown-spotted with age.

'Stab him,' she directed.

Lucas closed his hand on the knife. The blued-steel blade flashed, ugly; and he looked up from it to meet the glazed stare of the bound man beside Heurodis.

A smell of grease and old sweat came off the man; his ribs were visible under his shirt, and his yellow-grey hair marked him as only a few years younger than Heurodis.

'What are you waiting for?' the old lady demanded. 'A killing stroke – you would aim where?'

Lucas heard someone gasp behind him; refused to look back at the half-dozen other students. He nipped lower lip between tooth and incisor, frowning. The knife-blade chilled his thumb. A trickle of sweat ran down between his shoulder-blades.

'In cold blood?'

'This isn't a *game*, boy. If you think that it is, you have no business at the university!'

'I . . .'

He moved forward, boots loud on the scrubbed wooden floor. The bound man didn't move: drugged, dazed; the pulse beating steadily at the base of his corded throat. Heurodis leaned on her cane.

'I would cut the carotid artery *there*' – Lucas's free hand tapped the side of the man's throat – 'from the rear for preference, Reverend Mistress.'

He flipped the steel knife, caught it by the tip, held it out to her.

'But first I would make sure not to get into the situation. Or, if I had, that there was another way out of it. Or, if not, that I could stun rather than kill.'

Someone behind him muttered. A shadow flicked across the floor, from a bird passing the high windows; and far off a clock struck nine.

'Are you disobeying me, boy?' Her wrinkled face puckered into a smile. 'Good! The time will come when you have to kill to stay alive. But life is precious; you should always have a better reason for taking it than someone else's order.'

A tall girl stepped forward from the group. 'But we're here to learn, aren't we?'

Heurodis reached to take the knife from Lucas's outstretched hand. 'Certainly. And Reverend tutors mustn't be disobeyed, which is why Master Lucas will be scrubbing out the latrines this morning, as a punishment.'

Lucas wiped his wet palm on his shirt.

'As a point of reference,' the elderly lady said, 'we usually don't do any killing – knives, poisons, traps – until well into the second term.'

She gave the drugged man's tether to one of the hall-assistants, and as she passed Lucas he smelt frangipani and the scent of lilac. The old woman smoothed down her cotton dress.

'Pair off now. I want to see your techniques for

81

disarming someone who has a knife. Master Lucas, a word with you.'

The other new students began unrolling practice-mats. Lucas walked a few paces aside with the white-haired woman.

'I hear that you used some family influence yesterday to avoid the punishment for not attending.' She placed the top of her cane against Lucas's chest. 'Don't do that again. You could spend the rest of this term cleaning latrines.'

'I—' *was led astray by a dead girl*, Lucas finished the thought; and shut his mouth, and met Heurodis's smoky gaze. 'Sorry, Reverend Mistress.'

The cane rapped him familiarly under the fifth rib. She smiled, displaying long regular teeth. 'Good man.'

'When I've finished . . . *cleaning*' – Lucas's nostrils flared slightly – 'do I rejoin the class?'

'Yes.' Heurodis raised her voice inclusively. 'This afternoon you all have a session with Reverend Master Pharamond – and your first practice-session, out in the city itself.'

In the darkness, water dripped. Echoes ran off into the unseen distance. Cold moist air blew steadily now; and the stench of ordure was interrupted by scents of unbearable sweetness.

Rubble skittered across a hard surface. A grunt and an oath were succeeded by a splash.

'Zari?'

'My *foot*! My bare foot!'

The Katayan sprawled face-down across brick paving, half in and half out of a pool of water. She raised her head, pushing a chopped-off fringe of black hair out of her eyes, and then held up her hands, spread-fingered.

'Ei! I can *see*. It's light. Where's it coming from?'

She knelt up, wringing out the hem of her greatcoat. Her dappled tail cracked like a whip, and a fine spray of water flew into the darkness.

'Where are we? Can we get out of here?'

82

'I think it unlikely.'

Dim illumination shone on Plessiez, where the black Rat, drawn rapier in his hand, stood staring up a brick shaft that opened above his head. A cone of silvery light fell from it, on to a floor cluttered with broken bricks, stones, heaps of dried ordure, ossified branches and yellowing bones.

'Charnay, see if it's possible to climb here.'

The brown Rat emerged from the gloom. She put her fists on her furry haunches, craning her neck. The arched brick roof passed five or six feet above her head, and the shaft in it (easily thirty feet in diameter) opened without lip or ledge.

'It's smooth,' Charnay reported.

'I see that. Try if you can get a grip. *Climb.*'

Zar-bettu-zekigal stood up, shaking her dripping foot, and padded towards the light. The skeleton of a snake curved across the brick paving in front of her, entire, the delicate-branched vertebrae all intact; and she stooped to peer at the wedge-shaped skull.

It rose an inch, empty eye-sockets turning towards her; and glided smoothly under an abandoned heap of brushwood.

Zari took one step after the loose-rattling tail, hesitated, and limped over to the two Rats.

'Where's . . . ? We've lost Falke again,' she said.

Charnay's leap for the edge of the shaft connected briefly, and Plessiez stepped back as the brown Rat's wildly scrabbling hind foot swung past his head. Her tail whipped in wild circles.

'Damn the man.'

The brown Rat lost her tenuous grip, tangled a foot in her scabbard and tail on landing, and fell heavily on her rump. Plessiez side-stepped.

'I'm not his nurse!'

'Where *is* he?'

The shaft's dim light showed little around them but the walls. The scent of sweetness was stronger here. The

Katayan narrowed her eyes, discerning a phosphorescence patterning the brick vaulting. A paleness of brambles, toothed leaves, petals . . .

Zari stepped forward and stared up the shaft, hands shoved deep into her pockets. Dizzied by the receding circle of brickwork and the sweet stench, she stumbled back against Plessiez, grabbing the black Rat's arm.

'It goes way up, messire. I think it's elbow-jointed. What are the flowers?'

The priest fingered his pectoral *ankh*. 'A haunting of roses. One rarely sees such things above ground. I'd advise you to leave them alone.'

Her shivering communicated itself through his arm. Plessiez chose a dry area of paving, in the shaft's light, and pushed the Katayan woman to sit down.

'We're taking a rest now. Charnay, find Falke.'

The black Rat sheathed his rapier and reached up to untie his scarlet cloak. He swung it free, knelt down, and took the Katayan woman's freckled foot in his hands; drying it with the cloth, and examining it.

'Bruised. Can you walk?'

She withered him with a glare. 'Messire, of *course* I can walk.'

The black Rat dug thumbs into the ball of her foot, with hands upon which the rings were chill. His obsidian eyes glinted in the twilight.

'Honest assessment of your capabilities would be more useful than bravado, I think.'

Her calves ached with an infinitude of steps, passages, iron-rung ladders, and tunnels. 'I can walk.'

Plessiez swathed her feet temporarily in the warm lined cloak and sat down at her side. His lean wolfish face was thoughtful. In the twilight she could see how his scarlet jacket was mud-stained, and the plumed headband bedraggled. Only a twitching of his scaly tail showed his reined-in temper.

'Damn the man! This is his escape-route; he should know where it leads.'

Zari turned her greatcoat collar up, and sat hugging her knees. 'Messire, be honest. Did *you* stop to ask where this went, when it went away from those . . . things?'

'I did not.'

Plessiez removed his headband, scratching at the fur between his ears; and smoothed the broken black feathers. Two of the yellow nails on his right hand were broken. Scuffs and dishevelled patches showed in his sleek fur. He looked sideways at the young woman.

'I don't forget that your prompt action saved us.'

The Katayan shoved pale fingers through her hair, head bowed; and shook the black hair back from her face as she looked up. 'Falke did that, with his traps and false cellars.'

She knelt up, feet still swathed in Plessiez's cloak. She reached across, put her hands on the black Rat's shoulders, and absently began to knead the muscles that were tense under the sleek fur. Some of his rigidity dissolved. 'If this *is* a sewer system, then it's been here for *ever*—'

A sound thrilled through the dark.

Plessiez grabbed his rapier, scrambling upright. Zarbettu-zekigal half got to her feet, tangled herself in the cloak and sat down. Charnay's voice, nearby, said: 'So it's salt. Then you ought to be glad that I pulled you out, instead of bitching about it, messire!'

The brown Rat staggered into the circle of twilight, a man's body over her shoulder. With a grunt of effort, she knelt and eased him down on to the terracotta paving. Black overalls streamed water on to the brick.

'We've got to get out of here! If we don't, we'll starve!' Falke caught the harness of Charnay's rapier in a white fist. His translucent hair dripped, sleeked dark with oil and water, and his eyes, uncovered, stared wildly: velvet pits.

Plessiez sheathed his rapier, watching the pale fire of spectral roses.

'The last of our worries is starvation, messire.'

The brown Rat clapped Falke roughly on the back. 'No need for hysterics.'

Zari kicked her bare feet free of the cloak and scrambled upright. She seized Charnay's arm, as the brown Rat began to scrub water from her fur with a silk kerchief.

'It's wet!'

'So it's wet.' Charnay's tail whip-cracked, flicking water-drops off with an audible *spuk!* 'So what?'

Plessiez put his hand on the Katayan's shoulder, restraining her. 'Water?'

'Oh, yes, messire.' The brown Rat began cleaning dampness from her rapier.

'*Where?*'

Surprised, she said: 'Up ahead. Not far. Falke here found it the hard way, I don't know why; there was light enough that even a Ratling needn't have fallen in—'

Plessiez shoved Zar-bettu-zekigal back. The Katayan danced from foot to bare foot, hardly bothering to avoid the shivering Falke where he huddled, dripping.

'Light? Light from *what*, you dim-witted idiot!' the black Rat demanded.

Charnay sheathed her cleaned rapier, adjusted the hang of her cloak and looked down at Plessiez with a puzzled expression.

'The canal has lamps,' she explained.

Sun from the hard yellow sand dazzled him. Lucas sat on the lagoon wall, dealing cards on to the smooth stone surface.

White marble palaces shone under the luminous blue sky, rising up in terraces from the lagoon. Pink and blue banners hung from balustrades, from walls, from arches and domes. People on the streets made pin-pricks of bright colour. The thin thump of drums came down from a procession, up on a higher street, and the brass tang of cymbals. On the promenade, several black Rats in litters stopped to talk, blocking the way. The sun glinted off the cuirasses of their bodyguards.

'Play you at Shilling-the-Trump?' a voice offered.

Lucas nodded to the woman in sailor's breeches and

shirt, identifying her as a transient worker, and so allowed to carry coin. She set down her kitbag and sat on the carved balustrade beside him. He dealt, businesslike now.

'You're too good,' she said at last. Her yellow eyes narrowed suspiciously. 'You're not a student, are you?'

Lucas, lying only by implication, said deprecatingly: 'Only came in on the *Viper* two days ago.'

'I've been warned about students . . .'

The calm lagoon waters mirrored marble-white terraces and a clear sky. Gilding glinted from temple columns and dome-friezes. Far off, where the lagoon opened to the sea, masts were visible, and sailors loading ships, and merchants outside warehouses.

Here, on the flat-packed sand, immense oval shadows dappled the ground: airships tugging at mooring-ropes.

'Five shillings you owe me.'

The woman paid, and Lucas watched her walk away. Barely three o'clock, a dozen other students scattered across the promenades, and already five impromptu card-sharp games since his arrival . . .

None of them the meeting *she* foretold me. Still, she did say the station, and the docks, as well as here.

He dealt idly: Page of Sceptres, Ten of Coins, Three of Grails. A breeze whipped the pasteboard off the marble. He made a sprawling grab for the cards.

A hand the size of a ham slapped down on the stone balustrade, trapping the Page of Sceptres and smearing both card and stone with heavy streaks of machine-oil.

'Here.' A resonant good-natured voice.

'Of all the *filthy*—'

Lucas straightened up, the sun burning the back of his neck. On the sand-flats, crews were scurrying about a moored helium-airship; trolleys and small carriages scored ruts in the sand. Lucas's voice trailed off as he realized that all his view was blotted out.

The man wiped the Page of Sceptres on the lapel of his pink satin coat. Black oil smeared the satin. He peered at the card with china-blue eyes, and dropped a kitbag from his other ham-sized fist. It thudded on to the sand.

'Nothing wrong with that,' he remarked encouragingly, and handed the pasteboard back to Lucas.

'Just wait a damn minute—!'

'Yes?'

Cropped hair glinted the colour of copper wire. As he looked down over his mountainous stomach at the seated young man, his several chins creased up into sweaty folds. He beamed. The smell of the distant surf was overlaid by oil and sweat and garlic.

Lucas opened and shut his mouth several times.

The big man moved and sat down companionably on the balustrade. The marble shook as his weight hit it. He tugged his oil-stained silk breeches up, loosened his cravat and belched; and then gazed around at the surrounding city with immense pleasure.

'Architectonic,' he murmured. He scratched vigorously in his copper hair and examined his fingernails, flicking scurf away. 'Wonderful. Is all the city like this?'

'Uhhrh. No.'

'Pity.'

The man offered a plump fat-creased hand. His sleeve was coated in some yellow substance, almost to the elbow. Wet patches darkened under his arm.

'Casaubon,' he said.

Lucas managed to swallow, saliva wetting his dry mouth. Half-lost in thoughts, he muttered: 'You can't possibly be . . . *No!*'

'I assure you, my name *is* Baltazar Casaubon.' The big man enquired with gravity, over the noise of engines, voices and distant bells, 'Who ought I to be?'

'I'm not sure. I don't know.' Lucas closed his fist over the pack of cards. Badly startled, he began again. 'A seer foretold a meeting for me, here . . . Somehow I hardly think that you're the person in question.'

'Foretelling interests me.' Casaubon dug into the capacious pockets of his full-skirted coat and brought out a handful of roasted chicken-wings. Picking what remained of the meat from the bones, he said: 'I'll give you a shilling to help carry my gear, and we'll talk about it.'

Lucas stood up off the balustrade. Patience exhausted, the afternoon sun fraying his temper, he said: 'Oh, really! There are limits to what a prince will do!'

The big man looked down at the cards, and at the heap of small coins at Lucas's elbow. Through a fine spray of chewed chicken and spittle, he remarked: 'Are there? What are they?'

Lucas stared, silenced.

'Sir?'

A thin brown-haired woman in a frock-coat walked across the sand. Behind her, silver highlights slid across an airship's bulging hull. She snapped her fingers for a porter to follow: the man staggered under the weight of a brass-bound trunk. Two other men followed, carrying a larger trunk between the two of them, their boots digging deep into the sand. The woman made a deep formal bow.

'Ah – *Parry!* Here.' The stentorian bellow beside him deafened Lucas.

'I've summoned a carriage, Lord-Architect. Now, are you sure that—?'

Casaubon stood. He bulked large above Lucas, easily six foot four or five inches tall. He waved a dismissive hand at the woman.

'Parry, don't fuss. Go back, as arranged. And *try* to keep the Senate from bankrupting me while I'm gone, won't you?'

The woman, sweating in woollen frock-coat and breeches, gave a long-suffering sigh. 'Yes, Lord-Architect.'

One carriage rolled up, and the porters began to load it from the luggage piled up around the airship's steps. Case followed case, trunk followed trunk, until the metal-rimmed wheels sank inches deep into the sand. The precise woman snapped her fingers and beckoned another of the nearby carriages.

Casaubon strode over to supervise the loading, mopping

at the rolls of fat at the back of his neck with a brownish kerchief. Two of the men struggled to raise a square chest. He motioned them aside, squatted, and straightened up with it in his grip. He heaved it up on to the cart.

'Oof! We'll need another cart. Parry, you're about to miss your ship.'

The thin woman glanced over to where crews were loosening the anchor-ropes of the nearest airship.

'I'll manage,' the big man forestalled her. 'My friend here will call another carriage.'

The woman made a hurried bow, looked as though she would say more, heard a hail from the airship, and turned and strode away. Casaubon stared after her. Ponderously regretful, he shook his head, and then turned back to Lucas.

'Won't you?'

Lucas, a step away, hesitated. He scratched at his thick springy hair, and tugged the linen shirt away from his neck. The heat of the afternoon sun cleared promenade, sand-flats and streets; litters vanishing into cool court-yards, and men and women into cafés and bars. No-one now to be inveigled into a game of Shilling-the-Trump, and risk sunstroke.

He put a hand into his breeches pocket, and brought it out closed. 'I can only think of one way to tell if this is a waste of time.'

Lucas opened his hand. On his palm, heavy and intricate, glittering with sharp sun-sparks, lay a golden bee.

Falke shuddered as he walked through humid heat, arms tight about his body. One hand clenched, frustrated, lacking the sword that a Rat-Lord would kill him for owning. He flinched as wet petals brushed his face. Great single-petalled roses shone ebony in the gloom, each bramble and leaf and bud outlined in mirror-silver.

Their touch glided through his skin: substanceless.

'Here!' the brown Rat called from ahead.

Falke pushed sopping hair out of his eyes, staring into

the sewer-tunnel. Every noise – brushwood shoved aside, a stone kicked, the sharp sound of water dripping from the brick roof – thrilled through him. The reflexes of his illegal weapons-training made him twitch and start.

Stinking sweetness filled his nostrils, throat and lungs.

'Messire.' The young Katayan woman appeared at his side. Her pale skin glimmered in the tunnel's gloom. His dilated vision saw her face clearly.

She shrugged the heavy greatcoat back off her shoulders and swung it up to shroud him. 'You're shivering. Take it. Down here's the first time I've been warm since I came to your damn city!'

Hot humid air brushed his skin, leaving him clay-cold. He reached up, tugging the coat about his shoulders. The taste of copper lingered in his mouth.

The young woman, walking with a kick-heeled stride, plunged her hands into the pockets of her plain black dress. 'I thought it would get colder, the further down we went.'

The black Rat, outlined briefly at the mouth of the tunnel, stepped down to the left and vanished. Falke heard his voice, with Charnay's; and then Zar-bettu-zekigal slipped her arm under his, and steered him down two steps and out on to a sewer-quay.

The first oil-lamp, searing blue-white, hung in a niche in the tunnel wall. Above it, the ceiling soared thirty feet. Below, the brick went down in steps to the quay. Glass splinters of light pierced his eyes from the ripples. Other lamps shone, further off; gleaming on the filth-choked black quay and the massive tunnel that curved off to either side into the distance.

Oily water glistened and shifted. The Katayan woman coughed. 'The *stink* – it's like dead fish. Like the sea.'

Falke's heel skidded on the wet paving. He gripped her arm.

'Too much light. I can't see.' His clothes clung wetly to him, and he huddled down on the top step, the greatcoat wrapped round him, hands over his dilated eyes.

'Interesting.' Plessiez's voice came clearly. 'The oil has some way to burn yet. I wonder if these lamps are replaced at regular intervals?'

Zar-bettu-zekigal's voice said: 'If it's tidal, we're near the sea. Nearly outside.'

Falke raised his head, shading his eyes.

'No. Sea-water comes in a long way. There are hundreds of miles of sewer-system back of docklands.'

The black Rat paced back, lightly alert, drawn rapier shining in the lamp-light. His scarlet jacket, unbuttoned, gave him the raffish air of a duellist; little trace of the priest now. Only Falke saw how he shied away from black and silver phantoms.

'Charnay, you go two hundred paces up the tunnel, I'll go two hundred paces the other way; then come back and report.'

'Yes, messire.'

The brown Rat leaped down on to the lower quay and walked off. Falke heard her humming under her breath. He looked up to meet Plessiez's puzzled expression.

'Stay here, messire, with the little one. *No*, Zari, you're not coming. Stay where you are.'

The young woman brushed dirt from her dress with the tuft of her tail. 'Of course, messire.'

The black Rat padded soundlessly away. Falke watched the lithe figure merge into the wall's shadows; loping easily towards the bend in the tunnel. From the opposite direction, a loud curse was followed by the splash of some obstacle kicked into the water.

'Stay *quiet*!' He pushed his fist against his mouth, muffling his outburst.

Zar-bettu-zekigal flopped down on the step beside him. 'If someone hears her, that's a good thing. We want to get out of here.'

His laugh caught in his throat. He put both hands over his face, drew in a shaky breath; then took his hands away and clenched them, staring at his trembling fists.

Her voice came quietly. 'The acolytes frightened me, too.'

'It's . . . more than that. More than cowardice.' He chuckled, painfully, back in his throat. 'I am a coward, of course, but . . . '

The young woman's sepia eyes darkened now, with the concentration of a Memory. She put black hair behind her ears with both hands, and shifted her hip so that she sat close to him. Falke drew unadmitted comfort from the proximity.

'*Only, having once seen that, you never truly cease to see it.* Inside the Fane. But why here?' she asked.

Now the black Rat was out of sight, around the curve in the tunnel. Falke leaned forward to peer after Charnay, but she also was gone.

'When I made escape-routes from my hall, I only ever meant to get into the upper levels. Down here, do you know how old this is? These sewers – if you go deep enough, they're part of the catacombs under the Fane.'

Moisture trickled down from somewhere into the sluggish channel and, with the ripples, new stenches arose from the disturbed sewer-water. Saliva filled his mouth, prelude to nausea. He clenched his hand as if that could put one of the House of Salomon's illegal blades into it, and turned his dilated eyes on the Katayan.

'Once, six or seven years back, I was an architect on the Fane. Only a small addition to one wing, but I was proud of it – the tallest perpendicular arches yet, a hundred and eighty feet high, and flying buttresses as thin as lace . . . '

The Katayan bent forward and skimmed a stone across the quay. It struck a scorpion, that plopped into the water, threshing, and sank.

'I couldn't bear never to see it again after it was finished.' He pushed his fine white hair out of his face. 'How stupid . . . I was too old to be that stupid. I thought that I would conceal myself in it, as they came to take occupation, and see, and then I would know.'

Words tumbled out of him now, falling into the sepia gaze of her Memory.

'All the grimoires along Magus' Row couldn't hide a human soul from them. They dragged me out into the open. And took me in, into the heart of the Fane. Where nothing human had been since it was built, millennia past.'

He drew in a rough breath.

'Decans like The Spagyrus, that deal with humankind from time to time, become corrupt, become a little like us.'

Hot moist air pressed close. Muffled echoes came from some unidentifiable direction. Bones rattled and scuffled in the storm-flood piles of brushwood. Zar-bettu-zekigal's head rose with a jerk as the bright oil-lamp flickered.

'What else?'

'The noise. The *noise*. Agony. Torn flesh. Torn souls. Yes, the soul can be hurt.' He laughed: painful, embarrassed. 'Don't listen to me. I was afraid of nothing before that, and now I'm afraid of almost everything. The powers that are in there aren't corrupt with humanity. They're the Thirty-Six Decans, the Celestial Powers of hell, and they live on this earth, and we *build* for them!'

Zari turned towards him, cocked her head to one side, and stared into his eyes.

Falke said: 'Eyes that have seen the heart of the Fane are afterwards changed.'

Something in her body's stiffness cautioned him. He braced himself for her next words.

'See you, if it was me, I wouldn't make up stories about having been in the Fane to account for it.'

His heart beat once, with a white pain. Very still, he said: 'Stories?'

'Aw, Messire Falke! Go into the *heart* of the Fane? No-one ever has. You'd be squished like a bug.' Her dark eyes momentarily reflected storm-light. 'Or else you'd be lunch.'

Zar-bettu-zekigal stood up. The hem of her dress

brushed his face, and Falke caught a scent of dry grass and sweat; and he reached up and knotted a corner of the cloth in his fist.

'I don't like to be called a liar, girl!'

'Or a coward?' One freckle-backed hand ruffled his hair. He raised his head. Her white face and black hair stood out against black and silver roses. The brambles that trailed down across the air passed harmlessly through her arm and shoulder; and she stretched up, as if she would grasp them, arcing her back and tail.

'If I've worked it out, then messire will have, too. He probably even knows why you tell stories. If it isn't just vanity.'

She dropped down to squat on her haunches before him.

'Ei! I bet it impresses people, though. If they're gullible enough. Hello, messire, find anything?'

Plesŝiez stepped silently out of the gloom.

'More of the same. The lamps in that direction have less oil. Where's Charnay?'

'Fallen into the canal?' the Katayan suggested.

'Oh, I hardly think so. Strategy and tactics may be beyond her, but at feats of strength she's . . . ' Plessiez's voice trailed away.

Falke stood. A pounding fear filled his head, discovery and shock mingling; and his fingers fumbled as he began to fit his arms into the sleeves of the young woman's greatcoat, cold despite the moist heat. Grunts and snarls came from the far darkness of the quay.

Zar-bettu-zekigal hopped from one bare foot to the other.

'Oh, see you, *look* at that!'

Falke's dilated eyes searched the darkness beyond the lamps, first to find the approaching figure of Charnay.

For the first time, he smiled.

The brown Rat leaned forward as she walked, gripping a rope that ran taut over her shoulder, muscles straining under her brown fur. Ripples spread out from the water at the edge of the quay, following her, slopping thickly onto the brickwork. The Rat grunted. She planted both her feet squarely on the slippery quay, and heaved at the rope and the heavy object to which it was attached.

'Hell damn it!' Falke said. 'It's a boat.'

Lucas swung around as the carriage rattled under the arch, into the palace courtyard. He slid back on to his seat. The Rats in guard uniform took as little notice of him as they had when he had walked past them the day before, filthy with disguise.

He looked up at the white walls, the windows and the blue-tiled turrets and spires, an odd smile appearing on his face.

'So this is their idea of a palace . . . You're a stubborn man, Lucas.' Casaubon rested his bolster-arms across the back of the facing seat, turning his face up to the white sunlight.

His pink frock-coat fell open across his immense chest. Yellow sweat-rings marked his unlaced linen shirt, under the arms; and he scratched at the fine copper hairs on his chest with pudgy fingers. He leaned forward as the carriages halted in the courtyard, resting a forearm on his spreading thigh.

'Have you ever heard of the Invisible College?'

Lucas shook his head. 'Nothing to do with the University of Crime?'

'Oh, hardly, hardly.'

At the far side of the yard, another archway opened through to two successive courtyards, each surrounded by four- or five-storey blocks. The afternoon sun blazed back from white walls. Lithe black Rats in blue uniform jackets and plumes stood by every door opening into the yard, some carrying pikes and some rapiers. Heads turned as Casaubon's carriage drew up in a spray of gravel, followed by three loaded-down baggage-carts.

'I must go. I'm wasting your time and mine,' Lucas

'Time was when everyone recognized the golden bee.'

From *Summum Bonum*, Part IV, Robert Fludd, 1629. The inscription translates: 'The rose gives honey to the bees.'

observed. 'I'll go back to the airfield. I might be missing the person I *am* meant to meet.'

The copper-haired man's head came down, chin resting in rolls of fat. His bright blue eyes met Lucas's. Lucas judged him somewhere in his late thirties or early forties.

'Time was when everyone recognized the golden bee,' Casaubon said, 'which, I suppose, is why they stopped using it.'

He reached out an imperious palm. Lucas reluctantly dropped the metal bee onto it. Gold sparked in the sun, almost lost in the folds of Casaubon's hand.

The big man closed his palm. His eyes squeezed shut in immense concentration, vanishing into palely freckled cheeks. Lucas leaned forward anxiously, pointing at the approaching guards.

'They—'

'There!'

Casaubon opened his hand. A live bee, wings translucent and body black-and-brown-furred, flicked into the air and flew drunkenly off across the crowded yard.

'How did you . . . ? Then, you *are*—?'

'Can I help you, messire?' a uniformed black Rat enquired, strolling to stand beside the open carriage. Her hand was not far from her rapier-hilt.

'Yes. Find me whoever's in charge.'

The big man reached across with one ham-hand to push open the carriage door. He eased one thigh forward, then the other, and dropped to the ground with a grunt. The carriage rocked on its springs. Casaubon picked thoughtfully at his nose, gazing up at the windows.

'What the hell am I supposed to do now?' Lucas slid down to stand on the gravel beside him. 'I was in a dungeon here yesterday!'

'You do lead an eventful life, young Lucas.'

Casaubon hitched up his white silk breeches, fumbling to do up the top two buttons and abandoning the unequal struggle.

'But—'

A black Rat emerged from an arched stone doorway close by, slitting his eyes against the sunlight. His clawed hind feet scraped the stone steps as he strode down into the courtyard.

'Are you the architect?' he called.

He stood a head taller than Lucas: lean, heavy-shouldered and scarred. A blue sleeveless doublet came down to his haunches, so that it looked as though he wore black breeches; and a blue plume jutted from his headband. A basket-hilted rapier swung at his side.

'Are *all* these carriages yours?'

The copper-haired man felt inside his satin coat, dipping into voluminous pockets. A waft of garlic and dirty linen hit Lucas. Casaubon frowned, and turned down one of his great embroidered cuffs. He beamed, taking out a heavy black wax seal on a ribbon; and grunted with effort as he put it around his neck.

'Casaubon,' he announced, as the black Rat's tail began to twitch. 'Baltazar Casaubon, Lord-Architect, Knight of the Rose Castle, Archemaster, Garden-Surveyor—'

'You *are* the architect,' the black Rat interrupted. 'Good. My name is Desaguliers. Come with me. I'll show you what you have to do. How soon can you start work?'

Casaubon frowned, and looked as though he might be about to recite further titles in spite of the interruption. Instead he broke into a smile, clapped Lucas firmly on the back, and added: 'Master Desaguliers, this is Lucas – my page.'

The courtyard was crowded despite the heat, Rats and some humans passing through on business; and two or three of the guards stopped to exchange a word with Desaguliers. The black Rat turned back to Casaubon, and said briefly: 'Follow me.'

Lucas, rubbing his bruised shoulder, fell in behind the immense expanse of pink satin that was Casaubon's back. He glared at it as they walked into a cool white entrance-hall, neatly stacked on either side with firewood, and continued to fume as they followed the Rat into the spiral stone staircase jutting up through the centre of the building.

The big man slowed on the stairs, stomping up step by step, pausing to peer through the slot-windows cut in either wall. One side looked out into rooms; the other on to the other side of the stone double-spiral. Lucas dropped back a pace.

'I'm not your page!'

Casaubon said tranquilly: 'I know that.'

'Tell me how you did that, with the bee.'

'Tell me who gave it to you.'

The lean black Rat waited for them on the third floor. He strode across the tiles, between gilded-plaster walls, to where leaded casements blurred the afternoon sunlight. Reaching to swing one window fully open, he said: 'His Majesty wishes you to design him a garden. Here.'

Casaubon paused at the exit from the stairs. His cheeks and neck glowed pink, and he pulled out a filthy brown square of cloth and wiped sweat from his face and neck.

'I trust there is some challenge involved.'

Lucas followed him across to the window. It overlooked the eastern side of the palace. Black shadows of roofs, gables, oriel windows and tiled turrets fell on acres of rubble. Broken masonry, splintered glass and white dust ran out as far as the curtain-wall, two hundred yards distant.

'A wing of the palace has been demolished for the purpose,' Desaguliers observed.

The Lord-Architect said weakly: 'What *sort* of a garden does his Majesty want, exactly?'

The black Rat leaned up against the window-frame, arms folded. Sardonic, he said: 'Does it matter? You'll be paid.'

'It does matter! For one thing, I must know the intended function. Is it a Memory Garden, or merely illustrative of certain mythological and philosophical devices? Should it invigorate or relax? Does his Majesty wish to be entertained or spiritually instructed?'

Casaubon rested plump hands on the window-sill. Lucas, behind him, noted how one scuff-shoed foot scratched at his opposite calf, leaving marks on the silk stocking.

'I must know,' the Lord-Architect persisted.

Smoothly diplomatic, Lucas ventured to say: 'That can be discussed at the proper time, surely . . . my lord?'

Desaguliers spoke over him. 'You're familiar with garden machinery, Lord-Architect? Automata, water-organs, mechanical dials? His Majesty especially requires facility with machines.'

'Of course.' The big man sounded hurt. 'I think I should speak to the King, Master Desaguliers.'

He turned away from the window, resting his hand on Lucas's shoulder. 'My boy here will find me lodgings in the city. I prefer not to live where I work. Lucas, see to the unloading of the carts. Any box or chest marked with red chalk stays here; anything marked with blue chalk goes to my lodgings; anything unmarked you may return to the airfield, on the grounds that it isn't mine. Pay the men off.'

The black Rat seemed to notice Lucas for the first time. As he strode off, beckoning Casaubon to follow, he remarked: 'Boy, you do *know* where to find his Majesty's guest lodgings?'

'Yes, messire.'

Lucas looked up at the big man, meeting shrewd blue eyes. The Lord-Architect's mouth twitched, and a smile creased its way across his features.

'I do know where there's a room to let,' Lucas said hurriedly. 'I wish I didn't know why. The girl who lives there won't be coming back. I'll speak to Mistress Evelian and return here. There's one thing you ought to know.'

Casaubon, complicit in the necessity of their further meeting, raised a copper-coloured eyebrow. 'And that is?'

'I've heard of Desaguliers. Most people here have. He's a strange person to have developed a taste for gardening. Desaguliers is Captain of the King's Guard.'

A boat wallowed under vaulting brick roofs.

One oil-lantern, tied at the stern, shed illumination on a seated black Rat. His ringed right hand grasped the tiller. The other lay at rest on his stained scarlet jacket. Beside him, curled up with her spine against the warm fur of his flank, a young woman slept.

The other lantern, in the prow, reflected light back from oily water. A brown Rat drove a pole into the pitch blackness, strongly thrusting the boat forward; matched by the pale-haired man in black, poling on the boat's other side.

Zar-bettu-zekigal stretched, eyes still shut. Her pale

nostrils flared. She opened her eyes, sat up, and leaned over the side of the boat to spit.

'Pah! The *stink*!'

'It fails to improve,' the black Rat observed gravely.

Zari grinned. One hand and dappled tail extended for balance, she stood up in the boat. She scratched at her dishevelled hair. 'Is it tomorrow yet, messire?'

Falke, as the sweep of the pole brought him round to face her, said: 'Your friend Charnay thinks it's night outside. I say it must be day again.'

Zari leaned over the stern, peering down into clotted liquid. 'We can eat fish. If we can catch them. If there are any.'

'If we have no objection to poisoning ourselves.' Plessiez called towards the prow: 'Are we still following the lamps? Is there any other sign of occupation?'

Charnay wiped a hand over her translucent ears, and straightened up from the pole. 'You mean there are people down here?'

'I see no reason why there shouldn't be.' Plessiez leaned over, searching for some trace of the salty current. He sat back, remarking: 'After all, as our great poet once said, "there be land thieves and sea thieves, that is, land Rats and Py-Rats" . . .'

Charnay looked blank.

'Py-rates,' Plessiez enunciated clearly. 'Pirates. Pi . . . Charnay, education is wasted on you.'

'You're probably right, messire,' she said humbly. 'I think it's getting lighter up ahead, messire.'

'Where?'

'Ei! It *is*!' Zari scrambled over the planks, dipping a hand to catch the wildly rocking side of the boat, and flung herself down on her knees in the prow. Leaning out over the stinking water, she stared ahead.

'Falke – come *here*! Is that light? There?'

The black-clad man squatted down, following her gaze; shading his dilated eyes from the oil-lamps. He stood up. Charnay took her wooden pole and drove it into the mud simultaneously with his. The boat began to wallow forward.

Zari stuffed one sleeve of her greatcoat across her mouth and nose. She knelt up in the prow, intense gaze fixed on reflections in black water.

'*Ei, shit!*'

Light blazed. Zari fell back against Charnay. The brown Rat cursed. Eyes watering in an actinic glare, she took in one image of a vast brick cavern, quays on three sides ahead, tunnel-entrances; all weltering in sludge and nitre, and people: crowds of men and women.

With a noise like hail on corrugated iron, a metal-mesh net winched up out of the canal behind the boat. It rose rapidly, blocking the only exit.

'Shit!' Zar-bettu-zekigal pitched forward as the boat rammed, head-first over the side on to the quay.

Feet rushed towards her. A hand thrust her down. The torn-silk sound of a rapier drawn from its scabbard sounded above her. She sat up. Falke leaped for the dock. He swung the iron-tipped boathook up two-handed in a broadsword grip.

Tatterdemalion men and women ran down the quay, yelling. She saw ragged banners, raised sticks, swords; a woman screaming, a man leaping to avoid fallen rubble, and the white blaze of light began to fade. Yellow torchlight leaped.

'Stop—'

Zari ignored the voice, pushing herself upright, brick cobbles hard first under her knees and then under her bare feet.

'Guard yourself, messire!'

Charnay thrust coolly, sending her rapier into the shoulder of a man in ragged blue. Her brown fur shone in the torchlight. Bright-eyed, showing yellow teeth in a grin, she vaulted the quay steps and drove a group of men down the dock.

'*Stop—*'

Falke's iron-hooked staff cracked down on the cobbles.

Zari swung round. The boat drifted, empty, three paces out into filthy water. The boathook darted out, struck: a woman's face twisted in pain and a sword hit the ground.

'*Messire?*'

Zari fell forward. Something splashed into the canal behind her. A tall man in green met her eyes, grinned, swung up an axe into a two-handed grip. She crouched, snapping her left hand and tail, circling left, watching his stubbled face for distraction; scooped up a stone right-handed and skimmed it.

The man dropped the axe and clapped both hands to his face. Blood blossomed from his eye.

Her heel caught the shallow step leading up from the quay. She sat down abruptly. Plessiez shouted. The black Rat's rapier darted, his left arm wrapped in the scarlet cloak, feinting; he backed up against the edge of the quay, driven by three or four men.

'*Stop!*'

Yellow torches wavered.

Zar-bettu-zekigal put both hands over her mouth, muffling her suddenly audible breathing.

Slowly, eyes on the tattered men and women, she got to her feet. The sump (one canal and six tunnels opening into this great chamber) breathed a fetid quiet.

Heaps of black ash along the quays marked where flares had burned out. Men and women stood around the canal-end, tar-burning torches raised, the light falling on to black brick vaults, on to oily water and the metal net swaying from its winches. Most of the crowds carried swords, staves, banners. She let her eyes travel across them, tense, searching for whoever had shouted.

'Stop fighting and we won't kill you,' a man in red called from a tunnel-entrance. Five or six voices immediately added, '*Yet*,' and there was a rumble of amusement.

Zar-bettu-zekigal, slowly, hands held out from her sides, walked down to rejoin Falke and the Rats at the canal's edge. The white-haired man rested on his staff, free hand shading his eyes that ran with tears in the torch-glare.

Plessiez muttered to Charnay. She reluctantly lowered her rapier-point to the ground. The crowd grew minute by minute, pressing closer around them.

Abruptly banners at the back of the crowd jerked and moved aside. The tattered men and women fell back as a litter came through the crowd, carried by six men in ragged black clothing and remnants of unpolished armour.

'They're all human,' Zari muttered, not taking her eyes off the approaching litter.

'They are all pale,' the black Rat said, his tone thoughtful, although his chest heaved under the sword-harness. 'I think it some time since any one of them saw sunlight. Honour to you!'

The partly-armoured men set down the litter on its stilts, jolting on the brick quay. It was large, swathed in water-stained red curtains; and from an elongated corner-pole a banner painted with a sun hung in rags.

Plessiez bowed elegantly to the invisible occupant.

Zari stepped back as two men pushed forward with a carved oak chair. They set it down on the cobbles. A woman in armour shoved herself out of the litter, inch by strenuous inch, thumping the scabbard of a long sword down on the quayside, and using it as a support.

'Next person who doesn't *stop* I'll gut. That goes for you, Clovis. What have you found me?'

She stumbled in three great strides to the chair, sitting with a clash of armour, and waved away all offer of assistance. As she slumped back into the cushioned chair, two men came to kneel at either side of it.

The thin blond man at her left said: 'They came so close that we had to decoy them in.'

Her torn shirt and breeches were dark red, blood-red in torchlight; and vambraces gleamed on her forearms, greaves on her calves. Plate armour covered her torso; and she reached up and pulled off a horned laminated helmet, and shook her head, short greasy hair flying.

'Find out how they got here and then kill them.'

Zar-bettu-zekigal, hands in pockets, swirled the skirts

of her greatcoat about her, and stepped forward. Eyes glowing, she stood and gazed – at the woman's dirty sardonic face: the high cheek-bones, nondescript hair, the beginnings of crow's-feet.

Speaking over Plessiez's protest, and the armoured woman's next words, the Katayan said: 'Who *are* you?'

Silence. Two women with raised swords hesitated, looking to the armoured woman, whose slanting red-brown eyes narrowed. A frown indented lines on her forehead. She hitched herself forward in the chair, and Zar-bettu-zekigal smiled, dazed, dizzy with the fear that never touched her in the preceding quarter-hour.

'Who-are-you yourself,' the woman said laconically. 'I'm called The Hyena. I rule the human Imperial dynasty – what there is left of it.'

Dust rose up, yellowing the sills and steps all down Carver Street. Two carts rumbled past men and women (some in satin, some in rough cloth) who swore at the coating of flour-thin dust. Casaubon leaned back mountainously in the first carriage-seat and beamed at Lucas.

'Comfortable lodgings, I hope . . . ?'

Three harsh clangs drowned out his voice. Clock-mill struck the hour, its gold-and-blue dials revolving a notch; sun, moon and stars shifting to new configurations.

A great-maned lion rolled jerkily round on one set of rails, gilt flashing in the afternoon sun; passing a sleek silver hound on the other rail. From somewhere deep in the tower's mechanism, a mechanical *vox animalis* roared.

Casaubon sat up. 'An early Salomon de Caus—'

Lucas, muscles aching from getting from the palace to Carver Street and back again (by way of the Embassy Compound) to pick up the Lord-Architect, wiped his forehead and loosened the lacing of his thin shirt.

'Mistress Evelian should have the rooms cleared out,' he announced.

Casaubon winced as the carriage jolted to a halt. One of the drivers dismounted to see to the oxen, the second stepped down to put blocks under the wheels. Lucas beckoned one of the men.

'This load goes up to the first floor – through the street-door, there.' He slid down to the street, and glanced back up at the fat man. 'The person I mentioned, the White Crow . . . may not necessarily want to see you.'

Casaubon scratched at his crotch with plump fingers, still gazing up at the great dial of Clock-mill.

'Who knows?'

'Well . . . I'll make enquiries first.'

He left the big man gazing up at the clock, while the crates and chests and boxes were dumped on the cobbles beside him. The passage into the courtyard felt cool after the sun's heat, and he came out of the shadow blinking at the light beyond.

White sun warmed the wood-friezes; skulls, shovels and bones. He began to walk across to the far steps, towards the White Crow's rooms. Out of the tail of his eye, he caught a glint of red under the trees.

'Have . . . ?'

Lucas's voice dried up. A small square of brown grass under the cherry trees was the courtyard's only garden. Cinnamon-red hair tangled the sun in spidersilk fineness. The woman rested her head on her bare arms, gold lashes closed; and her white almost-freckled back and hips and thighs shone in the dappled shade. Her feet were a little apart, the cleft of her buttocks shadowed.

'Mmhhrm?'

The White Crow rolled lazily on to her back, one hand reaching for the spectacles that lay beside her, on the open pages of a hand-written grimoire. As she turned on to her back, Lucas saw her flattened breasts stippled with the imprint of grass, her dark aureoles, and the curled red-gold of her pubic hair. She pushed the spectacles on to her nose and raised her head without lifting her shoulders, momentarily double-chinned.

'You're not Mistress Evelian.'

'No.' Lucas shut his mouth on a croak.

Without any haste, the White Crow began to feel about for her cotton shirt, after some moments tugging it down from a cherry-branch and sliding the sun-warm fabric over her shoulders.

'Who were you looking for?' She eased her hips up to pull on thin cotton knee-breeches.

Her tawny eyes met his, and Lucas blushed sweaty red. He glanced up at the black-and-white half-timbered frontages and the blue sky beyond; and then couldn't help but drop his gaze back to her. The White Crow knelt up, tucking her shirt into her knee-breeches.

'I hear we have a new tenant. Know anything about that?'

'Very little.' He forced self-possession. 'And it isn't for want of looking in my uncle's confidential files, either. Have you ever heard of something called the Invisible College?'

The cinnamon-haired woman froze, one hand at her breeches waistband: her lips parted. Simultaneously Lucas heard Casaubon's heavy tread in the passage.

'I haven't said anything about you,' Lucas added hurriedly.

Casaubon stepped out into the sunlight. It glinted off his greasy copper hair, showed every stain and sweat-mark on his linen and satin coat.

Lucas turned back to the White Crow, one reassuring hand held out. 'He—'

'*Valentine!*'

Lucas spun round, deafened by the stentorian bellow.

The big man crossed the courtyard in half a dozen rapid strides, the cobbles shaking to his tread. The skirts of his pink coat flew wide. His shirt had fallen open, copper hairs glinting across the fleshy bulk of his chest; one silk stocking hung out of its garter. A great beam spread across his face.

'Valentine!' he cried happily.

The woman stood frozen, white-faced. His massive arms went forward, his hands seized her under the ribs; he

108

grunted with joy and swung her up, lifting her, tossing her up as if she were a small child. In a flurry of hair and shirt-tail and flailing arms, she soared skyward, six or seven feet above the cobbles – fell back and was swept into a massive hug, bare feet never brushing the ground.

'Valentine!'

'*Put me down!*'

Lucas snapped out of his astonishment and strode forward. 'Put her down – you heard her!'

Casaubon's grip loosened. The woman slid down, tiptoe on the cobbles; and he flung his arms round her again, pressing her nose into his sternum, grinning generously, laughing with unbelief. Looking down over the mountainous chins and the swell of his belly, he gripped her chin in his hand and bent down and kissed her, smackingly enthusiastic.

'*Will* you' – she elbowed room, and punched him smartly in the stomach – 'put me *down*?'

'It's you.' Amazement blazoned itself across his face. 'It's wonderful!'

'Casaubon!'

He loosened his embrace, still smiling happily. Lucas halted. Poised on the edge of violence or violent embarrassment, he looked to the White Crow for help.

She put tumbled red hair back from her face with hands that shook. Frowning disbelief, she shook her head, eyes for no-one but the big man; and suddenly clenched her fists and rested them against her lips, still staring at him.

Lucas, bewildered, said: 'But this is the White Crow . . . '

Casaubon's china-blue eyes filled with water. Tears overflowed, runnelling the dirt down his fat cheeks. He laughed, shook his head, laughed again.

'This is Master-Captain Valentine. This is a Scholar-Soldier, Valentine of the Invisible College.'

'*Not any more!*'

As if suddenly aware that she still stood within his embrace, the woman stepped back. A bare heel skidded on the dry grass; she caught her balance, one protesting hand stretched out against the fat man's movement to help.

'Don't!'

Casaubon clapped vast hands together, and then spread his arms expansively. 'Wonderful!'

Lucas reached out and closed, first, his right and (since it could not enclose the girth) then his left hand around Casaubon's wrist. Tensing muscles that had heaved the Lord-Architect's crates from an ox-cart, digging in his heels, he pulled the big man around in his tracks.

'Leave her alone.'

Casaubon blinked, blue eyes bright in his big, faintly freckled face. He scratched at his copper hair with his free hand, and looked down at Lucas; and suddenly swung his other hand around and clapped him on the shoulder, knocking Lucas six inches sideways.

'I've *found* her,' he beamed. 'It's wonderful.'

'She doesn't think so.'

Lucas felt muscles tense under his hands, in the hard fat that sleeved the man's wrist. He gripped more tightly, but the girth forced his fingers open. Lucas stepped back, seeing the red mark of his grip on the man's fair skin.

Casaubon, with no apparent resentment, remarked: 'Wonderful!'

'*Will you stop saying that?*'

Blind exasperation edged the White Crow's tone. Her arms fell to her sides, hands still clenched into fists. The sun through the leaves stippled her face with gold and shadow, and as she stepped out into the exposed courtyard her hair and linen blazed copper and white.

'I don't want you here!'

A stale scent of cooking wafted across the courtyard. Lucas heard Evelian's voice, singing, from one of the open casements; and panic stabbed through him, thinking that she or anyone might come outside.

'"Valentine" isn't a name on your file,' he protested.

The woman squinted at him briefly, lines webbing the corners of her eyes; her gaze hard now with a professional calculation. Lucas's heart thudded into his throat, and without any pride he said: '*Don't*.'

She took another step forward, glaring up at the fat man.

'Get out!'

Casaubon still smiled. He shrugged, massive weights of flesh shifting with his shoulders.

'I'll go.'

The gold-braid-edged skirts of his satin coat swirled as he turned. Lucas, bile and jealousy burning his gut, stared after the man as he strode ponderously towards the passage's archway.

The White Crow stared irresolutely at his retreating back. One hand went up to smooth her tumbled hair, straighten her spectacles – as Lucas was about to open his mouth, protest support and loyalty, she snatched off her gold-wire spectacles, gripping them in a fist.

'Where have you come from?' She raised her voice. 'Where have you been?'

Casaubon continued to walk away. The courtyard's quiet, born of sun and distant voices and the scent of dry grass, sifted down like dust.

'What the hell do you mean by just turning up!'

Lucas saw her fist tighten: gold-wire frames twisted. She stamped past him, flinched, reached out a hand to grip his shoulder and brush a stone from her bare sole.

'Damn you! Do *you* know what's gone wrong in this city?'

Lucas's dry mouth silenced him. He felt her warm hand; gazed at her profile, fine-textured skin, and darker freckles on her ears. Her long-lashed eyes fixed on Casaubon's departing back.

'And what *about* the College?'

Almost gone now, his scuffed shoe entering the shadow of the passageway that ran under Evelian's rooms.

'I used blood on the moon—'

She stepped past Lucas, ignoring his exclamation.

' – Are you the answer to my message?'

111

The shadow-line of the building slid down Casaubon's back, pink satin turning strawberry in the archway's dimness.

'*Casaubon!*'

The big man stopped and looked over his shoulder, a profile of forehead, nose, delicate lips; chins; belly swelling like a ship's sail.

'You want me to stay, then?'

'*Shit!*'

The White Crow stomped back past Lucas, stooped to pick up the grimoire from the grass, shut it with a clap that echoed flatly back from the courtyard walls, and stalked across the yard and up the wooden steps.

The outer door slammed violently behind her: a second later the inner room's door crashed to.

Lucas started as Casaubon's arm fell across his shoulders, greasy, massive, delicately light. He looked up. Orange-gold hair glinted, falling over a forehead where freckles were hardly visible under dirt.

The fat man glanced down at Lucas, beaming beatifically.

'She wants me to stay.'

Spiritual corruption crackled in the air. It tanged dry as fear in Plessiez's mouth. The black Rat priest's hand moved to the looped cross at his breast.

'I'll take that.'

The Hyena snatched the silver *ankh* from Plessiez's neck. He spun round, slender dark fingers reaching for the rapier that was no longer at his side; wincing as the chain cut fur and flesh.

The woman threw the jewelled chain carelessly away. 'A rich priest! How unusual . . . '

Plessiez shuddered, hardly aware of her sarcasm. Chains clanked above his head. All around the vast walls of the cavern, broken metal beams jutted out. From each beam hung chains, and in the chains hung corpses. Some showed bone and dried sinew only. The one above him was fresher.

'Messire,' Charnay leaned down to mutter. 'You're not afraid?'

Plessiez suppressed a shiver, fur hackling with horror and satisfaction.

Here, raw brick edges showed how a dozen sewer-chambers had been knocked into one, many-ledged and on multiple levels. Ragged sun-banners hung everywhere. Flames licked the soot-stained walls. They burned in apparently empty ram's-horns and wide dishes. Niches and ledges higher up gleamed with the spectral light of roses.

'The sheer power . . . ' Plessiez breathed, for once unguarded. 'Digging bones from crypts is well enough, but *this* . . . The Order should – I should have discovered this before now!'

Ragged men and women crouched around individual fires, between heaps of rubbish. Sullen, they watched. Ordure stank underfoot; the smells of decay and cooked meat choked the air.

Plessiez, unarmed, black eyes bright, took busy steps back and forth, peering at how woodlice and centipedes swarmed over the heaps of rubbish, active in the humidity. The delicate skulls of herons, mounted on poles, rustled with a ghost of feathers and air.

'Now, messire,' Charnay warned, 'your Order's plans are very pleasant in a tavern of a summer evening, but this is serious. Let me break some heads. We don't need swords to get out of here; they're a poor lot!'

'No!' Plessiez shook his head violently. 'Do nothing before I tell you. Think, for once in your life! What better place to raise plague-*magia* than *here*? Let the Cardinal-General weep; I'll be head of the Order before I'm much older.'

The walls sweated a dark nitre that stank of blood.

The brown Rat put her hand on his arm. 'Plessiez, we're old friends. Sometimes you're an ambitious *fool*.'

Furious, he swung round, and then lost his balance on the filth-choked earth as the young Katayan woman pushed him to one side. The thick light that swam in metal bowls shone on her dirty face and on her fever-bright eyes.

'Feed us!' She gazed up at the Hyena, hands still in greatcoat pockets, with a grin that might have been confidence or agony. 'Two days we've been lost. You brought us here. *Feed* us!'

The armoured woman leaned weight on her scabbarded long sword, all the metal glistering dully in the light. She spat. A globule of spittle hit the earth-choked brick paving by Plessiez's feet. It moved. It scuttled, and he set his heel on it, grinding the aborted by-product of *magia* into the earth.

She said: 'Won't waste food on you. You wouldn't have time to shit it out again before we killed you. *Clovis!*'

The blond man ran to kneel before her. She spoke rapidly to him.

Plessiez watched the men and women of the Imperial dynasty sleeping, eating and arguing in the shadows of gallows; never glancing up.

Wiry arms flung themselves around him. He swore, bit the words back. Zar-bettu-zekigal hugged, pressing the sword-harness painfully into his fur, resting the top of her head against his chest.

'Eeee!' The Katayan kicked a bare foot against the ground, and looked up with glowing eyes. 'She's *won*derful!'

'Damn you, Zaribet!' Plessiez's pulse jolted. 'Hell damn you, you little idiot!'

The Katayan beamed uncomprehendingly. 'I must be mad. She isn't a day over twenty-five; she's a *baby*. Mistress Evelian's all woman. This one's flat as a yard of tap-water . . . '

Exasperation sharpened his voice as Plessiez gathered his shaken self-possession. 'I grant you, if she were about to kill us, she would have done it immediately. *However*—'

The Hyena's voice cut across his.

'How long is it since we last caught someone down here?'

114

She reached up with her free hand, skin filthy in the yellow light, and jangled the gallows chains high above Plessiez's head. The stink of rot drenched the air. He coughed.

Something unidentifiable in the shadows fell from the gallows, hitting the earth with a squashy thud.

'About a month,' she judged.

Plessiez swallowed hard. Falke's shoulder shoved him back as the white-haired man pushed forward. He snarled at the armoured woman: 'Scare *me*, "Lady" Hyena. Try. These eyes have seen the heart of the Fane. Nothing *human* is going to make me afraid.' He dropped the hand that shaded his eyes, staring at the woman with pit-velvet pupils.

'Clovis!'

The armoured woman snapped her fingers. Two men in half-armour heaved a wooden block across and slammed it down at the Hyena's feet. The taller of the two drew a thin curved sword; light dripped along the edge of the blade. The other grabbed Falke's arms, twisting them up behind his back, and dragged him sprawling half across the block.

Plessiez narrowed his eyes to furry slits. He met the Hyena's gaze, and said softly and clearly:

'Honour to you.'

She stared, shook her head and made a bitter sound. 'To me? Messire priest, if I had any honour left, why would we be down here?'

Men and women mostly between the years of fifteen and forty watched, faces sullen. Plessiez ignored them, ignored Falke.

'These are offal, and you know it,' he said clearly. 'Since you're not blind or deaf, you can hardly mistake them for anything else. I'm not concerned with them.'

She limped, armour clashing, until her face came within an inch of his. He smelt blood; ghostly in the air about her. 'What can we humans *be* but your servants or your whores? You starve us and use us. What can we do? Leave the city?

No. Carry a sword, and defend ourselves when you kick us in the streets? *No*. Carry *money*, even? No!'

She scowled, black brows dipping; and a strand of lank hair lodged across her cheek, as her head moved with passionate anger.

'Work our guts out and then die while you sleep on silk; and even when we die we're not free of the city!'

Plessiez smoothed his fur with fingers that trembled.

' "We"?' he said delicately.

The Hyena struck backhanded without looking, and the nearer man let Falke pull free of his grip. The white-haired man stared up from under tear-dazzled lashes at the gallows.

'We,' she said, wiping the hair away from her face. Her hectoring tone gave way to puzzled suspicion. 'Yes, and you, too – the Decans are your masters.'

Plessiez nodded.

'Honour to you,' he repeated. 'People who are going to kill do it quite utilitarianly. A knife between two neck-vertebrae is efficient. Charnay will not admit it, I think, but I believe that humans may have a soldier's honour.'

Charnay straightened, tail lashing. 'Imperial horseshit! I don't care if they have stolen swords from somewhere; they're a rabble.'

Plessiez very carefully caught the armoured woman's eye, letting a little humorous resignation show. After a long moment, the Hyena's mouth moved in a smile.

'A priest, a King's Guard, a Master Builder and' – her red-brown eyes moved to Zar-bettu-zekigal – 'something from half the world away . . . It would be a shame to lose a ransom. I'll kill you after I've let you prove to your masters that you're alive. Then you won't tell them where to find us.'

Plessiez smoothed down his fur again, shooting a brief humorous glance at her; sure of himself now, and ebullient.

'I'll pay you more than a ransom,' he said. 'I'll pay you a King's ransom that his Majesty is far too mean to give.

116

Your people go under the city, don't they? Under the whole city? Let's talk. You can do something for me, and I can do much for you.'

'If you Rat-Lords kill each other, that's good, but it doesn't help us.'

'I belong to an Order within the Church,' Plessiez enunciated carefully, aware of knife-edge balance, 'and I fear, madam, that we have too short a time for me to retell thirty years of their history; but suffice it that we're not interested in factions at the court of his Majesty the King. Shall I say we're concerned with the city's strange masters?'

'The *Decans*?'

The woman glanced round, gripped the litter's pole with a gauntleted hand and slumped down to sit. She looked up at Plessiez from among ordure-stained drapes and cushions.

'A mad priest. We've found ourselves a mad priest. You'd fight god, would you? *Stupid* – and more fool me for listening.'

Plessiez let the chill humidity of the cavern sink in; the devil-light and the little hauntings. He took the risk quite deliberately.

'Fifty years ago the plague wiped out a third of the population. It didn't touch the Fane. Why should it? It only killed bodies. Since then the organization within the Church to which I belong has been studying *magia*.'

Falke hauled himself up by Charnay's helping hand, shading his eyes that were intent on Plessiez.

'Plagues may exist in flesh, in base matter, and bring bodies to death. And, we discover, there are other pestilences that may be achieved, plagues of the spirit and the soul.' His long fingers searched the fur of his breast for the missing *ankh*. 'And there are plagues that can be brought into existence only by acts of *magia*. They bring their own analogue of death – to such as our masters, the Thirty-Six Lords of Heaven and Hell: the Decans.'

117

The woman took hold of the ragged sun-banner hanging from the litter-pole. '*Death?* Theirs?'

'To the Divine? No. Naturally not. Lady, what we can and must do is make Them sicken, so that They abandon Their incarnations in flesh and remove to that Celestial sphere that is Their proper habitation, leaving' – his tone sharpened – 'the world to us.'

The Hyena, without any sign of hearing Plessiez, looked past him to the young Katayan woman. 'You – what are you?'

Zar-bettu-zekigal scratched her ear with the tip of her tail. 'A Kings' Memory?' she offered.

The woman stood, tossed her lobster-tail helmet under-arm: Zari caught it in both hands, and the Hyena took firm hold of her shoulder and drew the Katayan aside.

'You've been with the priest; *you* tell me what you've heard.'

Plessiez straightened his shoulders, sanguine in the haunting-light for all his ruffled fur. His brilliant eyes darted, missing nothing: the two women, dark-haired and dirty, almost twins, standing by poles decorated with the shifting-eyed skulls of cranes.

The older and taller bent her head, listening. The younger stood with eyes half-shut, in the concentration of Memory, the speech of Masons' Hall unrolling in smooth sequence. Plessiez narrowed his eyes, translucent ears swivelling; stood still, and listened.

'Vitruvius writes . . . '

Casaubon sprawled back in the sagging armchair, legs planted widely apart, a book held at a distance in his free hand. He bit into a gravy-soaked hunk of bread, chewed, and put the remainder of the bread down on the expanse of his spread thigh. Dark liquid blotted the silk.

'In *The Ten Books of Architecture*, writes of . . . ' He squinted, licked a gravy-stained digit and thumbed ponderously through the pages. '"*Hegetor's Tortoise: A Siege-Engine*." "*The Ballista*." Catapults, crossbows; "*The*

Automata of Warfare" . . . Military engineering. Hardly what I'm *used* to, but I can do it.'

'Casaubon!'

The White Crow smacked the side of his head. Lucas seethed as she pulled out the tail of her shirt, grabbed first one and then the other of the Lord-Architect's plump hands, and wiped each relatively clean.

'Master Desaguliers has put a factory production-line at my disposal.' He sucked a finger clean. 'And the King offers me ample funds.'

'The King's as interested in military engineering as Desaguliers?' The White Crow picked up her glass of red wine again. She left her shirt-tail hanging out.

'His Majesty are interesting people,' Casaubon remarked.

'Why don't you go back to your rooms and your books,' she enquired pointedly, 'instead of making a mess of mine?'

Casaubon's head turned as he surveyed the book-strewn, map- and chart-walled room. One eyebrow quirked up.

'Mess?'

Lucas took a deep swallow of wine, slid down in his chair and continued to glare at the Lord-Architect. Blue-grey storm-light blurred the window. The heavy air and wine made his temples throb.

The remains of a meal were spread across the round table. White Crow – or Valentine – walked restlessly about the room, glass in hand.

'In any case,' Casaubon added, in tones of injured reasonableness, 'the porters are still moving my belongings into *my* room.'

His fat arm reached up to the table. He grabbed two tomatoes from a dish and bit into both at once. Through a handful of red pulp and seeds, he added: 'Who does Master Desaguliers wish to attack, or defend?'

'Who cares?' Valentine paced back across the book-cluttered floor. She hitched a hip up to sit on the window-sill. 'Lucas will know. Won't you, Lucas? Tell us about the politics, Prince.'

He struggled to sit up, meeting her tawny eyes.

'Any news I had at my father's court will be eighteen months out of date. I'll have to speak with my uncle. He might be able to tell you something.'

'You do that, Prince.'

Her grin blurred; and she reached over to pick up the wine-bottle, nursing it on her lap before refilling her glass. Her eyes moved to the Lord-Architect, and Lucas could not read her expression.

'Why are you here—? Lazarus, no!'

Lucas shifted his legs as the timber wolf trotted in from the further room. Its ice-pale eyes fixed on the Lord-Architect, and it began to whine: a nail scratched down glass. Casaubon reached down and shoved his fingers through the animal's hackle-raised ruff, gripped the wolf's muzzle and shook it.

'There was blood on the moon,' he reminded the White Crow.

The timber wolf made an explosive *huff!* sound and curled up beside the armchair.

Lucas scratched through his springy hair and stood up, striving for calm or authority or anything but confusion.

'I saw,' he insisted. 'I saw that when I hadn't been in the city an hour.'

The White Crow nodded her head several times. She lifted one shoulder; the cotton slid across the curve of it and her breast. 'You're talented, Prince—'

Footsteps sounded on the outer stairs. Evelian put her head around the door. She knocked on the open door lintel. 'Messire Casaubon?'

' – He's here,' the White Crow finished.

'The porters can't get everything up to your room.' Evelian wiped a thick coil of yellow hair back with her wrist. Her smile showed pale; flesh bagged under her eyes. 'If you're not over in two minutes to sort it out, I'm telling them to leave the rest in the street!'

Her blue-and-yellow satin skirt flashed as she turned, and her footsteps clattered down the steps.

Casaubon tossed a handful of tomato-skins to the timber wolf. It snapped them out of mid-air, chewed – and immediately hacked the fruit back up, onto the carpet. The Lord-Architect stood, agile. He drew the skirts of his coat about him, bent to peer out of the casement, and held a fat palm out to test the air.

Heat-lightning whitened the rooftops, erratic as artillery. Spots of rain darkened the blistered paint on the window-sill.

'Brandy is good for aposthumes and influenzas,' he remarked hopefully. 'I'll return shortly, Lady Valentine. *Ah.* Excuse me.'

He bent ponderously and picked up an object from a corner of the room.

Lucas slammed his glass down, slopping wine; staggered across the room, and made it to the window at the same time as the cinnamon-haired woman grabbed the frame and leaned dangerously far out. He leaned out beside her, rain cool on his face.

Casaubon strode across the yard, coat flying, one massive hand gripping the stem of a lace parasol.

His head was high. He did not look up. As he disappeared into the passage Lucas heard his voice rumble, baritone, and the noise of a dropped crate.

'Oh!' The White Crow's arms clamped tight across her ribs. Mouth a rictus, she leaned against the casement and wheezed for air. Lucas opened his mouth to speak and caught the infectious laughter.

'Shit!' he said. 'Oh, shit, what a sight!'

The woman rubbed her eye with the heel of her hand. Storm-light gave a warmth to her fine skin, her dark-red curls; and from the open neck of her shirt Lucas breathed a scent of sun and grass and flesh.

He sat down on the opposite side of the sill. Laughter slowly stopped shaking her.

Finding words from nowhere, he explained: 'I thought that you were on your own in the city.'

'So did I.'

Relaxed, her mouth curved; and the terrible warmth of her eyes hit him in the pit of his stomach.

'I am,' she contradicted herself softly. 'Sometimes I look ahead, and I can see the days, each one a little cell. He knows me, you see. The clown. He thinks that if he entertains me I'll . . . '

Lucas picked up her hand and rubbed it against his face, feeling the warmth; the calluses on her middle finger.

'No.' The woman shook her head. 'The easiest thing in the world to say to you: stay. Don't listen to *la belle dame sans merci*. I won't listen to her, either.'

Lucas marvelled.

'I didn't think you knew I was here at all.'

She took her hand back, slid one cotton sleeve of her shirt to show the curve of her shoulder, and winked at him. Her breath was soft with wine.

'Ah, but now it wouldn't be because of you.'

'Valentine—'

'No. Not "Valentine",' she said. 'Not ever again.'

Not ever again beat in his pulse with the wine. Thinking how a Lord-Architect would not be here for ever, and how a student might be three years in the city, Lucas grinned crookedly.

Wood creaked with the returning tread of the fat man. The banisters protested his grip. The Lord-Architect and Knight of the Rose Castle stooped, still cracking his head lightly on the door-lintel.

'There was too little space,' he confided sunnily. 'I told the porters to store certain items in another room. The Lady Evelian suggested yours, young Lucas. I thought that particularly apt, since you're my page.'

The light is green, the colour of sunlight through hazel leaves in April. It shines on the frost-cracked masonry of a tiny cell. It shines on a thick rusty iron spike.

The air curls with vapours.

His hair is the same, gentle silver-white waves, and it

122

is an untidy thatch above the same creased labile features. Vulnerably swimming eyes blink, would turn away if they could. Instead the mouth stumbles to form words, responds to insistent questioning.

The iron spike is slippery, clotted with blood, plasma, mucus; stringy with sinews. Knobbed bone shows a gleaming red and white.

His head ends raggedly at the stump of a neck . . . torn muscle, wrenched vertebrae, split skin upon which age-freckles are still brown. His head is impaled on the iron spike.

Time has ceased in the stone labyrinths of the Fane. He is lost in a moment of butchery, endlessly prolonged; still balancing his endurance against the endless, endless demands for his knowledge.

The grey eyes brim with tears: not because of the moment's pain, but because the Bishop of the Trees has discovered that the tortures of the gods are infinitely diverse, and eternally prolonged.

'*I am not your page!*'

The White Crow rolled wine in her mouth, the numbness of alcohol pricking her tongue. The muscular young man stiffened, spine straightening; his black brows scowled: turning in a second from relaxed adult to tightly buttoned boy.

'He's a prince.' She sighed, the last vestiges of humorous teasing falling away from her. 'Princes can't be servants, you see.'

Casaubon placed one hand on his massive chest, and inclined his head in a bow to Lucas of Candover. His heel struck the door, and knocked it to.

'Page of Sceptres,' he said.

She walked to the reversed-mirror table, concentrating on the lifting and pouring of a bottle. Cool damp storm-air rustled the star-charts pinned to the walls.

'I know. Yes. Lucas is concerned in this somehow,' the White Crow admitted, clunking the bottle of straw-coloured wine down on the wood.

The Prince sank into the cleared chair at the table, his dark eyes not leaving her face.

'So.'

Casaubon grabbed a cold chicken-wing from the table as he passed, eased himself down into the creaking armchair, bit into the oily flesh and, in an indistinct but inviting tone, echoed: 'So?'

The White Crow walked to the street-side window. She leaned up against the jamb, banging her shoulder, and pushed the casement open. Rain spattered her face.

A yellow storm-light coloured the streets, and the roofs of the houses beyond. Past them, on the swell of the hill and horizon, running in a south-austerly direction to mark the quarter's boundary, a toothed line of obelisks and pyramids made a stark skyline.

Chitinous wings whir, too distant for human hearing. Like distant fly-swarms, acolytes darken the air over the distant stone.

She tasted rain on her lips.

'I know exactly what this is about.'

She heard the armchair creak, knew Casaubon's vast bulk must have shifted. The thinning rain glistened on the tiled roofs opposite; and an odour of straw and oil drifted up to her. She fisted one hand and stretched that arm, feeling the wine unlock the muscles.

'Here at the heart of the world . . . it's lazy, don't you feel it?'

Cloud-cover tore in the high wind. She tasted in her mouth how the skyline runs true on Evelian's side of the building: another black chain of courts and wings and outyards, the Fane cutting across aust-easterly to divide the Nineteenth District from the Thirtieth and Dockland.

From behind her Lucas's voice volunteered, 'We're souls fixed on the Great Wheel.'

The White Crow spluttered, wiped her hand across her nose and mouth, and turned around and sat down on the damp window-sill in one unwise movement.

'Now gods defend us from the orthodox!' She shook her

head. The room shifted. She set her empty glass down clumsily. 'Next you'll think you have to tell me that every thing that is is alive, and held in the constant creation of the Thirty-Six. From stones, bees and roses, to worlds that in their orbits move, singing with their own life that moves them . . . '

'Unquote.' The Lord-Architect belched. He settled back down into the armchair. 'Valentine, you've grown regrettably long-winded since we last met.'

The White Crow stood. Anger moved her precisely across the room, avoiding piles of books and the table.

'*Four times*.' Her index finger stabbed at him. 'The first time it happened was the first year I came here. It's why I stayed. Then another, three years later. And then *two* in this year alone: one in winter and one a month ago. Now, don't tell me the College can't read the stars as clearly as I can. Don't tell me that's not why you're here!'

Casaubon watched her with guileless china-blue eyes.

'*What* happened four times?' Prince Lucas asked.

She swayed, and reached out to steady herself on empty air. The stale smell of an eaten meal roiled her stomach.

'I'll show you.'

The White Crow walked unsteadily to where a chest stood against the wall. Leather-bound volumes weighed down the lid. A chair scraped: Lucas was beside her, suddenly, lifting the books and setting them down on the carpet. The smell of leather and dust made her nostrils flare.

She pushed up the lid of the chest, and took out, first, an old backpack, the straps cracked from lack of polish; and then a basket-hilted rapier, oiled and wrapped in silk.

'Scholar-Soldier!'

The White Crow ignored the Lord-Architect's muttered exclamation. She let herself grip the hilt, lifting the sword; and the memory of that action in her flesh made her eyes sting.

'You'll make me maudlin,' she snarled. 'Here, look at these.'

She flung the rolled-up star-charts at Casaubon. Lucas moved to stare over the Lord-Architect's shoulder as he unrolled them. The White Crow rose cautiously to her feet, and sat down in Lucas's vacated chair.

'The Invisible College must know', she said, 'that The Spagyrus practises Alchemy. Yes? Up there, in the heart of the Fane. While we turn with the Great Wheel, and return on this earth, *he* practises sublimation and distillation and exaltation, to discover the elixir of life – or so I thought, until this year.'

'Mmmhmrm.' The Lord-Architect swivelled a star-chart with surprisingly precise movements.

'And since there's no eternal life but the life of the soul, that would have been harmless enough. He is a Decan, eternal, divine. He'd be playing. You see?'

'Oh, yes. Certainly.'

She was aware of the dark-browed young man frowning. The White Crow leaned back, struts of the chair hard against her spine. A half-inch of wine remained in the bottle. She held the bottle, tilting it gently from one side to the other.

'Oh, Lucas . . . '

His body brushed her hair as he passed. 'Tell me.'

'There is a thing that men search for.'

She spoke into the rain-scented air, not attempting to watch him as he paced about the room.

'Although the Decans found it long since; or, being gods, never needed it. I mean the Philosopher's Stone: that same elixir that, being perfect in itself, cannot help but induce perfection in all that it touches.'

The after-effect of wine dizzied her, and she laughed softly.

'Including the human body. And a perfect body couldn't be corrupted. Couldn't die. Hence it's sometimes called the elixir of eternal life.'

The parchment star-charts crumpled in Casaubon's fist as the Lord-Architect heaved himself out of his chair. He knelt down beside the chest. The thud vibrated through

126

the floorboards. He lifted the leather satchel and the sword, laying them carefully in the trunk.

'You can still clean a sword,' he said, 'but I fear for your scholarship, if that's how you interpret these charts.'

She reached across to ruffle his orange-copper hair, and feel the massive shoulder straining under the linen shirt.

'No. *No.* I was just explaining to Lucas that . . . '

Light shifted from storm-cloud yellow to sun: the evening clearing. A cold air touched her. She sat at table, among the remains of the meal, still tilting the wine-bottle. A deep sky shone through the street-window. She looked at the black-obelisked horizon.

'Lazy, this heart of the world . . . I came here when I thought I would do nothing but listen to it beat, hear the Great Wheel turn; forget I had ever studied *magia*, wait to die and be reborn.'

She thumbed the cork out of the bottle with a hollow sound. The glass was cold at her lips.

'And then, a month after I got here, I saw it. Written in the sky, clear for anyone who could read the stars. A fracture of nature. I didn't know what it was; I hardly believed I saw it. So – ah.'

She laughed deprecatingly, and waved both hands as if she swatted something away from her; meeting Casaubon's gaze as he got to his feet.

'So just what you'd expect to happen happened. I'd thought I'd done with study. But I paid with labour for a room, and worked in kitchens and bars for what else I needed – optic glass and books mainly – and stayed here searching the *De occulta philosophia*, the *Hieroglyphika*, the *Corpus Hermeticum*, the *Thirty Statues* . . . Everything and anything. So much for Valentine's history, hiding out in case the College should find her.'

The Lord-Architect still held one chart in his ham-hand. The most recent, she saw.

'Four is too many to be accidental,' he remarked.

'Now, I believe that. I thought it might just be an accident, and the second time coincidence. There are

god-daemons on earth here in the heart of the world –
is it so surprising if miracles happen? Black miracles,' she
said. 'Black miracles.'

Lucas, tracing a finger down the annotated line of
the star-chart the Lord-Architect held, frowned in
concentration.

'It's a death-hour, isn't it? The heavens at the moment
of somebody's death?'

The White Crow reached up to take the parchment and
unroll it among the dishes and plates on the table. She
weighed one corner down with the wine-bottle.

'Not some *body*. Bodies die all the time, young Lucas.
The Great Wheel turns. We're weighed against a feather,
ka-spirit and shadow-soul both; and then the Boat sails us
through the Night, and back to birth.'

The last after-effects of the wine tanged melancholy on
her tongue. Workaday evening light glowed in through
the window.

'It's a chart of the heavens at a moment I've only
seen these four times. When the Great Circle itself has
been broken.'

'It's not possible,' Lucas denied.

'It is possible. Black alchemy, and an elixir not of
life but of death, true death . . . Four times the Great
Circle has been broken by a death that was not merely
the body's death.'

Her callused finger touched at the alignment on paper
of Arcturus, Spica, the Corona, the *sphera barbarica*. The
constellations of animal-headed god-daemons marched
across a sky of black ink on yellow parchment.

'In this city the soul can die, too.'

4

'But I must keep hostages,' the Hyena concluded. She turned her slanting red-brown eyes on Falke and Charnay and Zar-bettu-zekigal.

Plessiez's slender dark fingers moved to his neck, feeling in his black fur for the missing *ankh*. His piercing black eyes narrowed.

'I need Charnay; the Lieutenant's familiar with the plan. And the Katayan. Keep Master Builder Falke.'

The man did not stir. He sat with his back to the sewer wall, head resting down on his arms. Zari sprang up from where she sat beside him. Her dappled tail coiled around her leg, whisk-end wrapped tight about her ankle.

'I could stay!' she volunteered.

Plessiez hid an icy amusement. 'You will come with me, Kings' Memory, to repeat your record to his Majesty, and to the General of my Order; I will then send you *back* here, to tell your Memory to the Lady Hyena.'

'So long as I get to come back.' Unrepentant, the Katayan grinned.

The Hyena glanced up at Charnay. 'The Lieutenant stays here. You won't be concerned if I kill a man, even a Master Builder. If I kill a Rat, you will. She stays, with him.'

'Lieutenant Charnay—'

The brown Rat chuckled, and hitched up her sword-belt on her furry haunches, the empty scabbard dangling. She flexed massive shoulders.

'No problem, messire. I'll even keep your pet human alive for you.'

'How very thoughtful,' Plessiez murmured.

His eyes moved to the crowd of ragged men and women who pressed in close now. Sun-banners and skeletons' shadows danced on the walls, above their heads, in the flickering torchlight. The stench of unwashed flesh and old cooking made his mobile snout quiver.

'I can give no guarantees that I will achieve your demands.'

The Hyena swung round, one fist clenched. A babble of voices echoed off the sewer-chamber's walls.

'Our freedom—'

'To walk in the streets—'

' – To carry weapons—'

'Carry swords without being arrested, gaoled—'

' – Defend ourselves—'

'Trade—'

One of the raggedly dressed men drew his sword, holding it up so that it glinted in the light; a rust-spotted épée. Two or three other men and women copied him, then another; then, awkwardly, most of the assembled crowd.

'*Freedom!*'

'Ye-ess . . . ' Plessiez straightened, one slender hand at his side, head high. He gazed around at human faces. Each one's eyes fell as he met them: subservient, angry, afraid. 'I'm not impressed by third-rate histrionics.'

He turned back to the Hyena, adding: 'If only because I know how effective they are with the General of my Order, and with his Majesty the King . . . Lady, you could kill me now. You could let me work to gain you the concession of returning to the world above, carrying arms, and then do nothing of what I've asked.'

Her dark face glinted with humour.

'That may happen, Plessiez. Or we may let you try to work your necromancy. Let me warn you: we go above ground secretly, and we know the city. If you don't get the truce for us, we'll stop you dead in your tracks.'

Sweetness made saliva run in his mouth. The stench of roses leaked down from the sewer walls, gleaming with a phantom sunlight.

'Come here.'

As Zar-bettu-zekigal came to his side, Plessiez rested clawed fingers lightly on the shoulder of her black cotton dress.

'Memory, witness. The Lady Hyena's people to carry arms, to walk the streets above ground, to be free of the outstanding penalties against them as rebels and traitors.'

The Katayan nodded once.

The woman folded her arms, metal clicking. 'We do nothing until that happens. Very well. Memory, witness. Certain articles of corpse-relic necromancy to be placed at septagon points under the heart of the world, for the summoning of a pestilence . . .'

'Which will happen before very long,' Plessiez added smoothly. 'I have already placed two; the rest are yours. And if no plague-symptoms appear soon, Desaguliers' police will have words with your people, lady.'

Her slanting eyes met his. 'If your Order's *magia* does work, messire priest, then it's everyone for themselves.'

The hunger on her dirty face made hackles rise down Plessiez's spine. He abruptly turned, snapped fingers for Charnay's attention, brushing aside humans who sought to stop him. He waved Zar-bettu-zekigal away.

'Charnay and I are old friends. She may have messages for her family . . .'

He caught the scepticism in the Hyena's expression, and the last inches of his scaly tail tapped a rhythm of tension.

'Lieutenant, give me as many days as you can before you escape from here.'

The brown Rat matched his undertone. 'I'll stay, messire. To tell you the truth, I'd sooner duel Desaguliers' Cadets any day of the week. These scum are amateurs. Just as likely to stab you in the back as fight . . .'

She dropped her resonant voice a tone softer. 'Give it a couple of weeks, let the plague get a grip down here, and I'll come out in the confusion. Don't worry, messire! I'll do it.'

His hand closed on her brawny arm, dark against the glossy brown fur. 'If it's from you that they discover they're not immune to this plague, I swear I'll have you gutted at the square and chasing your own entrails round a stake!'

She nodded, good-humoured, still smiling. 'Plessiez, man, give me credit for sense! I want to die as little as you do. The only way they'll find out is when they start burying each other.'

Plessiez looked up at her. 'See that's so.'

He stepped back, adding in a louder tone: 'We'll leave you now.'

The blond man, Clovis, squinted at the woman in ragged armour. 'Lady, who'll lead him out?'

'I will.' The Hyena pointed. 'Take those others and give them food.'

A man in the tatters of a satin suit jeered. Youths scrambled to follow Falke and Charnay as they were led off, scooping handfuls of ordure to throw, screeching insults. Plessiez bristled, tail cocked high.

As she turned away, he spoke unpremeditatedly:

'*And give me back my sword.*'

The armoured woman beckoned, not turning to see if she was obeyed. The great silence of the sewers pressed against his ears. The substanceless brambles of roses brushed his fur.

'No,' she said. 'Feel how it is to go unarmed, messire, in the presence of your enemies.'

Above, in the city, clocks strike four in the morning.

Footsteps echoed down the main aisle of the Cathedral of the Trees.

'You!'

The novice sleeping on the oak altar started awake. Bright starlight showed his patched water-stained robe. He rubbed his eyes. 'The cathedral's closed.'

The brusque voice said: 'We don't close the cathedral.'

She moved into the starlight, monochrome through

night-stained windows. The novice saw a black-skinned woman in her twenties. Her tree-embroidered robe had a wide belt, cinched tightly, so that she seemed an hour-glass: round hips and buttocks, round shoulders and breasts. Her short hair tangled darkness in loops and curls.

'Archdeachon Regnault, I beg your pardon!'

He slid down from the altar, an awkward bony young man.

'I didn't know you were back from the Aust quarter.'

Regnault smiled briefly. 'We remain a church, in despite of all they can do to us. Are you the only one here?'

'The others are out looking for Bishop Theodoret.'

'So am I,' the Archdeacon said. 'The old man's put his head in the Decan's mouth once too often. We'll have to do what we can to get it out.'

'You think . . . you think he's alive, then?'

The Archdeacon tugged at the waist of her robe. Her dark hand brushed the hawthorn spray pinned on her breast. Her fingers splayed in a Sign of the Branches.

'Where's your faith?' she asked.

'Ei!'

Feathers swooped down and flung into an upward curve. Zari crooked up an arm. Wings splayed like spread hands in front of her face. She flinched away as the bird skirred past, burring up to the unseen roof.

'Little one?'

'Oh, see you, it's nothing.'

Her voice died. The black Rat stopped, and she cannoned into his elbow. Humidity had slicked his fur up into tufts. She pressed close to his side.

A few yards ahead, the Hyena swivelled, pivoting on the scabbard she used as a crutch. 'Keep moving! I told you that we'd have to cross the bridge.'

Cloud and blue vapour drifted across the stonework. Here, in older tunnels, the brickwork had given way to masonry. Zar-bettu-zekigal reached out to trail her fingers across one immense pale-blue block of Portland stone. Chill wetness took the print. A wind gusted into her face, lifting strands of black hair.

'Messire, where are we?'

The black Rat limped now, weary with four hours' walking, and his tail dragged in the stone-dust. Thrown ordure marked his scarlet jacket. His dark fingers continually reached for his empty scabbard.

'In Hell. I—' His arctic calm shattered. *'What's that?'*

Zar-bettu-zekigal scurried three steps to the Hyena's side. She pushed past the woman in red cloth and armour, skidded, slipped to one knee, tail crooked out for balance; pointed ahead.

'That—!'

Great wings beat, a thirty-foot wing-span: dipping down so slowly that the up-curve of flight-feathers clearly showed at their tips. Zari fell to hands and knees. The sharp beak and amber eyes soared towards her. Gleaming black, only wing-tips and head feathered white, the condor rose on a column of air that blew in her face, scattering the white clouds and blue vapour.

It scored the air towards her, rising, too large for the narrow tunnel. Wing-tips thirty feet apart brushed through the blue stone walls and ceiling. As the feathers passed through the substance of the stone, the stone crumbled away, falling on the downsweep into newly created void.

Zar-bettu-zekigal craned her neck to follow as the condor soared over her head. The great bird vanished into mist. She looked down again, to see in its wake – sky.

'Messire Plessiez!'

She knelt up, tail tucking around her knees.

Ahead, voids of empty air opened up. The walls and roof of the tunnel crumbled, blue stone falling into blue air.

Zar-bettu-zekigal stared at the masonry of the floor, momentarily solid and spanning the gulf. Emptiness began to eat into it, stone melting like frost in sunlight.

'But we're underground,' she protested.

Slender strong fingers grasped her shoulder. She looked

up to see Plessiez gazing ahead, black eyes narrowed.

'*What is this?*'

'You're under the city,' the Hyena said. 'You're under the heart of the world.'

Zar-bettu-zekigal stood, brushing dust from her black dress. She pulled the greatcoat firmly around her. The vast gulfs of air pressed in on her, swelling her skull with emptiness; until she swayed, and caught hold of the woman's arm, steel vambrace cold under her hand.

Miles below, a plain stretched out into blue mists. She gazed at a middle region of cloud, eyes squinting against a cold wind. The breath she took smelt of burning.

A steel-gauntleted hand pushed Zari in the flat of her back.

'Move, or you'll never cross.'

Zar-bettu-zekigal stepped forward, bare feet testing the Portland stone. Chill water slicked the surface. The stone bridge diminished into distance and perspective before her. She lifted her head and saw, where vapours shifted, the ragged ends of arches and stone groynes hanging down into the void.

'*Look*,' she breathed.

Masonry towers ended above her, hanging their sealed cellars down from the underside of the city into the gulf. Blended with brick, and with steel girders; and structures the shape of building-foundations. And random jammed-together masses of stone and mortar and wood. Further off, raw rock jutted down into the sky: the undersides of hills.

Zar-bettu-zekigal strained her vision, searching the vapour.

Between the underside of the city and the plain, a waning moon stood flat and white in a blue sky. A second half-globe hung behind it, larger and more pale. Within the larger moon's curve, Zar-bettu-zekigal saw the fingernail-paring of a smaller satellite.

She looked down, off the slender span of stone.

Her stomach wrenched. Six miles below, the plain

135

burned with visible flames. Licking orange-and-yellow fires, hearth-fire welcoming; until she made out how condors and eagles soared in the depths under the bridge.

Plessiez's fur brushed her shoulder. Water pearled on the Rat's glossy black coat. The priest walked steadily beside Zar-bettu-zekigal, hand gripping her arm. She looked up and saw that his eyes were clamped shut.

Behind them, the woman laughed.

The masonry floor of the tunnel shifted, etched away piecemeal by the air. Zar-bettu-zekigal peered over the edge again as she walked, heels kicking the slick stone, and stopped.

'How much time do we have?'

A whisk of metal and leather sounded, yards behind. She spun round as Plessiez did. The woman leaned now on a naked sword, some yard and a half long, that spanged light from its outside curve. She rubbed a hand across her filthy face.

'Not long,' she said, 'and we can't turn back. Now let's *move*.'

Clock-mill strikes four-thirty.

Stars hieroglyphed the night sky, blotted by rainclouds.

A large figure trod stealthily across the dark courtyard, smelling of fresh soap. The Lord-Architect padded towards the steps in the far corner, the silken tail of his night-robe flapping in the wind.

He rubbed thumb and middle finger softly together. Faint gold light glimmered, died. His shoulders straightened. Invisible in the night, he smiled. No natural magic tripwires guarding the steps to Valentine's rooms . . .

He put one foot on the bottom step, hesitated as the wood creaked. Her window showed dark. He climbed another step, and another.

The Lord-Architect's foot caught a metal rim. The handle of the saucepan flew up, cracking his shin. His other foot came down firmly inside a pot and, as he stumbled, two cans rattled and clanged down the wooden steps.

The Lord-Architect exclaimed, '*Helldammit!*', arms wheeling, flailing massively. Another pan clattered from stairs to cobbles.

Upstairs, a woman rubbed cinnamon hair from her mouth with one wrist, rolling over in bed on to her stomach; eyes glued shut, smiling in her sleep.

Lights came on in several windows round Evelian's courtyard: flints struck, copper lamps groped for and lit; fingers burned, swearwords muttered.

With immense dignity, and his left foot jammed tightly into an enamelled chamberpot, the Lord-Architect Casaubon clanked back to his own rooms.

'I'll be back!'

Zar-bettu-zekigal clung with both hands to the iron ladder's rails. Looking between her feet, she shouted down the narrow shaft again:

'Don't forget me!'

Far below, a woman laughed.

'Come, little one.' The black Rat leaned over, standing above her where the ladder hooped over to the head of the shaft. Light shining up from the depths illuminated his snout and brilliant eyes.

Hunger dizzied her as he reached down. Her foot slipped. She whipped her tail around the ladder, grabbed the Rat's sword-belt, and felt her greatcoat ride up over her shoulders as Plessiez grabbed her under the arms, hauling her up on to a flat brick floor.

Far, far below, the laugh modulated out of the sound a human voice makes: raked up into higher, yelping registers; echoed away in whoops, giggles, vixen-yawps.

The light that shone up the shaft began to fade. Zari raised her head, peering at the surrounding dark.

'I've seen places I liked better.' She stepped out of the Rat's inadvertent embrace, pushing lank hair out of her eyes.

This shaft opened into a brick chamber some twenty by thirty feet, empty in the fading illumination. The black Rat reached up to the ceiling, eighteen inches above his head, testing each of the interlocked metal plates.

'She was laughing at where we'll come out,' Zari guessed. 'It *has* to be in the city still. When I came in on the ship it took five days just to sail up the estuary, and the city all around us all the way.'

Fading light showed her his face, lean and drawn with hunger, with the weariness of climbing shaft upon shaft of the endless sewers.

'Ah!'

One plate swung up and over, vanished with a *clang!*, and Plessiez sprang to hoist himself up through the now-open trapdoor. Zari danced from one foot to the other beneath.

'What is it? What's there? Where are we?'

Plessiez began to laugh.

Zari leaped up, hands gripping the sides of the trap; got one bare foot up for leverage. She heard him laugh again, a loud uninhibited guffaw: part awe, part admiration. Metal clanged. Rapid footsteps went back and forth.

'*What?*' Huffing, she pulled herself up through the trapdoor.

'But this is wonderful!'

Plessiez's expression changed from enjoyment to second thoughts. He stood in a passageway lined either side with barred rooms, and had been banging on the iron-studded door at the far end of the passage.

'Amazing. Little one, these are the oubliettes of the Abbey of Guiry.'

Zar-bettu-zekigal rubbed at green stains on the sleeves of her greatcoat. 'The Abbey what?'

A last gust of laughter shook Plessiez.

'My Order is the Order of Guiry, the Guiresites,' he explained gravely; and swung round and struck the door an echoing blow. 'Guards! What, *guards ho!*'

There were green stains on the soles of her feet, Zari

discovered, as she balanced precariously on one leg. And stains on her black dress.

Over the clatter of approaching feet, the black Rat said: 'Listen to me, Kings' Memory – you stay with me, now, and only with me. Above all, you say nothing except when I direct you to.'

'I'm a Kings' Memory; I speak to whoever asks me.' She buttoned the great overcoat, covering the worst of the stains. 'Messire, can we have something to *eat*?'

The rattle of the door unlocking was followed by a rush of black and brown Rats into the corridor. Zari gazed at their sober black dress. The first Rat, plumed and wearing a black jacket, came to a skidding halt when she saw Plessiez; grabbed the *ankh* at her neck, and exclaimed: 'Plessiez! Cardinal-General Ignatia told us you were dead—'

His glance crossed hers. Zar-bettu-zekigal saw the black Rat grin, showing sharp incisors. Amusement, triumph, and a febrile excitement gleamed in his eyes.

'There's much that Cardinal-General Ignatia doesn't know, I assure you.'

A brown Rat pushed to the forefront of the guards and priests, looked Plessiez up and down, and with an air of triumph concluded: 'You're not dead, are you?'

Plessiez smoothed down his torn scarlet jacket. '*No*, Mornay – and nor is your sister Charnay. Hilaire, order my coach brought to the front of the palace. Lucien, ride immediately to his Majesty and say that I must have an immediate audience. *Now*. I want no argument. I must see the King.'

Zari grinned at the startled faces. Plessiez's slender-fingered hand swept her along, trotting beside him while he fired orders to left and right. Her calves ached sharp protests at the steps up from the oubliette to the guardroom.

'Fetch Reverend Captains Fenelon and Fleury. They'll be accompanying me to the King. Lay out my best clothes in my rooms. Also my sword. Sauval, come with me; I'll want you to take down a dictated report as we go—'

'Food!' Zari yelled succinctly above the confusion.

' – and have the kitchens bring something to eat.'

A black Rat some years older than Plessiez pushed through the crowd, past Zar-bettu-zekigal. She had little enough of the priest about her: her plumed headband was gold and white, and her jacket white with gold piping. 'I'll have to inform Cardinal-General Ignatia, Plessiez. You can't ask to see the King if she doesn't know why.'

Plessiez hesitated at the guardroom door, head cocked, translucent ears tensing. Zari saw him listen to some interior voice urging caution and discard it.

'The Cardinal-General Ignatia', Plessiez said, 'is a useless old bitch.'

'*What?*'

Zar-bettu-zekigal put both hands on separate Rats' shoulders and shoved them aside. Sunlight dimmed the candles in the corridor outside, patched with colour the coats and embroidered scabbards of the priest Rats. She blinked water from her eyes. Pushed, shoved, ignored by the quarrel rapidly forming, she thrust a way out of the group and padded across the white-walled corridor to the nearest window.

The sun hung a hand's breadth above the horizon. Sharp-edged clouds glowed, indigo above, translucent pink below. She pushed the casement open. Cold air flooded her lungs – the chill of evening or the dew-damp of dawn? She scrunched her fingers through her hair, and twitched the kinks from her black-and-white furred tail.

'Morning or evening?' She caught a passing Rat's arm. He stared at her, and she jerked her head at the window. Light as cold and clear as water covered the city, that stretched out unbroken to the horizon.

'Dawn. Messire—'

Plessiez's voice ripped the air. 'Silence! Captain Auverne, you may make yourself useful by taking a squad of guardsmen and investigating the sewer-shaft that opens into our cellars. But use all possible caution. I want a day-and-night guard kept down there from now on.'

140

The white-and-gold-clad Rat snarled something under her breath, reluctantly turning away to summon guards.

'And I am most disturbed to discover that you knew nothing of this entrance, Captain Auverne. Kindly report to me later with the explanation. Zari.' Plessiez turned his back on the indignant captain.

'I'm here, messire.'

'Come with me.'

She followed the priest as he strode off through the whitewashed stone corridors. A faintness of hunger sang in her head, cramped her guts; and at every sunlit window they passed she grinned and skipped a half-step. Each window gave her a wider view of the dawn: the pale sky deepening to azure.

Inside the doors of extensive apartments, the small group grew to a crowd, augmented as other Rats came running. Plessiez's voice rose over the noise, his rapid-fire orders sending junior priests off on errands. Zari flopped down on a satin-covered couch, her attention taken up with a tray of bread and goat-cheese, and a flagon of cold water.

'Steady, little one.'

She looked up, jaws clamped on a crust; tore and swallowed and nodded, all in one movement.

'I know, I know . . .' Cramps from too-rapid eating griped in her gut.

The outer doors swung closed. Sunlight blazed in the white low-roofed rooms; on carpets, tapestries, desks, globes and icons. Plessiez dictated to his secretary as Rats sponged and brushed his filthy fur. Zari switched to sitting cross-legged on the couch, gazing round at the royal-blue drapes, the silver goblets and plates.

'It isn't', she said into a gap in Plessiez's dictation, 'an austere Order, the Order of Guiry.'

Plessiez chuckled. He slipped his arms into a crimson jacket slashed with gold and, as a brown Rat servant buttoned it up to his throat, remarked: 'An academic Order, little one; and austere as – ah, as all academics are.'

The silver rim of the water-jug chilled her mouth. She drank, colicky; and belched.

'*Plessiez!*'

'Here.' The black Rat acknowledged the yelp of joy, raising his arms while a servant buckled and adjusted his sword-belt and basket-hilted rapier. He shrugged himself back into it, hand going at once to rest there. The junior priests and servants fell back before two newcomers.

Zari switched round to kneel upright on the couch. She put both hands over her mouth, muffling a giggle. A short plump black Rat slitted her eyes, her gaze passing over the Katayan silhouetted against the rising sun.

'You're going to see the King?' she asked Plessiez.

'Fleury, of course he is!' A tall and very thin Rat, with raffish black fur and a cheerfully unworldly look, slapped Plessiez's shoulder. 'Must have worked out, eh? When do we give the word to move?'

With a start, he noticed the Katayan.

'Zar-bettu-zekigal,' she said gravely, scratching her ear with her tail. The Rat bowed.

'Fenelon,' he said.

'Fleury, Fenelon, you'll come with me to the King.' Plessiez beckoned. 'Little one.'

Zar-bettu-zekigal got off the couch, and bent to rub her calves with both hands. 'I'm dead beat!'

'Rest in the coach. Come.'

'Messire Plessiez!'

An elderly black Rat stood in the doorway, the white-and-gold-clad captain beside her. Her ears showed ragged, her muzzle grey. The sleeveless open robe over her jacket glowed emerald. Lace foamed at her wrists and at her throat. A gemmed pectoral *ankh* hung between her rows of dugs.

'I regret I cannot stay to serve the Cardinal-General,' Plessiez said, picking up his scarlet cloak and plumed headband. 'The Cardinal-General will excuse me.'

'What are you doing?' Cardinal-General Ignatia frowned, bewildered. 'Captain Auverne reports you asked for an audience with the King. You must, of course, first report to myself anything concerning the use of *magia*—'

'Is my coach there?' Plessiez asked Zar-bettu-zekigal. She padded across to the window.

'There's a coach waiting in the courtyard, messire.'

'Good.'

'Messire Plessiez, you will explain yourself!'

Zari saw the black Rat's tail sweep into a jaunty curve. With a studied recklessness, Plessiez faced the Rat in the doorway.

'The explanation would be a little too complex for you, Ignatia. Short of force, you won't stop me seeing the King. And you won't use force.'

The black Rat that Zari identified as Auverne stepped forward. Fleury's sword scraped out of the scabbard: a ragged raw noise. The Cardinal-General held up her hand.

'Really, Messire Plessiez, the haste, if nothing else, is most unseemly; and, even without that rashness, protocol demands that your superior in the Order first hears whatever information you may possess.'

Zar-bettu-zekigal rubbed her eyes, planting her bare feet four-square on the floorboards; dazzled by whitewashed walls and daylight. The sun-warmed wood thrummed, once, and she winced: the tensile memory of the skin on the soles of her feet still tingling with the dissolution of stone.

'That child has seen *magia*!' the Cardinal-General protested. Zari opened her eyes to find the elderly Rat peering at her.

'Yes, *magia*. Thirty years' study should at least enable you to recognize it when you see it!'

Plessiez snarled, not slowing as he approached the Cardinal-General.

'Or has it been something in books for too long, Ignatia? Don't you care for it raw? Now, while you've been poring over the Library for decades, I've *acted*.'

The elderly Rat involuntarily stepped back.

'This is your old talk of power under the heart of the

143

world? Plessiez, you demean yourself, you behave no better than a Tree-priest. We have our God at hand, their *gaia* is nowhere to be seen, and as for beneath the city—'

'Messire Plessiez,' a guard interrupted, as he pushed his way through the crowd at the door. 'That sewer-shaft. We've investigated. It goes down about six feet. Then it's completely choked by new rubble.'

Zari's feet tingled, remembering the floorboards' tremor. She tried to catch Plessiez's eye, but the black Rat only beckoned her and Fleury and Fenelon.

As they passed the Cardinal-General, Zar-bettu-zekigal glanced first at her and then sympathetically up at the raffish Fenelon.

'End of a long fight?'

'About six years' worth,' he agreed. He put himself between Zar-bettu-zekigal and Auverne's novice-guards.

Plessiez carried his slim body taut, swinging cloak and headband from his free hand. As Zari caught up, he called back over his shoulder: 'Make the most of your time, Ignatia. I'll be asking the King to appoint a new Cardinal-General of the Order of Guiry.'

Far into the Fane, day and night are lost memories. The light that shines on the stonework is cool green. There is no slightest hint of decay in the air.

– Why did you betray your people?—

He hears no audible voice. It writes, instead, in lines of blood forming behind his shut eyelids. The Bishop can croak air through ripped vocal cords. But he will not speak.

His wrinkled lids, blue-veined, open to disclose rheumy eyes. No matter how he tries to look down (head held immobile by the iron spike upon which it is impaled) he cannot see the peripheral obstructions of chest or shoulders. They no longer exist.

– Why did you betray the Builders' conspiracy?—

Lines of blood, forming in the empty air.

His creased lower jaw works. Drying blood and sinews constrict his throat.

– How did they think to threaten god-daemons?—

'I . . . don't . . . know . . .'

– Answer and it will count well in your favour. Those are coming who need to ask no questions, all-knowing and all-seeing. The Decans will be less kind than we who are only their servants.—

'Lady . . . of . . . the . . . Woods . . .'

Unable to see his interrogators, unable to move anything but that once-eloquent mouth, the Bishop of the Trees begins to pray.

The heat of the early sun drew vapour from the black wooden sill. Earth and cobbles in the courtyard below steamed, the previous night's rain drying. The young man on the truckle-bed rolled over. Half-asleep, sweating, he got up on one elbow. The vibrations of Clock-mill striking eight jarred his brown eyes open.

'Awshit,' Lucas of Candover muttered. 'Awshitshit . . .'

A long *cre-eak* disorientated him. He kicked free of the sheet and sat up. Something large, pink and swathed in wet towels loomed over the bed. Lucas swallowed the foul taste in his mouth.

'Wh—?'

The Lord-Architect Casaubon said: 'Step across the landing for a moment, Prince. I need help.'

'Mmhrm – *What?*'

The door to Lucas's room creaked shut. He rubbed granules of sleep from his eyes, staring around the tiny room. Only the smell of steam spoke of recent occupation. He groped for his breeches.

'*Shit!*' Struggling into his clothes, he barged out and across the tiny landing to the Lord-Architect's door. 'What is it? What's wrong? Is it her – White Crow?'

The Lord-Architect sat on his creaking truckle-bed, towelling his hair vigorously. A claw-footed iron bathtub in one corner was surrounded by sopping-wet towels. Crates and brass-bound trunks occupied what space that was left. Through the leaded window, a blue summer sky grew pale and hotter by the second.

145

'*Is she in danger?*'

'What?' The Lord-Architect emerged from his towel, wet hair standing up in red-gold spikes. He beamed at Lucas. 'Some ridiculous ordinance in the city – a human being can't hire *servants*! Of all the pox-rotted pig's-tripe. Hand me my vest, will you?'

'Servants?'

'Body-servants,' Casaubon amplified. He pushed himself up from the bed, and the wooden frame creaked a protest. The wet towel joined the others on the floorboards. Pulling a vest over his head, he repeated from the depths of the folds of cloth: 'Hand me *that*, there.'

Lucas glared. 'I'm a Prince of Candover and no man's servant!'

'Hmm?' The Lord-Architect thrust his head out of the muffling cloth. 'Hurry it up, will you? There's a good lad.'

Something in the Lord-Architect's tone convicted Lucas of dubious manners at best. Lucas picked up the canvas garment hanging over the back of a chair and passed it across. He caught a jaw-cracking yawn, stifled it, and combed his sleep-tangled curls with his fingers.

'This is what you woke me up for? Of all the *insolence*—'

He stopped, and stared at Casaubon's back. The fat man's vest rode up over slabs of thigh and buttock as he fitted the canvas garment over his head, tugging it down over the full-moon swell of his belly.

'Poxrotted-damned-cretinous—' One elbow jammed in the air, the other caught in the laced-up garment. 'Lend a hand, can't you, boy!'

The court of Candover requires tact and diplomacy from a prince. Lucas sniffed hard. 'Is that a corset?'

'Damned-poxrotted full-dress *audience*—'

Lucas looked at canvas, bone-ribs and thick cord lacings, almost as bewildered as the older man. He bristled, caught between the insult to his dignity and the sneaking suspicion that his lack of knowledge was about to make a fool of him.

'The Princes of Candover don't dress themselves!'

He reached out and tugged tentatively at the bottom hem. Casaubon's elbow slid free. The fat man pulled the garment lower, huffing, until it girdled his stomach.

'Can't hire a damned servant, can't get a decent meal.' He turned, glaring down at Lucas. 'Does your poxrotted landlady *ever* serve anything without boiled cabbage in the meal?'

'I don't know,' Lucas shot back with satisfaction. 'I've only been here a week!'

The Lord-Architect chuckled resonantly. His companionable beam took in Lucas, the summer morning, the bell-notes of birds in the courtyard.

'Pull,' he ordered, presenting the Prince of Candover with his back and the lacings of the corset.

Lucas stepped closer, staring up at the fat-sheathed muscles of the Lord-Architect's shoulders and arms. He tugged the two flaps of the corset towards each other across the broad back.

'Right,' he said. '*Right.*'

He grabbed the two cords and pulled, sharply. The Lord-Architect grunted and braced his massive legs apart.

'She doesn't want you here.' Lucas emphasized his speech with a hard pull on the lacings. 'She's only talking to you because you won't answer her questions!'

The top of the corset, under the fat man's arms, began to pull together. Lucas, sweating, poked at the lacings further down; hooked his fingers under a point where they crossed over, and heaved.

'What's more, you're bothering her, and I don't like it.'

Casaubon grunted. He scratched at his newly washed hair, spiking it in tufts. Craning to look back over his cushioned shoulder, the Lord-Architect said mildly: 'Now, if I'd answered her questions when I arrived, what would she have done?'

'Told you to—' Lucas trapped his finger between tight lacings. He swore under his breath. 'To go away.'

'Precisely.' The Lord-Architect sucked in his breath and belly. The two edges of the corset creaked closer together. 'Now, how else could I get a bad-tempered impatient woman like Valentine to stand still and hear my message?'

Lucas glowered at the Lord-Architect's back. He wrapped the cords around his fist, put a knee at the cleft of the fat man's buttocks and pulled.

'What message?'

'Valentine will be asking herself that.'

Lucas whipped the cords into a secure knot, and sat down heavily on the Lord-Architect's bed, panting. Casaubon picked up a ruffled shirt and slid his arms into it, the bone-ribs of the corset gently creaking.

'I said . . . you're bothering her . . . and I don't like it.' Lucas rested his arms back, propping himself up, chin on his chest. Outside, the heat whitened city roofs, turned the air dusty. He sweated. The sour smell of bathwater and wet cloth filled his nostrils.

'You're right,' Casaubon said contritely. 'It was too sudden.'

He fastened the toggles on his shirt. The tails hung down almost to his massive calves. Lucas shook his head, and handed up the bright-blue silk breeches laid out on the bottom of the bed.

'Much too sudden!' The Lord-Architect stopped, one foot in his breeches, the other wavering in mid-air. He beamed widely at Lucas.

'I shall woo her,' he announced.

His foot hit the floorboards with an audible thump. As he fastened his silk breeches, he added: 'Do you think she likes poetry? I'll write her a sonnet. Two sonnets. How many lines would that be, exactly?'

Lucas fell back across the bed, wheezing, water leaking out of the corners of his eyes.

'Have that hay-fever treated,' the Lord-Architect advised. He cumbrously hooked his braces to his breeches, and over them eased an embroidered waistcoat on to his massive torso.

The attic-room's airless heat increased. Lucas rolled across the bed and pushed the casement window open.

Mud patched the courtyard, remnant of the storm. The White Crow stood up, two battered saucepans under her arm, and waved as she saw Lucas. He stared after her as she climbed her steps, picking up another can on the way. He realized he hadn't waved back.

'*What* message? If you're getting her involved in anything dangerous . . . '

The sun tangled in her hair that, he saw now, shone red without a gleam of gold or orange in it. Her white shirt hung out of the back of her brown knee-breeches.

The door swung to behind her.

Casaubon came to the window, shrugging into a royalblue satin coat, deep-pocketed, with turned-back embroidered cuffs. It fitted across his corseted stomach like a second skin. The full skirts swirled. Lucas, momentarily petty, enjoyed a thought of how hot and uncomfortable the Lord-Architect was going to be at a formal audience.

'Valentine has faced danger for the College since she was fifteen,' Casaubon said soberly. 'The woman enjoys it. Foolish child.'

Lucas stood. The Lord-Architect still topped him by six or eight inches.

'My uncle the Ambassador has a fairly efficient intelligence service. If I want to find out what's going on here, I can. Suppose you tell me.'

Casaubon lifted the corner of the bedsheet, peering under the bed. He padded to the other side of the room in stockinged feet.

'Can you see a shoe?'

Lucas scratched his chest. Muscles slid under sweaty skin. Almost despairing, he burst out: 'If you care about her so much, why won't you take help when it's offered? I'm a prince. I can command my people who are here. I could help!'

'It was here somewhere . . . '

Lucas picked up an extremely large black shoe from

149

behind a crate. Acting on nothing but impulse, he walked around the bottom of the bed, put his hand on Casaubon's chest and pushed. The Lord-Architect sat down heavily. Wood screeched. Lucas squatted down on his haunches in front of the fat man.

'You won't get rid of me.' He grabbed one stockinged foot, shoving the shoe on to it. Casaubon grunted. Lucas snared the other high-heeled court shoe from under the bed and fitted it on. 'So you might as – uh – might as *well* get used to me. There.'

Casaubon rested his elbows on his massive thighs, and rested his chins in his hands. China-blue eyes met Lucas's.

'I am about to go and give Valentine her message,' he said gravely. 'Would you care to come with me, before you leave for the university?'

Lucas stood. 'Yes! Yes . . . '

'Good.'

Hazarding a blind guess, Lucas said: 'You'll take her with you, to your audience with the King?'

'I have an audience,' the Lord-Architect Casaubon agreed, 'but not with the King. I have an audience at eleven, at the Fane.'

'No, true, my eyes are a natural condition. Permanently dilated pupils. My grandmother suffered them, too.'

Falke pulled down the sleeves of a slightly overlarge grey leather doublet, shrugging his shoulders into the new garment.

'Do you blame me for impressing the gullible? You must know what it's like to grub for every scrap of influence, the dynasty being powerless these many centuries . . . I tell them: every guttersnipe in the city walks into the Fane to talk to God; but I don't mean antechambers or building-sites, I mean the infinite interior of what we build . . . I say: *I've seen*. It works.'

Silver buckles clinked at his wrists, and he fastened them; thumbing back the dove-grey silk that protruded through the slashing on the leather sleeves. Pinpoints of brilliance reflected back from the metal into his vision. His eyes watered.

'And, gullible or not, I have a large number of people who listen to what the House of Salomon says. You need support. Your numbers are comparatively small — compared to our masters the Rat-Lords, that is.'

A last movement, tucking grey breeches into new boots (the leather a little bloodstained still at the toes), and he straightened; dry and clothed, now; gambling; meeting her red-brown eyes where she sprawled across the carved chair, under the torches and banners and bones.

'I've listened to you.' She snapped her fingers, not looking at the blond man who ran to her side. 'Clovis, feed him. I'll speak to him again later.'

'What about the Lieutenant?' Clovis asked.

'Nothing. I must think. Go.'

Falke followed the man through the makeshift camp in the vast chamber, walking easily across shadowed broken earth. A warm wind blew in his face, with a stench of carrion and sweetness on it; nevertheless he expanded his chest, drawing in the air.

'There.'

Clovis jerked his head towards a wide brick ledge. Falke leaped up lightly as the man walked away towards cooking-pots on tripods.

Charnay opened shining dark eyes. She lounged back against the brick wall with something of a disappointed air, furry body half-supported against sacks and barrels, her long-fingered hands clasped comfortably across her belly. 'Didn't expect to see you again. Who gave you the new kit?'

'The Lady Hyena.'

Falke reached up to tie his silver-grey hair back into a pony-tail with a length of leather thong. Fingers busy, facing into the great cavern, arms up and so unprotected. 'There's always a way, and I found it!'

The Rat rolled over on to one massive brown-furred

flank. 'I wouldn't trust one of you peasants to find your backside with both hands and a map.'

A pottery dish clunked on the edge of the brickwork. Clovis walked away without a word. Falke watched him stumble over rocks plainly visible in the sombre torchlight that mimicked night.

He chuckled quietly, back in his throat.

Squatting, he scooped up the stew-bowl and prodded the mess of cooked weeds with his forefinger. Warm, greasy; the smell made his stomach contract. He shoved a messy fistful into his mouth, spilling fronds down the front of the leather doublet, and spoke between chewing.

'She knows, now, that I've been inside the Fane. Something your messire Plessiez can't claim.'

'What use is that to her? You fill your breeches at the mention of daemons.'

Falke stopped chewing. 'True, but that's not to the point now. A *magia* plague, a plague to send into the Fane. Very good. I like that. House of Salomon will approve. *I understand the Fane.* Listen, and try to understand me, Lieutenant. Messire Plessiez would want you to support me in making an alliance with this woman. She has a number of people down here; she can be useful.'

Shining black eyes shifted. The Rat lumbered to her hind feet and stood over him, looking down. 'Too late. He has his bargain with her already, boy. He doesn't need you now.'

Warm shivers walked across his skin, raising the small hairs. Cramps twisted his gut. Falke turned his back on her momentarily. Shadows shifted. Hauntings whispered at the edges of light. A jealousy shifted in his breast. Across the vast brick chamber, under a ragged sun-banner, two men circled each other, sparring: light sliding down the blades of broadswords.

'You think so? It isn't the first time Rat-Lords have used me. I may surprise them yet.'

The anvil-clang of weapons-practice echoed in the sewer chamber. Stenches drifted up from the distant canal.

Falke, hands tucked up under his armpits, stared across the expanse of camp-fires, brushwood heaps, gallows, and men and women. Each speck of light pricked at his unbandaged eyes.

'I shall live to thank Messire Plessiez for abandoning me here.'

He missed what she rumbled in reply, still staring out at the armed camp.

At human men and women carrying swords, pikes, flails, daggers. Carrying weapons and practised in their use.

The fox-cub nipped at the White Crow's wrist. She swore, put the feeding-bottle down on the mirror-table, and the cub back in its box. She reached up to the herb shelf for witch-hazel to put on the blood-bruise.

'Where did I . . . ?'

The silver wolf padded across the room, pushing over two precarious piles of books. They slid to rest in the sunlight slanting whitely in at the street-side and courtyard windows, and at the roof-trap. Light fell on opened books, star-charts propped up with ivory rods, wax discs scattered in three heaps, and discarded hieroglyphed scrolls.

'Here.'

She tapped the wolf's muzzle. Pale eyes met hers. It gaped, letting her finger the socket where a rotten tooth had been removed. Its head twitched irritably.

'Lazarus, you only come to me to get your teeth fixed,' she accused. 'I'd wait a day or two yet—'

She heard footsteps, and raised her voice without looking up: 'We're shut! Go away!'

The door swung open. She raised her head to see the dark young man open it with a mocking flourish, and bow most formally. The Lord-Architect Casaubon strode in past Lucas without a blink of acknowledgement.

'Valentine!'

The White Crow looked down at the timber wolf. 'No. *I* don't know how he does it.'

'I must say', Casaubon remarked, 'that you could keep this place a good deal tidier.'

She put her fists on her hips.

'I've been up since dawn working on the last batch of Mayor Spatchet's talismans, which aren't finished, which *won't* be finished today unless we're all very lucky, and so I advise you not to make critical comments of any sort, because my temper is not of the best, is that clear?'

The Lord-Architect tugged at the turned-up cuffs of his blue satin coat. 'I had something of a disturbed night myself.'

'Aw—' The White Crow sat down heavily at the table, sinking her chin in her hands. Bright eyes brimmed with laughter, fixing on Casaubon; she snuffled helplessly for several seconds.

Lucas's dark brows met in a scowl.

'Good morning . . . Prince,' the White Crow said.

Lucas picked up one of the discarded wax tablets. 'Talismans?'

'Oh . . . ' She took it out of his hand. 'Easy enough making something to warn when Decans exercise their power. The difficulty is making one the god-daemons' acolytes won't immediately feel being used and flock to.'

A light wind lifted papers as it brushed past her. She anchored one heap on the table with the handful of talismans. A number of crates stood open under the table, carved wood and incised wax talismans nesting in oakum. Her hand went to the small of her back, rubbing. She looked past the young man's earnest face to Casaubon.

'Now I suppose you'll tell me why you're here?'

The Lord-Architect stood by the open street-side window, face intent. He whistled through chiselled lips. The White Crow stood and walked across to sit on the sill, drawing her feet up, bracketed by the frame.

'There have been three other Scholar-Soldiers come to the heart of the world', Casaubon said, 'since you disappeared.'

154

Feathers rustled by her head. She flinched at the fluttering.

Bright chaffinches flew to perch on the Lord-Architect's extended plump fingers. A thrush's claws scored his head, pricking sharp through his hair; and a humming-bird the same brilliant blue as his satin coat hung so close before his face that his eyes crossed watching it. He whistled again.

She met his gaze through vibrating wings.

'None of them survived a half-year,' he concluded.

'I didn't know. This place is scaring me shitless.' The White Crow lifted her chin. 'You're not helping.'

'I have a message from the Invisible College.'

She reached forward, past her raised knees, touching the wooden window-frame. Sun-warmed, barely damp now. She breathed the acrid smell of street-dust. Heat already soaked the sky: people hurrying past kept to the buildings' shadows. Clock-mill's half-hour chime came from the far side of the building.

'I haven't written on the moon in ten years. Believe that I wouldn't have sent out any warning unless I had to. If I'd known it would bring *you*—'

His cushioned arms pushed between her back and the window-frame, and under the arch of her knees. She grabbed wildly, balance gone; blindly lurching back from the one-storey drop. His arms tightened. The White Crow knotted fists in his shirt as the fat man lifted her, holding her across the swell of his stomach.

'I am not in the habit of being a messenger-boy! Sit down, sit still, shut up and *listen!*'

Her bare feet hit the floor stingingly hard.

'*Get the hell out of here!*'

Lucas's voice came from the corner of the room: 'How does an invisible college find itself, to send messages?'

'Oh, what!' Exasperated, the White Crow swung round. She met his dark gaze, seeing both amusement and calculation. She nodded once. As she tucked her white shirt into her breeches, she said: 'Well done, Prince. But you won't stop the two of us quarrelling. As to your question, the College is wherever two or three Scholar-Soldiers happen to meet. Often you never *do* find out just who suggested what.'

A last sparrow flew out of the street-side window. The Lord-Architect rubbed absently at his sleeves, smearing guano across the blue satin. Wet patches of sweat already showed under his arms.

'You're promoted', he announced, 'from Master-Captain to Master-Physician Valentine.'

She felt an amazed grin start, and touched clasped fists to her mouth to hide the joy. 'You're joking. No, really.'

'I'm telling the truth,' Casaubon said.

'I never thought they'd ever— But I've *left* the damned College!' She sat down at the table and looked at Lucas. 'Yes, and your next question is *How do you find the College to leave it?*'

The Lord-Architect rested his hand on Lucas's shoulder as he walked around to face her. 'The Invisible College's rules are strict. We travel incognito, Prince, and never more than two or three together.'

'Oh, this is quite ridiculous.' The White Crow pressed the heels of her hands into her eyes, lost in a sparkling darkness. Evelian's voice sounded out in the courtyard, talking to her daughter Sharlevian. It came no nearer. A bee hummed in through one window, out through the other.

'Stupid.' She took her sweat-damp hands away from her face. 'I did leave. You knew it; so did Master-Captain Janou. You can't make me a Master-Physician, because I won't let you.'

The young man squatted down, fiddling with one of the chests against the wall.

'You know what's truly stupid?' She turned her head towards Casaubon. 'What's stupid is that it comforted me, sometimes, to think that I might be part of the College still – whoever we are, and however many there

156

may be of us. I had to leave you, but I lost something when I left.'

'And so did I.'

The White Crow felt her cheeks heat. She rubbed her flat palms against her face.

'And so did you . . . And now I don't want anything to do with this. I sent that warning because I want nothing to do with this; I wanted someone wiser to come here and *do* something about it!'

Casaubon *tsk*-ed ironically. 'Poor Valentine.'

Lucas's hand passed over her shoulder, and she sat up as a long bundle clattered on to the mirror-table.

'I asked the Lord-Architect about Scholar-Soldiers,' the young man said. 'You should be carrying this.'

She ignored Casaubon's startled look. Her fingers undid the wrappings, sliding scabbard and sword onto the table. The sweat-darkened leather grip on the hilt fitted her fingers, ridged to their exact shape. The weight on her wrist when she lifted it, familiar and strange now, made her throat ache.

'Why does the College need a Master-Physician here?'

'I would like to know that,' Casaubon said.

She rubbed her finger along the oiled flat of the blade. Cold metal, cold as mornings walking the road, or evenings coming to an inn. The smell of the oil mixed with the smell of the ink on the table, drying on the hieroglyphed parchments.

'What could possibly need *healing?*'

In one flawless movement she clicked the rapier home in its scabbard. The straps and buckles of the sword-belt tumbled across the table.

'I'm frightened.'

The Lord-Architect's voice rumbled above her head. 'That makes me afraid.'

'Well, that's sense enough.' Hands still on the scabbard, she looked across at Lucas. 'Oh, and if I wear this in the street I'll be in the palace dungeons before you can say *his Majesty*.'

'You need to wear it,' he insisted. 'You need to. Not for protection.'

She looked down at hands tanned and with a fine grain to the skin, the blue veins showing faintly under the surface. She flexed her fingers.

'A wise child. My lord, you have a wise child with you.' She took Casaubon's cuff between thumb and forefinger. The sweat-damp satin smelt of an expensive scent. 'Something formal, is it?'

'The Fane. An audience, at the eleventh hour.'

'*What?* Who with? The Spagyrus?'

The Lord-Architect spread padded hands. 'How can I tell you that? You've left the College.'

The White Crow drew in a breath, saliva tasting metallic. Gaining time, she stood, her practised fingers unbuckling the straps of the sword-hanger and belt. She muttered irritably, waving away Lucas's offered help; and busied herself for almost two minutes in slinging straps over her shoulders and around her hips, buckling the scabbard so that it hung comfortably across her back, hilt jutting above her right shoulder.

'If I accept Master-Physician?' she queried.

Casaubon pushed the piles of paper from the table onto the floor, spun the table to its mirror side, and began to comb his copper hair into a neat Brutus style. Before she could get breath to swear he straightened, and pulled white cotton gloves from his capacious pockets.

'I am told' – Casaubon tugged glove-fingers snugly down – 'that I shall be seeing the Thirty-Sixth Decan, whose Sign is the Ten Degrees of High Summer.'

The White Crow worked the belt around her waist, made an alteration of one notch to a buckle. Then she reached across and brushed the Lord-Architect's fingers away, and buttoned his gloves at the wrist.

'Lucas . . .'

She crossed the room and hugged the young man, having to stand up on the balls of her feet and stretch her arms around his muscled back. His eyes shone. She

158

stepped back, reaching up to touch the hilt of her sword, where it hung ready for a down-draw over the shoulder.

'Thank you,' she said, and to Casaubon: 'I'll come to the Fane with you. Lucas, can I ask you a favour? I need you to go and see your uncle, the Ambassador.'

Blinding and imperceptible, the sun rose higher.

Pools of rain in Evelian's courtyard shrank fraction by fraction. The heat of the sun drew mosquito nymphs to the water's surface. The wooden frieze of skulls and spades grew warm, and hosted colonies of insects swarmed out of cracks.

Wings skirred: one of the Lord-Architect's sparrows fluttering to the eaves.

Beyond Clock-mill, lizards sunned themselves in corners of streets left drowsy and deserted. White dust and white blossom snowed the streets of the city.

The sparrow flicked from eaves to tiles to roof-ridge, crossing the quarter. Where the Fane's obelisks cut the sky, the bird scurried for height, lost in the milk-blue heavens; flying swiftly south-aust.

Down between marble wharfs, heat-swollen helium airships tugged at mooring-ropes. Crews rushed to the gas-vents. The bird's bead-black eyes registered movement. A dusty-brown mop of feathers, it fell towards an airship's underslung cabin.

Aust, north, south, east and west: the city stretches away below, reflected in the sparrow's uncomprehending vision.

A day later, one woman crewing an airship will find the bird, half-frozen, and feed it drops of warm milk and millet. Thinking to keep it as a pet, when the airship's long overseas voyage is done.

The Lord-Architect's sparrow rests, cushioned under her shirt, between her breasts. The bead-black eyes hold a message that is simple enough for those with the power to read it.

*　　*　　*

159

'Carrying a sword?' the Candovard Ambassador exclaimed.

'It was wonderful. *She* was wonderful!' Lucas sobered. 'At first . . . I don't know what she's seen to cause her so much fear. But she's going to the Fane at eleven this morning.'

'A sword,' Andaluz repeated.

'Well, yes, technically she shouldn't, but . . . '

Andaluz scratched his salt-and-pepper hair. One stubby finger pointed at his Prince.

'This is the heart of the world, not the White Mountain. Candover sees its Rat-Lord Governor only once or twice a year, and you're let carry weapons there because who else could? Here, every Rat with pretensions to gentle blood carries a sword. Gods preserve men or women who trespass on their privileges!'

Dust drifted in from the compound. Flies haunted the ceiling, undeterred by the *wck-wck-wck* of the fan.

'I . . . didn't realize.' Lucas, who had carried his shirt in his hand, slung it about his neck like a towel, and tugged it back and forth to mop up sweat.

'Your father could never bear it. I discourage him from travelling here.' Andaluz pushed his chair back from the big desk. 'Lucas, dear boy, here I'm the ambassador from savages – yes, *savages* – who are suffered to live with only minor supervision, because we're far away and beneath the Rat-Lords' notice.'

'And I told her to carry a sword.' Lucas's eyes showed dark in a face gone greenish-white. 'I'll have to warn her!'

'If this White Crow woman has been five years in the heart of the world, I assure you that she knows.'

'She *needs* it. To be what she should be.' Lucas looked up from the dusty patterned carpet. 'She asked if you would attend at court today. I told her that you would. I told her that you'll use all of Candover's influence with the King, Uncle, if she's troubled or arrested.'

'Yes, Prince.' Andaluz made a face. 'What there is of it. Ah . . . the university?'

'I'll take care of that. Reverend Mistress Heurodis has her own way with students,' the young man said. 'I'm coming with you to court. A prince's word may carry weight.'

'Aww, this sun's too bright. Hold on a minute.' The cinnamon-haired woman clattered back up the stairs from the street-door.

The Lord-Architect Casaubon waited by the carriage, easing his shirt away from the rolls of flesh at his neck. Sweat trickled down his back.

She re-emerged holding a white felt hat, wide-brimmed and with a dented crown. It had a black band, and small black characters printed into the felt. She clapped it on to her head and tilted it, shading her eyes.

'And you say *I* have no dress sense.'

She smiled. 'No sense of any kind, as far as I could ever make out . . . You know what this hat needs?'

'Euthanasia?'

'A black feather. Tell me if you spot one.'

She leaned automatically up against his arm, sparking backchat off his deadpan replies with the ease of habit and practice. Now he saw her frown. She moved away.

'Master-Physician.' The Lord-Architect very formally offered a glove, handing her into the carriage.

He settled himself opposite her, with his back to the driver, the carriage sinking on its springs. The oxen lowed and pulled away. The red-haired woman tilted her hat further down towards her nose, and rested one heel up on his seat.

'The Decans', she said, 'won't swallow any story about your being a travelling horologer or garden-architect, or whatever nonsense you gave Captain-General Desaguliers. Who have you said you are?'

'A Scholar-Soldier of the Invisible College.'

He beamed, seeing Valentine reduced to complete speechlessness. 'They'll know, in any case,' he added.

'And you think they're going to let us out of there after that!'

He smiled.

'Casaubon!'

Casaubon dug in one pocket, thumbed ponderously through a very small notebook, extracted a pencil from the spine, and began to write, with many hesitations and crossings-out. The carriage jolted into wider streets.

The White Crow stood it for all of three minutes. 'What are you writing?'

His blue eyes all but vanished into his padded cheeks as he squinted in concentration.

'Poetry,' said the Lord-Architect, 'but I can't think of a rhyme for "Valentine".'

His formally buttoned black doublet left Lucas dizzy with the heat. He fingered the short ruff, moving a step closer to Andaluz. Loud talk resounded from almost two hundred and fifty Rats and humans crowding the main audience chamber.

The clover-leaf-domed hall soared, and Lucas lifted his head, gaping up at the four bright domes. Andaluz's pepper-and-salt brows dipped in the family frown.

'Two of the – no, *three* of the Lords Magi are here,' he said, looking through the crowd at black Rats in sleeveless gold robes. 'And most of the noble Houses . . . And all seven Cardinals-General of the Church . . . '

Rows of paired guards in Cadet uniform lined the interlocking circular walls, black fur gleaming. At regular intervals ceiling-length curtains were drawn across windows that, none the less, admitted chinks of sunlight.

'Whatever this is, it's blown up fast as a summer storm.'

'What . . . ?' Lucas moved away from the main entrance's staircase. He began walking towards the point where two of the four semi-circular floor areas intersected.

A treadmill stood a little out from the blue-draped wall,

on the spindle of some panelled and bolted metal machine. Blue-white sparks shot out of the metal casing.

The treadmill itself stood eight feet tall. In its cage, two men and a woman, stripped to breech-clouts, trod the steps down in never-ending repetition. Lucas, shoved by the press of assembled bodies, turned away. He saw two more treadmills over the heads of the crowd.

Thick cables wound up from the machines to the ceilings. In the four hollow domes, a stalactite-forest of chandeliers hung down. Lucas saw clusters of glass, wires burning blue-white and blue-purple, and lowered his gaze, blinking away water.

'Impressive,' Andaluz said. 'If they didn't have to close the curtains to show it off, and stifle all of us.'

The actinic light wavered down on Rats in the sleeveless robes of Lords Magi, on the jewelled collars and swords of nobles and soldiers, the red and purple of priests.

'Uncle . . . ' Lucas turned. Startled, he met the gaze of a youth much his own age. The young man smiled. Fair-haired, stripped to breeches and barefoot, he wore a studded collar round his throat. From it hung a metal leash. A middle-aged black Rat robed in yards of orange taffeta held the end of the leash casually in her hand.

'Bred from the finest stock,' Lucas heard her say to another female black Rat, 'and trained fully in *all* skills.'

She trailed the chain-leash over one furry shoulder, and tugged the metal links. The fair-haired young man squatted down on his haunches at her side.

'A pretty little thing, yes.' The second black Rat, slender in linen shirt and breeches enclosing furry haunches, her rapier slung at her side, turned to eye the treadmills. Two men and a woman in the wheel plodded, heads down, gripping the central bar with sweat-stained hands.

'Don't stare,' Andaluz murmured. 'You're being provincial.'

The Rat in linen and leather swaggered a little, by the treadmill, hand on her sword, ears twitching. The other

163

Rat tugged the leash, walking away with the young man trotting at her heels.

'I must confess', Lucas heard his uncle saying to a robed man as he rejoined them, 'that I feared an incident of some magnitude. For one of your King's daughters to be killed here . . . '

The South Katayan Ambassador shrugged.

'I knew Zari briefly.' Lucas met the man's pale amber eyes. His white robe had been slit at the back, and a sleek black tail caressed the tiled floor.

'King's daughter is hardly a unique position. South Katay's full of them.' The Ambassador, off-hand, reached to pick up a wine glass from a passing brown Rat servant's tray. 'The King will naturally be grieved to hear that Zar-bettu-zekigal could not complete her training as a Memory.'

'She—'

The Katayan Ambassador caught a tall Rat's glance across the crowd and murmured: 'Excuse me. I must speak to Captain-General Desaguliers.'

Lucas slid a court shoe across the gold-and-blue tiles. Black and brown Rats surrounded him, in formal silks and jewelled collars and cloaks; he stood lost in the noise of their voices. A few inches shorter than most, he could not, from this corner by the full-length windows, see over heads and feather-plumes to the throne.

'She made me laugh,' he said. 'She didn't give a damn for anyone. Maybe I would have liked her, if I'd had time.'

Andaluz nodded gravely.

'Keep your eye on Desaguliers,' the older man directed. 'If there are any arrests, Desaguliers' police will be making them. He'll be notified. If we can see when that happens, I can try to bring it to his Majesty's attention.'

'Right.'

Casually keeping the South Katayan Ambassador and Desaguliers in sight, Lucas threaded his way through the crowd. A word here and there to other ambassadors, as

164

his training inculcated in him; pitching his voice above the chatter, side-stepping the jutting scabbards of rapiers, the trailing silk-lined edges of cloaks.

'Mind out!' A brown Rat pushed him aside, jerking his tail out of the way. 'Why they let these peasants in, I'll never know . . . '

Lucas bowed formally, one hand clenching in a fist.

Brass horns shattered conversation. A uniformed brown Rat at the head of the stairs announced lords whose names Lucas didn't catch. Satin and lace flurried as the Rats walked forward to make their brief bows to the Rat-King. Conversation resumed.

Desaguliers, shedding the South Katayan Ambassador, pushed his way towards the centre of the hall. High above, the clover-leaf of domes intersected in a fantasia of vaulting. Lucas fell in a few paces behind, taking a glass from a passing tray; all training in unobtrusive crowd-movement coming to him without thought.

'—let the Kings' Memory speak—'

He cannoned into the back of a tall Rat in grey silk. The Rat's hand cuffed his ear, jewelled rings stinging, and a drop of blood fell onto his ruff. Lucas only continued to stare. Using elbows, he shoved two brown Rat servants aside and forced his way to the front edge of the central crowd.

Drapes soared tent-like from a central golden boss to hang down the intersecting walls. Where the lights struck, they glowed sea-deep in shadow purple as evening. Framed by this canopy, the white silk of a great circular bed gleamed.

Sweet incense reached Lucas's nostrils.

Dais steps went up to the bed-throne, where the Rat-King lay among cushions and pillows of silk. Eight scaly tails showed dark in the middle of the Rats' groomed fur and silk jackets: gnarled and knotted, grown together.

Lucas ignored the dozen Rats of various rank and dress who knelt on the dais steps, talking to the Rat-King. Tense, he willed the long-coated figure to turn around . . .

Black hair fell lank to either side of a sharp face. The skinny young woman stood barefoot, scuffing her toes down on the tiled floor below the dais, head about on a level with one of the silver-furred Rats-King. One hand stayed thrust in the pocket of a stained and torn brown greatcoat. The other gestured fluidly.

'*Zari?*'

He stood some four yards from her, but names draw attention: the Katayan's head turned, and she nodded once in his direction.

' . . . *the Lady Hyena's people to carry arms, to walk the streets above ground, to be free of the outstanding penalties against them as rebels and traitors,*' she concluded, the concentration of Memory leaving her voice.

The silver-furred and the bony black Rats-King spoke in tandem to a kneeling Rat priest. Lucas made covert frantic signals which Zar-bettu-zekigal ignored.

He looked again at the priest. A black Rat, down on one knee on the dais steps, his scarlet jacket blazing against the white silk of the bed. He held his plumed headband clasped in one slender-fingered ringed hand. His mobile furry snout quivered, speaking to the silver Rats-King in a rapid monologue.

'It *is* her. *She's alive!* And the priest is Plessiez,' he muttered to Andaluz as the older man reached him. 'The one we met in the crypt. I'm certain of it.'

He read hunger and exhaustion in her face – high on tension, high on hardship – and glanced again at Plessiez. The same, better-concealed, showed in the black Rat.

'We can't speak to her now . . . '

Lucas caught the approach of Desaguliers out of the corner of his eye. He nudged the Candovard Ambassador's arm, and faded back a rank or two into the crowd. Practised, he lost the Captain-General's attention, thinking furiously. He ducked past a fat female Rat in mauve satin and came out by the wall and the edge of the drapes. A brawny Rat edged backwards into him, muttered an apology without turning to see she had apologized to a man. Lucas became aware that most of the front rank of the crowd tensed, eavesdropping; and he slid his black-clad form behind the brawny Rat, and strained to listen.

'Your Majesty will appreciate the necessity,' the black Rat, Plessiez, said.

The silver-furred Rat rolled on to his left side, scratching idly at one furry haunch. 'Indeed we do, messire. Messire Plessiez, in view of what you say, we have decided to grant your request. For a preliminary trial period.'

Lucas saw Zar-bettu-zekigal straighten, enthusiasm in the line of her narrow shoulders. Plessiez rose to his feet, bowing, and backing unerring down the dais steps.

'Then, with your Majesty's permission, I'll send the delegation and the Memory to inform the Lady Hyena of your decision.'

Lucas scowled, bemused.

'Go. We do so order.'

In the gap between Plessiez's snout and Zari's head, Lucas glimpsed the South Katayan Ambassador clutching Desaguliers' arm, muttering rapidly at the Captain-General. A short plump Rat blocked his view. She and a raffish black Rat flanked Zar-bettu-zekigal as Plessiez directed the Katayan to leave.

Zar-bettu-zekigal passed close enough for her greatcoat to brush Lucas's leg. The briefest glance of helplessness and humour darted in Lucas's direction. She left a scent on the air of water, stagnant and stale. Lucas pondered the nature of the stains on her coat, scowling to himself.

'Her ambassador didn't seem pleased,' he said as Andaluz reappeared through the crush.

'Ger-zarru-huk's a bastard at the best of times. Strictly off the record.'

'I have to talk with Zari.' Lucas put a hand against his side, still expecting to find a sword there. He scowled.

'You resemble your mother greatly when you do that,' Andaluz remarked, 'and gods know she's a stubborn enough woman. This student romance of yours—'

'No. By no means that.' Lucas stopped the older man. 'Uncle, what have you got on file for the Invisible College?'

Andaluz blinked, matching his nephew step for ratiocinative step. 'Mendicant scholars and mercenaries spread rumours that there is such a thing. All mythical, of course. It's been quite fully investigated.'

The buzz of conversation rose by several levels. Lucas, pressed between two black Rats, side-stepped a dagger-hilt at one's belt and slid back to the Candovard Ambassador. Doubt jolted him, as sudden and shocking as stepping off a stair in the dark.

'But—'

Brazen horns blared. This time the sound echoed from the high vaulted ceilings, bright sound in artificial brilliance; muffled itself in drapes and hangings; and blew again, redoubled, in a shriek that cut through every Rat and human voice. It sounded a final time and fell silent.

A black Rat in major-domo's robes rapped her garnet-studded ivory staff on the tiles.

'*Hear his Majesty the King!* The hall is to be cleared of all below the rank of noble. All servants, ambassadors and other humans will leave immediately. *Hear the word of the King!*'

The mounts spooked as the carriage jolted under the fifth arch on Austroad. The driver swore. The White Crow gazed up at the shaking roof of the carriage and the unseen coachman, and lifted her black-and-white hat in salute.

Through open shadowed windows, the chitinous hum of insects echoed in the canyon between wall and high wall.

She saw Casaubon lean back in his seat, rummaging through an inside pocket. He brought his hand out, ink-stained fingers all but concealing a silver hip-flask.

'Give me that,' the White Crow said, reaching across. She tilted her head back, drank, coughed, and wiped her nose. 'You're *still* drinking this stuff?'

The Lord-Architect took the hip-flask back. He made

'*Mendicant scholars and mercenaries spread rumours that
there is such a thing. All mythical, of course.*'

From the tomb of Christian Rosenkreuz

to replace it in his capacious pocket, shook it close to one freckled ear, listened – and up-ended it down his throat.

'*Casaubon* . . . '

He raised it to drink again, spilling the sticky metheglin down his embroidered blue-and-gold waistcoat and blue silk breeches. He cracked a phenomenally loud belch.

'You can't leave me to do this on my own,' the White Crow protested.

The Lord-Architect stowed his empty flask away, and looked down owlishly at the small notebook lying open on his spreading thigh.

'"Valentine,"' he mused. '"Eglantine" . . . ? "Porcupine" . . . ?'

The White Crow ran her tongue over the back of her teeth, wincing at the aftertaste.

'"Turpentine"?' she suggested.

The strokes of ten clashed across Nineteenth District's tiny south quarter. Reverend Master Candia took his hand away from his face. The unfamiliar open sky shocked him. He looked at the blood on his palms.

'Did They brand me?' His voice croaked. 'I should be marked.'

Pigeons scuttered up into the air, their shadows and guano falling into the alley at the back of the deserted Cathedral of the Trees. Slumped into the corner of wall and door, masonry bruised Candia's shoulders and buttocks.

'Bastard!'

'Down him again!'

'Here, Sordio, let me—'

'He's *mine*. No-one else's!'

A hand grabbed his collar. His loose lacy shirt ripped. Candia pitched forward on to hands and knees, groaning; and yelled with pain as a boot slammed into his ribs. He scrabbled and caught the iron drainpipe stapled to the wall, pulling himself up on to his knees.

A familiar voice rasped: 'I might have known we'd

find you slumming around this place. Thirty-Six! Why did you *do* it?'

Candia rubbed the back of his wrist across his mouth. Stale food crusted his straggling beard. His own breath came back to him, stinking; and he coughed, tears running from the corners of his eyes. A spurt of fear pushed him to his feet, eyes wide.

He staggered forward, other hands grabbing him before he fell.

'*Why?*'

A taste of copper in his mouth faded to the taste of old vomit. Candia smiled shakily. He reached out and stroked the face of the man who held him by the shoulders: a crop-haired man with his own sandy colouring; a man with dust-sore eyes; large, furious, utterly familiar.

'Sordio.' He patted the older man's cheek. 'And Ercole here, too. Is all the family—?'

Out of nowhere, a fist slammed into his face. Agony blinded him. Vision cleared, and through pain's water he saw a dozen men in silk overalls, some with sticks, all much of an age with Sordio; and he brushed uselessly at his own filthy clothes. Bruises purpled his fingers.

'Brother—'

'You're no brother of mine.' Sordio's hands flexed. 'We should have drowned you at birth.'

'*Damn you, do you know what I had to do?*'

He stared down silenced faces. Sun beat into the alley. He shifted scuffed boots, tucking his ripped shirt back into his breeches, fastening his thick leather belt on the third attempt. All the university's training gone, driven from his head; even the instinct that had brought him back to Theodoret's cathedral eradicated now. He held Sordio's gaze.

'We saw you.' Sordio said flatly. 'Over at the hall, in the rubble.'

The remembered texture of broken planking and bricks woke in his hands. Candia raised them and stared at ripped nails, bloody fingers.

Sordio's gaze went past him to the barred cathedral door. 'Do you think our mother never knew that he put you up to that place?'

'Bishop Theodoret is my friend.' The words left him unprompted. Candia opened his mouth in a gasp, tears filling his eyes, and giggled. 'Yes, he helped me to get into the university. Yes. The old bitch'd be proud of the return favour I've given him for that—'

He laughed helplessly. One dark man swung a splintered piece of two-by-four; he caught it on one up-raised arm, twisted it free of the man's grip, and whacked it back against the cathedral wall. The dull *crack!* echoed. The man stepped back. He stared at Sordio.

'Leave me alone!'

'You bastard, you brought them down on the Hall, you did that!'

Heat from the morning sun soaked into his bruised shoulders. He swallowed. His mouth tasted foul, but with the foulness of humanity: no copper-coin bitterness now.

'I'll say this.' He watched Sordio. A little older now, this last year gone by, a little stouter, with the muscles of a builder; wearing now the gold ribbon of the House of Salomon openly on his overalls. 'I went to the Lord Decan. I told him what was happening at the East-quarter hall. *You* told me.'

'Thirty-Six, you're my *brother*. I thought I could trust you!'

'You could. You can.'

A black beetle crawled in the dust on the cathedral's back step, abandoning the rubbish piled in the corner of the door. Masonry chilled his back where he leaned against the door-arch. Candia tensed. His body shuddered, shuddered uncontrollably; the thin beam of wood falling from his hands to the paving.

'I know exactly how many people died at that hall. I can tell you their names.' He shut his eyes, dizzy; opened them again to a blue-stained sunlight, and Sordio's sweating red face. 'It was better that some people should die now than

172

most of the District die later. We had to take that decision. That was what we said. It's better—'

He swallowed with difficulty.

'Damn you, do it, then! Here I am. I'm telling you, the Lord Decan could wipe you out like *that*.' His boot crunched the black beetle into a chitinous smear. 'And what are we to them? They wouldn't waste time sorting out who's in the House of Salomon conspiracy and who's innocent. Remember Fifth District? A massacre!'

Somewhere, far away, a clock struck the quarter-hour.

A spar cracked across Candia's hip and stomach. He screamed. Two men moved in with fists. He staggered, tried a spin and kick; fell forward into Sordio's grip, gasping.

His brother's fist sank deep and hard into his stomach. Candia bent double, vomiting. Water blurred his vision, and he clamped his eyes shut.

Far above, a rustle of dry wings electrified the noon sky; and a line of blood incised itself across the inside of his eyelids. A distant mockery hissed in the sun.

– *Twice traitor!*—

'Clear the chamber,' Captain-General Desaguliers ordered. '*Move.*'

Sleek black Rat Cadets split up, crossing the great clover-leaf audience chamber. Desaguliers took up a stance under the vaulting of one intersection, watching ambassadors complain: Ger-zarru-huk protesting volubly, leaving at last with two cadets gripping him firmly under the arms, his tail lashing; the Candovard Ambassador forcing his own contentious prince from the hall.

His scarred face creased, the smile sardonic.

'Messire, the generators? The human servants?'

Desaguliers picked his incisors with a neatly trimmed claw. Unlike the Magi, Lords and priests, he wore severe black sword-harness and studded leather collar.

'Leave 'em,' he directed the young Cadet. 'His Majesty'll spit blood if the precious lights don't stay on. When this is

173

over, sling 'em in gaol for a week or two, until they forget they ever heard anything here today.'

The Cadet smartly touched her silver headband.

Desaguliers shoved through the press of bodies, checking for humans. The hot curtained morning brought a shiver to his spine. Premonitory, his scarred face creased into a frown. His black eyes, anxious for once, sought through the crowded ranks for a red-jacketed priest: one among many.

'Plessiez,' he muttered.

Hands resting on his plain sword-belt, he strode towards the dais and the King: narrow powerful shoulders thrusting a way between black and brown Rats. The four sets of double doors clanged shut. Cadets slid lock-bars into place, then moved to position themselves against the walls. Heat slicked Desaguliers' fur up into tufts. The noise and confusion of two hundred nobles, Magi and priests washed over him, and he wiped the fur above his eyes.

'Secure.' He made a low bow at the foot of the dais.

The Rat-King looked up from ordering pages to clear the silks and cushions, several pairs of eyes turning towards Desaguliers. The Captain-General's spine stiffened. Standing on the lowest step of the dais by one silver-furred Rats-King, Plessiez folded sleek hands and smiled.

'Messire Desaguliers.'

'Your reverence.'

The actinic lights brightened. Desaguliers heard a thong crack at the back of the hall, and a treadmill creak faster. Points of hard light shot back from diamond collars, from rings, from sword-hilts and from the black eyes of Rats. The smell of heat and fur made his snout tense rhythmically.

Lords Magi took their places in the first rank of the circle surrounding the bed-throne, and he moved a step aside as the seven Cardinals-General joined them. Across the room, he met Cardinal Ignatia's gaze, vainly searching for some hint of the future.

The Rat-King stood, one brown Rat offering a hand to the bony black Rat, the rest rising with some dignity. The knot of their tails stood out stark, scaled, deformed. With one movement the assembly bowed. Desaguliers, straightening, saw the Chancellor crack her ivory staff against the tiles.

'Hear his Majesty!'

All voices silenced, the only sound came from the hum and spark of the generators, the creak of the turning treadmills. The Rat-King stood in a circle, each Rat facing out across the assembly. Pages hurriedly finished draping the shoulders of each with cloth-of-gold cloaks.

The bony black Rats-King spoke.

'Captain-General.'

Desaguliers bowed, hands resting on his plain sword-belt. 'Your Majesty desires?'

'It seems Messire Plessiez survived the attack from the Fane.'

Tension and the fear of ridicule walked hot shivers up Desaguliers' spine. He glanced around, tail twitching. A few faces showed incomprehension. His eyes swept the Lords Magi and the Cardinals-General, seeing knowing smiles.

'Yes, your Majesty.'

Desaguliers made a low bow, going on one knee on the dais steps. His sword-harness clashed. That and his studded black collar were his only ornaments: a lean ragged black Rat in middle years. He lifted his head to meet the Rat-King's gaze.

'We should have been most interested to discover—'

' – what was said at that hall,' a brown Rats-King concluded. 'But you could not tell us, messire.'

'You could not tell us', the bony black Rats-King smiled, 'that we knew of Messire Plessiez's mission. That he had our authority.'

Desaguliers studiously kept his face turned away from the little priest.

'I've done my best to investigate,' he judged it safe to say.

The black Rat glared down at Desaguliers, who began to sweat.

'Messire Plessiez made it clear just how long you were present at that meeting, before the Fane's acolytes attacked. You heard all of what was said there, and thought fit not to inform us of that fact.'

Desaguliers' whiskers quivered. His dark-fingered hand clenched by his side.

'We don't care to be deceived. We think that such an offence deserves summary dismissal—'

' – but that the little priest's evidence is not unbiased,' one of the silver-furred Rats concluded sardonically, leaning over from the far side of the circular bed. He fixed Desaguliers with eyes dark as garnets. 'We might advise you to prove your innocence, messire, and in fairly short order.'

The jabber and laughter of the Lords Magi and nobles washed over him. He rose to his feet, and nodded once sharply: 'As your Majesty wishes.'

The bony black Rats-King turned his head, searching the ranks of nobles, Lords Magi and priests. Desaguliers breathed hard, sensing a respite but no escape.

'Cardinal-General Ignatia.'

The elderly female Rat stepped forward from the six other Cardinals-General of the Church, straightening her emerald-green robe.

'Your Majesty, I must protest at this sudden action of Messire Plessiez. He has been acting entirely without the authority of the Order of Guiry—'

'He has acted at all times with *our* authority and full knowledge.'

'I don't understand, your Majesty.'

Desaguliers smoothed his whiskers down, studying Ignatia's genuine bewilderment. A hot temper flared in his gut, and a fear. Whispered comments in the crowd located the fear: that something so obviously long-planned

176

could occur without Desaguliers' police knowing of it.

The bony black Rats-King waved one hand, rings flashing in the artificial light.

'It seems to us', he said mildly, 'that the pressures of the generalship of the Order of Guiry stand between you and your excellent scholarship, Cardinal Ignatia. We therefore promote a new Cardinal-General into your place, to enable you to spend even more of your valuable time in the Archives.'

Ignatia opened her mouth, closed it again, and fell to grooming the fur of one arm for a few seconds. Desaguliers caught her eye as she looked up, her gaze now lustreless.

'As your Majesty wishes. Who is my successor?'

Under his breath Desaguliers could not help muttering: 'You must be the only one in this room who doesn't guess!'

'Messire Plessiez,' the black Rats-King said sardonically, 'we invest you Cardinal-General of the Order of Guiry. Remembering always that poor service merits loss of such a position.'

Plessiez's head turned. He stared directly at Desaguliers.

The Captain-General's temper flared. 'I think his Majesty has no reason to complain of my service!'

In the crowd, several people sniggered. Desaguliers bit his lip, straightened and, having walked into the priest's trap, chose bluster to see him through it. He swept a curt bow to the black Rats-King.

'I *do* think you have no reason to complain of my service. If your Majesty doubts me, my resignation is tendered now, this morning – this moment. Let St Cyr have the Cadets.'

The silver-furred and the bony black Rats-King exchanged glances. Desaguliers stood with his spine taut. One hand caressed the hilt of his sword. His black eyes flicked to each one of the Rat-King, bright with calculation.

'Yes . . . ' The silver Rat smiled. The black Rat continued: 'Yes, we agree. For a while, Messire Desaguliers,

177

we accept your resignation. Order Messire St Cyr to us after we have spoken to this assembly. It will be politic to have him conduct this investigation. You will resume your post when proved innocent of any deception of your King.'

Desaguliers opened his mouth. His jaw hung slack for a second; then snapped shut.

'Furthermore,' a black Rats-King said, 'St Cyr is to have the overseeing of the artillery garden. Send your imported architect to him as soon as is convenient.'

Desaguliers gave the briefest bow and turned away, not waiting for a dismissal. Fury scoured him. He shouldered past five or six Rat-Lords. Their laughter cauterized him.

At the far end of one clover-leaf, by the barred doors, he abandoned caution and summoned one of the Cadets with a fierce look.

'We must move earlier than I expected.'

'Messire?'

'St Cyr is to have the cadets.' Desaguliers' scarred face twisted into a smile. 'You might say I was fool enough to give his command to him . . . Next time I'll make *sure* Plessiez is a corpse. Call the others together. We'll meet at noon. All plans will have to be advanced. Pass word on.'

The tall black Rat bowed, and slid away into the massed assembly.

Desaguliers caught his breath with some difficulty, stared down the dozen or so Rats nearest to him; and then cocked his ears as the brass horns rang out again, silencing the assembly.

'We have called you here, also, to witness the promulgation of a new law.'

The taller of the silver-furred Rats-King spoke, voice dropping into the expectant silence. His incisors showed in a smile.

'It is not our intention to explain our policy, but to be obeyed in what we say.

'For the immediate future, and for however long it may chance to pass—'

' – and because we are a generous sovereign, wishing nothing more than to be loved by our people—'

' – we hereby revoke the penalties of treason and conspiracy outstanding against the human rebels now fugitive here in the heart of the world.'

A rumble of protest rose up into the vaulted roofs.

Desaguliers stared across the heads of the crowd, between translucent ears and nodding feather-plumes. The bright gold-cloaked figures of the Rat-King spangled light back, dazzling the assembled nobles.

'Therefore,' continued the other silver-furred Rats-King, his voice proceeding with the slightest-possible stutter, 'and as a gesture of goodwill, we promulgate the following law: that all men and women under the gold-cross banner of the Sun may be permitted to carry weapons in the streets and dwellings of the city.'

'*Never!*'

Against the crescendo of shouting, the Rats-King said something to the Chancellor, and that Rat slammed her ivory-and-garnet staff against the tiles and cried out: '*This audience is over!*'

Lights dimmed, cadets wrenched curtains open, and sun and air poured in. Desaguliers pushed through the dazed assembly to be first out. He caught one glimpse of Plessiez as he went. The little priest stood on the dais steps, deep in conversation with the silver-furred Rats-King, smiling.

The carriage drew up outside one of the smaller and older of the Thirty-Six temples of the Fane. A clock down in North quarter struck quarter to the hour of eleven.

'Shit,' said the White Crow.

A granular sea-mist greyed the stone cornices and columns. The air below the mist made street-level humid, warm as bathwater. She hooked one bent frame of her spectacles in the V of her buttoned shirt, and pushed the brim of her hat up.

'I don't think this is one of your better ideas,' she remarked, dismounting from the carriage. Its springs

179

creaked as the Lord-Architect got out after her.

'What's more—'

She turned her head to add another word of disquiet and stopped.

The Lord-Architect Casaubon ponderously moved to position himself beside the rear nearside wheel. The White Crow's jaw slackened as he unbuttoned the flap of his blue silk breeches, reached down, stared absently back down the hill, and urinated fully and at some length over the wooden wheel-spokes.

'Oh, really!' The White Crow's exasperation gave way to laughter. 'There is a time and a place to exercise ancient privileges, and this isn't either one of them!'

Mist dissipated. Above the cityscape gliders flinked brilliance from their wings, circling about a central column of air.

'Nervous,' Casaubon explained, buttoning himself up.

'*You?*'

'Wait for us,' the Lord-Architect directed the carriage-driver.

The White Crow took a pace. Shadow fell cool across her back, where her linen shirt plastered sweaty skin. As if it were a talisman she raised her hand to her nostrils and inhaled human odours of heat.

A hooped arch broke the Fane's brown brick wall. Stepping under it, she saw other arches in other walls opening off to left and right. Across a small courtyard, an arch's bricks burned tawny in sunlight. Beyond, another lay in shade.

'Well, then.'

She stretched all fingers on both hands, palms taut, flexing sinews, in a gesture that she did not remember to be one church's Sign of the Branches. After that she tipped her speckled hat back slightly, and glanced up at the Lord-Architect.

'Suppose we leave this until another day?' she suggested.

'Suppose we don't.'

Brief shadow cooled her in the archway. In the small

courtyard, heat bounced back from the worn brickwork. Silence drummed on her ears. Glancing back, the White Crow faced a blank wall: no sign of the arch by which they'd entered. She smiled ruefully.

'That one,' Casaubon said.

She walked towards the further archway. The Lord-Architect's blue satin frock-coat brushed her arm at every pace. Her left arm. Her right hand swung free, and she reached up to touch the hilt of her sword, and smiled to herself again.

'You never did miss a trick,' she observed.

The sky overhead curdled hot and yellow. Storm-lightning flickered above the windowless brick walls, almost invisible in the bright day. White Crow matched Casaubon stride for stride, through three enclosed court-yards: ears tensed for any noise, eyes searching for any movement.

Her saliva began to have the metallic taste of fear. Sweat made her skin tacky at elbow and knee joints, above her lip, and on each upper eyelid. She reached up and pulled her sword from its sheath.

'Valentine.'

'No. I need to,' she said. White sun flashed the length of the blade. Its grip fitted into her palm; and the weight of its pull on her shoulder felt comfortingly familiar. Anxiety tensed her back, prickled down her vertebrae.

She grinned.

'Last-minute rescues.' Her voice bounced back from the bricks of a fourth enclosed courtyard. 'Frantic escapes, reprieves on the gallows-steps, victory or defeat at the final instant, on the eleventh minute of the eleventh hour of the eleventh day . . . '

Casaubon's copper hair gleamed as he nodded. 'In short: the Decan of the Eleventh Hour.'

Urgency and excitement radiated back from the walls with the heat and light. With long-practised ease she reached up and slid the blade back into her shoulder-scabbard.

She turned her head to do it, and to look at Casaubon as she spoke, walking under yet another arch of the brick labyrinth. Turning back, she stopped in her tracks; Casaubon's cushioned arm bumped her forward a step; and she stumbled, wincing at her bare feet on gravelled earth.

The heart of the maze of the Thirty-Sixth temple opened before her.

The White Crow moved forward slowly into the large courtyard. High walls enclosed her, of small bricks once dark brown and now sun-bleached to ochre; the sky empty and sun-filled. Black dots floated across her vision. One of them landed on her arm, crawling among the fine red hairs.

'The old English black bee . . . ' She raised her arm, blew softly, and the bee flew off.

'Made extinct in an epidemic.' Casaubon's hand rested on her shoulder. 'Master-Physician.'

All the ground lay marked in ochre and yellow and brown gravels, a labyrinth of patterns on the earth. She began to walk the knotted pattern. She did not raise her eyes yet, to see what lay in the centre of the courtyard.

Black roses thrust briars into crevices of the brickwork. The pattern brought her close to one wall, and she reached up to touch: black stem, black thorns, black petals; cold as living onyx or jet. The tiny bees swarmed about her. Their noise filled her head. She reached behind without looking, left-handed, and Casaubon's hand enclosed hers.

The soles of her bare feet burned with the hot earth. She stepped from that to brick paving, reaching the centre of the marked patterns. The Lord-Architect came to stand beside her. The yellow sun drenched the enclosed garden. A smell of hot earth and hot brick reached her nostrils.

A statue loomed in the centre of the courtyard, bees swarming over its crossed front paws. Brown unmortared bricks rose up into leonine shoulders, flanks, haunches, and a tail curved over one slightly stretched hind leg. Around the shoulders and head, drape-work delineated in curved brickwork surrounded an almond-eyed face. The swell of breasts showed above the crossed front paws.

The White Crow shifted, eyes aching from staring up into the sun. The sphinx towered some sixteen or eighteen feet above her; shaped brickwork smoothly curving, sun-bleached, and crumbling here and there where bees nested in crevices. She sat down, cross-legged, ignoring Casaubon's expostulation; energy sucked by the heat.

Drowned dizzy, she wiped her red face and reached down to scratch her bare legs under the knee-breeches. The fingers of her left hand pricked with pain. She glanced down to see angry red pin-pricks where she had touched the bristles of the black roses.

Casaubon's voice, half-drowned in the silence of sun and bees, said: 'Time.'

She heard no clock. The hour sounded as invisibly as ripples under water, pulsing through her.

The sphinx's curved brickwork eyelids slid up.

Pupil-less ochre eyes gazed down, twelve feet above the earth. She saw herself and the Lord-Architect reflected there, in shining sand. Some frontier irrevocably crossed in her mind, the White Crow succumbed to a casual bravado that might pass for, or might become, courage. She removed her hat. She laughed.

Long lips curved up, and the great front paws moved, dust haunting the hot air.

'*You are too early.*'

The Lord-Architect knelt beside the White Crow. She stared at the back of his neck, the yellow-stained linen and heat-flushed skin.

'What do you mean, "too early"!' Casaubon protested indignantly. 'I might have been too late!'

The White Crow gripped the crown of her speckled black-and-white hat and fanned herself with the brim. Still sitting, she called up: 'Lady of the Eleventh Hour, who is Lord of the Ten Degrees of High Summer!'

The sphinx's eyes shifted to the red-haired woman.

'I'm the Master-Physician White Crow,' the White Crow

183

said, 'and this is Baltazar Casaubon, Lord-Architect, Knight of the Golden Rose, Scholar-Soldier of the Invisible College . . .'

'*Yes.*' The ancient eyes filled with amusement. '*I know. I summoned him.*'

A stillness touched the White Crow; only her eyes shifting up to the man who knelt beside her. What she had forgotten of his wit and strength (not merely a very fat man, but a very large man also fat) came back to her with the rush of five years' forgetting.

Brick paving jolted as Casaubon sat down heavily. Peeling off the heavy satin frock-coat, and unbuttoning his embroidered waistcoat, he wiped his already-wet shirt-sleeves across his face, and gazed up at the Decan.

A heat-shimmer clung to the shaped bricks. The folds of the head-dress fell across leonine shoulders, framing a face more than human. Articulated, impossible, the great body shifted to one elbow, hind leg stretching.

The White Crow ignored Casaubon's attempts to speak now that his immediate indignation had run dry. She gazed up at the god-daemon, not able to keep her mouth from stretching in a smile of pure joy. She put her hat back on the masses of tangled red hair, tilted it to shade her eyes. Her fingers flexed. They tingled for the act of an art so long unpractised.

The Decan's full-lipped mouth smiled. Her robed head bent, and her shining sand eyes fixed on the White Crow.

'*Child of earth.*'

'Lady.' The White Crow laughed. Sweat trickled down between her sharp shoulder-blades. The Decan's sun unknotted tensions in her body, smoothed them into a trance of heat.

'You sent for an architect and a physician of the Invisible College.' Casaubon, doggedly rolling up his shirt-sleeves, addressed his remarks to the sphinx-paw resting on the earth beside him. The paw lay large as a cart on the earth. Brick claws flexed.

'Divine One,' he added, as an afterthought.

Heady, as if she were ten years younger and still the woman who would speak her mind although god and daemon waited on it, she poked her finger into Casaubon's damp shoulder.

'Oh, now, you, hold it – *right* there. A *Decan* sent for the College's assistance? And you didn't tell me that?'

Sunned in the warmth of amusement radiant from the brick courtyard, the Lord-Architect said: 'Now, Valentine. You wouldn't be here if I had. I know you.'

'Yes.' The White Crow uncrossed her legs, rubbing at cramp in one calf. 'Yes . . .'

She rested her elbow along his shoulder. His shirt showed sopping patches under the arms and down the middle of his vast back. Sweat and metheglin reeked on the air.

'This is not the appointed hour.'

The White Crow made a grab for the Lord-Architect as he rose majestically to his feet.

'You're lucky I'm here at all!' he rumbled, ham-hands planted on hips. 'I bring you the best pox-rotted physician there is (who doesn't want to come), and the best living expert in architectonics (and *I* didn't want to come either, if your Divine Presence doesn't know that), and I get us both here, now, through *magia* run wild, and what thanks do I get for it!'

He stopped, swept up his satin coat, rescued the hip-flask from one pocket, and stomped to the edge of the brickwork to stare out over the knotted gravel patterns of the courtyard and coax a drop or two more of metheglin from the flask.

The hot brick paving quivered. The other paw of the sphinx fell lightly, so that, from where she sat between them now, the White Crow could have reached out a hand to touch both.

'The best living – but I can raise the best of the dead. You passed a world of dangers – but we could unseam the world from pole to pole, in a heartbeat.'

The White Crow laughed.

She was aware that Casaubon turned, that the freckles on his heated face stood out in a sudden pallor. All else vanished in the sandstorm and dust-devil gaze of the god-daemon, as the Decan lowered her head and focused her close gaze on the White Crow.

Nails digging into her palms, the White Crow said: 'Lady, and begging your Divine Presence's pardon, I know the Decans could unsoul the sky, untie the bonds that fasten the earth, untune the dance of the heavens; for all that is is held within the Degrees of the Thirty-Six.'

The brick lids blinked.

'And I also know', the White Crow ended, 'how difficult it is to get thirty-six of anybody to agree to anything, and act as one.'

Furnace heat scoured the courtyard. Softer than the hum of black bees and the rustle of the roses, the White Crow heard the rare laughter of a Decan. She climbed to her feet. The muscles at the backs of her legs trembled.

'She is a Master-Physician, to know the conflict and contention among the Stars so well. You have performed adequately, child of earth, in bringing her here. Welcome.'

' "Bringing"?' the White Crow queried.

' "Adequately"?' the Lord-Architect bridled.

She could feel him clinging to his refuge of obtuse pride and alcohol, as she clung to wit or a studied carelessness: some scant refuge against the presence of the god-daemon informing mortal matter. Casaubon's plump knuckles brushed her chin, moved up to lift the tumbled mass of hair, silver-white at the temples. The power of ten degrees of the sky infused the courtyard: permitting no evasions, nothing less than truth.

'I made you keep me here. I made you listen to me. I made you come with me. Valentine.'

'Oh, I knew how you were doing it,' she said, 'but I let you, just the same . . . I did the hard bit when I hid here and researched the heart of the world for five years, alone.'

The White Crow pushed the brim of her hat up. She

grinned, sun-dazed. 'And I'll do the rest that's hard when we leave here, and if we're alive at the end of it I will still thank you for finding me. But as for now—'

' – for now,' the Lord-Architect Casaubon picked up, turning to look into the Decan's slanting desert-eyes. 'I would be cautious, Divine One, with what I said before mortal kings. You, who read hearts and minds, know mine.'

The great paw moved slightly closer. The White Crow felt a radiance from it through her arm, ribs, thigh, and the left side of her body. She took a breath. Half air and half the soul of heat, it burned in her lungs.

'I wrote with woman's blood on the moon, because I saw the Great Circle four times broken.'

'*It will be broken again.*'

The god-daemon's breath touched her face, and the White Crow smelt bone-dust.

'*You are too early. For all things, there is a certain hour to act: that hour and no other.*'

The White Crow swayed. Black bees filled the air, mica-wings glittering. They flew exactly the sun-hot courtyard's patterns, holding the air above the gravel labyrinth. She reached out to knot the linen of Casaubon's shirt in one hand. Ghost-lines of darkness began to pattern the sky.

'*Shall pestilence in the heart of the world be healed? I have seen infinite generations board the Boat to be carried through the Night and back to birth. This is nothing in the eyes of the Thirty-Six Powers.*'

'Pestilence?' The White Crow frowned: calculating, bewildered.

The shining salt-pan gaze of the god-daemon fell on the White Crow. A black geometry starred the sky. The White Crow rubbed her sweat-blurred eyes.

The Decan's robed head tilted to look down upon Casaubon, where the Lord-Architect stood between her paws.

'*Shall we permit Salomon's House to be raised in the heart of the world, that it become the New Jerusalem? These things*

187

pass. The Temple has fallen once, and will fall again. This is nothing in the eyes of the Thirty-Six Powers.'

'Ah. I don't know about that . . . Divine One.' Casaubon wriggled his index finger in his ear, took it out, looked at the wax under the nail and, as he wiped it down his embroidered waistcoat, said: 'I ruled a city once. All of it built by line, by rule, by square; by order of hierarchy and just proportion of harmony. They tore it down. It's a republic now. The Lords-Architect are gone.'

The White Crow watched time-worn brick move as living flesh; the pocked and crumbling leonine body tense.

'We are who we are, and not to be vanquished by the reshaping of stone-masonry! That is nothing. But – The Spagyrus, the Lord of Noon and Midnight – shall He break the Dance?'

The White Crow slid her hand up to rest on Casaubon's forearm. Fine copper-haired flesh, sweet and sleepy: human. She reached up and removed her hat. The heat of the sky above the Thirty-Sixth temple struck at her neck and the crown of her head.

'It *was* broken.' Casaubon's arm slid around the White Crow's shoulders.

'A black miracle.' She rubbed her mouth with her hand and tasted salt. Her dry voice creaked. 'A Philosopher's Stone that gives eternal Death, death of the soul.'

'Such things unloose the sky and earth; untie the forces that hold world to sun, and flesh to bone.'

The White Crow's skin smelt to her now of sweat and sweet age, of middle years and high summer, of dreams enacted and powers taken up into unused hands. She brushed hair away from her eyes. The heat of it burned her fingers.

Casaubon's mouth at her ear, warm with alcohol, breathed: 'The face . . . Does she have the face of your mother?'

'How did you know that!'

'Because she has the face of my mother, too.'

'*All things happen in a certain hour. An hour to act, an hour to fail or succeed.*'

The courtyard hummed with the flight of bees, ceaselessly rising and falling. The scent of black roses hung in the heat-soaked air. The sphinx blocked all light, Her robed head raised against a yellow sky pocked with the black geometries of constellations: the hieroglyphs of reality.

'*Do what you will, children of earth. In one hour, there will be a* magia *of pestilence. In one hour, the founding stone will be laid of the House of Salomon. In this one same hour, do what you will.*'

The White Crow shivered, standing in the shadow of the god-daemon. Lips curved, the baking-hot brick crumbling dust onto the air. Lids slid widely open upon eyes as pitiless, amused and deadly as earth's wastelands.

'*The hour of that day is not yet. You are come before your time.*

'*In that one hour, the Lord of Noon and Midnight will once more break the great circle of the living and the dying: I prophesy. And in that one hour the Wheel of Three Hundred and Sixty Degrees will fly apart into chaos: I prophesy. Stone from stone, flesh from bone, earth from sun, star from star. There shall not be one mote of matter left clinging to another, nor light enough to kindle a spark, nor soul left living in the universe.*

'*In that one hour.*'

Movement caught her eye: the White Crow wrenched free of Casaubon's arm, her hand going up to her sword. She froze, fingers outstretched to grip. Above, in the yellow heat-soaked sky, black lines etched animal-headed god-daemons with stars for eyes.

'*I give you both the day that holds that hour.*'

The sky shuddered.

A sense of turning sickened her. She slitted her lids to block out the sky, and the sun that *moved*: shifting thirty Degrees across its arc from the Sign of the Lord of Morning to the Sign of the Lady of High Summer.

Cramps twisted her womb, and she bent over, grinding a fist into the pit of her belly, the pain of the moon waxing and waning in a heartbeat.

'*At the precise moment that the Great Circle is once again broken – then act!*'

The great paws of the god-daemon closed together.

The White Crow flung out both arms, pushing against the sun-hot brick that writhed beneath her palms. She staggered, slipped to one knee, sneezed violently as cold air forced its way into her lungs; and scrambled to her feet.

A wall of tiny ochre bricks blocked her vision. Her dusty hands rested flat against them. She pushed away, her eyes following the brickwork up . . . to where it hooped above her head in an arch.

The first entrance-arch cast a dawn shadow into the street. No coach waited outside. The White Crow stood alone, shivering in air that felt cold only by contrast with the soul of heat. Her womb ached with the loss of time passed.

'*Shit*-damn!'

Her voice echoed.

The White Crow swung around, taking in the dew drying on the cobbles, the dawn-mist turning the blue sky milky. 'Evelian! My rooms! Who's been feeding my animals while I've been gone?'

A citizen, out early, skittered past one corner of the Fane, and the White Crow yelled: 'The day, messire?'

Without turning or stopping, the man called: 'Day of the Feast of Misrule.'

'*That* long?'

She swung back, stabbing a dusty index-finger at the Lord-Architect, to realize that she stood alone and faced a blank gateless brick wall.

' – Casaubon?'

5

Light spreads out across the heart of the world.

Down in Eighth District North quarter the barter-stalls open early, candy-striped awnings pearled with dawn's dew. Men and women argue the value of rice, portraits and chairs against pomanders, shoes and viola da gambas. The barter-markets will close in an hour: it is the Feast of Misrule.

In Thirty-First District morning is advanced. Children dig the heavy clay earth of allotments, unearthing shards of pottery with a peacock-bright glaze, where sun sparkles from the edges of broken telescopic lenses. Parents call the children in; it is the Feast of Misrule.

At the royal palace light slants into wide gravel-floored courtyards, glares back white from walls. Echoing: the clatter of guard-change, the rattle of hoofs. Even this early, heat soaks the thick-walled chambers where Rats await a special morning audience.

And down where Fourteenth District meets the harbour the sail-less masts of ships catch the first yellow fire of the sun. Tugs anchored; wherries moored; light stains the lapping water where ships lie idle, even the transients part of the preparations.

Ashen, the dawn touches the Fane. Light curdles, chitters; sifting to fall upon the ragged wings of daemons: acolytes rustle and roost. Storm-bright eyes flick open.

Light spreads out across the heart of the world, the dawn of the day of the Feast of Misrule.

Reverend Mistress Heurodis said: 'I cannot stay so long as I thought. It would hardly do for me to be seen with you.'

Archdeacon Regnault sat on the gutter step, sandal in one dark hand, fingering the ball of her aching right foot. She raised her head when Reverend Mistress Heurodis spoke, and laughed mirthlessly.

'I'm told by the novices that Reverend Master Candia took equally great care not to be seen with Bishop Theodoret of the Trees.' She pitched her voice to carry over the constant ringing of a charnel-house bell. 'They were together, I know that. I know nothing else. And that was thirty days ago!'

She stood, clutching one sandal in her hand.

'My time to search grows less. I'm needed back at the hospital now. We've never needed to heal so many sick with pestilence as this High Summer.'

Beckoning Heurodis with a nod of her head, she limped across the wide, tree-lined avenue towards the illegal cafés of the human Eighth District Southquarter, just opening or shutting with the dawn.

'If your Church didn't insist on healing those the god-daemons fate for death and rebirth' – Heurodis seized the trailing edge of her blue cotton dress, and picked a neat way between fallen leaves, cracked roadstones, and fresh dung – 'you wouldn't now stand between poverty and ignominy.'

Two- and three-storey sandstone buildings took a warm light from the sun, the cafés' shield-shaped signs glowing blue, crimson and gold. The smell of fresh water rose from newly washed pavements. Where the soapy liquid trickled into the gutters, it accentuated the dung-odours of the avenue.

The Archdeacon paused on the far pavement, waiting for the old woman to catch up. She squinted up at the milky sky, sighed, anticipating heat and the distances to be walked across the heart of the world when one's Church is too poor to afford carriages.

'A Sign's passed, but I won't give up. Tell me one thing', she persisted doggedly, 'before you return to the university.'

The old woman in the neat cotton dress turned smoky-blue eyes on the Archdeacon.

'I have honest work teaching at the University of Crime,' Heurodis said, her thin voice firm. 'Why should I jeopardize it by becoming concerned in the dubious activities of the Church of the Trees?'

The Archdeacon stepped into the shadow of a eucalyptus tree, hearing its leaves rustle above her head. A rush of water from a shop-front wet her bare foot, and made Heurodis step aside with an irritated mutter. She made to take the old lady by the elbow and guide her.

'Ah! I didn't mean—' She shook her wrist, rubbed her elbow and stepped back from the Reverend Mistress. The white-haired woman smiled.

'What is it you have to ask me, girlie?'

The Archdeacon brushed the shoulder of her green cotton dress, and touched the scrolling bark of the eucalyptus for comfort. She cinched her belt in another notch. The dappled shadow and light of leaves fell across her black skin. She pointed down the avenue, to one of the bars that, open all night in the heart of the world, now began to close its doors.

'*Is* that Reverend Master Candia?' she asked.

Heurodis brushed tendrils of silver hair away from her face, and shaded her eyes with a brown-spotted hand. The Archdeacon followed her gaze into the open frontage of the café. Broken mirrors lined the walls. Among tables and shattered bottles and the fumes of hemp, a heavily built café-owner stood arguing with a man slumped into a chair.

'Yes.' Heurodis rubbed her bare corded arms, as if with a sudden chill.

The Archdeacon slipped her sandal back on her bare foot and strode towards the café. The Reverend Mistress hurried after her.

'We'll take over here.'

The burly man turned a scarred face on the Archdeacon and the Reverend Mistress. He nodded his head to Heurodis.

'If this bastard's a friend of yours, he's got a score to settle . . . '

Heurodis looked around, and slapped her hand down on Candia's table. The burly man's voice died as she lifted her palm. Six or seven silver coins gleamed on the scarred wood. Snake-swift, he brushed the money over the table-edge into his hand, fisted it, and glared at the old woman.

'You're mad! Using *coin*! The Rat-Lords will hang all four of us.'

'Then you'd better not tell them.'

The bar-owner met Heurodis's occluded gaze for a second, turned, and stomped to the back of the café to oversee the haphazard cleaning.

'Candia!'

The blond man sat slumped down so that his head was below the back of the chair, his booted legs sprawled widely. His uncut beard straggled to his collar. The buff-coloured doublet, open to show filthy linen, had more slashes than sufficed to show the crimson lining. He twitched at Heurodis's sharp tone.

'Reverend Master!'

The Archdeacon leaned forward. His warm foul breath hit her in the face. She reached out, wound a dark hand in his hair and jerked his head upright. Blond hair flopped across a face all pallor but for sepia-bruised eyes.

The man muttered something inaudible.

Heurodis folded her hands neatly in front of her. 'It takes more than days to get into this state.'

The Archdeacon straightened, looking around. Morning light showed unkind on upturned tables and the deserted bar. Dark wood scarred with knife-cuts and slogans reflected in shards of mirrors. She reached out and took a pail from one of the cleaners as he passed, and up-ended dirty water over the slumped man.

'Where's Theodoret? Where's my Bishop?'

The blond man reared up from the chair. Swearing, he threw out dripping arms for balance, opened his eyes and turned an uncomprehending gaze on the café and Heurodis and the Archdeacon. He stooped. One filthy hand went out to the nearest wall for support. An expression of amazement and embarrassment crossed his pale features.

Candia bent forward and vomited on the floor.

Broken mirrors at the back of the bar reflected the owner in conversation with two men. Both newcomers wore gold-and-white sashes; both wore clumsily adjusted rapiers and sword-belts.

Over the noise of retching, Heurodis said: 'Those are Salomon-men . . . We should move him from here, before they begin to question us.'

Gritting her teeth against the stink of vomit, alcohol and urine, the Archdeacon pulled one of the blond man's arms across her shoulder and guided (not being tall enough to support) him out into the avenue. A few yards on he fell against her, and she let him slide down to sit with his back against one of the eucalyptus trees.

Candia frowned, lifting a drooping head. He opened his mouth to speak and vomited into his lap, covering his doublet and breeches.

'It would be better, for his sake, not to take him back to the university.' Heurodis blinked in the sunlight.

The Archdeacon stepped back to join her. The blond man lay against the tree-trunk, head back, legs widely apart; moaning.

'Where did you go with the Bishop?'

She squatted down a yard from Candia.

'The novices saw you leave together. *Where did you take him?*'

A ragged band of crimson cloth had been tied about one of his wrists; days ago, judging by the dirt. A half-healed scar showed under the edge of it.

'He's been missing for nearly thirty days,' the Archdeacon persisted. '*Where did you leave him?*'

A light tap on her shoulder got her attention. She stood and faced Heurodis. Carts clattered past on the rough avenue. A few early passers-by turned to look at Candia.

'It's been nearly thirty days since the Reverend Master attended at the university,' Heurodis confirmed. 'I have not the least idea what he would be doing in the cathedral with low-life, but it seems a strong possibility that he *was*.'

The small old woman showed no disgust when she looked at the blond man sprawled on the pavement.

'He will need treatment, I'm afraid, before he can walk; and we can hardly carry him.' Heurodis's smoky gaze found its way to the Archdeacon's face. 'I have a basic grounding in medicine. And I, too, can remember drinking to drive away pain.'

'I can help him temporarily.'

Heurodis sniffed. Without a crack in her façade of disapproval, she nodded. 'Very well, then, but be quick. To be seen with one of you is bad enough, but to be present in public while you actually . . . Get on with it, girlie.'

The Archdeacon knelt down in front of Candia, one hand on his shoulder, one on the trunk of the eucalyptus.

Dawn mist cleared now, over roofs and alleys, and carts passed every few minutes, jolting over the broken paving-stones. All the drivers were human; no Rats visible. Heat began to soak up from the pavement, ripen the smells of the gutter.

Leaves rustled, rattled together.

A faint green colour rippled across the Archdeacon's black fingers. She brushed Candia's dirt-ringed neck. He stirred, straightening; his eyes opened and blinked against the sunlight. A smell of green leaves and leaf-mould momentarily overpowered city odours.

Water brimmed in his eyes. A tear runnelled the dirt on his face. She saw him focus into himself; the loose-limbed sprawl tensing. She let a little more of the power of green growing things clear his sodden head and veins.

'Can you understand me?'

His thin dirty hand came up and touched hers. As if the faint green colour of spring leaves pained him, another rush of water brimmed over his eyes.

196

'He . . . did that, and it didn't save him . . . '

The Archdeacon glanced up at Heurodis. Healing momentarily forgotten, she tightened her grip on Candia's shoulder and shook him.

'Who did? I talked to builders, some of the builders on the Fane – they say they saw my Bishop there. Was that you? Were you with him? What happened to him?'

He groaned. Sweat broke out on his forehead, plastering blond hair down. His other hand came up and gripped her wrist.

'Ask – why did they let me go . . . and not Theo . . . '

'He's at the Fane? Is he alive and well?'

'Yes . . . no . . . '

His breath stank. The effort it took him to speak made the Archdeacon shake her head in self-disgust.

She reverently touched the eucalyptus-trunk, centering patterns of veins in leaf and flesh, letting energy rise. After a moment she let the colour fade from her hands, and pulled Candia's arm across her shoulder again, and lifted. He came up on to his feet with difficulty, weight heavy on her.

Heurodis's chin rose, looking up at him, flesh losing creases momentarily. 'Take him to my house.'

Trying not to breathe in his stink, the Archdeacon put her arm around Candia's body to support him. Under his shirt her fingers felt each rib prominent. His pelvic bone jabbed into her side. Heurodis, irritable at the increasing number of people on the avenue, moved to hook the Reverend Master's other arm in hers and push him into uncertain steps. He swayed as they walked, slow yard by yard.

'If I do anything, it's what the Thirty-Six want me to do . . . what they let me go loose for . . . ' His voice slurred. 'People *talk* when they think you're drunk . . . I'm not drunk. I've heard things. Not as drunk as I'd have to be . . . '

His arms flopped loosely over the two women's supporting shoulders. His head dipped. His eyes shifted to the sky, watching under wary brows, afraid. The Archdeacon shifted her grip. His head turned, and he focused on the hawthorn pinned to her full bodice.

'Fuck your church! Fuck your arrogant beggarly church—'

He lurched free of the Archdeacon, ignoring Heurodis. His hair flew as he turned his face to the sky, to the Fane that blackened the south-aust horizon.

'Put *my* head on a spike like his, why don't you! Ask *me* why we betrayed the House of Salomon!'

A pulse of shock chilled her.

'Drunken hallucination,' Heurodis whispered.

'If one of the Salomon-men hears him . . . ' The Archdeacon wiped vomit-stained hands down her dress. Bright, rising over roof-tops, morning sun dawned on the Day of the Feast of Misrule, warming the sandstone streets.

'Ask *me*. I know.' Candia sank to his knees on the paving. Tears slid down his filthy skin. He rubbed helplessly at his ripped doublet and breeches, and wiped his nose on the back of his bandaged wrist.

The Archdeacon steeled herself to walk forward and grip his arm. Head down, he muttered at the broken paving. She only just understood what he said.

'Heurodis, Heurodis, I don't have the courage – no, I don't have the *talent* to do what we should do now.'

Dawn sunlight slid across the dial of Clock-mill as the loaded mules passed by its waterwheel. The balding man in the darned jerkin mopped his brow in the early heat and tugged the lead mule's rein.

Above, the blue-and-gold dial showed three hundred and sixty Degrees marked with the signs of the Thirty-Six Decans. The clock-hands stood at five-and-twenty to six.

Mayor Tannakin Spatchet turned the corner out of Carver Street in an odour of mule dung. Two apprentices in silk and satin stopped and jeered. He stiffened his spine. A third girl, the gold-cross sash tied about her waist, shouted, and they ran off down the cobbles, bawling insults, late for their site. He drove the four mules around another corner as far as a narrow door, where he knocked.

One of the mules clattered its hoof against the cobbles, loud in the quiet street. The Mayor gazed up past the black wooden frieze of skulls and gold-chests and ivy to a window that stood an inch open.

'Lady! White Crow!'

He hammered his plump fist against the street-door. Distantly, above, he heard footsteps.

'Unh?'

A thin girl of fifteen or so opened the narrow door. Her yellow hair straggled up into a bun, and her blue satin overalls appeared to have a coating of orange fur and damp spots down the front.

'Unh?' she repeated.

Tannakin Spatchet, displeased at seeing the widow's daughter, drew in a breath that expanded his chest, showing off the verdigris-green Mayor's chain. 'Sharlevian, I wish to see the White Crow. Immediately. Fetch her.'

'Ain't here.'

'When will she—?'

'Ain't *living* here,' the girl snapped.

A voice from the darkness up the stairwell called: 'Sharlevian, who is it?'

'Aw, *Mo*ther . . . it isn't anybody. Only the Mayor.'

'Come back up here and finish feeding these blasted animals!'

Tannakin Spatchet heard Evelian's irritated voice grow louder, coming down the stairs, and glimpsed her blue-and-yellow satin dress. The buxom woman thrust a half-grown fox-cub and a feeding-bottle into Sharlevian's hands, ignoring both their whines, and nodded briskly to him.

'Tannakin.'

He raised a finger, pointing at the upstairs window. 'Is she coming back?'

The buxom woman stepped down into the street, closing

199

the door behind her. Her gaze took in the four mules and the roped tarpaulin loads that stood almost as high again as the animals' backs. One fair brow quirked up.

'I don't know that she *isn't*. What's all this lot? You've come for more talismans?'

'It's taken us thirty days to collect this to pay for the last ones, and now you say she's gone . . . Is there another philosopher in the quarter who can make protective talismans?'

'You're joking! Magus' Row is bare as a Tree priest's larder, and no wonder, after the last Sign.'

Evelian prodded the packing, and spoke without turning:

'Sharlevian's talking of nothing but this House of Salomon. All the apprentices are the same, and she – it's all these fool boys she hangs around with. A bitch on heat, if I say it who's her mother. I wish I didn't think that I'd be better off with friends among the Salomon-men, but I do.'

Tannakin let her vent the heat-bitterness of high summer.

'I've lost three lodgers in the last thirty days. I'm told the little Katayan's *alive*, but I've seen nothing of her. As for the White Crow . . . this is all hers?'

Tannakin Spatchet sighed. With his own bitter resentment, he said: 'It's little enough. Brass pans, some shelving, an old clock, some lenses, four cheeses—'

'I can smell the cheeses.'

' – a dozen tallow candles, and a ream of paper. The other loads are much the same. Mistress Evelian, in no way do I support the Salomon movement, in no way at all, but there are times when I would give my Mayor's chain not to have to barter, to be able to carry money and do with it what the Rat-Lords do.'

He saw her smile, but did not entirely understand why.

'We'll have to lug it all up these stairs and store it in her room. *Sharlevian!* If the White Crow doesn't come back,' the yellow-haired woman said, 'it can stand as my back rent.'

'Always the businesswoman—'

Tannakin Spatchet broke off, staring down the sunlit street into morning haze. Dark specks buzzed about the aust-west horizon: acolytes swarming about the angled Fane.

Evelian shaded her eyes. 'How often do you see that? Master Mayor, we're all going to need more than talismans to get through the next Calendar Sign.'

'Hear me!' The Hyena's voice crackled through the loudspeakers. The din of the crowd momentarily drowned out her words.

Zar-bettu-zekigal sat down on the step and unbuttoned her new greatcoat, cautiously letting the sun's early radiance warm her. She rested her chin on her fists.

The greatcoat, as matt black as her hacked-short hair, spread out on the marble step and the thrown-down yellow carpet. She curled her tail tightly to her body. The wash-faded black cloth of her dress began to grow hot in the morning sun, and she smiled and shrugged a stretch without moving from her sitting position. She kept one bare foot firmly on the stock of her musket that lay on the step below.

'We *will* build the Temple again, our temple, the House of Salomon: with just rule and line, for the Imperial dynasty to rule justly over our own people! We will build for ourselves, and never again for the Thirty-Six!'

Zar-bettu-zekigal yawned into her fists. Memory tracking automatically, she shifted an inch closer to the Hyena's plate-clad legs to watch every word. She gazed up, murmuring under her breath: 'Oh, you're beautiful! But see you, you're a child; just a baby!'

The Hyena stood on woven carpets, under gold silk canopies held by ragged silk-clad soldiers.

'We have been the servants of servants, the slaves of slaves, forbidden the least right, hidden in darkness, condemned to toil only for others! Now our buried birthright is uncovered, is come into the light; our day dawns, *this* day!'

She walked forward to the edge of the steps. Against the milk-blue sky, the armoured shoulders of the woman glittered silver; her scrubbed young face shone in the morning light. Zari watched the movement of her mobile mouth, the passion of her face; chopped-short brown hair flying, slanting red-brown eyes narrowed against the light.

'For them, now, nothing! We cut no more stone. We lay no more bricks. We dig no foundations. We draw no plans! Oh, they can force us to work – who denies it? But, if we're strong, who can force us to sleep or to eat?'

Behind the Hyena, gold-cross banners of the Sun shone: ranks of ragged soldiers crowding onto the steps of the Thirty-Second District square. The stink of gunpowder still hung in the air from a few enthusiastic musket-shots. Sword and sword-harness chinked.

'And when we die and are carried again on the Boat through the Night – who will they have then to build their power? Oh, who? None. For when we come again we will act as we do now: *we will not spend all our lives digging our graves and building our tombs!*'

The crowd's roar bounced back from the marble walls of the Trade Guild Meeting-halls, empty of their Rat-Lords now; together with the echoes of the Hyena's loudspeaker. Zari swivelled back on the step and faced forward, looking out across the heads of ten or fifteen thousand civilian men and women. In silk, in satin; their callused hands still carrying rule, trowel, wrench, or hod.

'But not only *I* tell you this.' The Hyena's voice dropped from passion to a passionate honesty. 'If it were only me, how could I ask you to act? I have hidden in darkness. I have hit and run, struck and fled again, damaging the Rat-Lords but never confronting them. I have not starved. I have not died, to refuse the Thirty-Six my labour. If it were only me, and these soldiers here, why would you listen?'

202

'*We cut no more stone. We lay no more bricks. We dig no foundations.*'

Frontispiece to *Sphinx Mystagoga*, Athanasius Kircher, Amsterdam, 1676

Zar-bettu-zekigal put in Memory the shouts in the crowd: half-audible, encouraging.

'So listen to one of your own,' the Hyena called out loudly. 'Listen to Master Builder Falke!'

Her foot kicked Zari as she stepped aside, and the woman looked down and grinned an apology. As the white-haired man moved out from under the shade of the silk canopy, the Hyena squatted down on her haunches beside Zar-bettu-zekigal.

'Hot.' Zari put the flat of her hand against the plate armour; the metal stung her palm. The woman pulled up her dark-red kerchief, shading her neck. A soldier two paces away held her laminated steel helm. The ragged Sun-banner drooped on a staff strapped to his back.

'Be hotter yet. This is early. It's going better than the last rally. Have you heard enough yet?'

'The Cardinal will want to know it all. He always does.'

A single line of Sun-banner soldiers kept the crowd back from the steps. The Hyena clanked down to sit beside Zari. The Katayan sat up and slid her hand along the hot steel to the woman's shoulders and, a little behind her now, began pressing her fingers down between armour and neck, finding points to release muscle tension.

'It had to work here.' The Hyena's voice rasped. 'After the last thirty days . . . Tell your Plessiez I gave the final order today. We're officially abandoning the areas under the city. Too much . . . *corruption* there.'

Zari dug her fingers in. 'See you, weren't there always hauntings?'

'Not like this!' The woman's plate gauntlet clacked against her breastplate. 'I wonder . . . I do wonder, now, what it was Plessiez had us do when we ran his underground errands. We don't get this sort of aid without our previous help being worth a lot. But after today it won't matter. We take charge today.'

White hair glinted in the sun as Falke stepped forward.

His booted foot just missed Zar-bettu-zekigal. She glanced up over her shoulder.

Falke walked with gravitas, thumbs tucked under his new sword-belt. His white-silver hair, longer now, he wore scraped back into a pony-tail and confined by a heavy silver ring. The morning sun showed up the lines around his mouth.

Black silk strips criss-crossed his eyes. He moved uncomfortably, sweating in the sun's heat, with a sword hanging from his belt, and a mail shirt and surcoat over his padded grey leather arming doublet. Embroidered insignia caught the sun and blazed across the square, on his breast not a ragged Sun but the House of Salomon's golden Rule.

'My friends.'

His voice crackled out across the square, half-humorous, and self-mockingly indulgent.

'My friends, *I* have not gone into voluntary exile. *I* have not trained men and women to be warriors. *I* have not sabotaged the Rat-Lords, lived starving and tireless, fought without hope until I saw this day. No, I have not done these things. For that, you must go to the Lady Hyena and her people. And, conscious of that, I speak humbly after her.'

The flesh under Zari's fingers tensed. She began to rub her thumbs at the base of the Hyena's skull. The woman rumbled: 'And three weeks ago he was gibbering with terror in a sewer. Gods, but that man can make capital out of anything.'

'See you, you're absolutely right.'

Lost in the contact of flesh and flesh, Zar-bettu-zekigal grinned dreamily to herself. She cocked an eye at Falke, looking through his legs at the crowded square.

He raised the microphone to his mouth again.

'You've heard good oratory from many of us this morning. I'll disappoint you; I'm a plain speaker. I'm one head of one hall in the east quarter of Nineteenth District. That's one quarter out of a hundred and eighty-one; one

District out of thirty-six. That's all. But I've learned things you have a right to know about.'

His head lowered for a calculated moment, then lifted to face sun, sky and the assembled thousands.

'From today, we do no work on any site. We have no choice. You have heard, and I have found out it's true, that his so-called Majesty the King will send in their troops to fire on you. And the priests of the Orders of Guiry, and Hildi, and Varagnac will come, and they will damn you with all ceremony. Let them! We can withstand it. We are stronger than that. We have no choice.'

Falke's voice rose.

'You will bear with me. None of you is a fool. We know the Rat-Lords exploit us and make us slaves, and we are old enough in the ways of the world not to expect better. But now we have – yes, I tell you today, now, this moment! – *now* we have the wisdom for which we searched. All of you know the Mysteries. You know the Interior Temple and the Exterior Temple are mirrors of each other, and of the greater Order.'

He rested one hand on his breast.

'If we had the knowledge, we said, we would build thus. Build in the shape of our souls, and compel the Divine to acknowledge us. We have been kept dumb and blind by the Rat-Lords, forbidden to build for ourselves, forbidden the knowledge of it; but no longer. Now, today, we have at last recovered the knowledge we lost – the knowledge they hid from us so long ago. Now, today, *we have the Word of Seshat!*'

A susurrus of words filled the air. Ripples of sound: lapping through the hot morning and the square, out to the pillared porticoes and marble frontages of the Trade Guild Meeting-halls.

'Look at them! There isn't a building site in the city that'll be working today.' The Hyena grinned. Her armoured heel hacked down on the marble. She turned a heat-reddened face to Zar-bettu-zekigal, impervious to the Katayan's skilled fingers.

206

'One minute everything's the same as it's always been, and then—' Her fist smacked into her palm. 'By the end of today we'll have a general strike. No building, no trains, no servants. Tell Plessiez that. And tell him Falke and I *must* know when his necromancy will take full effect.'

'I'll tell him.'

'Tell him I must know what happens at the Fane.' Her slanting red-brown eyes moved, some hidden fear stirring and suppressed in a blink. 'I must.'

'Shall I go to him now?'

The Hyena glanced up to where Falke still spoke, pale hands gesturing. The Sun-banner soldiers still stood, but much of the crowd sat on the paving-stones: clusters of people growing closer together with the steady increase in their numbers.

'Yes, and hurry back. Falke and I – we can start this, but we can't stop it once it's begun. It'll cross the city like fire: every slightest whisper will carry it! It's out of our hands.'

Zar-bettu-zekigal stood, picked up the musket and laid it back across one shoulder, and sketched a mock salute. 'Anything for you, Lady. Anything at all.'

'Leave that gun here!'

The woman put her fingers to her shoulder, only now sensing a tactile memory. The laminated steel plate blazed back sunlight. Zari blinked. The woman looked up at her.

'Take it, then, Kings' Memory. And take care.'

The airship and the warm bosom of the aircrew-woman long left behind, Casaubon's sparrow flies through skies where vultures rise on mesa-winds. Heat is a hard arrow under the bird's heart, piercing, piercing.

To either side rise up the cliffs, sand-banded mesas: ochre, scarlet, orange, white.

Reflected in the bird's obsidian eye is desert, blue sky, great horizons; the jagged battlements of a castle built into the mesa-side; the drowsy noon emptiness of a courtyard; the tower-window overlooking it.

The sparrow falls arrow-straight, kicks up a spurt of dust

*on the stone window-sill, hops on to the ring finger of the hand
outstretched to receive her.*

Hot morning sun and warm air poured in through the
open windows of the palace corridor. Zar-bettu-zekigal,
musket confiscated at the gates, swung her greatcoat off
her shoulders and slung it across her arm as she walked.
Her dappled tail curved up, poking through the slit at the
back of her knee-length black dress.

'Messire!'

Plessiez raised a ringed hand in acknowledgement as he
walked towards her. He gestured with finality to the four
or five priests with him, giving orders, sending the last
hurrying off as he came up with the Katayan.

' . . . and tell Messire Fenelon to attend me in the
Abbey of Guiry in an hour. Honour to you, Zaribet.'

'I just came from the Abbey of Guiry, messire. Fleury
told me you were here in attendance on the King.'

Outside the open windows, sun put a haze on the
blue-tiled turrets and spires and belvederes of the royal
palace roofs. The roofscape spread out, acre upon acre.
Mist rose up from drying pools of water: the previous
sundown's thunderstorm. Cardinal-General Plessiez drew
in a breath, bead-black eyes bright, muzzle and whiskers
quivering. He folded his arms and leaned up against the
white stone corridor-wall.

'I have just had an audience with his Majesty, yes.'

A silver band looped above one of his translucent-
skinned ears, below the other; a black ostrich-plume
being clipped into it at a jaunty angle. A basket-hilted
rapier hung at his side: leather harness black, buckles
silver. Zar-bettu-zekigal grinned, seeing how he tied the
cardinal's green sash rakishly from left shoulder to knot
above right haunch; tail carried with a high swagger, silver
ankh almost lost in his sleek neck-fur.

'I've much to do this morning. Now, the overseeing of
the artillery garden . . . Zaribet, come with me; I shall
need you as Memory then—'

'But not right this minute.' Zar-bettu-zekigal's eyes gleamed. 'Shouldn't Messire St Cyr be dealing with the artillery garden?'

Plessiez snapped his fingers as he turned, not looking to see if the young Katayan woman scurried down the corridor at his heels. Zar-bettu-zekigal tossed her greatcoat into the window embrasure and left it. She caught him up after a few skips, revelling in the sun-hot corridor-tiles under her feet.

'What did the King say, messire?'

Cardinal-General Plessiez slowed rapid steps. He clasped ringed fingers behind his back as he paced, and began evasively: 'Messire Desaguliers once removed, it would obviously be his second-in-command, St Cyr, who gained control of the Cadets . . . St Cyr is not Desaguliers' man; he is mine. I put him in as lieutenant some years ago; hence he leaves to me what I desire to oversee; hence . . . I have said I will deal with the artillery garden.'

'And the King?'

Zar-bettu-zekigal smoothed back her matt black hair from its centre parting with both hands. She grinned up at the Cardinal-General: watching his severity and wry humour and affected military air with the delight of a connoisseur or an admirer.

Two approaching priests robbed her of what answer he might have given. Plessiez stopped to issue orders. Zar-bettu-zekigal leaned back against the double doors at the end of the corridor, palms flat against the black oak, her dappled tail coiling down to her bare ankles.

'Be Kings' Memory now,' Plessiez cut her off as he rejoined her. She pushed the doors open for him to pass through. Leisurely, she repeated the standard pronouncement: 'Messire, you have an auditor . . .'

Plessiez walked through the next hall to where, white in sunlight through leaded casements, the double-spiral stone staircase rose up through this wing of the palace. He paused under its entrance-arch for the young woman to catch up.

'You hold all our secrets.'

She glanced up from her footing on the warm stone steps, descending in front of him. 'No secrets, messire. What I'm asked, I tell to whoever asks me. When I've heard it as Memory.'

'And not otherwise?'

'Oh, see you, messire! I wouldn't take a question like that from anyone except you.'

Here in the stone shaft, air blew morning-cool. The Katayan rubbed her bare arms. Plessiez watched her with what, eventually, he had identified as a certain awe; as if she were some hawk come tamely willing to his hand without capture.

'That may be why we all use you as a confessional.' He caught the flash of her eyes, knowing and innocent; and his snout twitched with an unwilling smile. 'Or does the Lady Hyena, as yet, share more than the ear of the Kings' Memory?'

The Katayan woman fisted hands to thrust in greatcoat pockets no longer there. Instead she put them behind her back, tail coiling up to loop her wrists.

'I'm working on that . . . She wants to know when anything's going to happen at the Fane. And, see you, Master Falke is lying his head off.'

'Falke tells no lies that I don't know about.'

The jerk of her head, chopped-off hair flying, took in all the thirty-six Districts of the city invisible beyond palace walls. 'Her "Imperial dynasty" and the Salomon-men – they've started something they can't stop down there in the city.'

'I know,' Plessiez said. 'It will be soon. It has already begun.'

Leaving the stairwell two floors below, walking through a cluttered salon, he nodded a greeting to passing black Rats, to one of St Cyr's uniformed Cadets, and to an aide of one of the Lords Magi. The Katayan beside him skipped to keep up with his strides. Plessiez eased the green sash where it crossed the fur of his shoulder, onyx and silver rings clinking against the *ankh*.

In the next salon all the full-length windows had been flung open, and heat slid in on tentative breezes, bringing the noise of hammers and forges and Rats shouting. Outside the windows, a ruined marble terrace gave way to the artillery garden. Blue haze coiled up from stretches of mud not yet dried by the sun.

A brown Rat passed across the terrace, and the Katayan woman checked. 'I thought . . . it might have been Charnay.'

'No. Not yet.' Plessiez's finger tapped irritably against his flank. 'I believe the Lady Hyena's admission that she released her. That means Charnay is off on some fool plan of her own. And that's when one knows there'll be trouble.'

The ormolu clock at the far end of the salon struck seven times. As the tinny notes died, a Cadet pushed the doors open. He bowed deeply to Plessiez.

'Lord Cardinal, the military architect is here to see you.'

'Finally! Show him in.'

'He . . . ah . . . '

Plessiez glimpsed a shadow out on the terrace. The previous night's rain stood in pools, flashing back white sun through the rising haze of steam. The mud, rubble, broken joists, and the machines of the artillery garden were blotted out by the bulk of a man. The big man glanced in at the window, nodding to Plessiez. His copper hair shone. He hooked his thumbs under the lapels of his blue satin frock-coat.

'Messire priest, I am Baltazar Casaubon, Lord-Architect, Scholar-Soldier of the Invisible College, Surveyor of Extraordinary Gardens, Knight oftheRoseCastle*and*', the immensely fat man got in before Plessiez could interrupt him, 'Horologer, Solar and Lunar Dial-maker, Duke of the Golden Compasses, and Brother of the Forgotten Hunt. Where is Messire Desaguliers?'

Rubble and hard earth jarred the base of his spine.

Candia's eyes jolted open. Sunlight spiked into his head. He moaned, lying back and leaning his face against rough-pointed brickwork.

' . . . it *is* a priest!'

'Not a real one.'

'We ain't got one, but we got her. Ei, priest, over here!'

Voices resounded in the warm air above his head. Yellow grass beside him grew up through shattered paving-stones. Silk- and satin-clad legs milled in front of his face: scarlet and azure and cloth-of-silver dazzled.

' – need any sort of a priest; we—'

' – see how things are here—'

' – necessary exorcism—'

' – a priest, *now*!'

Candia uncovered his face. A factory's sheer brick soared up into a blue sky. Above and beyond, he saw smokeless chimney-stacks. His head fell forward. Six inches from his nose, in the folds of a faded, tree-embroidered, green cotton dress, a black hand clenched into a fist.

A voice just above him said: 'I'll send you someone else from the Cathedral of the Trees.'

'No. We can't wait!'

'Not while they come all the way from Nineteenth District!'

Candia raised his head with an effort. He focused on a burly woman, arms folded, the gold Rule embroidered on her overalls catching the sun painfully bright.

'No,' she repeated. 'We want you, Archdeacon, before it's too late.'

Candia pushed his shaking fingers through his lank hair. As he moved, the cloth of his doublet and breeches cracked with dried liquid, and he smelt the stench of old urine and vomit. He pressed his shaking hands into his eye-sockets.

'Who? Where?' His weak voice cracked.

A familiar tart voice at his other side said: 'You're a fool, Candia. The university officially suspended you ten days ago. What did you do that was worth getting yourself into this state?'

He felt a slow heat spreading across his face. For a second his shame would not let him look up at Heurodis. Veins pulsed behind his shut eyelids, the colour of light through new leaves. The invading presence of that healing could no longer be denied.

'Heurodis . . . ' He took his hands from his face, braced his shoulders against the wall, and pushed himself upright against the rough brick, ripping his buff doublet again. Morning sun dazzled. The young black woman beside him argued furiously with the burly carpenter. Workers crowded around in the alley, the movement confusing him.

'Stay here.' The black woman moved a step towards the factory, glancing at the locked gates at the end of the alley, and then at the elderly Heurodis and at Candia. 'I'll come back for you.'

'No . . . ' Gesture and voice died; he leaned weakly against the wall, brushing fair hair from his eyes, ignoring filth.

'Yes.' Heurodis put her wrinkled hand protectively on Candia's arm, and kept it there until the black woman turned away. She raised one faded eyebrow at the Reverend Master then.

'Help me,' Candia said shakily. 'Now, while they're arguing. I've seen, and I've heard . . . Heurodis, I have to get back inside the Fane.'

'Of course,' Plessiez heard the Lord-Architect observe, 'I left numerous and very *detailed* plans . . . '

The Lord-Architect rested one ham-hand on a joist of the machine, some four feet above ground-level, and bent to peer under the platform. His left foot came free of the artillery garden's white mud with a concussive suck. He looked absently down at his dripping silk stocking and shoe.

' – which the factory could have accurately followed.'

213

'What caused your absence?' the Cardinal-General demanded.

'I assure you, messire, the last . . . ' Casaubon paused invitingly.

'Thirty days.'

'The last thirty days have, for me, gone past in the blink of an eye. You may say, indeed, they passed in the space of a heartbeat.'

'I am well aware that you must be busy.' Plessiez, waspish, whipped his tail out of the mud, taking a firmer stance on the artillery garden's rubble. The immense shadow of the machine fell cool across his sun-warmed fur. His left hand slid down to grasp the scabbard of his rapier. He gestured for Zar-bettu-zekigal to approach. 'Are you suggesting that these particular engines have been built incorrectly? Is that where the difficulty of operation arises?'

'Oh, not *incorrectly*, not as such . . . '

The Lord-Architect rapped his fist against the lower joist near the massive rear wheel. The iron plates of the wheel casing quivered. His blue-coated bulk tipped lower as he moved a step forward, under the platform of the machine.

'. . . merely minor adjustments . . . '

As Plessiez watched, the fat man gripped a strut in one hand and pivoted, slowly graceful, easing his body down. One massive leg slid forward. He swung down to sit in three inches of semi-liquid mud and, on his back, pull himself further under the axle-casing with massive white-gloved hands.

'. . . a few days' work . . . '

Plessiez frowned. Picking his way across the rutted site, he stooped to look under the machine. The Lord-Architect Casaubon lay on his back in the mud, his blue satin frock-coat spreading out flat, soaking up rain-pools. As Plessiez started to speak, the fat man fumbled in the pocket of his embroidered waistcoat and brought out a miniature hammer. He reached up and tapped the iron axle. A sharp

214

metallic click echoed back across the artillery garden from the royal palace wall.

'I don't have "a few days", Lord-Architect. These engines must be ready to move later today.'

Plessiez, irritated, straightened up and looked for the Kings' Memory. The young Katayan woman had her heels on the wheel-rim where it rested on the earth, eight inches above ground, her back to the axle, stretching her arms as far up the spokes to the metal casing as possible. The top of the wheel curved a yard and a half above her head.

Her chin tilted up, pale, as her eyes traversed the bulk of the engine above her on the wheeled platform.

'Zari!'

'I'm listening, messire.' The Katayan's chin lowered. She grinned.

Plessiez urbanely repressed the fur rising down his spine. The tip of his tail lashed an inch to either side in a tightly controlled movement. 'I repeat: I do not have days.'

The fat man grunted amiably. His large delicate fingers probed the gear-wheels above the axle. He took his hand away, staring at a glove now caked with black grease. He began to ease himself forward on hands and heels and buttocks, until he cleared the mud with a succession of squelches. The Lord-Architect stood up, cracked his head against the underside of the platform, and spread oil and mud in his copper-gold hair as he rubbed the crown of his head.

'Days,' Casaubon repeated firmly. He ducked out from under the platform. His silk knee-breeches dripped. Taking one hem of his frock-coat in a gloved hand, he cracked the cloth and spattered mud in a five-yard radius.

The Katayan wiped the tuft of her tail across her cheek.

Plessiez looked down at the glutinous white mud spattered across his fur and cardinal's sash. 'You may find this behaviour acceptable. I do not. It is possible, Messire

Casaubon, that these tactics are designed to obfuscate your inefficiency. I assure you that they fail.'

The Lord-Architect laughed. He swung a gloved grease-stained hand to clap Plessiez on the back. The Cardinal-General stepped away smartly, his heel coming down on a broken paving-stone filmed with mud.

'Wh—?'

Plessiez skidded, flailed limbs and tail to stay upright; a rock-solid hand closed around his arm and steadied his balance. Chins creased as the big man smiled, innocent.

'Careful, messire.'

'I am always careful. Thank you.' Plessiez met Zar-bettu-zekigal's gaze. The Kings' Memory leaned her fist hard against her mouth, eyes bright. Plessiez took a step back, gazing up at the metal-plated casings and turrets and ports and beaks of the siege engine.

Morning sun dazzled off the row of nineteen others ranked beyond it.

'Not my preferred line of work, really. Trained in it, of course. Could do you ornamental garden automata,' the Lord-Architect offered hopefully, 'or hydraulic water-organs . . . '

Plessiez narrowed his eyes to furred slits and studied the large man. Coming in moments to a conclusion that (had he known) it had taken the White Crow years to arrive at, he smiled, nodded an acknowledgement, and observed: 'Very well, we understand each other. I am somewhat in your hands, being at the mercy of your expertise, and you have a price which is not entirely orthodox. It may be granted, if it is not too impossible, messire.'

Casaubon beamed, blue eyes guileless. 'I could work faster if I knew what these engines are *specifically* needed to do.'

Morning light shone back from white earth, from distant windows and multi-tiered roofs, with a promise of later heat. Small figures dotted the perimeter of the site: engineers being kept back by St Cyr's Cadets. Their impatient voices came to Plessiez across the intervening distance.

'We *do* understand each other. Very well,' Plessiez conceded. His muzzle turned towards Zar-bettu-zekigal as she stepped down from her perch on the wheel. 'But, I regret, not in your presence, Zari. For the present this must be between his Majesty and myself – and now you, Messire Casaubon.'

'Must she go?' The big man's face creased in disappointment. 'Such a beautiful young woman. And a Memory, too? Lady, you should have told me.'

The Katayan leaned her elbow against the wheel-rim and her cheek on her hand. 'I did tell you. I yelled it in your ear. You had your head in the rotor-casing at the time, but I did tell you you had an auditor. Didn't I, messire?'

'Certainly.' Plessiez, sardonic, folded his arms, sword-harness chinking; looking from the King's Memory to the Lord-Architect, and absently picking pieces of drying mud from his left elbow-fur with his right hand. 'Is there anything else either of you would wish to know?'

'*I'd* like to know what these machines are for.' The Katayan inclined her head to the fat man, her tail cocked high. 'Zar-bettu-zekigal. Are *you* liable to need a Kings' Memory, messire architect?'

The Lord-Architect Casaubon took the young woman's hand between the tips of filthy gloved fingers and thumb, inspected it for a moment, and bowed to kiss it. 'Baltazar Casaubon, Lord-Architect, Scholar-Soldier of—'

Plessiez cut the man off in mid-flow: 'If you listen, Zaribet, you do it as a private person.'

The Katayan nodded vigorously, hair flopping over her black-hook eyebrows.

Plessiez let his weight rest on one haunch, thumb tucked into sword-belt, eyes narrowed against the sun; something of his poise returning.

'There are thirty-six of these engines. I've directed the production-line workers for the past week, getting sixteen engines on-station in the further Districts. These that remain must be functioning and able to move by noon, to

217

be in position – at the entrances to the airfield, the docks, the underground rail and sewer termini, the main avenue to the royal palace, and at as many points overlooking the Fane as possible.'

He saw Zar-bettu-zekigal's head come up, her pale eyes raking armour-plating, gunports, stacked muskets on the platform, beaked battering-rams.

'You're going to attack the Hyena's people!' she accused.

'We face no serious threat from a few of the servant class who've latterly learned to hold a sword by the correct end.'

'No.'

Plessiez, startled, looked up from his footing on the rubble to meet the china-blue eyes of the Lord-Architect. The fat man absently wrang mud out of his coat-tails and shook his head again.

'As I understand it, these are spiritual machines.' Plessiez shrugged. 'Designed to protect my people against attack – by the servants of the Thirty-Six: the acolytes of the Fane.'

A shudder walked down Plessiez's spine. He momentarily shut his eyes upon a memory of Masons' Hall, butcher-red, a shambles. The early sun fell hot on his fur. He opened his eyes to the distant sparks of light from palace windows. The silence of work suspended hung above the artillery garden, as it had been poised above all the city since dawn.

Zar-bettu-zekigal's eyes narrowed against the brightness of the empty sky. She smoothed her dress over her narrow hips with both hands. Her dappled tail hung limp.

'Tripe!' boomed a bass voice: Casaubon shattering the quiet.

Plessiez, tight-mouthed, shifted his ringed hand to his belt-dagger. A momentary breeze unrolled like a gonfalon the hooded silk cloak of a Cardinal-General. 'Messire, if you would confine yourself to architecture and engineering—'

A large hand hit Plessiez squarely between the shoulders.

218

The black Rat twisted his head, feather-plume blocking his view, to see a muddy glove-print on the back of his robe.

'*Complete* rubbish,' the Lord-Architect Casaubon beamed. 'That being the case, you'd only cover the Rat and Mixed districts. Wouldn't bother with a siege-engine for every district, including the Human.'

Plessiez opened his mouth to prevaricate, saw Zari hop from one bare foot to the other, grinning wildly, and Casaubon twinkle at her: 'I don't doubt he plans protection from the Fane. I'm no fool, Messire Cardinal. I can see thaumaturgy plain in a set of blueprints. As for *these* – a jerk of the head at the towering siege-engines that set his multiple chins quivering – 'I'm an architect. I followed your exact design. Put these in strategic locations and you protect *everybody* – as far as that's possible. Yes?'

Cardinal-General Plessiez shut his open mouth. He lifted his snout, raking the large man from copper hair to mud-dripping high-heeled shoes, and bringing his gaze to rest on the amiably smiling face. A brown smear of oil covered freckles, continued up into the cropped hair. The black Rat met the man's eyes.

'I assume that you need to know that,' Plessiez said, 'because I don't indulge idle curiosity, not with a matter that has taken years to conceive and execute, and which, besides, involves his Majesty the King. Even the curiosity of an excellent architect, messire.'

The Lord-Architect Casaubon inclined his head gravely, waiting.

'Yes,' Plessiez said. 'The intention is to protect as many people as we can, regardless of who and what they are. Rat or human. Or, if it comes to it, acolyte. You are liable to see apocalyptic matters today, messire, and if any of us survive it will be thanks to these machines which his Majesty has desired and I have designed.'

The Archdeacon's sandals scuffed on the concrete of the yard. Tawny grass sprouted up through the cracked surface. She raised her eyes to the tops of the surrounding

219

factory walls. Grass rooted there, against a blue morning sky. A stink of oil and furnaces made her broad nostrils flare.

'A daylight possession? And not susceptible to talismans?'

'We've tried everything. It keeps growing.' The burly woman wiped sweat from her eyes. 'There have been small corruptions breaking through for ten days or more, but now the Rat priests and the Fane won't answer our messages.'

Inside the nearest factory-hangar door men and women leaned exhaustedly up against walls or lay on benches. The Archdeacon glanced back over her shoulder, seeing the alley; the Reverend Mistress and the blond Candia safely penned in by a locked gate and factory workers regarding them with suspicion.

'This way.' The burly woman in carpenter's silks led her past moulding and milling engines, standing silent and reeking of oil, towards the back of the building. In the unaccustomed silence, the bells of the nearby charnel-houses rang clearly.

'Your sick people here' – the Archdeacon pointed – 'is it the pestilence?'

The carpenter glanced back at her co-workers where they sprawled or staggered. The Archdeacon saw a whiteness of skin under the woman's eyes, a certain luminosity and sharpness about the broad features. Vagueness crossed her eyes from moment to moment.

'I'm Yolanda.' The woman stopped at the back wall. 'Foreman over in the next workshop. Well, priest—'

The Archdeacon pointed to a canvas-shrouded bundle in the corner, among broken glass and waste metal and sacking. The length and shape of the human body: on it, blotted red dried to blotched brown. 'Is that a victim of the possession here?'

A proud note came into Yolanda's deep voice. 'Garrard? He fainted and fell under the ore-carts out in the sidings. Hadn't eaten for five days, to my certain knowledge. We had a Sergeant of Arms down here, running back to the Rat-Lords, closing us down. We tried to get a real priest.'

She stopped, shrugged, eyes still on the shroud. 'Already on the Boat by now, and travelling through the Night. He always did like sailing . . . The possession is here, Archdeacon.'

The Archdeacon remained standing staring into the corner of the factory hangar. 'This man died because he tried to work without food or sleep?'

Yolanda folded her arms. 'He died because the Decans fated him to die today. More fool them. No foundries means no tools, no scaffolding, pretty soon no more building on the sites – no more Fane. They'll soon know how it goes. We're *willing* to work. Just not able.'

The Archdeacon cracked her dark knuckles, loosening the muscles in her hands. 'If the plague carries on, you won't need to starve or fatigue yourself, Fellowcraft Yolanda.'

'Here.' Yolanda pushed the small back door open.

Light from a clerestory window picked out the darker green threads woven into the Archdeacon's cotton dress: the pattern of roots, trunk, branches, leaves. She pulled her wide cloth belt taut. Her fingers touched the energy centres at her dark temples, at her breasts and groin and each opposite wrist.

'For all you despise my Church, I can't refuse to do my duty here. My name is Regnault.' The Archdeacon's voice sounded clear, cold. 'If I should be injured and can't do this, you must see to it: take Master Candia to the Cathedral of the Trees. Tell them Candia is to be questioned about Theodoret.'

'Candia is to be questioned about Theodoret—' Yolanda flinched back a sleep-dazed step as the door in the back wall began to drift open. She turned and walked rapidly towards the front of the factory, gesturing to other workers to stay back.

Regnault touched fingers to the peeling white paint of the door. She wrinkled her nose. A smell of rotten vegetation came through the open door: not honest decay, but touched with a corruption of flesh.

She entered, took one slow step into the long white-tiled room, and halted, the door swinging closed behind her, her eye caught by movement. A young black woman in a faded dress faced her from the far end of the room. Round-breasted, round-hipped; bushy hair throwing back a myriad points of gold light from the clerestory windows. Archdeacon Regnault gazed at her reflection in the spotted mirror, at the long row of porcelain urinals on the wall to her left, and the row of closed or open cubicle-doors to her right. Darkness prickled at the edge of her vision. Cold struck up through the tiling and her sandals to impale the soles of her feet.

'Root in Earth protect me.' Her whisper fell on dank air. She put her fingers to her breast, to the spray of hawthorn pinned there. She pressed the pad of her index finger against the thorn, piercing the skin. A bead of blood swelled.

'Above, beneath: branch and root—'

Breath-soft, she began the Litany of the Trees; letting her power push the pepper-scent of hawthorn out into the tiled room, expunging the smell of urine and faeces, tasting still a faint corruption in her mouth.

'Pillars of the world—'

Light brightened: sun through high windows. A watery *glop* sounded, close at hand. The Archdeacon padded forward, and suddenly stopped.

Her reflection in the fly-spotted mirror had not moved.

' – branch and leaf—'

The reflection raised a head subtly disfigured, and smiled with teeth too long and pointed.

' – leaf in bud: shelter and protection—'

The Archdeacon splayed the fingers of her left hand in the Sign of the Branches. Her right index finger throbbed. Blood fell to the floor-tiling in small perfect discs and ovals.

Something buzzed, close at her right hand.

222

Regnault halted between one step and the next, glancing sideways. The cubicle-door beside her stood half-open, opening inwards, disclosing muddy porcelain footstands in the floor-basin and the china throat of the open drain.

A furred body as large as her two fists hung above the toilet-hole, angrily buzzing. Yellow and black stripes, light glinting from whirring wings, multi-faceted eyes.

The Archdeacon turned from the mirror, stepping towards the cubicle. Water blinked in the open floor-drain: a dark eye in the stained white porcelain. The giant wasp shifted in the air, shifted again, faster than she could react. She stabbed her finger against the hawthorn again and sketched a sign in blood on the air.

' – the protection of the Branches that support the sky—'

The wasp lifted, buzzing, the vibration reverberate from the walls; rising level with the Archdeacon's head. Regnault flung both hands out at a level with her shoulders, spread her fingers and slowly closed them.

Dints appeared in the furred body-segments. Diaphanous wings glimmered emerald, the colour of spring leaves, and crumpled. The soft heavy body fell, still crumpling, to smack against the glazed china surface; slid down the shallow slope and blocked the open drain, feebly burring.

Sweat trickled down between Regnault's shoulder-blades. The step forward had brought her into the cubicle. Eyes still fixed on the dying wasp, she reached out a hand behind her to pull open the swung-to door.

Her outstretched fingers touched fur.

She twisted around, flattening her body against the pipework of the back wall. Her bare ankle brushed over the dead wasp. The door swung closed an inch, a foot, weighed by the heaviness of its burden.

Bulbous shapes – no, *a* shape – clung to the inside of the peeling cubicle door. Fragile insectile legs shifted for purchase. The throbbing soft segments of the torso glowed black and yellow, the glassy wings shattered a rainbow

223

spectrum. The Archdeacon pressed herself back against the wall, heel kicking at the pipework.

The wasp's body, as tall and solid as she, clung quivering to the door, arching slightly at the division of its bulbous body, sting pulsing under the lower torso. Regnault's skin crawled. She looked up wildly to see if the cubicle walls could be climbed. Beyond the partition a deep buzzing note began, joined by another, then another. Sun through the clerestory windows glinted on rising wings.

The wasp that clung to the back of the door thrummed a raw increasing shriek.

' – heart of the Wood protect, the Lady of the Trees defend—'

A sharp click sounded outside the cubicle, at the end of the long room. She recognized the sound of a sandal stepping down on to a tiled floor from a small height: the height of, say, a wall-mirror.

She reached up, hands shaking, and carefully pressed each finger in turn to the hawthorn spray. With bloody hands she unpinned it from her dress, marking the cloth, tearing it into two handfuls of twig and leaf. Her skin cringed away from the insectile form clinging to the door, its translucent guts throbbing with half-digested food.

Poised, dizzy, she took a breath of oxygenless air.

Outside the cubicle, pacing footsteps traced a staccato inhuman rhythm. She glimpsed a brown ankle under the cubicle door, and a foot with claws.

Wetness touched her bare leg.

The fist-sized body of the dead wasp no longer blocked the drain. From its open throat a tendril of wet dark nuzzled. It touched her ankle, numbed the skin, left white puckered marks.

'Heart of the Wood!'

Both hands clenched on crushed hawthorn, she pivoted on one heel and struck the cubicle door solidly with her other foot, a hand-span from the thrumming wings. The door banged shut, rebounded concussively inwards. She pitched into a forward roll through the door, hands tucked into her sides, bruising her shoulders.

The wasp ripped up into the air, its chainsaw buzz shattering the glass in the row of clerestory windows.

Regnault came up on to her feet, crouching on the tiles; threw her left hand's bunch of hawthorn full in the sharp-toothed liquid-fleshed mirror-face that fleered above her.

Bloody leaves, stained blossom: for a second outlined in green-and-gold brilliance. Light blinded. She dropped to one knee, edging back towards the urinals. Something black fell from the high ceiling. Shrieking above the saw-buzz of wasp wings, she flung her right hand's hawthorn, slipped, fell full-length on the floor.

The last whole windows imploded.

Black clotted liquid spattered her dress and skin, scalding hot. A rain of ordure pattered down for thirty seconds. She raised her head. Fragments of wing and black fur floated in the air: the wasps were no longer there.

Archdeacon Regnault put her wrist to her nose and wiped away blood. She smiled with the satisfaction of the craftsman. Silence pressed in on her eyes, deep and echoing. Slowly, painfully, she got to her feet; fingers throbbing and still bleeding, clots of faeces sliding to hit the tiles.

The wall-mirror hung shattered in the pattern of a hieroglyph. She read it; frowned suddenly.

'"Oldest of all, deepest of all, rooted in the soul of earth; who dies not but is disguised, who sleeps only—"'

The tiles under her feet rippled, ceramic shifting like water, and she fell to one knee.

A black stain oozed out from under the furthest cubicle door. Black liquid ran down from the urinals. A stink of blood and urine constricted her throat. She clenched her fists, forcing concentration out of pain, muscles tensing to push her towards the exit.

Her legs could not move.

The ceramic tiles under her foot and knee shattered, thin as cat-ice on a puddle. Tears ripped from her eyes as

225

she fell into corrosive vapour. She clawed at the edge of the floor as she fell past it, caught a joist with one bleeding hand for the briefest second.

She stared down into vaulting flooded with liquid darkness, heard the voices calling her, saw in the glistening surface far below the reflection of her face: feral, sharp-toothed, grinning—

The joist grew wormy, holed and friable in the space of a breath. It crumbled under her clenching fingers.

She fell.

A sepia twilight, hot and brown, clings to discarded furnace-mouths, broken bains-marie and alembics. The Bishop of the Trees views them through the open door of his cell: unable to move, or turn away, crusted blood and sinew tightening below his impaled medulla oblongata.

'Why . . . will . . . you . . . not . . . let . . . me . . . die?'

He forces each word out with what breath he can gather into his withered cheeks.

Wings rustle in the heat. Basalt pinions settle to huge flanks as the Decan of Noon and Midnight who is also called The Spagyrus lays his tusked and tendrilled head upon vast paws.

– You're bait—

'Wh . . . ?'

The ebony lids slide up from basalt eyes.

– My servants questioned you for their pleasure. I am a god and a daemon, a Decan of the Thirty-Six: I know all that you could ever know. Still, I allow the acolytes their play—

Scales rustle as the immense head settles still further, yellow-crusted nostrils twitching.

Theodoret, Bishop of the Trees, turns his sandpaper-gaze to where the Decan looks. Down in the wall of the Fane, above the deserted alchemical workshop, is set a glass bubble – no, a congeries of glass bubbles, each with their variant image of the heart of the world enclosed . . .

They cast a bluish-white light upon The Spagyrus, where the Decan sprawls under the Fane's crepuscular vaults. Perhaps it is that light – or the sun's not being in his Sign – or perhaps it is instinct: the most primitive instinct is smell, and Theodoret has that sense left to him still.

Each breath is rasping pain, each word formed through a torn throat and split lips; still, Bishop Theodoret forces words into the hot silence of the heart of the Fane.

'You . . . know . . . all . . . my . . . Lord— I . . . who . . . know . . . nothing . . . will ask you . . . a . . . riddle . . . What . . . can happen . . . to . . . make . . . a god . . afraid?'

6

Light advancing, mid-morning of the Day of the Feast of Misrule.

Rafi of Adocentyn rolled over on the rug, kicking a foot against one of the Lord-Architect's locked abandoned chests.

'If I'd known we had theory-tests on Festival days, I'd never have joined the university! What is all this junk anyway?'

Lucas chose deliberately to misunderstand. From where he sprawled on his bed, surrounded by open books, he muttered: 'Geometry, one would hope.'

'Witty, Candover, witty.'

The languid king's son from Adocentyn hoisted himself up on an elbow on the rug, and plotted a course across a page with a dirty finger.

'Lucas, just *listen* to this question: *"The Five Points of the Compass lie upon a circle of 360 degrees, each one at a ninety-degree angle from the next . . . Draw a compass rose, and enter North, West, East, South and Aust at the appropriate positions."'*

Lucas shifted into a patch of morning sun, knowing he would be grateful later for shade. He gestured for Rafi to continue. The other dark-haired student propped the book up on its spine.

'*"Now draw the following quadrilateral triangle . . ."'*

Lucas leaned down, grabbed a sheet of paper and a lead pencil, and sketched for a few seconds. 'Like so.'

'You think so?' Rafi of Adocentyn sat up, scratching at

the cleft of his buttocks. 'We're going to be sweating our arses off in Big Hall today.'

'The way things are here, lucky if that's the only problem we got.'

'Yeah, the Feast of Misrule won't be up to much.'

Lucas got up and stood at the open window, thumbs hooked in the back pockets of his knee-breeches. The warm air soothed his sun-scalded chest and shoulders. He looked down into the street. A mist so milky blue as to be almost purple clung to the roofs.

'At least you haven't been scrubbing latrines for three weeks.'

Rafi bellowed, thin mobile features convulsed. 'Shit, that Heurodis bitch has got it in for you!'

'*And* the rest.'

'I think it's funny,' the other king's son said, 'but then, nothing that happens to me here is ever going to get back to Adocentyn if I can prevent it.'

The wooden frame creaked under Lucas's grip as he leaned out of the window, one knee up on the sill.

'What is it this time? Ei, *Luke!*'

He fell back into the room, struck the door-frame with his shoulder on the way through, ignored Rafi's shout, and hit every third stair going down to the street-door.

Heat struck down from a cloudless sky. Apprentices clattered past at the Clock-mill end of the side-alley. His rapid breathing slowed as he went barefoot over the cobbles to the other end of the alley and turned the corner.

Voices rang across the street: Evelian's snotty daughter, Evelian herself, and a woman just now halted with her back to Lucas.

Sun tumbled in cinnamon hair.

'I want my rent!' Evelian shouted. 'And where's your friend the Lord-Architect?'

'The gods know! No – they probably do. *I* don't.'

She stood, now, with one arm outstretched to the brick-and-plaster wall for support, her white shirt-sleeve half-unrolled. Sweat soaked the underarms; her uncovered skin glowed pink-red. Slung across her back, worn straps cinched tight, a sword-rapier caught the morning light.

'White Crow?'

His whisper cracked soprano, inaudible.

She brushed grit from the sole of her right foot with her free hand. Brick- or stone-dust powdered her smooth calves and the hems of her knee-breeches. A hat lay upturned at her feet, white felt speckled with black hieroglyphics; and she bent and turned and scooped it up, and her tawny eyes focused and met his.

'Lucas!'

She strode the few yards between them, flung her arms around his chest: breasts and belly and legs pressed the length of his stirring body. Her rib-cage moved rapidly as she panted, hyperventilating in the heat. He buried his face in her hot-odoured white-streaked hair. Careful of blade and harness, as careful of her fine-lined skin and solid flesh as of porcelain, Lucas closed his arms across her back.

'You're sunburned.' The White Crow swatted his chest with the brim of her hat, stepping out of his embrace. 'The mysteries of elapsed time . . . What the hell has happened to the trains and carriages? I've had to walk from the Thirty-Sixth District, and it's taken me hours.'

'You must be new here,' Evelian snarled sarcastically. 'Haven't you heard about the strikes?'

The White Crow smiled. 'I've been away, remember?'

Lucas watched her lips move in the sunlight. A fine line marked her lower lip: a thirst-split. More fine lines webbed the corners of her eyes and cheek-bones. Her cinnamon lashes blinked over pale eyes, in eye-sockets whitened by heat and sweat.

He bent his head, smelling the sweet odour of her skin, and kissed the gritted corner of first one and then her other eye.

'Grave-robber!' A possessive mutter from Sharlevian.

He straightened, ignoring the girl. The White Crow's

mouth moved in some reaction too complex for easy interpretation. Shock still reverberating through him, Lucas yelled: '*What happened? What did the Fane do to you?*'

Sharlevian gasped; he saw her mouth gape comically. Evelian scowled. The White Crow pitched her voice above Mistress Evelian's renewed questions: 'I was gone, I'm back; I'll be gone again shortly, and after that I don't know!'

'But—'

Noise interrupted Lucas: a dozen apprentices clattering down the alley, cutting through the street to a Dockland site. A gangling dark boy snapped a punch at Lucas in passing; an older man jeered: 'Student!'

'What are the gold-and-white sashes?' the White Crow said at his shoulder. 'And was that *weapons* they're carrying? Openly?'

Lucas stared the gangling youth out until he turned, spitting, to follow the others. Of the dozen or so passing men and women, fully half had a striped sash and sword-belt around their shoulders or waists.

'The new Order of the – *Shit!*' A thrown pebble struck his knuckle. He jammed it into his mouth and sucked the cut. 'Of the Poor Knights of the House of Salomon. We've had street-fights with them at the university.'

'I did wonder. No-one called me out on this.' The White Crow reached up, touching the hilt of her sword. Sunlight shone on the blue metal, the sweat-dark leather binding; and on the curve of her uplifted arm. 'It seems that the House of Salomon has changed greatly since the Mayor told me about them.'

'*Those* aren't Salomon men,' Lucas added. 'Just their followers. White and gold are their colours. They're the sort who say you can wear the gold cross as protection against the plague.'

'There *is* a plague?'

Disquiet touched her face. Lucas regretted the drama-tization.

'Not really. Just the High Summer fevers are worse than usual. It's all rumour.'

'I need to know . . .' She shook her head, sun-silvered red hair falling about her shoulders. Lucas noted the falling cuff of her shirt: a stain of red wine not yet faded.

'. . . What *don't* I need to know!' she finished.

'Wait there, right there!'

'I'll be up in my rooms. Evelian—'

Lucas raced back around the corner of the building, up the street-stairs, into his own rooms, physical effort for the moment masking his wild excitement.

'The test's in an *hour*,' the king's son of Adocentyn grunted, arms full of texts, as Lucas shoved past him to rummage in a heap of revision-papers. 'They'll sling us out if we don't pass. Luke!'

'Yeah, yeah. *Got it.*'

He sprinted back, out into the morning air, seeing Evelian and her daughter still arguing in the street; leaping for the stairs and skidding up through the kitchen and into the White Crow's main room.

'Here. This'll tell you all you need to know about Salomon. It's put out by the woman who claims to lead the imperial dynasty.'

'The *what?*'

'You must know. Where have you been?' And then he froze, at the implications of that casual question.

The White Crow squatted, glancing into the fox-cubs' box. The chill of disuse and her absence cut through High Summer heat in the newly opened room. Junk stacked the corners, piled on chairs.

The mirror-table shone, glass side up, feeding-bottles scarring rings across its cracked surface.

'Fuck!' The White Crow bent to check the broken magus-mirror.

'Evelian wouldn't let me in here, or I'd have looked after it.'

The White Crow straightened. Her head came up as she turned a full circle, taking in neglected books and charts and lenses. The slightly fat-blurred line of her chin made his throat constrict. She prodded a heap of hand-scrawled messages resting on the table, tilting her head sideways to read one.

'I must follow up some of these names. And talk to Evelian about people she knows. Now . . . ' She reached for the pamphlet he still held out, and her fingers touched his hand. He grinned foolishly.

'Damned black letter printing . . . Let me see. *Liber ad Milites Templi de Laude Novae Militae*. "In Praise of the New Knighthood"?'

'The Salomon men are behind the organized hunger-strikes up at the Fane. They've almost stopped all building going on.'

'Casaubon knows more about the Secret Orders than I do. Whenever he's been put now . . . ' Her mouth quirked up. '"One crucial hour" – and it turns out to be the Feast of Misrule. Lucas, don't let anyone tell you the gods have no sense of humour.'

Lucas scratched under his open shirt at sweaty hair. Bewildered, he said: 'There won't be much of a festival, with the sickness and the strikes. What do you mean, *when*ever?'

She absently folded the black-letter pamphlet, creasing it sharply, and put it in her pocket. 'I don't know for certain that the Decan did do the same to him. Pox-rotten damned idiot that he is, why didn't he tell me what he was up to! I wonder if it's too late to contact any more of the College?'

She rested both fists against her mouth, tapping them softly against her teeth, in the gesture of thought that brought Lucas's heart to his mouth. Then, still absently, she reached up to a shelf for a wooden box, opened it, and took out three small talismans on chains.

Cut into tear-translucent moonstone: a sickle moon. Into pearl: a nereid's trident. And into black onyx: the cold Pole Star. Some of the sweat-blotched red and white left her face as she put them around her neck.

She stretched, and all but fell into a sitting position on the courtyard-window's sill.

'That's better. I'd forgotten what High Summer's like, here in the heart of the world . . . '

Lucas said softly: 'Are you well?'

She shoved her spread fingers through her hair, pushing it back from her face. The white at her temples gleamed. Resting with her back against the jamb, one bare foot up on the sill, she smiled exhaustedly up at Lucas.

'Yes, kind sir, I thank you for asking. But no,' she said, the smile vanishing, 'I'll have to be moving again. Damned transport would be out now, when I need to get across half the city. And I hate to break a strike.'

Lucas looked round at the star-charts curling on the walls, the cracked mage-mirror table, the stacked volumes of Paracelsus, Michael Meier, Basil Valentine. He walked to stand beside her, looking across the top of her head and out into the courtyard. Yellow grass sprouted up between the flagstones. A dark patch on the earth showed where Evelian irrigated the cherry trees; morning light dappling their long oval leaves.

'Lady, you don't need to be told how much I missed you, or how I feared you dead. I even ordered poor Andaluz to make enquiries at the Fane of the Thirty-Sixth Decan. My uncle is afraid of the Decans. He was not admitted, in any case. But you had been allowed in . . . '

She raised her face, and he lost track of his thoughts. He grinned: a rictus.

'I believe that I even missed your friend the Lord-Architect, gods alone know why; but I find myself hoping that he's well, as you are.'

The White Crow blinked as if thrusting away some disturbing image. 'I hope so, too.'

The heat and the white light that came in at the window dazzled Lucas. He rubbed his eyes.

'How could I forget what you said? *In this city, the soul can die, too.* I don't have to be a Kings' Memory to remember that. Lady, I've spent the days studying,

234

learning, at the university; and all the time wondering: has it happened again? Has someone else been taken by The Spagyrus into the Fane and died – died, with no rebirth? And, if it had happened, had it happened to you?'

Lucas, having rehearsed the conversation for a dozen nights, lost the distinction between fact and fantasy, let the tips of his fingers touch her fine hair that the sun made hot.

'No, and no, is the answer. Believe me, you'd know! None of us would be here . . . ' She slid off the window-sill to pace across the room, remove her leather backpack from its chest, and begin to throw into it gem-talismans, amulets, herbs, parchment and tiny bottles of strangely composed inks.

'And I suppose I'd better take Cornelius . . . ' She slid a book into the satchel, paused, and added another. 'And the *Ghâya*.'

'What did the Decan tell you?' Lucas touched her shoulder as she passed him; the cloth of her shirt rough under his hand. 'You don't seem changed, and you've spoken with god.'

'You haven't been in the heart of the world long enough, Prince. You get used to living on god's doorstep, and you get used to some very practical divine intervention, when you live here. Hasn't anyone told you *this is Hell*?'

'I didn't know what they meant.'

'They might equally well have said *this is Heaven*. The gods are here, on earth. Live here, and you live cheek-by-jowl with what moves the living stars in their courses, and the sun, and the earth. When you die, Prince, you'll travel through the Night, and that's the same Night that exists within the Fane, *is* the Fane, grows with the Fane as it's built. Yes, I've spoken with god. Around here, that isn't too unusual.'

Lucas swallowed, wet his lips, touched by something that still clung to her, a scent as of sun-hot courtyards and the silence that stone breathes off under great heat.

'What will you do?'

The cinnamon-haired woman bent to pick up another piece of chalk and tuck it into the side-pocket of her leather backpack.

'I don't know what to do, except that it must be something a Scholar-Soldier *might* do – so I take this.' She touched her pack, her sword. 'And I don't know where, or when; but since it's The Spagyrus who caused this I suspect it's at the Fane, at noon or midnight. And, if I start now, I might just be able to walk to the Fane-in-the-Twelfth-District by noon.'

She tilted the mirror-table, catching sun from the sky-light. Reflections danced on her neck and the underside of her chin. Her mouth twisted in a sideways smile.

'So much *magia* in the air! If I tried to use this, I'd be as deafened and blinded as when the acolytes attacked that hall. And it's the one time I would have risked *magia* to go from here to there without going between . . .'

Lucas frowned, thoughts racing. 'What did the Decan say you should do?'

'Heal. What else would a Master-Physician do? Of course, it would help if I knew who I was meant to be healing. And why the Decan wants them healed, instead of dying on their Fated day and passing through to rebirth.'

'You have a whole sick city to choose from.'

'Oh, Prince.' She straightened up from unfastening her sword-harness and slung the rapier and scabbard across the mirror-table, careless of further damage. 'That was gruesome enough to come from the Lord-Architect himself. You're learning.'

'Growing up,' Lucas said acidly.

'I have never doubted you were grown.' She twinkled. Shifting her attention before Lucas could say any of what crowded on his tongue, she added: 'I am to heal, and Casaubon, I think, is to handle the builders. The strike, I wonder, or the House of Salomon? She revealed nothing to him, nothing to me. Only assured us that we're in the right moment to act. And She should know, being a Decan.'

236

Lucas scowled. 'But if the Decans know what will happen in the future, then why—?'

The White Crow grinned. 'They make the future. They turn the Great Cycle of the Heavens: in the thirty-six divisions of Ten Degrees. *But* . . . many of the Decans are in opposition to one another.'

'With us as game-pieces.'

'Oh, Prince, it's real life; it isn't a game.'

She was a little fey, he thought; and still with that air of the god-daemon about her, as if she could taste the power in her mouth, feel it crackle through her like static. He noticed how she favoured her left hand, the fingers pierced and slightly swollen, pin-pricked with black marks.

'White Crow, I can tell you something. You, or it might be more useful to the Lord-Architect.'

The savour of the knowledge had gone now, gone with the fantasy of her gratitude when she should receive it. He concentrated only on being as plain as possible.

'It started with my wanting to talk to Zari. Knowing she's alive. I haven't seen her yet, but I have seen that priest she went off with – the one that was supposed to have been killed, and now he's a Cardinal?'

'And?' She bowed her head, adjusting the sword-harness so that she could buckle it about her waist, out of the way of the backpack.

'Plessiez and my uncle are old friends. I've met the Cardinal now. Between that and the Embassy files, I'm certain that he's got some very close connection with the House of Salomon, and with the woman that wrote the pamphlet, the one who claims to be leader of the imperial human dynasty.'

She nodded slowly. 'Yes. Lucas, I want you to do something for me. Find your friend, the Kings' Memory, Zar-bettu-zekigal. If your uncle knows her present employer, you should be able to manage it somehow. And if you can't bring her to me, try to find the Lord-Architect and take her to him. He'll need to know everything he can about the House of Salomon.'

237

'I'll do it,' the Prince of Candover said, 'after I've gone with you to the Fane. There are the acolytes. It's too dangerous for you to go on your own.'

She opened her mouth, and he cut off the sharp reply he saw in her eyes: 'Scholar, yes; soldier, yes; but have you been trained at the University of Crime?'

The White Crow's eyebrows went up. 'Well. You might have a point there, prince.'

He watched her for a few more minutes, packing with the ease of practised preparation. The half-grown fox-cubs whined from their box.

'And if it happens again?' Lucas asked.

'It will. Once more. I have it on—' The White Crow paused. 'On very good authority. I can tell you the prophecy. *The Lord of Noon and Midnight will once more break the circle of the living and the dying: in that one hour the Wheel of Three Hundred and Sixty Degrees will fly apart.* What I want to know is, if the Decan of Noon and Midnight knows what that will do, which he must know, then why do it?'

The White Crow broke off. Then: 'She cares nothing for plague. That was apparent. So if She doesn't want me to heal the sick, who am I to heal?'

'If The Spagyrus's alchemy—'

'I know what you're going to say. That that wouldn't be the healing of a body from sickness, but of a soul from The Spagyrus's black miracle: true death. I'm good,' Master-Physician White Crow said, with a smile that never reached her eyes. 'I probably know more about *magia* than anyone now in the heart of the world, the Lord-Architect included. And I've done necromancy in my time. But I wouldn't even know how to go about raising the truly dead.'

Lucas at last identified the energy that moved her: excitement, and a wild fear.

'She said there would be a moment to act. She did not', the White Crow said, 'tell us what we should do. I wish Casaubon were here . . . but I can't wait for him.'

'I'm coming with you.'

238

The woman made no objection, which at first pleased and then badly frightened him. She hefted her pack onto her shoulders, thumbing the straps into place, and walked past him towards the window as she did up the buckles.

'There's more,' she said. 'Something new.'

The White Crow turned her head slightly, so that she looked down into the courtyard and not at Lucas. Her fingers reached for the warm wooden frieze interrupted by the window-frame: the carved skulls and spades.

'Walking here this morning . . . I feel it every time my foot touches the ground. There are focuses of ill and sickness, under the city. Seven of them. Plague-*magia*, I think – corpse-relic necromancy. Either cast while I was gone, or grown stronger in the meanwhile. And becoming more violent with every minute that passes.'

'Necromancy.' Lucas swallowed, saliva suddenly thick in his mouth. 'Lady, I think I can tell you something about necromancy and Cardinal-General Plessiez.'

The heat of mid-morning stifled the small audience chamber. Lengths of fine linen, dyed blue, shaded the great windows; and brown Rat servants cranked the blades of a ceiling-fan. The Cardinal-General of Guiry waved other servants aside as he strode down the azure carpet.

'Your Majesty.' Plessiez knelt, with a flourish, on the dais step of the circular bed. 'I have news, best discussed confidentially.'

The Rat-King sprawled on silk covers. One dictated a letter to a secretary; another held out an arm for a young brown Rat page to groom it; two more played with tarot dice, spilling the bright enamelled cubes on the cushions they lay against. One plump black Rats-King sat himself grooming the knot of their eight tails.

'News?' The bony black Rats-King opened an eye. 'So we would hope. It grows—'

' – late, Messire Cardinal,' finished a fat brown Rats-King, this morning next to the black. He snapped his

239

fingers, dismissing the servants to the five corners of the chamber. 'Well?'

Tension, like static in fur, crackled in the heat-heavy air.

'I have spoken with the architect, your Majesty, and corrected the fault in the drive mechanisms of the remaining siege-engines. They can be set to move whenever you command.'

The formal phrasing came easily. Plessiez kept his eyes fixed on a point just over the black Rats-King's shoulder. Before the King answered, he spoke again:

'Your Majesty, this was done by your will. I have always acted so; I trust that I always shall. You have had your necromancy performed, and by the end of this day there will be no-one who does not perceive the result of it.'

One of the silver Rats-King put down the scroll he was reading. 'Then, all is well, messire.'

'Your engines are ready to be put in place, to ward off the acolytes if they attack.' Memory touched Plessiez's spine with a cold claw. 'But I beseech your Majesty, again, to approve the plan the Order of Guiry has suggested, and spare several such engines for the defence of Human districts.'

Heat soaked in through the linen curtains, and in the silence Plessiez heard the servants whispering in the corners of the audience chamber. The long-bladed fan turned slowly, as if through clear honey.

'St Cyr came to me today.' The bony black Rats-King spoke without acknowledging the Cardinal's last words. He smiled. 'The conspiracy of Messire Desaguliers – or perhaps *coup* is better, since he plans Our removal and replacement – is ripe now. St Cyr believes he and his disaffected friends will act in the next two days.'

'Remove the fool now, your Majesty.'

'I may yet have a use for Messire Desaguliers. But we did not—'

' – ask for your opinion in this, Messire Plessiez.' The fatter of the brown Rats-King spoke again. 'What else?'

Plessiez mentally shrugged, shifted one furred knee on the steps where it began to ache, and reported: 'It's five days, now, since anything at all was observed leaving or entering any part of the Fane. Your Majesty, I believe that means the *magia* begins to work upon them. We should protect ourselves.'

Three of the Rat-King spoke together.

'The humans—'

' – this High Summer fever is our pestilence in disguise. It begins—'

' – to thin down their numbers.'

'They will prove more tractable to our rule if there are fewer of them.' The bony middle-aged black Rats-King shifted, easing over on to his other haunch. 'Yes, Messire Plessiez, we are aware that you find that unpalatable. Government is a hard art, harder than your *magia*. Very well, order the engines to move out – between the hours of eleven and one, when the heat will empty the streets.'

Plessiez, rising to leave, adjusted the hang of his scabbard, and the cardinal's green sash; and at the last couldn't keep from his warning: 'Your Majesty, I know, may hope by this to weaken our masters' power, or even, it may be, to drive them to abandon their incarnation here amongst us. But consider that then we lose not only their oppression of us, but also their protection.'

'We *have* considered it,' the bony black Rats-King said. 'You may go, and do as we order, messire.'

Plessiez bowed deeply, backing across the carpet to the doors. The brown Rat servants opened them soundlessly as he turned and passed through. The airless chamber slicked down his fur with heat. He paused for a moment in the palace corridor to groom.

'Lord Cardinal, a message for you.'

He took the folded paper from the brown Rat, expecting it to be Reverend Captains Fleury or Fenelon, or perhaps something from the military architect. He unfolded it and read:

I have urgent news but can't meet you now, messire. Be

on the Mauressy Docks by noon. The laboriously printed
signature spelled out *Lieutenant Charnay, King's Guard.*

'It's taken me an hour and a *half* to walk here.' Breathless,
Zar-bettu-zekigal sat down heavily on the camp-bed. The
trestles gave out a sharp creak.

'What does the Cardinal-General say?'

'Tell you in a . . . in a minute . . . '

The Hyena paced the length of the temporary pavilion.
Sepia light through the canvas walls sallowed her face. Her
scabbard clashed as she moved. Her plate armour hung
discarded on a frame in the corner of the tent; the woman
wore only her dark red shirt and breeches, sweat-marked
in the close heat.

'Well?' She passed the document-covered desk, ignoring
it for the moment, and finished standing beside the trestle
bed, looking down at the young Katayan woman. 'What
did he tell you?'

Muffled, clocks struck eleven. The harsh strokes barely
penetrated the folds of the pavilion tent.

The young woman leaned back on her elbows on the
bed, looking up. Her pale arms and legs glowed golden
in the sunlight sifted through the canvas. Black lashes
dipped once across dark eyes, before she shifted on to
one elbow, reaching with her other hand for the shoulder
of her black dress.

'I can't believe it: it's so *hot.*'

The Hyena folded her arms, with difficulty keeping a
smile from her face. 'You're a Katayan.'

'I'm still hot!'

The younger woman, eyes holding the Hyena's, undid
with accurate fingertips the hooks-and-eyes that ran down
the shoulder and side of her black dress.

'You're as subtle as a brick.'

'Oh, but, see you, it *works.*'

Amused, exasperated, the Hyena shook her head. 'I
don't have time for this, not now of all times. Tell me
about Plessiez.'

The Katayan lifted her legs on to the trestle bed and rolled over onto her front, so that she lay on the discarded flattened dress, head pillowed on her pale arms. The matt-black hair of her head grew in a tiny hackle down her neck and the pale knobs of her spine, to transform into fur where her tail (wide as her wrist at the coccyx, but flattened) coiled down black and white.

'Don't you ever give up?'

'Never!'

The Hyena seated herself on the unsteady edge of the bed. She reached out and began to rub the younger woman's shoulders. Zar-bettu-zekigal lowered her head, lay with her nose in the crook of her arm. Something brushed the Hyena's shoulder; she started; realized it was the tuft-tipped tail.

'I'm ordering camp struck. Well enough for the Salomon men to fortify their halls, but the dynasty's used to hit-and-run.' She paused. 'We may need to be invisible before the end of today, to attack with no warning of our coming.'

Zari's head came up far enough for her to say: 'That why you shifted the tents down here? To Fourteenth District?'

The Hyena pushed her thumbs into flesh that barely cushioned sharp shoulder-blades, hot under her hands; bracing her fingers on the Katayan's skin. Shadows crossed the tent. No breeze moved the canvas walls. Outside, she heard the shouts of civilian infantry being drilled, spared a moment's thought for the sewer-taught soldiery and this district's militia.

'The Fane.' Her fingers dug into smooth skin.

'Messire the Cardinal says: *Memory, hear: To the leader of the imperial dynasty this message. His Majesty's own precautions will have taken place by noon. If you wish no retaliation, make no attack on them; they are not designed for use against your people . . .* '

The Hyena nodded impatiently. 'I know about the engines in the artillery garden. Zari—'

Still soothing the younger woman's muscles in rhythmic

243

strokes, she found her hands moving as Zar-bettu-zekigal rolled over onto her back, until they rested on her small high breasts. The Katayan put her hands under the back of her head and grinned. A dappled tuft of hair marked her Venus-mound, and pale freckles dotted her belly. The Hyena moved her hands down over the sharply defined rib-cage.

'Your own people's protection I leave to you. My best experts in magia foretell this noontide to be the moment of the Great Wheel's turning. Now, whether it be for the favour of my people or yours, I know not, but such a confusion is cast over all readings for our strange masters the Decans that I confidently anticipate—'

Hardly holding in her impatience, she said: 'Yes? Yes?'

' – anticipate that our bargain reaches its conclusion here. Lady, when the Fane falls—'

The Katayan winced. The Hyena withdrew fingers that had spiked flesh, nodded.

'When the Fane falls, which I believe will be noon today, then, it being everyone for themselves, I bid you farewell, Lady.'

'Damn it, it is, it *is* today! Now – I'll give the alert.'

She sat back, moving to stand. Pale hands reached up. She stared absently down at the young woman, suddenly pulled her up to sit on the bed and threw her arms about her in a fierce embrace. Zar-bettu-zekigal yelped in her ear.

A voice outside the tent called: 'Lady Hyena!'

Ignoring Zar-bettu-zekigal's oath, she shouted back to the sentry: 'What is it, Clovis?'

'Vanringham's on his way through camp,' the muffled voice called. 'You said this time you'd see him, Lady.'

'Send him in.' She stood, strode to the desk, suddenly spun round in her tracks. 'Zari, out!'

'Ei, what?'

'You can't be allowed to talk to him. Out. Come on, out now!' The Hyena pulled her up by the wrists, and the Katayan came unwillingly to her feet.

Fists on bare hips, she glared. 'Oh, *what!*'

'The back way. Now!' She bundled up the crumpled black dress, thrust it into the younger woman's arms, head turned to catch the announcement of entrance. 'Vanringham's from one of the news-broadsheets. You can't talk to him.'

The dress dropped to the floor. The young Katayan woman's shoulders straightened. She glared up from under her fringe of black hair, taut with anger. 'I'm a Kings' Memory. I talk with whoever asks me—'

'Exactly, and you're not talking to the press. Now, *out* when I tell you!'

A horn blared outside the pavilion. The sound of mailed tread approached. The Hyena took a step forward. She watched as Zar-bettu-zekigal bent and scooped up the dress, clutched it to her bare stomach, and then hesitated.

The sentry outside called: 'Lady Hyena, the representative of the Nineteenth District broadsheet.'

The Katayan's head turned as the canvas wall of the tent quivered. Her chin came up. Hooking the dress on one finger, she slung it over her shoulder, sepia light sliding down her naked shoulders, breasts, hips and legs; and walked with something of a swagger to the curtained exit.

'Zari.'

Loud enough to be heard, the Katayan spat: 'If you didn't want a Kings' Memory, you had no business talking in front of one!'

Tail flicking, she strode out as the sentry and the new arrival came through the canvas passage; nodded a casual greeting at the gaping men, and walked out into the blazing sun.

The Hyena brushed the lank hair back from her face, sighing. The man escorted in, small and middle-aged, with white hair that stuck up like owl's feathers, turned his head back from following the Katayan's exit.

'*Do* you have a Kings' Memory in your employ, Lady?'

245

She ignored his question. Passing Clovis on her way to sit down, she said quietly: 'Call in the council of captains.'

Sepia light gleamed on the banners of the dynasty, draped white and gold at the rear of the tent. A flash of white light glinted from the armour-stand as Clovis lifted the curtain on his way out. The Hyena walked slowly round to sit behind the desk, facing the broadsheet publisher, the gold-cross banners at her back.

'Messire Vanringham, I want to show you something.'

She uncreased a folded broadsheet that lay on the table, on top of unfolded maps. Her own face looked up at her in shades of grey from the paper, slanting brows made heavy by shadow.

'I do not ever recall telling you, Messire Vanringham, that the army of the human dynasty is made up from "criminals escaped from oubliettes, the disaffected, the lunatic; and the young enticed by drugs or seduced by treason". Nor that "their leader, claiming imperial blood, is in fact the child of a shopkeeper and a Tree-priest" . . . '

The man scratched at his head, spiking the hair into further disarray, and then rubbed his nose vigorously and dug in the pockets of his stained doublet for his notebook. Unembarrassed, and possibly unafraid, he said: 'I print what I have to, Lady. Else I lose my printing press to the Rat-Lords.'

'Criminal.' She let sweat shine on his forehead before she added: 'But you need no longer suffer it.'

Light and heat momentarily glared as Clovis re-entered. Armour and swords clashed, the tent suddenly full of bright metal and gold-cross surcoats: eight or nine other captains entering with him. They knelt before the Hyena.

A little uncomfortable, Cornelius Vanringham looked at her across their lowered heads. The Hyena waited until she could see the professional hardness re-enter his gaze.

'We're ready to make the announcement today, messire. I want you to put out a special edition. Print it now, send it out to the five quarters here, and to as many other Districts as your delivery-men can reach—'

He made a protest patently not the one in his mind. 'But the strike?'

'The people will break it. This is for the human dynasty and the House of Salomon. And don't worry about your masters and your printing press.' She waited a heartbeat for the doubt to clear from his face. Seeing it would not, knowing the man's reservations, she grinned.

'Don't forget how far and how fast I've come. You'll believe me by the end of the day, Messire Vanringham. The story you'll print shall be this: that the imperial dynasty is at last ready to resume its place as the ruling power in the heart of the world.'

Heat-haze lay over the lagoon and the expanse of dock-yards. Zar-bettu-zekigal hooked together the last hook-and-eye on the shoulder of her black dress, the cloth hot under her fingers.

'Bitch! Cow! Shitarse!'

She slammed her fists down on the balustrade of the bridge. A fragment of stone plopped into the canal below. She leaned over, staring down into the ripples. All the docks stood deserted. No barges sailed down from the arsenal; the booms and cranes of the Moressy dock-quay stood silent.

Faint but audible across the half-mile distance came the noise of the impromptu camp: imperial soldiers and the House of Salomon.

'Bitch . . .'

She leaned her elbows on the bridge, on clumps of grass that grew in the pointing. Eyes unfocused, she watched sun dance on the lagoon. Haze obscured sails on the horizon. Her gaze dropped, and her eyes abruptly focused.

'Oh, what!'

She put one foot on the rough brick, hoisting herself up; then slid down, ran barefoot down the further steps and ducked into the shadow of the canal bridge. 'Charnay!'

Cold metal slipped across her shoulder to lie against her neck.

'Don't be ridiculous!' she snapped. 'It's *me*.'

The rapier lifted. A deep laugh sounded in her ear. She turned. Burn-patches and scars marked the big brown Rat's fur, and her cloak and uniform were missing. She gave Zar-bettu-zekigal a confident smile. 'You've come from Messire Plessiez?'

Zar-bettu-zekigal shook her head.

'I sent a message,' Charnay complained, resheathing her rapier. 'He should have been here at noon.'

'That's an hour yet!' She saw the big Rat scowl. 'Charnay, where have you been? What's been happening?'

The brown Rat raised her head, listening for footsteps. 'Take me to Plessiez.'

'Can't. Kings' Memory business. Got to go back and find out if the bi— If she's got messages for him.' Zar-bettu-zekigal brought her tail up to scratch her upper arms, tingling from the sun. 'Isn't as easy as it sounds, but I have to. Charnay, where *were* you?'

'With the Night Council.'

'Who?'

The brown Rat opened her mouth as if to speak, then shut it. Transparently awkward, she cast about for something and finally pointed out into the lagoon. Heat lay white on the blue sea, on the sand-bars that lined the horizon. The sails of the small fleet of ships hung like faded washing, casting for every faint breeze.

'I've been watching that fleet come in. No pilot-ship?' Charnay said wonderingly. 'No tugs?'

Zar-bettu-zekigal narrowed her eyes and did her best imitation of Messire Plessiez. 'Charnay, someone once told you about changing the subject, but you never got the hang of it, did you? That's the strike. Now, what's this "Night Council"—?'

She grabbed Charnay's arm, and the big Rat winced as her fingers tightened.

'Charnay, wait! I *know* one of those ships. Those are the banners of South Katay!'

A smell of *magia* haunted the air like burning.

The White Crow tensed her fingers against the hot leather of reins, halting the brown mare. Hoofs broke the silence with hollow concussive noise. Something drifted past her field of vision, and she reached out with her free hand, snatching; and opening her hand on a black feather. She blinked back water, staring at the empty furnace-sky.

'In which it is seen', she murmured, 'how a prince turns horse-thief. Very useful, your university training; we may yet make the Fane by noon.'

She pulled the brim of her black-and-white hat down firmly to cut the glare, squinting at the walls and shuttered windows of the Twenty-Third District's deserted street. Almost at the brow of the hill now. Despite talismans of cold, she wiped a face hot and sweaty.

'I hear something.' Lucas reined in the black gelding.

'I sense something.'

She lifted her leg over the saddle and slid to the street, slipping off her sandal and resting her foot on the flag-stones. Stone burned her bare toughened sole.

'Seven focuses of plague-*magia*.' Two hours' riding left her throat sandpaper and her head pounding. 'And, yes, it's more than a summer pestilence. There are diseases of the flesh that have their resonances in soul and spirit.'

'How far away?'

'They're widely scattered. Even the nearest is a damn long way off.'

She forced concentration: cut out the weight of the leather backpack, the swinging scabbard at her hip, the mare's head lifting beside her shoulder and tugging on the reins.

'They're coming up to crisis-point now, I can tell that much. I could try to reach one – but if I even try to go for it, I'll miss The Spagyrus at noon. Damn. *Damn.*'

Lucas slid down from his stolen hack to join her. A red head-band had been tied raggedly about his black hair, and a knife jutted through the belt of his knee-breeches. He hissed as his sandals touched the cobbles, and grabbed for the talisman at his neck.

'I meant that—'

A grinding roar drowned his words.

The White Crow straightened. The mare skittered back; reins jolted her arm and shoulder-joint. Hoofs hit the cobbles inches from her feet. Automatically searching for *magia* words, she hesitated; her wet hands lost grip as the mare reared. Lucas swore, ducked back as the gelding kicked. Both horses clattered in circles in the street, the noise echoing from white porticoes; diminishing as they cantered back down the hill.

Lucas swore steadily and vilely under his breath.

'What-the-fuck-is-*that*?' he finished.

A machine rumbled towards them.

It towered level with the flat marble-balustraded roofs. The White Crow pushed back the brim of her hat, staring upwards at the bright metal housings that shot back highlights from the sun; at the two beaked rams like claws at the front, and the metal-sheathed ballista at the rear: a rising scorpion-tail. Brown and black Rats crouched on the carapace-platform carrying muskets.

'It's a siege-engine . . . It's a *Vitruvian* siege-engine . . .'

Noise thrummed through the flagstones of the street and the bones of her chest; she felt in her belly the juggernaut weight of it. Its massively spoked iron wheels turned with a ponderous inevitability.

Lucas's arm flattened her back against the wall. The noise roared into her head, spiking her ear-drums. She stepped back up onto a doorstep. As the engine drew level, the platform some eight feet above their heads, two of the blue-clad Rats lowered their muskets to point at the Prince of Candover and the Master-Physician.

'What—' Temper lost left her breathless. 'What about my fucking horse!'

Lucas's hand shook her arm. She turned to see him mouthing, inaudible, eyes bright; some convulsive emotion twisting his features. She shook her head, cupped her hand over her ear. He took both her shoulders in his hands, and turned her to face the front of the engine.

The throbbing machine backfired in a cloud of sweet-smelling oil and cut down to a tickover. She fingered her ear, wincing. In the comparative quiet, a voice above her said: 'Is it damned *passengers* now?'

The White Crow lifted her head. A metal trapdoor stood open in the upper casing. Filling every inch of the gap, an immensely fat man in rolled-up shirt and eye-goggles leaned massive elbows on the trapdoor rim. He reached up and shoved the goggles off his eyes, into his cropped orange-red hair.

A white mask of clean skin crossed the Lord-Architect's face at eye-level, clearly showing his freckles. The rest of his face, hands and arms showed black with oil and grease. He dabbed at his chins with a rag, small in his plump fingers, that appeared once to have been an embroidered silk waistcoat.

'Valentine!' He beamed. 'And my young Page of Sceptres, too. This city is remarkably short of trans-port at the moment, it would seem. Can I offer you a lift anywhere?'

Andaluz eased a finger under the tight ruff of his formal doublet, sweating in the docklands heat. Sun flickered up off the harbour water. The Candovard Ambassador stepped away from his private coach, signalling his clerk to attend him, and walked down the wide marble steps to Fourteenth District's north-quarter quay.

'But it's almost deserted. Dear girl, where are the other ambassadors?'

The clerk, a thin red-haired woman in black, shrugged.

'They were notified of the putative Katayan state visit, Excellency. Pardon me, Excellency, I don't even see a Rat-Lord here to greet them.'

Voices drifted on the wind. Andaluz risked a glance behind, across the sands of the airfield and the deflated airships, to where the marble buildings opened out from a great square. The size of the crowd, to be heard at this distance . . .

'They would have overturned us, simply for breaking the transport strike. I hardly blame the Rat-Lords for not being on the streets,' Andaluz said drily.

Across the lagoon, under the noon heat that leached all colour from the blue water and the bright flags, the unwieldy galleons spread all sail to catch the scant wind. Andaluz's pepper-and-salt brows met as he frowned, estimating. How long to come to safe anchorage at this deepest quay? He cocked his head, listening to a distant clock strike the half-hour.

'Noon,' he guessed. The clerk bowed.

'Excellency, if there are no lords here from the heart of the world, and no other ambassadors, I foresee that the King of South Katay will ask you many awkward questions.'

'Simply because I'm here? Dear girl, I can't ignore our duty because of that unfortunate fact.' Andaluz folded his hands together behind his back. Without a tremor of surprise, he added: 'But *this* young lady should be able to tell you considerably more about South Katay than I can. Claris, you'll have seen her with Cardinal-General Plessiez and myself.'

The clerk murmured: 'She's the one Prince Lucas wants to see? Shall I follow her when she leaves?'

'Of course,' Andaluz confirmed, mildly surprised; and raised his voice to call: 'Honour to you, Mistress Zarbettu-zekigal.'

The Katayan woman trotted down the wide flight of steps to the quay, a brown Rat following her at a distance. She nodded absently to Andaluz, squatted down on the marble quay beside a silver mooring-bollard, and rested her arms on the metal and her chin on her arms.

'*Some*thing's wrong. See you, messire ambassador, when were you told this was happening?'

'Three days past, when the fleet passed the mouth of the estuary. You heard nothing from your august father?'

'Oh, if he's here three months after me, he must have left soon after I did. Takes close on a year to get here from South Katay.' The young woman straightened up and turned to sit on the bollard. As the large brown Rat joined them, she indicated the harbour with a sharp jerk of her head.

'See you, *some* of those are Katayan flags. That one isn't. Nor's that. And as for that last ship . . . '

Andaluz found the red-headed clerk at his elbow. She stooped slightly to speak in a low tone.

'Excellency, the last ship's banners are from New Atlantis. I recognize them – from my history studies at the University of the White Mountain.'

The Candovard Ambassador's head came up, chin and small beard jutting. He put a reassuring hand on the clerk's arm. Half his attention fixed on the King's daughter – she now leaned up against the big female Rat, pointing to the ships, chattering in an undertone – and half his attention on the ships.

'My dear,' he interrupted Zar-bettu-zekigal, 'will you do something for me? Will you count how many ships there are?'

'Oh, sure.' The Katayan's dappled tail came up, tuft flicking to point at each one. 'The one with Katayan banners, the one with the high poop-deck, the one with blue flags, one with bad hull-barnacles, and one with what your friend calls New Atlantis banners – six.'

Her tail drooped.

The big brown Rat guffawed, clapping her on the shoulder. 'Call me stupid, girl? You've added up five and made six!'

Andaluz numbered them softly over in his head.

'One,' he counted. 'And one, and another one . . . another one, and one more . . . and I see six of them still.'

The clerk nodded. 'So do I, Excellency.'

The brown Rat, still frowning, moved back towards the steps, as if she had business urgently elsewhere. She carried her rapier unsheathed now, and Andaluz had not seen her draw it. The young Katayan ignored the Rat's muttered question. One pale fist knotted in the cloth of her dress, black fabric bunched.

Her pale eyes met Andaluz's gaze. 'Those are oldstyle Union-of-Katay banners. Not my father's.'

The Candovard Ambassador nodded. He planted his feet apart, tugging his doublet straight, gave a glance to the sun's position, and then stared out across the half-mile of water separating ships from the dock.

'My dear, it seems to me that one of those ships must be the Boat.'

Beetles and centipedes scuttled across the marble paving, fried by the approaching-noon sun. Something rustled on her arm, and the White Crow's fingertips brushed chitin: a locust skittering away. She wiped her upper lip free of sweat. She could hardly look up at the sky. The shadow of the siege-engine fell on her as welcome shade.

'This really is the most amazing machine to drive.' The Lord-Architect Casaubon beamed under oil-smears. His head lifted, chins unfolding, as a clock chimed the half-hour somewhere down towards the docks. The White Crow bit her lip to keep a grin off her face.

'How long have you been now? Here?'

He gazed down from the engine-casing, rocked a podgy hand back and forth. 'Since dawn, this day?'

'Yeah, that's about when I found myself.'

Catching the Rats' attention on her, she switched to a language of more distant origin.

'I'm trying for the Fane-in-the-Twelfth-District, to enter at noon. If not, it'll have to be at midnight.

254

But I don't think we have that much time. And then there's . . .'

She flicked a brief gaze to the hot flagstones. Casaubon ponderously nodded.

'What lies below? Oh, yes. And almost ripe, by the feel of it.' His bulk shifted. 'Valentine . . . Pox rot the Decan; She robbed us of a month! We could have discovered the nature of this *magia*, and how to prevent it.'

'I can hazard a better guess than the great Lord-Architect Casaubon?' The White Crow wiped her wet forehead. 'Amazing. But talk to Lucas about the crypt under Aust-quarter. This is a plague-*magia*, responsible among other things for this High Summer pestilence. I believe I know who made it, but I don't know why. What advantage is it to the Rat-Lords to have humans sick now?'

She shifted one bare foot scalded by the hot paving, and raised it to slip on her shoe. 'And, if I go after it now, I'll miss entry to the Fane.'

The Lord-Architect rested bare arms on the engine-casing, wincing at the heat of sun on the metal, obviously feeling for a foothold in the bowels of the machine. Slowly he heaved his immense torso upwards. His shirt snagged on a rivet, tore free.

'Pox rot it, She gave me my own task to do; and I *must* do it. I must see the builders. If you haven't returned after noon, I'll come for you.'

He sat up and swung his massive legs over, slid down to the main part of the platform, and knelt to offer the White Crow a hand to climb up.

'If I can meet you, yes, we'll debate what we do next. If noon's the crucial time, then act as and how you can. I don't like the feel of the day.'

Metal rungs hot under her tender palms, she climbed the ladder; grasped his hand and swung to stand on the steel-plated platform. The Lord-Architect rose to stand beside her. Somewhere he had shed one stocking, and his shoes were caked with white mud.

'I wish', the White Crow said, 'that She had been a *little*

255

more forthcoming in what She wants us to do.'

From the height of the platform she could see how, ahead, the street opened up. She stared down the hill to the lagoon, the airfield and the rising slope of marble temples beyond, and – highest, farthest – the black aust-northerly horizon of the Fane-in-the-Twelfth-District.

'I do what I can, Master-Physician. I am only' – Casaubon put one massive hand on the stained shirt over his heart – 'a poor Archemaster and Master-Captain.'

'This is *serious*. Lucas . . . Lucas?'

Glancing down, she missed the Prince of Candover. His voice came from the rear of the engine-platform, as he scrambled up the metal ladder near the ballista and hailed a black Rat.

'Messire Cardinal!'

The Rats in Guard uniform fell back from the edge as the black Rat signalled. Sleek, a few inches taller than Lucas; he rested his ringed hand on the hilt of his rapier. The Rat stood lightly, tail cocked, black feather-plume at a jaunty angle, with a silver *ankh* at his collar, and only the rich green silk sash to mark him more than a priest.

'Where's Desaguliers?' The White Crow touched Casaubon's sweat-warm shirt-front. 'Those are Guiry colours. *That's* the Cardinal-General of Guiry? That's Plessiez?'

The Lord-Architect opened his mouth, shut it again, shook his head and made *later* gestures with his plump fingers.

The Prince of Candover walked down the platform, apparently unaffected by the sun-heated metal under his thin sandals. 'Messire Cardinal-General Plessiez. We've met, you may recall it. At the Embassy, with my Uncle Andaluz.'

The black Rat's snout wrinkled in a smile. 'And also, Prince, I think we met in the crypt below Nineteenth District's Aust quarter. But that I have not yet discussed with your uncle the Ambassador.'

'In a crypt!' the Lord-Architect snorted *sotto voce*.

Lucas's gaze moved across the White Crow's face, his own blank as any diplomat's; and she watched with a professional appreciation that momentarily, pleasantly, masked her urgent fears.

'The very question I wanted to raise, Messire Plessiez,' Lucas said. 'You'll recall I was with a Katayan girl then. Mistress Zar-bettu-zekigal – Zari. Her friends have been afraid she was dead. I'd very much like to speak with her again.'

The black Rat raised one furry brow.

About to speak, the White Crow hesitated as she felt Casaubon's voice rumble through his massive torso: 'I, also, think it would be rewarding to speak with the Kings' Memory. Valentine, you'll be unaware of it, but I met her this morning, in company with the Cardinal here. A most *delightful* young lady.'

She blandly ignored his last comment. The Lord-Architect's apparent smugness gave way to apparent pique. She smiled.

'You may be overstepping an archemaster's privileges, Messire Casaubon.' The black Rat's expression flickered, the glint of anger in bead-black eyes.

'But,' Plessiez continued smoothly, 'in point of fact, I was about to suggest the same thing. I sent Mistress Zaribet to the great square in Fourteenth District with a message, and she may still be there. Perhaps, Prince Lucas, I could beg you to accompany us?'

Still in a distant language, the White Crow murmured: 'That one won't get as much out of the Prince as he hopes, though I see he'll try.'

'And your delightful foreign friend,' Cardinal-General Plessiez continued, 'who I take to be a practitioner of the noble Art? Madam, if you seek employment, I could find a use for a prognosticator of fortunes.'

'As well as for a Lord-Architect?' the White Crow challenged. 'Who you seem to have riding in this monstrosity as well as building it—'

'Driving, not riding,' Casaubon corrected with mild

257

hurt. 'Master Plessiez here has promised me an intro-
duction to the leader of the House of Salomon, one
Master Builder Falke, in the great square. Therefore I
accompany him.'

'Falke?' The White Crow put her palms back against the
hot metal casing of the upper engine, supporting herself.
Between tension and delight, she grinned at Plessiez. 'So
this Master Falke came out of the Eastquarter hall alive?
I was told he died. But, then, I was told *you* died there,
your Eminence. One can't trust rumour!'

Brown Rats in King's Guard uniform leaned at their
stations on the engine's carapace, shading eyes against
the brilliance, or checking the loading of muskets and
calivers.

'You know Falke, madam?'

'I know of him. I know of you.'

The click of a rifle-bolt echoed back from the house-
fronts. A sweet stink of oil choked the air, throbbing up
as the siege-engine ticked over. Plessiez glanced over his
shoulder at the Prince of Candover.

'I see . . .'

The Lord-Architect Casaubon interrupted: 'We can
drive to our destination by way of the Twelfth District,
Valentine. Certainly! You'd be late if we left you to walk.'

Plessiez opened his mouth to protest.

'Oh, certainly,' the White Crow deadpanned. 'I'll never
get Lucas to steal me horse and tack again in the time left.
Of course, if it weren't for this *thing*, we'd still have the
mare and the gelding . . .'

Hot sun beat down. Marble roofs and frontages, gold
and white against the blue, breathed back the silence that
comes from hot stone. The tickover of the siege-engine
came back from street and alley walls like the beating
of surf, mingling with the offhand talk of the Guards as
they patrolled the platform or squatted down against the
shaded side.

The Cardinal-General frowned with an expression
condemning bad taste.

258

'Madam, this is not a day upon which to make jokes.'

'I know, your Eminence. I know that better than you appreciate.' The White Crow tilted her hat-brim down to shade her eyes. 'Let's speak of necromancy, shall we?'

Desaguliers walked past the turning treadmill, not pausing even to brush the sparks from his fur as they fell from the crackling chandeliers. One sweating human face turned towards him. He slapped the end of his tail against the bars. 'Get working.'

'Scum!'

Unbelieving, he swung back to throttle the whisper out of the naked straining worker. Before he could reach her, a Lord Magus in a golden robe appeared at his elbow.

'All's arranged.'

He felt a small hard object pressed into his palm.

'Watch me, then. Don't miss the signal.' Desaguliers, sweating in the heat of midday, the audience hall's closed curtains and artificial light, let a cynical smile appear on his lean features. 'I've known too many of these affairs be messy failures. This one has to succeed. If I go down, I'll take all of you with me.'

'We never doubted that, messire.'

Desaguliers left him, walking under the clover-leaf vaults of the great chamber, now bright with the flare of generated lights. He pushed between two Rats, one in blue satin, one in linen and leather; both feeding by hand and from the same dish their leashed human slaves.

A flurry in the thick crowd caught his attention. A tall Rat in the gold of the Lords Magi, awkwardly riding the shoulders of a female brown Rat-Guard, yelled a drunken toast to the four or five hundred packed into the hall: 'The King!'

Different voices chorused: 'The King and victory!'

'To our future without masters!' the Magus echoed, slipped, and slid to vanish from Desaguliers' sight into the crowd and a roar of laughter.

Pushing onwards, elbowing, the former Captain-General

259

worked his way towards the circular dais-throne. The crowd grew thicker. He thrust a way between four female Rats in Guard uniform, a priest, a cluster of gallants quarrelling; stepped down hard on the long-toed foot of a dazed-drunk brown Rat and opened a gap in the front row.

The Rat-King sat among wine-stained cushions, under the incandescent glare of the lights. Receiving toasts, congratulations; waving away a messenger, talking to a priest in the robes of the Abbey of Guiry, bright-eyed with victory celebrations . . .

'Messire Desaguliers!' The younger of the silver-furred Rats-King raised a wine-goblet in ironic salutation. 'Have you come seeking your co-conspirators?'

Silence began to seep into their immediate circle.

'Conspiracy?' Desaguliers asked mildly.

'Janin, Reuss, Chalons,' the silver-furred Rat-King enumerated. 'And, of the Guard, Rostagny and Hervet—'

' – Volcyr, Perigord, de Barthes,' the bony black Rats-King picked up, turning away from the young female Guiry priest. 'If you have come enquiring for them, I recommend you seek them out in the palace oubliettes. But, then, you'll—'

' – be there in their company soon enough.' A brown Rats-King flopped down on his belly, tail cocked high, and wrinkled his nose dazedly. 'Drink, man! We'll settle your execution tomorrow. Things will be different tomorrow.'

'They certainly will.' Desaguliers spoke over the nearest of the crowd's ragged cheers. He made a low formal bow and, as he straightened up, added: 'You were well informed about the conspiracy, your Majesty. If not quite well enough.'

'Shilly.' The brown Rat-King closed his eyes suddenly.

'Are you still a danger, then?' the bony black Rats-King said. He sprang to his feet, dragging the knot of co-joined tails painfully towards him. Standing knee-deep in the silk cushions, he flung out a hand.

'Enough leniency. *More* than enough. Shoot him!'

The Rats nearest Desaguliers started, whiskers quivering; backed up hard against the packed crowd. The Guards around the dais raised their loaded muskets, struck tinder for the fuses. Someone at Desaguliers' elbow screamed. The Rat-King pointed again, shrieking: '*Shoot!*'

Elbows rammed into his ribs; feet clawed him, pushing away. Desaguliers, swordless, grinned a ferocious grin and kept his feet; watching the smouldering musket-fuses, praying that the Lord Magus' lent magic would – *once*, it only needs to be this once – work for him.

He flung up his hand and crushed the tiny glass sphere that he carried in his hand. '*Now!*'

The sputtering chandeliers died momentarily; then blazed up with a glare that lit the closed draperies like a gunpowder-flash. Hot splinters of glass rained down among screams. Desaguliers threw himself flat as a musket discharged, heard the shot whistle past his head and *thunk* into something with a noise like a butcher's cleaver hitting bone. Wet blood spattered his fur.

On his knees, jaw aching from some unrecognized blow, he heard what seemed at first to be a continuation of the bulbs breaking. The full-length windows shattered, draperies billowing inwards. Daylight blazed in, and dust.

Through clouds of dust and stone-fragments, Desaguliers saw the metal-tipped beak of a battering-ram. Panicked Rats all but crushed him as, now, they struggled as hard away from the windows as they had from the dais. Desaguliers sprang across the intervening distance and landed on the Rat-King's throne.

'*Nobody move!*'

The spur of the battering-ram, joined by a second, pushed collapsing wall and window-frames into the audience hall. Dust rained down on silks and satin and fur. Screams and cries echoed. A silver Rats-King sobbed. The vast bulk of a siege-engine rumbled through the destroyed wall and on to the inlaid-wood flooring, grinding up planks as it came. It blocked the shafts of sunlight spearing the dust.

'Here!' Desaguliers held up his hand, signalling to the Rats in Guard uniform crouching on the main platform, who now, swords in hand, leaped down and began shoving the crowd together in smaller, terrorized groups. One group remained on the engine-platform, firing a musket-volley into the King's Guards.

The leader, St Cyr, picked a way from the siege-engine between the wounded through to the throne, fastidiously wiping blood and dust from his black fur.

'Saw your signal,' he said. 'The rest are in position at the back of the building.'

Desaguliers looked down at the bony black Rats-King, crouching at his feet in the silken cushions.

'Your intelligence was good,' he advised, 'but not good enough. Think about how many more of these engines we may have stolen out of Messire Plessiez's control. And then you can be thinking about how the Rat-King, tomorrow, will still have a master. The senate of our new republic.'

The gangplank grated as it hit the quayside.

Six or eight very young children leaned over the Boat's rail, screeched, slid back; and the Candovard Ambassador heard their shrill voices calling, bare feet thumping on the deck, high above and invisible.

'Sir?'

Andaluz looked at the red-headed clerk at his elbow.

'My dear girl, you don't suppose that – No. He would be on the Boat when it docks under the White Mountain, not here. I mean my son.' A sea-breeze gusted in his face. He rubbed absently at his hair, feeling it stiff with salt. 'My late son. You'd recognize him easily, Claris. He bore a remarkable resemblance to my nephew.'

Noon shadows pooled on the white marble quay; from the brown Rat, the Katayan, and the two Candovards. Ropes strained from the bollard beside the four of them to the moored ship. Black tarred planks rose up above the Ambassador's head, plain and solid in the sun. He craned his neck and read the name of the Boat cut deeply into the hull. *Ludr*.

'An old word: it means "ship",' he said, 'and "cradle", and "grave" . . . The other ships are gone?'

The tall young clerk squinted into the light off the harbour. 'Yes, sir.'

Zar-bettu-zekigal pointed. 'It's still flying a Katayan flag!'

'Among many others.' Andaluz rested his hand on her shoulder, restraining her impatience.

'I don't understand.' The brown Rat, Charnay, padded back down the marble quay steps and halted beside Zar-bettu-zekigal. 'When those five galleons were coming in, we couldn't see this one; and now we can see this one the others have vanished.'

'Oh, what! Haven't you ever seen the Boat before?' Zar-bettu-zekigal leaned back on her bare heels, tail coiling up to scratch at her shaggy-growing hair. 'See you, must be hundreds of 'em on board. Boat hasn't been in all this summer.'

Above, furled sails gleamed an ochre, sand-coloured white in the midday sun. From the decks came the clamour of children's voices.

'I can't stay here for this,' Charnay protested. 'I must find Messire Plessiez. The Night Council want him!'

Andaluz let their voices fade into the background. The sun beat down on his uncovered head; he blinked away heat-dazzles in his vision, sweating. Sounds came clearly: the shift of the horses, restless in the shafts of the coach up on the promenade, and, far off across the airfield and the square, the roar of voices . . .

The gangplank creaked.

Andaluz straightened, unconsciously assuming the position of formal greeting. Then his ramrod spine relaxed. He smiled wistfully.

A child some two or three years old staggered down the plank. Another followed it, dark as the first was fair; squatting to prod at the sun-softened tar on the plank.

When she stepped onto the quay she took the other child's hand. Both walked away.

'They . . .'

Andaluz held up a hand to arrest Claris's words. He peered up at the light-silhouetted deck, seeing another child, two more; a group of a dozen Ratlings, burnished pelts bobbing in the sun. They clattered barefoot down the gangplank, swarmed for a moment about him, so that Andaluz looked down on the heads of small children, surrounded.

All silent now, all solemn; looking up at the Katayan woman, the Rat and the Candovards.

He knelt, reaching out, almost touching the arm of a small boy no more than two. The child looked with blue eyes, dark blue eyes so nakedly curious and real that Andaluz shuddered. He sat back, slipped, reached up to grip his clerk's arm. By the time he rose to his feet, the crowd of human and Rat children were beginning to back up on the gangplank. He stepped to one side.

'They forget. Travelling through the Night, they forget.'

One cried shrilly. Another laughed. All children, all under the age of three; they ran, suddenly, in the bright sun – running off along the quay, up to the airfield, down towards the promenade, scattering like a school of fish.

'No shadows.'

'What?' He looked where Claris pointed, at a small girl who plumped down trying to unpick threads from the mooring-rope: the hemp wider around than her small wrist. He saw only a tiny rim of black about her feet.

'They grow 'em in a few minutes.' Zar-bettu-zekigal stood on the tips of her filthy toes, peering up at the deck. The flood of children swept around her like a tide. Andaluz saw her reach out absently from time to time and touch a fair or dark head. He glanced around for Charnay. The brown Rat stood staring to and fro along the quay.

'He might have recognized me if he were here . . .'

A silence breathed off the tarred planks, muffling the creaking of the mooring-ropes. The voices of the children, not yet having speech, cried like distant gulls. Andaluz took out a kerchief and dusted his nose with some energy, wiped the corners of his eyes, and squinted up at the sun-drenched Boat.

A figure appeared at the top of the gangway, walking slowly down to the quay. A tall man, thirty or so, with long black hair; his bony hand holding the paw of a brown Ratling. Andaluz, glancing down, saw neither had a shadow.

'Sir, I greet you.'

Their eyes met his, and Andaluz inclined his head, falling silent. A shadow of night still lay in their gaze. He stepped aside, bowed. The man and the Rat child walked past without a glance at Claris, Zar-bettu-zekigal or Charnay.

Another man appeared from the deck, then a sun-haired woman; two black Rats, fur dulled with the salt breeze; a young man with cropped black hair. Andaluz felt his pulse thud, once, before he recognized it as only a chance resemblance.

'I've waited a long while.' He looked at Claris. 'I can wait, it seems, a little longer.'

'If we're not needed, sir, may I suggest that we would be safer back in the Residence.'

The disembarking humans and Rats momentarily separated him from his clerk. Andaluz turned, brushed shoulders with Zar-bettu-zekigal, who stood gazing up at the pennants streaming from the mainmast.

'Lady, if you're going back into the city, may I offer you a ride in my coach?'

'Right!' She spun around, pivoting on one heel with dappled tail out for balance. Her grin shone in the sun. 'I need to get back to the square in Fourteenth's north quarter. So does Charnay. Can you drop us off there?'

Forming a tactful evasion, Andaluz began to speak, and cut himself off as he saw her gaze go over his shoulder and her sepia-brown eyes widen.

A voice shouted: 'Zar!'

Andaluz saw the recognizable Katayan speech sink home into her as an arrow does. Caught with one heel resting on the stone quay, weight on the other bare foot, tail coiled down, she for a moment looked all child, bewildered as the embarkees from the Boat. He waited a second to see if he would have to catch her as she fainted.

Zar-bettu-zekigal whispered: '*Elish?*'

'Necromancy . . . '

The White Crow said: 'You heard me, Eminence.'

The Lord-Architect reached down one oil-black hand and touched her dark red hair, frowning. She saw Lucas's head turn, and his startled expression.

The black Rat, Plessiez, murmured urbanely: 'I fail to follow you. What would a Cardinal of Guiry know about such heresies as necromancy? Come, come, you know as well as I do: there is a weak *magia* of the dead played with the discarded shells of souls, that is, bodies; but it has no power, and so is not worth speaking of.'

'And if souls died like bodies?'

The Cardinal-General appeared frankly angry. 'What nonsense. I won't listen to blasphemy. Under our masters the Decans, the dead travel through the Night and return on the Boat; there is no other death.'

The White Crow held his bead-black gaze.

'I'm a Scholar-Soldier, your Eminence, and while we travel you and I should talk.'

The black Rat suddenly laughed. His sleek jaw rose, light gleaming from his fur. The black feather on his head-band swept the heated air.

'A Scholar-Soldier! Oh, come now. On this day of all days, to present me with some mythical human organization—'

'This day?' The White Crow hooked her elbow over the steel rungs of the nearest ladder. She leaned back easily. 'Your Eminence, today's the Feast of Misrule. When servants beat their masters, Apprentices give orders to Fellowcrafts, Rat-Lords serve feasts to their human slaves, Cardinals tend humble priests – and the Thirty-Six Decans, it seems, leave the solving of cosmic riddles to poor, blind, stupid human scholars.'

She wiped her mouth, dry with the day's air; grinned at him with sweat-ringed eyes.

'And the Rat-Lords loose a plague amongst the human population of the heart of the world. Your Eminence, please. I *do* know about these things.'

Expecting no honest answer, she shivered when he inclined his head, his glittering black gaze still holding hers.

'Do you? Well, then, madam scholar. What can it alter, now, for it to be known? – There is unrest. Order must be restored. With so many humans passing onto the Boat to begin their journey through the Night, they will be weakened beyond opposition to the King. Do you see?'

The White Crow absently lifted her free hand to her mouth, sucking dusty rose-scarred fingers. 'Truly, Eminence?'

The sleek Rat, black fur almost blue in the intense sun, shrugged lithe shoulders and gripped the hilt of his rapier. 'Madam scholar, what I have done I have done with my King's authority, and my own full knowledge. Now, if you will be so kind as to excuse me, I must finish the matter.'

'No. I won't excuse you.'

Her mouth curved up, a smile unwillingly rising; and she flipped her arm loose from the side-ladder, took the black Rat by the elbow and ushered him a dozen steps into one of the protruding sections of the upper platform that served as a shield against forward attack. She glanced back, seeing them out of earshot of the others.

He made no resistance, meeting her gaze with contained amusement.

'Well, madam scholar?'

'Master-Captain, as it happens.' She grinned. 'White Crow is my name.'

Above, the sky tilts towards midday. The weight of

267

its heat lies heavy on her shoulders. The White Crow breathed a deep scent of oil, dust and harbour wind; shuddered with an instinct that presaged some manifestation of a *demonium meridanium*.

'Eminence, how can I convince you to talk to me? I've spoken to the Candovard Prince, and to others. I could probably give you the names of those who attended a meeting in Fourteenth Eastquarter's Masons' Hall, and tell you what was said there.'

She shifted, aware of the straps of her pack digging into her shoulder. The hilt of her sword-rapier scraped the metal carapace; the black Rat raised a furry brow.

She said: 'Someone had to be supplying the raw materials.'

All his lithe body stilled.

'Materials?'

'I've been asking myself questions while I was riding, your Eminence. Such as: What was a priest of Guiry doing with bones in an Austquarter crypt? I'm a Scholar-Soldier; I know that there have been four true deaths in the heart of the world. I may have known that before you did; I've been in the city a while.'

Some fragile accord, born of the hot sun and urgency and the knowledge of crisis, hung unspoken in the air between them. The black Rat nodded, approving.

'Master-Captain, you are a true practitioner of the Arts.'

She reached for the talismans at her throat, gripping them as if she could squeeze chill into her flesh.

'I guessed at where the bodies might be. In the city crypts. Where else do you put a corpse? And what other kind of corpse would give you the raw materials for necromancy? Hence this plague-*magia*. There's more to it, yes, but I believe what I'm saying is true.'

He smoothed down the Cardinal's green sash with a demure humour. 'Yes, Master-Captain. I think that I, also, believe that what you say is true.'

The White Crow touched his arm. Sun-hot fur burned her fingers.

268

'Eminence, tell me. *You need to*. I know. Don't ask me how I know. Not all the talents of a Scholar-Soldier are easy to analyse.'

The lean bulk of him blocked the sun, brought a certain coolness to her. The tender flesh of his nostrils flexed, vibrating wire-thin whiskers; and his voice, dropped to the threshold of audibility, contained a grating endurance.

'Can you take the weight of it, do you imagine?'

She shrugged.

'Messire, when one arrives at our age, it's with a baggage of emotional debts – and they're rarely repaid to those whom we owe. Others have taken the weight for me in the past. I'll do it for you now.'

He looked away, squinting at the bright sky. 'You are older than me, I think.'

'Am I?'

'Old enough to forget. What it is to *win* – you forget that. I can tell by the look of you.'

Wiry muscles shifted under the sleek pelt as he straightened, hind feet in the balanced stance of the sword-fighter. The blue sky glimmered beyond his sparkling gaze.

'I can have anything I want.' Plessiez laughed, musing. 'Luck put the Austquarter crypt in my way, and yet I have years enough of study to know what use to put it to. Luck put Guiry into my hands, and I had wit enough to take it. And if luck gives me a lever with which to move the Thirty-Six Themselves – well, why shouldn't the universe give me what I want?'

The black Rat exhaled. She smelt his breath, musky and metallic.

'So. I take a great part in this, and as great a responsibility. And, if I am honest, greater ambition – but I perceive you are aware of the goads of ambition yourself.' He looked back at her, nodded once. 'Oh, yes. It's apparent, if not relevant. And, to fall to the matter in hand, there have been others in as deep as I.'

The White Crow shut her mouth, which she had not been aware hung open.

269

'True. There were two other leads I'd have followed, if I'd had the time: a Reverend tutor of the University of Crime, and a priest from the Cathedral of the Trees.' She paused. 'Messire Cardinal, I don't know you, and I wish I did. I would like to know if *you* know what will happen, now, with your plague-*magia*.'

Softly he stressed: 'Not mine. Not mine alone.'

'No . . . '

They stood in silence for a moment. The black Rat snorted quietly, and gazed at the Guards manning the siege-engine with immense satisfaction.

'I have some conception of what approaches. But what is one to do? We have strange masters. And one may sometimes hope to outwit them.' Amusement, amazingly enough, in his voice. 'Madam, having come so far and so fast, and through such strange occurrences, I am ready to credit the existence of an Invisible College. Tell me, if you hazard a guess, what is to happen now?'

Fragile accord bound them for a moment in the sunlight.

'I've . . . been away. Eminence, this is how it seems to me.' Her acute gaze flicked towards him. 'I think noon will see another true death. Caused by that *magia* which you, and perhaps his Majesty? yes – which you have scattered under the heart of the world . . . '

He motioned with one hand, as if to say 'Go on'.

The White Crow took off her hat and fanned herself with the brim, and replaced it on her head. The sun burned hot on her hair. 'Only I don't know, messire, if you know all of what that *magia* is intended for.'

A sardonic stare met hers: as curious, and as cynical. The White Crow swallowed. Her shirt clung to her breasts, wet under the arms, her own sweat rank in her nostrils.

'I spoke with the Lady of the Eleventh Hour,' she said. 'We all speak with Decans, your Eminence. Me with mine, you with the Decan of Noon and Midnight, The Spagyrus.'

'The Order of Guiry's relations with The Spagyrus

have always been most . . . cordial.' Cardinal-General Plessiez straightened. 'That really is enough, Master-Captain, unless you have practical advice for me.'

'You know what another death of the soul could do?'

'I conceive some idea.'

'Truly?' She stared. 'You knew what you were doing?'

A chill entered the Cardinal-General's voice. 'I believe I did.'

Their fragile accord parted as spider-thread parts in a summer breeze.

'I can't believe that *anyone*—'

The siege-engine shook, motor roaring.

The White Crow gripped the jutting shield-wall. Plessiez's warm body brushed hers as he grabbed at the same support. She twisted to stare over her shoulder. The Lord-Architect had vanished: the engine-trapdoor stood open.

'*No* – I permit it!' Plessiez snapped an order; the Guards remained at their stations. The motor coughed a cloud of blue smoke and groaned as the wheels gripped the cobbles. Noise increased, plateaued. The beaked rams swivelled as the siege-engine ground to point north-aust.

The White Crow regained balance; the weight of pack and sword heavy on her. 'You'll allow this?'

The siege-engine thrummed, gathering speed. Streets flowed past. She rocked with the velocity. Ahead the sky turns ashen with the first finials of the Fane-in-the-Twelfth-District.

'It is no great detour. I have the time – and, possibly, I admit, the necessity – to indulge my expert engineer. I regret,' the Cardinal-General's voice rasped, pitched to carry over the metallic clash of gears, still with a mockery in it, 'I regret what you will find when we leave you, madam. It has been so for five days, for all of us; even for your kind – the Fane is closed to all entry now.'

Zar-bettu-zekigal pushed past Andaluz, dodging the Boat's speechless passengers; and he shaded his eyes against the

271

glare. A Katayan woman of medium height and in her middle twenties walked down the gangplank, peacock-blue satin coat and white breeches gleaming in the sun.

Her shadow lay on the plank, sharp-edged and blue.

'Elish? Oh, what! What are you *doing* here? How come you're on the Boat? You haven't been through the Night!'

'I did die, little one. I'm back now.'

Short black hair fell in curls over her pale forehead, a lace cravat foamed in ruffles under her chin; and she whisked a tail as black as her hair through the slit in the satin coat. 'Father told me the court seers predict ill fortune for you. I came to do what I could. How else could I get here and not spend a year travelling, except on the Boat?'

'Elish!'

Zar-bettu-zekigal flung her arms around the older Katayan woman, hugging her violently. The older woman patted her back. She raised her head, and Andaluz saw her smile as she met his eyes. He straightened his doublet and executed his best formal bow.

'Madam, I take you to be from the South Katayan court? May I, on behalf of the Candovard Embassy, welcome you here, and offer you any assistance that you may need?'

'Sir, I thank you. I—' The Katayan woman prised Zar-bettu-zekigal's head out of her lace ruffles. 'Zar'! Behave. What have you got yourself into *now*?'

Still with her arm about the woman's waist, the young Katayan faced Andaluz. 'This is my best full-sister, Elish-hakku-zekigal. Elish, this is Ambassador Andaluz; he's Lucas's uncle. Oh, dirt! You don't know Lucas. Or messire the Cardinal. We have to talk! I've been working as a Memory. Messire Andaluz, may my sister come in the coach with us?'

Andaluz smiled. 'Of course, child.'

'We'll have to take Charnay up to the square with us. *Charnay!* Get over here, you dumb Rat. And then there's the Hyena – Elish, you have *got* to meet her, she's wonderful!'

The black-haired Katayan smiled tolerantly.

'Another one of your true loves, Zar'? Messire Ambassador, I apologize for my sister. I would be extremely grateful for your hospitality; there are matters that I wish to discuss. I have some informal status as plenipotentiary envoy from South Katay.'

Andaluz lifted his head, scenting on the breeze something at once sweet and nauseous. It faded. He looked around at the sun and the sea and the white marble of the docks, deserted now but for the last travellers on the Boat, walking away into the city. The brown Rat had her snout lowered, listening to something that the clerk explained with short abrupt gestures. Andaluz saw both of them glance up the steps towards the airfield sands.

'You've walked in on a critical moment, Madam Elish-hakku-zekigal. I think the wisest thing that I can offer you and your sister is the protection of the Embassy Compound.'

'Oh, *what*!' Zar-bettu-zekigal stepped away from her sister, planting her fists on her narrow hips. 'I have to find the Hyena and Messire Plessiez. I've got work to do!'

'I really would advise—'

A screech ripped into his ear. Andaluz jerked around, one hand automatically clapped over his left ear, blinded by the sun off the lagoon-harbour. A blaze of red and yellow flapped in his face. He stumbled back.

A new voice called: 'Careful! You'll frighten him! Here, Ehecatl; here, boy.'

The brilliant-feathered bird scuttered in the air, circled, and fell to perch on the shoulder of a woman who stood halfway down the gangplank. Andaluz brushed furiously at his guano-spotted doublet and breeches.

'Madam, I really must protest!'

'Really? Then, please don't let me stop you.' The woman tapped her way down the gangplank, leaning on a bamboo cane.

Andaluz looked down at her as she approached. Skin shining a pale ochre, braided hair shining white, she stood barely as tall as his collar-bone. Lines wrinkled about her eyes as she smiled up at him, a woman some years short of sixty.

'Sir, I apologize. The journey's been hard, and I fear I've not arrived in time. Elish, help me with my baggage, please. I have two trunks on deck. Can you and your – sister, is it? – fetch them down here?'

The young Katayan gaped, then followed the elder with trepidation up the gangplank and leaned over to grab two cases, careful not to set a foot on the deck of the Boat. Andaluz rubbed his mouth thoughtfully, managing to conceal a chuckle.

'Sir, I don't know who you are.' The parakeet clung to her shoulder, guano spotting the crimson, purple and orange-patterned linen robes that swathed her. A small humming-bird hovered around her head, brilliant blue; and from a fold in the robes at her breast a dusty sparrow peered out.

'Candovard Ambassador, madam. My name is Andaluz. Welcome to—'

'An ambassador? How marvellous! *Just* the man I wanted to see.' She snapped her fingers. 'Elish, help your little sister, will you? Those cases must *not* be damaged, and they're heavy. Now, messire – Andaluz, is it? – kindly call me a carriage, and make sure that the horses are lively. I've much to do.'

The woman tapped past Andaluz, his clerk and the brown Rat. Andaluz caught a glimpse of gold sandals under the trailing robes. Sprays of scarlet-and-blue feathers had been braided into her long white plait. Now three bright humming-birds hovered in the air around her.

'Make haste!' She snapped her fingers again, and the two Katayan women fell in behind her, each with a small brass-bound trunk on her shoulder.

'Madam, I—' Andaluz moved forward, and found himself running up the quay steps to catch up with the

274

woman. 'I don't think you understand. It's dangerous to be on the streets today. If you'll come with me to my Residence . . . '

Breath failed him at the top of the marble steps. The small woman paused, looking up at him with eyes bright and amber as the parakeet's. Laughter shifted in the lines of her round face. Shadows fell across her: high and distant, circling wings. Andaluz glanced up into an empty sky. When he looked down, the shadows remained.

Speaking with an inborn respect for *magia*, he asked: 'Lady, may I know your name?'

The older Katayan woman shouldered her trunk, sweating in the heat, and said: 'Messire Ambassador, this is the Lady of the Birds.'

'Luka to you, young man. Now . . . '

She smiled, disclosing crooked but white teeth, and rested her light hand on Andaluz's; a smile of such sweetness that he forgot his breathlessness and concern.

'First,' the Lady Luka said, 'I need to find my son. I believe he's here in the heart of the world. You may know of him. He's a Lord-Architect. His name is Baltazar Casaubon.'

The acolytes swarmed, their flight warping sky and light.

Warm dust skirled about the White Crow's ankles, blowing across the lichen-covered steps. Heat slammed back at her from the stone. Swinging the backpack from her shoulders and squatting, frog-like, she rummaged for a strip of paper written over with characters.

'C'mon, girl, come *on*; you haven't got all day—'

Echoes of her mutter clicked back double and triple from the Fane of the Decan of Noon and Midnight. Arches, pinnacles and buttresses reared above and around, blackening all the north-aust sky. She irritably rubbed the hair out of her eyes; pinned the thin strip of paper in a tight four-way loop about the hilt of her rapier.

A cracked elderly voice called: 'Here's another fool! Another one as mad as you are, young Candia!'

She risked a glance down the steps. The abandoned scaffolding shimmered in the heat. The path ran back between pyramids of bricks, gleaming like black tar under the sun; vanished among abandoned piles of half-dressed masonry. At the foot of the steps of the Fane a man stumbled as he walked, supported by the arm and shoulder of a white-haired woman.

The White Crow stood. 'Get *up* here. No, don't argue; get up here in the shelter of the arch. I don't know who the hell you are, but if you want to stay alive to regret this, *move!*'

She slung the pack up on her shoulders and gripped the hilt of her sword. The corded grip fitted her palm easily, smoothly; with the hard feel of something right and fitting. She raised her head.

High above, circling, swarming, no larger than birds or insects at this distance, acolytes flew restlessly up from pinnacles, gutters, high Gothic arches. One beast swept low, gargoyle-wings outspread, bristle tail lashing the air. High-pitched humming chittered in the heat.

'Oh shit . . . *move!*'

A small old woman in a blue dress limped up the steps, one arm tightly hooked about a fair-haired man in his thirties. The White Crow grabbed the man's arm, thrust him under the overhanging carving of the great arched door; reached a hand to the old woman and dodged back with her, eyes still fixed on the sky. The acolyte hovered, wings beating, raising up dust.

'Saw you on the road behind me. What in gods' names possessed you to come here?'

'We might ask you the same thing, missy.'

The man's voice, amazed, said: 'She's a Scholar-Soldier.'

Heat reflected back from the dizzying heights of stone above, and from the great brass-hinged wooden doors. The White Crow coughed, smelling a sweetness of roses. She risked an eye-watering glance at the sun. Overhead: closing fast with noon.

'Not fast enough. Now, there's an irony.' Her pulse thundered away the minutes, beating in her head. She fingered the talismans with a sweat-slick hand, *magia* protecting against heat, not against fear. 'And if the damn place is closed anyway—'

'*Where were you?*'

Startled at the man's intensity, she backed a step or two into the archway and glanced up at him. Fair hair flopped across his bruised-looking eyes. With one hand he made an attempt to pull a stained and stinking doublet into some kind of order, a gesture that degenerated into helplessness. His blue eyes glared.

'*Why* didn't you come to the university a month ago?'

Warm alcohol-stinking breath hit the White Crow in the face. Turning, eyes on the wheeling gargoyle-shape now riding an updraught, she snapped: 'Should I have?'

'We sent out messages for a Scholar-Soldier! We tried to contact the Invisible College for months!'

'Damn.' She stopped dead. 'Are you *Candia*? I've been asking Evelian about you—'

'Now wait *just* one moment.' The old woman's face creased into a frown, smoky-blue eyes darkening with anger. 'Do I understand you, Reverend Master? You've been in contact with these vagabond scholar-mercenaries? In direct contravention of university regulations? And just who are *we*?'

The man lurched forward. The White Crow grabbed his shoulder one-handed, found herself supporting half the man's weight. Now four shadows wheeled and skittered across the stone steps.

'Get back, rot you!'

Her left hand throbbed. She thrust him back, gripping the rapier, eyes never leaving the movements above, point mirroring flight by instinct and long practice.

His voice came from behind her. 'We prayed you'd come in with the new intake, a month ago. When I told Bishop Theodoret there was no-one . . . '

Something that might have been a sob or a gasp of pain

interrupted; his voice picked up after a second.

'I have to rescue him or kill him now, lady. *Where were you?*'

'Me? I've been here all along. The Invisible College never has been the best-organized—'

Cold air screeched across her skin; she whirled, thrust upward, darted back. The blade sank home, ripped free. A bristle-tail lashed the steps. White stone chips flew up, stinging her cheek. The lichen on the steps began to glow with a yellow luminescence. The beat of wings hissed in the air. Dark bodies dropped down from the soaring flock.

'We're going to miss noon by minutes.' Frustrated, she stared down at the heat-soaked abandoned building site; seeking cover, seeing only temporary salvation. Feeling through the soles of her feet the *magia* in the depths, necromancy boiling to crisis, that stirred the servants of the Fane to bloodlust. 'Minutes, unfortunately, will be enough. Damn, I think he was right: the Fane *is* closed.'

A spot of blood dripped from the rapier to her bare foot. She winced at the caustic impact. Waiting: waiting for the circles of Time to slide and interlock, mesh into the Noon that will open the Fane-of-the-Twelfth-Decan to mortals. Eyes running water, she stared up through circling wings at the sun still minutes short of midday.

'Girl!'

The White Crow swung round. The old woman stood at the great carved doors, one veined hand just leaving the bronze ring. At her touch the black wooden slab swung open a yard, and another. Sun-dusty beams of light slanted into the interior of the Fane.

'It's not time!'

Above, the chittering rose to shrieking-pitch. Dark wings tumbled across an air suddenly yellow and sere.

'Heurodis,' the woman said, folding a thin strip of metal and secreting it back in her cotton sleeve. 'Reverend Mistress, University of Crime. *I* have no intention of waiting out here to be attacked.'

The White Crow wiped her sweating face, pushing the silvered red hair back behind her ears. Aware that her mouth gaped open, she shut it firmly; caught the blond man's elbow in her free hand, and stepped smartly after the old woman, shoving the door to with her heel as she crossed the threshold into the Fane.

Silence shattered.

Raggedly at first, then in a roar, a hundred thousand men and women began to cheer.

' – *And now!*' Falke gripped the loudspeaker microphone tightly. '*The Feast of Misrule's truly started! With our strike-carnival!*'

The square rippled.

His silk eye-bandage blurred Fourteenth District's great square with black. Textures of cloth overwove the sunlight, snared the blue sky in threads. Falke blinked, strained vision.

The mass of people seethed.

He clenched his own hand at his side, seeing so many arms flung up, so many hands waving. Sweat ran down between his shoulder-blades; the heat of his mail-shirt robbing him of breath. Cheering racketed back from the distant façades of buildings.

'Listen to that!'

'I hear it.' The Hyena jostled his elbow, steel vambrace hard and hot in the sun. Through his shielding silk the visor of her helm flashed as she slid it up; red-brown eyes sharp. 'I see it. Now?'

'Now.' He wiped the sweat from his forehead, grinning. Abruptly he signalled.

Shadowless heat hammered him from the north-aust.

All this fifth side of the square lay demolished. Mansions torn down, ragged edges of brick and masonry and dug-up foundations cast aside in great heaps. Cranes and earth-movers rested, poised. He rubbed the silk tighter against his face, through blurred vision making out the sixty-acre clearance, the scaffolding at its entrance – and the great block of granite held in a cradle of rope and steel wire.

'Now, my baby . . . '

He shook his head and chuckled. A wind blew from the square behind him, carrying the smell of human sweat, of beer and sharp wine and the powder from muskets.

'Now's our time.'

The rope cradle creaked, inching round. He squinted at the cranes, unable to see the workers. Only the yellow-and-white Salomon colours. He paced four steps along, four steps back, booted heels kicking.

He cut the air with his hand: the lateral swing ceased.

Hieroglyphics shone on the great foundation-stone, newly incised; gleaming redly, as if the cut stone filled up with blood.

He turned his face up to the sky, letting the breeze cool his sweating face, turning back as the granite block stilled. Packed faces: painted, masked, laughing, calling; the rows of silent Rat-Lords at the nearer buildings' windows.

He touched the Hyena's steel shoulder. 'Wait for me here.'

He ran careless of obstacles down the rutted steps to the front of the site, the microphone clasped in his fist. Soldiers in imperial mail and citizen militia shoved the crowd back. Men and women reached between them, over their shoulders, hands outstretched; and Falke waved good-naturedly, trotting along some yards until he swung and faced out into the crowd.

'*Long live tradition!*'

His voice echoed back from far walls, soft as surf in sewer-tunnels that riddle the docks. Paper streamers soared up into the air, and bottles; and he turned his face full up to the sun, careless of dazzlement.

'*Long live tradition, long live the Feast of Misrule!*' He paused, letting them quieten a little. '*Yes, the great and ancient Feast of Misrule . . . This annual day when all's turned upside-down – and we, yes, today, WE turn the world upside-down! Only this time, it STAYS this way! You see the stone. It is our stone, it is our foundation-stone:*

280

the founding-stone of the New Temple of Salomon!'

Cheers broke out, doubled and redoubled.

He strode another few yards along the steps. A paper streamer glanced across his shoulder; he gripped it in the same hand as the microphone, waved it, grinned at the feather-masked boy, dimly seen, who'd thrown it. The boy pulled off his mask, eyes bright, mouth a round O.

'The world turned upside-down – you've all heard that prophecy.' The metal of the microphone, warmed and dampened by his breath, chilled his lips. *'Hear it and believe it! Oh, not the Rat-Lords; they don't matter now – although they may still think they do.'*

Falke paused, lifting a hand in ironic salute to the black Rats lining the overlooking windows. One looked down at a broken flower in his hand. Another, head-band in hand, smoothed a feather. None spoke.

'You will say they have been challenged before, these masters of ours. So they have. So they have. I was a part of that summer, fifteen years gone. Fifteen years ago, in Fifth District, when they cut us down in the streets – rode us down, for daring to refuse our labour!'

Now he dropped his tone caressingly; walking down the scarred marble steps to the line of soldiers, touching hands with the people beyond as he walked along the front row, invisible to more than those few but letting the loudspeakers carry it.

'I have never forgotten. You have never forgotten. Now we can erase it from our minds. Now, today, we labour only for ourselves.'

He halted, lowering the microphone.

Faces, hands, swords, mail-shirts: the front row of the crowd a tapestry, sun-bright and raucous. His mouth dried. He swallowed with difficulty, blinking; the touch of silk strange against his lashes. He reached up and pulled the bandage free.

'They have always betrayed us.'

Tears streamed hot down his cheeks; a bubble of laughter in his chest for this final public hypocrisy.

He snatched breath suddenly, tears of the bright sun becoming the wrenching tears of a man who assumed, until then, that he only cries for appearance's sake.

'We can be true to ourselves.'

Warm wind bathed his fingers as he held up his hand, poised; cut the air with one decisive stroke. He let his hand fall to his side.

Through his feet he felt the vibration of the Temple's foundation-stone settling into its place on the site behind him.

'The foundation-stone is laid! Now feast and rejoice. Feast and rejoice – and build the New Temple of Salomon!'

He laughed, recklessly reaching into the crowd again to grip hands; his tear-streaked naked face dappled with paint, daubed on by small children held up by their parents.

'Now drink! Eat! Rejoice! BUILD THE TEMPLE!'

Breathing hard, he stumbled back up the steps. A glare of silver: he seized the Hyena's plate-clad arm for support; leaned with his head down for a moment, breath sobbing, and then nodded.

'At last.' She signalled.

The imperial soldiers fell out the rank that held the crowd back. First one, then ten, then dozens of men and women ran forward and up the steps to the open site; meeting there the Fellowcrafts of the Masons' Halls. Falke gazed at the river of silks and satins, masks thrown down and trodden underfoot as the skilled workers swarmed over the foundations and scaffolding and cranes.

The Hyena held up her gauntleted hand, the soldiers linking arms again to thin the flow.

Falke covered his eyes, between sweating fingers watching the tide of masons, carpenters and builders spread out across the open ground behind him.

Exhilarated, the Hyena swept her arm in an arc. 'Look at it! We've done it.'

'I . . . hardly believe it.'

He retied his black silk bandage. The last of the first

282

shift of workers walked across the steps to the site. The rest settled: men and women sitting down where they stood; bottles and food brought out, masks pushed up so that eating and drinking could begin. The noise of their singing, clapping and shouting beat back from the distant walls.

The Hyena yawped a laugh. 'No going back for us. Not now, whatever happens.'

The rising tide of sound drowned thought. He wiped his nose on the sleeve of his grey doublet, and rested both hands on his wide sword-belt. The ring-guards of the sword-rapier brushed his knuckles. Standing with feet apart, welcoming the weight of weapons, he peered through black silk at the crowded day. Faintly, through the shouting and music, a clock on the far side of the square chimed quarter to the hour.

'Ahead of schedule.' He smiled, finding his voice thick with the aftermath of weeping.

'*Ah.*'

'What is it?' He peered at the Hyena, straining to see which way she faced, what she stared at. 'Lady?'

'I think – right on schedule.' Amused surprise rounded her tone. 'This is effrontery of the first order. What *does* he think I'll do? Clovis!'

Clovis and a dozen other soldiers doubled up the steps to join her. Falke frowned. Shoved back, he elbowed his way to the Hyena's side, demanded:

'What is it? What's happening?'

The woman shaded her eyes against the sun, staring out across the great square. Frustrated, Falke followed the direction of her gaze. Waving arms, thrown hats and occasional muzzle-flashes from muskets: the rest a cloth-shrouded blur.

A groaning vibration came to him through the earth he stood on.

'All King's Guard by the uniform.' The Hyena's grin widened. 'Good firepower, but they're somewhat outnumbered. We'll accept their surrender. Clovis, take a squad

283

down there and escort them here. Master Falke, can you see? There.'

A deep-throated mechanical roar drowned crowd-noise; and he wrinkled his nose at the stench of oil. Light glinted – from windows, stone surfaces. Swords? Gun-barrels?

Fine detail faded into sun-blaze.

Counting on a second's view before blindness, Falke snatched away the eye bandage. Tears ran down his face.

Shockingly close, rearing above the impromptu tents of the Hyena's camp and the crowd: beaked rams, hammered steel plates, curving ballista.

Midday sun gleamed from the blued-steel barrels of muskets, from unsheathed swords, and from the harness of Rat-Lords seemingly as small as children, crouched on the platform of a great armoured engine of war.

'There must be two hundred thousand people here!'

Lucas leaned tight into the steel wall-shield of the siege-engine, the metal platform hard under his knee. Curving hot metal sheltered his body ahead and to the side. From where he crouched, he could see the other King's Guard behind the shelters.

Tens, dozens, hundreds of faces turned upwards. Looking at the siege-engine. Faces caked with white lead and yellow ochre, the colours of the House of Salomon.

The engine's noise drowned all but the tolling of the charnel bells, coming raggedly from the quarters beyond Fourteenth District's square. His grip on the support-strut grew sweat-slippery. Blood pounded in his head, and his hand went automatically to the talisman at his neck.

'Casaubon! Lord-Architect!'

Lucas rapped on the hot metal of the engine-hatch. Heat throbbed from a bright sky.

'Slow down! If we hurt anyone, the rest'll tear us to pieces!'

'Pox rot it, I'm doing what I can!'

The thudding vibration of the machine diminished,

the juggernaut wheels slowing. Heat shimmered across packed bodies.

The Lord-Architect Casaubon heaved himself up through the hatch, swore as his bare arms touched metal, and lifted his immense buttocks up to rest on the rivet-studded platform.

'And at that, we're almost too late.'

His stained linen shirt and corset obviously discarded somewhere in the engine compartment, sun pinked the slabs of fat cushioning his back and shoulder-blades. Black smears of oil covered his faint freckles, glistened on the copper hairs on his chest. He picked his nose and wiped the result on the metal hatch-casing.

'Let me get this thing on to its station and primed, and I'll shake the truth out of that sleek ruffian who calls himself a Cardinal! *Then* we'll see!'

The Lord-Architect reached up. Lucas stretched out a hand, gripped his; steadying the immense bulk as the man rose to his feet.

He let go, wiping his now-oily palm on the back of his breeches.

Casaubon drew himself up to his full six foot five, lifted his foot, brought it down, and with his stockinged toe hooked his discarded blue satin frock-coat across the platform towards him.

Sun hammered Lucas's scalp. He blinked rapidly.

'Nearly noon. The White Crow. She will be all right, won't she?' His voice thickened. 'Stupid question. She won't be all right unless she's very lucky. And that goes for all of us, doesn't it?'

The Lord-Architect reached into the voluminous pockets of his once white silk breeches and brought out a silver flask. Lucas reached across as the big man offered it, up-ended the flask down his throat, spluttered into a coughing fit, and at last managed to hiss: 'What *is* this?'

Casaubon scratched at his copper hair and examined his fingernails for oil and scurf. 'Turpentine?'

'What!'

'I beg your pardon,' the Lord-Architect said gravely, 'metheglin is what I meant to say. She's a Master-Captain, boy, and a Master-Physician. More than that, she's Valentine.'

'What . . . ? I don't . . . '

As Lucas watched, bewildered, the fat man slid down to seat himself with his broad back against the ram-casing. The Lord-Architect screwed up his eyes almost to the smallness of raisins against the glare off the page, and began to write painstakingly in his notebook, resting it against his bolster-thigh.

'There.' He tore the pages out with a delicate concentration, folded them, retrieved a gold pin from the lapel of his rescued jacket and pinned the paper shut.

Lucas hunkered down, resting his brown arms across his thighs. 'Well?'

'We arrive, but in time to do nothing.' Casaubon lifted his head, losing at least one chin. 'Get over to the University of Crime. Rouse the students. Give this to the Board of Governors – no, *don't* argue with me, boy. Tell them it's no use their thinking all this pox-blasted foolery is beneath them; they must act, and I'd be obliged if they'd do it *now*.'

'Explain to me just exactly how I . . . ' Lucas stopped. 'You're serious, aren't you? I don't know why, messire, but the White Crow thinks you know what you're doing. Tell me how I get away from here and I'll give it a try.'

'Prince Lucas!'

The Lord-Architect lifted one copper brow at the new voice. 'Monstrous inconvenient.'

Cardinal-General Plessiez stepped out from the group of Guards on the platform and approached Lucas, pitching his voice over the crowd-noise. Sun shimmered from his black fur, from his *ankh* and green sash.

'An interesting woman, your magus, Prince Lucas. What can she hope to say to the Twelfth Decan?'

Buildings blocked the view behind them now; no sign of the marble terraces and the hill they had descended. Sun blurred Lucas's vision; he rubbed his eyes. Nothing to see from here. Not even that last glint of sun from her sword, herself a tiny blob of colour walking into heat-shimmer.

Sudden, clear, he feels the shade and cool interior of the house on Carver Street; a holistic flash of white walls, piled books, cracked mirror-table, and the woman's heat-roughened voice.

'According to you, there's no way into the Fane.' He attempted to eradicate hostility from his voice, achieved only sullenness. 'What's it to you, priest?'

'Still intransigent. I should have known when I met you. A King's son.'

Lucas frowned. On the north-aust horizon, around the Fane's black geometries, the summer air swarms thick with acolytes; gargoyle-wings beating as they hover, sink, aimlessly circle.

The smooth voice insinuated. 'And yet you're not with her now, messire. Did she just need a university student to steal her a horse when there are none to be had?'

The siege-engine creaked past the façades of ornate buildings lining the square. Pale plaster shot back sunlight and heat. Lucas stared grimly up at ornaments, strapwork, hanging flower-baskets. Rat-Lord spectators crowded balconies and windows. A brown Rat flourished a plumed hat; two drunken black Rats began tossing broken flowers down from pots on to the heads below.

'I can thieve,' he said. 'I don't have *magia*. She'd have been wasting her power protecting me. That's why I'm here and not with her.'

'But a magus—'

Something slithered across Lucas's bare ankle. A coiled paper streamer drifted across the platform, snagged, then pulled away.

Casaubon slammed his hand against the side of the machine. Iron echoed. 'What's happening, Plessiez? Where's your damned Master Builder? And young Zaribeth?'

A brown Rat called: 'Your Eminence!'

287

'You see we face some delay. The crowds,' Plessiez said silkily; and before he could be answered strode back to take a report from the Guard.

Lucas glanced back with a casual intensity, seeing the blue-liveried Guards positioned at each of the metal ladders. At the foot of the engine the crowd massed concealingly thick. The Lord-Architect beamed and prodded Lucas's chest with a fat finger, nearly overbalancing him.

'It'll work. You'll see.'

The black Rat, Plessiez, standing with the Guard, cast speculative glances up at the gleaming beaked rams and the high cup of the ballista. He murmured: 'We *must* stay on-station here at the south-aust side, at least until the stroke of midday.'

'Yes.' The Lord-Architect sounded grim. 'We must.'

Canopies of silk rose on this side of Fourteenth District's great square, great tents shining white and painted with the gold cross of the House of Salomon and the Sun of the Imperial Dynasty. Light glinted off laminated armour. Beyond the soldiers, scaffolding rose, great spider-structures of poles and platforms and cranes.

Lucas stood and shaded his eyes. 'Will you look at that!'

'It may have been wise to bring more men.' Plessiez walked to the front of the platform just as the Lord-Architect rose to his feet.

Heat shimmered over desolation.

A spiderwork of girders and scaffolding stretched away, covering sixty or more acres, the site rawly hacked out of the classical buildings surrounding it. Lucas stared at men and women swarming over heaps of brick and masonry. A great granite block towered in the foreground.

Lucas felt his skin shudder as a beast shivers. Realization hit hard and sudden: a jolt of cold injected into the blazing heat.

'They've started building.'

He shot a glance over his shoulder, knowledge of foundation rites brimming on his tongue; silenced himself in

288

the face of the Rat-Lords, and turned back to stare at worked stone, sunk in the earth, cut in proportion and inscribed.

'There is your revolution,' Plessiez remarked acidly at his side.

The Lord-Architect's head swivelled ponderously, surveying. His chins creased as he beamed, looking down at the Cardinal-General, nothing but innocence in his blue gaze.

'Wonderful! Obvious why they've started building now, of course. Someone's given them the Word of Seshat.'

Plessiez's fur, where it brushed Lucas's arm, prickled with a sudden tension.

Lucas looked up, met his black gaze. 'Yes, my uncle told me you have an interest in architecture, your Eminence. Human architecture. Speculative *and* operative.'

Plessiez stood four-square on the iron platform, balancing on bare clawed hind feet. A smile touched his mouth, the merest gleam of incisors. His head came up, the line of snout and jaw and sweeping feather-plume one clean curve in the midday heat. He turned his black eyes on Casaubon.

'Being a Lord-Architect, I suppose that would become immediately apparent to you. Yes. It's true that I put Messire Falke in the way of finding the lost knowledge he sought. I did not, until now, know the name of it. So the lost Word to build the Temple of Salomon is the Word of Seshat?'

'Mistress of the House of Books,' Casaubon said reverently, 'Lady of the Builder's Measure.'

The siege-engine inched forward, slowing now to a crowd-pressed halt. The Lord-Architect swung his arm around until it rested lightly across Plessiez's shoulders. He looked down over the swell of his belly at the black Rat.

'Why, Master Cardinal?'

A kind of relaxation or recklessness went through the black Rat. Lucas saw him look up at Casaubon, fur sleek

'*Mistress of the House of Books, Lady of the Builder's Measure.*'

From *Rituale Aegypticae Nova*, Vitruvius, ed. Johann Valentin
Andreae, Antwerp, 1610 (now lost – supposed burned
at Alexandria)

and shining in the sun, one ringed hand touching his
pectoral *ankh* while his scaly tail curved in a low arc
about his feet.

'I thought it not amiss, in this time when all changes,
if your people had a Temple of their own. You have built
for our strange masters, and for his Majesty, and never for
yourselves. I thought', Plessiez said, a self-mocking irony
apparent in his tone, 'that it might stave off at least *one*
armed rebellion. We shall see if I am right.'

Obscurely angry, Lucas demanded: 'What did he pay
you? This man Falke, you didn't give him what he
wanted as a gift.'

290

Plessiez invested two words with a wealth of irony. 'He paid.'

'*You – halt!*'

The immense sweating crowd pulled back. Lucas stared down from ten or twelve feet high on to the square's paving stones. Across them clattered a woman.

The sun blazed back from her. He twisted his head aside, after-images swimming across his vision. Her mirror-polished armour blazed, sending highlights dancing across the metal carapace of the siege-engine and the Guards' uniforms.

Plessiez put up a narrow-fingered hand to shield his face. 'Lady Hyena.'

The woman looked up, a slanting-browed face framed in the open sallet helm. Her sheathed broadsword clanked against her armoured hip.

'Here in person, Eminence?' she grinned toothily. 'A miscalculation, maybe.'

The black Rat beside Lucas shot one glance upwards, at the sun. 'I have no quarrel with you, Lady.'

'Nor with—?' She turned bodily, the sallet restricting her neck-movements, and pointed back to a man on the distant steps at the edge of the building site. 'Nor with the head of the House of Salomon? Don't make me laugh. Well, will you fire on the crowd or not? What say you? Do you take the chance?'

Lucas stared at the stranger. An excitement familiar from exercises at arms in Candover tingled through his body. Readiness, anticipation – and no arms, no defences; and the black muzzles of armed Sun-banner men pointing full at the siege-engine. Lucas shuddered. The excitement still would not be killed. He knelt up, leaning one arm on the steel shield-wall, grinning fiercely at the human troops.

'Madam, have I offered you violence?' Plessiez said mildly.

The woman deliberately surveyed the towering engine, now coughing clouds of blue exhaust; the baroquely-cast

291

beaked rams and the catapult. Sardonic, she observed: 'That's a fair offer of it!'

Now his thoughts slipped back into the taught mode, Lucas easily picked out snipers behind the tents, musketeers in the cover at the edge of the building site, armed men and women massing behind the first unarmed rows of the great crowd.

'I require nothing but to station this here as protection,' Plessiez said.

'What will you do now — sit quiet and watch Falke's builders?' She chuckled. 'Do that, then. I have a proclamation of my own to make, now that it's midday.'

At Lucas's elbow, the Lord-Architect Casaubon dug in his pocket and fumbled out a watch, flicked open the casing, and rumbled: 'Not yet. A few minutes.'

'White Crow said—' Lucas cut himself off. Imaging the woman, dark red hair tumbling, at the doors of the Fane: under the skreeing circles of daemons in flight. Noon. The Lord of Noon and Midnight. And which is it?

'Clovis, where's Cornelius Vanringham? Bring him. I want him to hear this.' The armoured woman, moving surprisingly lightly, strode to the front of the siege-engine. Lucas gazed down at her heat-scarlet face, dripping with sweat. She stared past him. 'Well, priest, you may as well hear it, too. You'd hear it before the end of today, be certain of that.'

Conciliatory, the black Rat bowed. 'As you wish, Lady. I shall be most interested to hear what you have to proclaim.'

'Only our independence.' Sardonic, her voice went harsh and honest. 'Only our freedom.'

Lucas shivered: a deep motion of the flesh that never reached his skin, that seemed to reverberate in his chest and gut. He looked to Casaubon.

'Go now,' the big man said quietly. His plump-fingered hand closed over Plessiez's shoulder, as the black Rat opened his mouth to call, tightening warningly.

Not pausing to consider trust, Lucas ducked back and

slid on his buttocks past the Lord-Architect, hidden by the man's bulk. He stood, walked to the rear of the siege-engine; sat and slid and let himself fall from the edge of the platform in one movement. He staggered into the crowd with stinging ankles, thrusting between people with his elbows, tense for a shout, the crack of a musket behind him.

Bells chimed from the five corners of the square.

Noon.

Chill fell across him, cooling his chest, arms and back, welcome as cold water in the press of sweaty bodies. He felt muscles relax that had been tensed against the hammering heat of midday. Shadow swept across the square. And again, deep in his gut, his flesh shuddered.

A great intake of breath sounded around him, a simultaneous sound from the thousands gathered. Like wind across a cornfield, faces tipped up to the sky, ignoring the building site and the foundation-stone. Lucas raised his head, the corners of his vision filling with yellow dazzles.

Brilliant blackness stabbed his vision. Ringed with a corona of black flames, a black sun hung at the apex of the sky.

All the sky from arch to horizon glows yellow as ancient parchment. The twelfth chime of noon dies. Transmuted, transformed, in a fire of darkness: the Night Sun shines.

7

'How the hell did you *do* that?' the White Crow demanded over her shoulder, padding down the steep flight of steps. 'You can't have done that; it isn't possible!'

The blond man touched one hand to the pale stone wall for support, leaning forward, frowning.

'It's . . . light . . . in here. I don't recognize any of this.'

He recollected himself and offered his hand to the old woman. Heurodis put one foot down, lowered her other foot to join it, then lowered herself cautiously down the next steep step. Her smoky eyes met the White Crow's.

'We don't do it often. We – that's the university, girlie – we can do it whenever we want to. That's something you indigent scholar-bullies will never master.'

'But you *can't—*'

The White Crow half-missed her footing. She turned her head, seeing white stone steps descending to an archway and a stone-flagged door just visible beyond. Above, the high ceiling of the passage glowed pale and deserted.

'It *is* light,' she said. 'And it wasn't for the first few minutes after we got in. I think I know what's happening outside . . . Reverend Mistress, you don't understand! It isn't a lock that keeps that threshold closed. It isn't *magia*, either; it's the power of god, the power that structures the universe. The interior of the Fane of Noon and Midnight doesn't *exist* outside those times; you can't just pick the lock and get in!'

'*We* can.' Heurodis grinned, showing all her long teeth.

Reverend Master Candia took Heurodis's hand and

294

rested it on the White Crow's left shoulder. The age-spotted hand gripped with some strength. Candia loped down to the bottom of the flight of steps. His slashed jerkin shed fragments of lace, leaving a smell of stale alcohol on the air.

'And I thought seeing the impossible done couldn't surprise me any more!' The White Crow laughed aloud. Echoes hissed up the passage. 'I've always wondered why the university doesn't depend on Rat-Lords or human patrons. If you can do that, you don't have to. *How do you do it?*'

Heurodis stepped down off the last step and took her hand from the White Crow's shoulder.

'We're gods' thieves,' she said. '*And* we've stolen from the gods themselves, missy. Under divine sufferance, no doubt, but we have done.'

'Crime's a high Art.' Candia gripped the lintel of the arch, leaning to peer into the chamber beyond. One hand went to his belt, clenched into a fist. 'Heurodis is a great practitioner.'

'Here.'

Drawing her small knife from the back of her belt, the White Crow passed it to the blond man. His hand, which had seemed to search quite independently of his will, closed about the hilt; he stooped slightly as he looked down at her, nodding with a wide-eyed surprise.

'You trust me, Master-Captain?'

'I don't think this is a place for anyone to go unarmed.' She hefted the rapier in her right hand, with her left reaching up to push a coil of red hair back under her hat. A wetness brushed her cheek. She rubbed her stinging fingers across her skin and looked down at a bloody hand.

'Lady, you're hurt.' He took her hand by the wrist, turning her palm upwards. A bead of blood oozed from the life-line.

'No. Or not just now anyway.' The White Crow winced, raising her left hand to her mouth, sucking at the pin-pricks made by black roses in the Garden of the Eleventh

Hour. 'The stigmata of *magia*. Messire Candia, do you recognize any of this?'

'None of it, lady.'

Stone dust gritted under her sandals. The White Crow reached down and flipped them off, feeling the tension of stone under her bare feet. She padded forward into pale light.

Squat pillars spread out, forest-like, into the distance. From them great low vaults curved up, in arcs so shallow it seemed impossible the masonry of the ceiling should stay supported. The sourceless white light arced the ribs of the vaults with multiple shadows.

Her nostrils flared, catching a scent of roses.

'Why did you and . . . ?'

The blond man complied. 'Theo. Bishop Theodoret, of the Church of the Trees.'

'A Reverend tutor. And a Tree-priest. Of course.'

The White Crow knelt and strained her vision. A breath of warm air feathered her cheek. Distance blurred pillars, low vaults, more pillars. No windows: the light not the light of sun or moon.

'Why did you need Scholar-Soldiers?'

Heurodis, catching the question, snapped: 'Why indeed? What young Candia here thought he was doing asking help of the Invisible College, I'm sure I'll never know. Ignorant children, all of them. You, too, missy.'

Heurodis wiped a bony finger along the surface of the nearest pillar, sniffed at the dust, and wiped it down her blue cotton dress. In tones of waspish outrage she added: 'How the University of Crime could begin to trust an organization that doesn't even work for *gain*—'

Reduced to complete speechlessness, the White Crow leaned her rapier against her leg, reached to pin her tumbling hair up out of the way under her wide-brimmed hat, and at last managed to say: 'You'll have to take that point up with one of the others. Come to think of it, I'd like you to talk to the Lord-Architect Casaubon. Rather, I'd like him to have the experience of talking to you . . . '

She walked forward as she talked, letting the words come almost absently, centering herself to the familiar heft of the sword in her hand, the weight of the backpack. Light slid about her like milk. The air grew warmer, out under the low-vaulted ceiling; and a glimmer of blue clung to the edges of ribs and pillars.

'If I had to guess, I'd say that noon brought us the Night Sun.' A quirk of humour showed as she glanced back at Heurodis. 'After today, I'm cautious about expressing an opinion.'

'Listen.'

She glanced up, seeing lines deepen in Candia's face; the blond man's air of permanent injured surprise giving way to an unselfconcerned anxiety. He stumbled as he walked past her, away from the wall.

'What—? No, I hear it. Wait . . . ' The White Crow moved forward and caught the buff-and-scarlet sleeve of his jerkin, halting him.

A deep wash of sound re-echoed from the pillars, hissing through the milky-blue air, losing direction against the white pillars and white vaults and white light. It died. The White Crow strained to hear. She walked forward, head cocked sideways, tracking it for some faint hint of direction.

'There . . . '

A faint green luminescence shone down one side of a low pillar, far off, where distance made the pillars small as a finger at arm's length. Again the sound hissed, growing from inaudibility to a harsh breath of pain. It sawed the warm air. Her chest tightened, attempting to match that arhythmic breathing. The White Crow frowned, mouth open.

Candia grunted as if he had been punched. 'Theo.'

The White Crow looked to Heurodis. The old woman shook her head, moving forward to take the blond man's elbow. His face held some abstract expression of pain and memory that defied analysis. The White Crow began to walk, hearing their slow footsteps behind her.

Pillars shifted, perspective moving them in her peripheral vision. Dry warm air rasped in her lungs. Deliberately barefoot, she walked lightly on the balls of her feet, letting the sensations of the flagstones guide her.

Between pillars, away in the milky light, she glimpsed a far wall. She walked faster.

'Master-Captain!'

The hissed whisper broke her concentration. She gestured shortly with her blood-wet left hand, ignoring Heurodis. More shifted in the light than perspective could account for. Small hairs hackled down the back of her neck. She slid from one squat round pillar to the concealment of the next.

Greenness drifted into the granular milky light, coiling as if it were steam or smoke and not luminescence: a light the colour of sun through a canopy of new leaves. It touched the skin of her arms, goose-pimpling them with cool. A stink of old blood caught in her throat.

'Stay back.' The White Crow touched one bloody finger to her backpack, stepping across the flagstoned space towards a door that opened into a tiny stone cell. She looked inside.

Candia, behind her, whispered: *'Theo . . .'*

Shock hit: her sweaty skin going cold between her shoulder-blades and down her arms. The White Crow bent forward and retched. One hand to the door-frame, the other leaning for support on her rapier, eyes blind with the tears of nausea, she vomited up the bile of a day's fasting.

'Oh shit . . . Don't come in. Somebody keep watch outside.'

She spat, wiped her nose with the heel of her hand, took in a breath, and stepped into the white stone cell. Its low step caught her foot. She stumbled, staring ahead.

Stark against her sight, an iron spike curved up out of the masonry wall. Blood and pale fluids had dried in streaks below it. The White Crow stared at the head of a man impaled on the iron spike. Undecayed, spots of blood

298

still dripped from the neck-stump to the stained floor. White hair flowed down to where, red-dappled, it stuck to drying knots of vertebrae, slashed cords and tendons.

Only the head: the cell held no truncated body.

Dappled light shifted, green and gold. For a second the White Crow sensed the rush of branches, birds, steps through leaf-mould. A shriek of ripped wood echoed, the light shifting. She knelt, staring levelly at the creased labile face.

At his open conscious eyes.

Heurodis's sharp indrawn breath sounded above her head. The fair-haired man fell to his knees beside her. One dirty hand reached out as if he would touch the severed head. The White Crow caught his wrist.

'No, messire, I'm sorry. Not with the power here.'

Tears brimmed over the lower lids of Candia's eyes. Absently moving his knife, he picked with the tip of it under one thumbnail. Green light gleamed from the blade. 'My lord Bishop . . . Theo, tell me how. I'll do it.'

The White Crow got to her feet, eyes never leaving the severed head. Heurodis whispered, 'Take more than a knife, girl, when it's a god keeping that thing alive,' and the White Crow nodded, and risked a glance over her shoulder.

'Rot it! I thought as much.'

Outside the cell, the pillars of the crypt had vanished. The cell now opened onto a gallery, forty feet above the floor of a high-vaulted chamber large as the nave of a cathedral, white and gold stone gleaming in sourceless brilliance. The White Crow touched a knee briefly to the floor, kneeling to look up and out past the low arch of the cell's doorway.

Shafts of golden light curved over clustered pillars, soared down from perpendicular arches in dust-mote-filled curtains. And in all the hull-shaped nave no windows: light shafting from unappreciable sources. The White Crow tilted down the brim of her speckled hat, shading her eyes, squinting. High fan-vaulting and hollow arches hung bare, empty of roosting acolytes. Below, all the wide floor stretched out deserted.

'Leave . . . here . . .'

She shivered. Breath echoed back from the stone behind her, forced into painful speech: an old man's weary voice.

'Leave . . . here . . . Candia . . . I am . . . bait . . . for . . . you . . . Go . . . Go!'

The White Crow got to her feet. She turned. The man in buff and scarlet still knelt, facing the severed head. She winced, seeing how the features of Theodoret *moved*: wrinkled eyelids blinking, the wide mobile mouth shifting.

Heurodis's hands clenched in the folds of her cotton dress.

The White Crow sheathed her rapier and took off her pack, tossing the speckled hat down beside it on the flagstones. She unbuckled the straps, fumbling, hands shaking; breathed in to calm herself, and took out a cotton handkerchief and a metal water-flask.

'Well, I'm here to see The Spagyrus. I assume.' A ghost of sardonic humour touched her voice. 'This should bring him.'

She stepped past Candia and knelt, unscrewing the top of the flask, covering it with the kerchief and tipping it up. Water chilled the cloth and her fingers. She reached up and, with the damp cloth, moistened the cracked lips of the head.

She kept her eyes on that vulnerable mouth, shivered inside; finally lifted her gaze. Swimming with light, his grey eyes met hers, saw her plainly; and the old man's lips moved into an attempt at a smile.

'Pitiable . . . and . . . grotesque . . .'

'No, messire.'

The White Crow moistened the cloth again and applied it, words coming as randomly as her thoughts.

'Mistress Heurodis got me in here. She saved all our lives. Master Candia tells me you sent to the Invisible College. Tell me what you wish, messire.'

The Bishop of the Trees spoke slowly, painfully. 'Bless . . . you . . . child . . . '

All else put aside, the White Crow sat back on her heels, staring up into his creased face. The edges of her vision glowed with the light of forests.

'My name is Valentine. White Crow. I come from the Invisible College. I was fifteen years a Master-Captain; I'm a Master-Physician now. Tell me quickly. If anything at all is possible now, would you die, or would you have me try something other?'

Abrupt and arctic, silence dropped on the square, darkling under the black sun.

'Don't fear! We *know* what that means.'

The Hyena screeched. She flung her free hand up, pointing at the sky that now shone a deep and pitiless blue as the Night Sun took hold.

'The Night Sun! The sign! The hour has come. We are free of our strange masters, free of the god-daemons, free of the Decans, free of the Thirty-Six! You all hear it, you all see it, you all feel it!'

Her voice flattened against the still cold air.

She swung round, pushing between packed men and women, shoving her way from the siege-engine towards the steps. No lips moved. The crowd, silent, parted by unspoken consent to let her through.

'Feast and rejoice! Feast and rejoice and *build*. Hold our celebration while the Night Sun shines. And when it passes you'll see the day's light shine on a Fane standing open and empty, the Thirty-Six abandoning the heart of the world. And that heart of the world given over into our keeping, here: the imperial Sun dynasty!'

A middle-aged woman raised her head. Her silk carpenter's shirt hung in strips. Her face, caked thick with yellow and white paint, showed raw sores around her mouth and nostrils. She met the Hyena's gaze and showed her teeth.

'Clovis, damn you!' The Hyena strode up the steps,

armour clattering; the only noise but for the siege-engine's throbbing motor.

Faces turned to follow. Silk and satin work-clothes hung in strips and tatters. A burly man stumbled from her path, face covered by a feather-mask. Many masks gleamed in the crowd: brilliant or dust-covered feathers clinging to faces, masking eyes, leaving mouths and sores uncovered. And still no sound: not a shout, not a whisper.

The blond man, Clovis, met her on the top step.

'Lady . . . what have we done?'

'*Plague Carnival!*'

The voice echoed down from the nearest building, where on balconies black and brown Rats gazed down with arrogant equanimity.

'Why not sing?' one called down. 'Why don't you dance now, peasants?'

Another pointed into the vast mass of people. 'A silent carnival! A plague carnival!'

'You don't amuse us!'

'Dancing's a sovereign cure for the plague, they tell me!'

'*Quiet!*' The sky shimmered from yellow to blue in the corners of the Hyena's vision. A smell of sickness breathed up from the flagstones. She rubbed her nose, eyes watering at the stench.

'Lay down fire across the building if they speak again. Over the heads of the crowd.'

A young boy stepped from the silent crowd and threw a handful of broken petals towards the balcony. He whisked a mask of owl's feathers from his face, sun gleaming on red hair and on his sores weeping white pus. Other masked revellers stood in silence, jammed shoulder to shoulder, crowding the dry basins of fountains. The Hyena followed the direction of every gaze.

In the pitiless blue sky, coronas of black fire licked out across the empyrean. Midnight at noon, night-fire: the black sun blazes.

'Clovis. Set up sound-broadcast. I'm going to tell them

this is what we've been waiting for.' She spared one glance for the Rat-Lords on the siege-engine platform. Picking out an emerald sash, some humour curved her lips. 'We can all use . . . coincidences. Where's Falke?'

'Here.'

The man stepped silently to her side. He slid the black silk bandage from his eyes, raising his face to the sky. She saw momentarily in his unnaturally dilated pupils the twin reflections of darkness.

'We must hold the ceremony of the shadow. The building *must* continue.'

Her slanting red brows lifted. Directing troops to their places by hand-signals, she spoke now without looking at him, in a measured tone only a fraction from hysterical laughter.

'Whose shadow? Yours? *Have you seen what's in front of you?*'

The man gazed blindly across the building site.

'I've done without all else. I can do without my shadow to keep the Temple of Salomon standing.'

She pointed at their feet, then fumbled her hands back into plate gauntlets.

'Oh, damn your Craft mysteries . . .'

All their shadows fell bright, brilliant; fell through the dark air to shine on the broken stone.

'It's impossible. *Look*. You've to nail a shadow to the first-raised wall to keep the Temple standing. *All the shadows are lights!*'

Falke frowned, brushing a hand across his lips and the several tiny weeping sores at the corners of his mouth. The cagework-shadows of scaffolding fell bright across his surcoat, and the Hyena held out both gauntleted hands, glinting darkly.

'See! You have to depend on my troops now!'

She met his eyes, and his gaze blurred.

Falke stumbled against her, and she caught him with one steel-clad arm; spun to grip his shoulders and lower his dead weight to the broken paving. His eyes rolled up and showed only thin white lines below the lids.

'Damn pestilence, it's thinning us out faster than we can fight or build. Let's have some help here! Ho!'

The Hyena pushed greasy hair out of her face, pulled off her plate gauntlet to feel for his pulse. She glanced up for her lieutenants. Two of the people in her immediate sight – a dark-bearded man, a young boy – slid down on their knees and fell hard across the stones. She gaped.

Above on the scaffolding a scream sounded, and the thud of a heavy body falling.

'*Falke?*'

She grabbed his dark-streaked hair, pulling his head up, and stopped as he sprawled limply back against her; head falling back, mouth falling open. Tatters of black flesh ran across the skin of his face from mouth to temple, spread down his neck to vanish under his collar. Crisped, sere: as if plague-fever could burn up flesh in heartbeats.

She touched her bare fingers to his throat. No pulse.

Dark flames licked down into her vision. The Hyena stared across the open square. To left and to right, men and women sprawled across the paving; others leaped up or shouted for aid. A coldness chilled her bare hands.

With a child-like puzzlement, she looked down and touched the face of the man dead in her arms.

Brightness moved in his mouth.

The Hyena snatched her hand away. Antennae moved in the dead man's open mouth, quivering, wavering. Insect feet scraped for purchase on his lips. It crawled between his teeth, first a velvet body, and then the spreading black-and-white-mottled wings of a death's-head moth.

Frozen, not even able to push his body away, she watched the moth shake out its wings and sun itself on his tattered cheek.

A scrap of colour bobbed past her vision. A scarlet butterfly, wings dusted with gold, sharp against the blue sky . . . The Hyena looked at the boy collapsed on the next step down. From between his lips a pale blue butterfly crawled, took flight.

The death's-head moth flew up past her face, skull-markings plain on its dried wings. She covered her mouth with her hand, sick and afraid.

Under the generative chill of the Night Sun, all the air above the square glimmered, red and blue and black and gold, alive with whirling columns of butterflies and moths rising up from the mouths of the plague-dead.

'It's a bad joke!' Candia exclaimed. He rocked back on to his heels, standing up.

The White Crow grabbed at her arm as he caught it, pulling her up on to her feet. She twisted out of a grip that would leave bruises, glaring up at the blond man.

'*No*—'

Candia reached down to knot his fists in her shirt, leaning over her, breath stinking in her face.

'Break a Decan's power? Theo – you can't kill him, you can't heal him. How can you joke, and in front of him! I'll have no more of it. Hear me?'

'Messire—' The White Crow cut herself off. As gently as temper would let her, she closed her hands over the Reverend Master's fists, conscious of the pain in her left hand, of the dry warmth of the stone cell. 'Candia. I mean what I say.'

Flickers of green pushed at her vision, marbling the pale masonry walls. The blond man released his grip, reaching up to push hair out of his bruised-seeming eyes, gazing down bewildered. The White Crow tugged creased cloth straight.

'Lady, he . . . Death would be an act of mercy.'

'Trust me.'

'Trust a Scholar-Soldier?' Reverend Mistress Heurodis's acid voice sounded from the low arched door, where she peered out into the golden nave. 'Well, girlie, it doesn't matter; I think none of us will leave here, but you may try to end his pain.'

The White Crow turned and knelt. The stone, hard and

warm under her bare knee, beat with an imperceptible tension. She looked up again at the severed head. The old man's eyelids slid half-shut over swimming grey eyes, and his mouth clenched.

'I . . . needed to . . . die . . . before . . . He . . . called . . . me . . . bait.'

Some choking pressure in her chest resolved itself into pity and anger, and she put out a hand and touched his soft skin, echoes of pain resounding on cellular levels. 'Take time to decide. We've got a little time.'

She sat back, grabbing the leather backpack and sorting through the books and papers inside.

Candia said thickly: 'Bait? For who?'

Heurodis's voice sounded above the White Crow's head. 'For all of us?'

The White Crow stood and moved to the door. She squatted, dabbed the gummed end of a paper strip at her tongue and pasted it across the threshold. Her sallow fingers worked rapidly, fastening the character-inked strips across the jamb and lintel. A certain growing tension in the air held itself in abeyance.

She stood for a moment with her back to the three of them, staring out into the golden shafts of light in the nave.

'My lord, I haven't heard you answer.'

'So . . . much . . . suffering . . . '

The White Crow turned and took two rapid paces across the cell, catching up her sword as she knelt, resting her hands on the hilt and her chin on her hands, words falling rapidly into the full silence.

'I don't think I should help you die. I mean . . . ' She gave a helpless shrug. 'I don't know if I *can* give you anything better than death. I'm a Scholar-Soldier; I can't work miracles. But, see, someone is going to die soon – truly die, my lord, the soul, too – and that's when the Circle is broken, and I can't . . . if it's you . . . if that happens, we . . . I was told by the Decan of the Eleventh Hour to act. But not how.'

306

Theodoret's creased features moved. Long seconds passed.

'My lord,' the White Crow said very softly, 'you're laughing at me, I think.'

The severed head's bright eyes moved, meeting hers; and the Bishop of the Trees, as if there were no-one there but the two of them, no old friend Candia, no Reverend Mistress, said: 'Do . . . your . . . damnedest . . . woman . . . I would . . . live . . . like *this* . . . if . . . I . . . thought . . . it would . . . hurt . . . The . . . Spagyrus . . .'

Reverend Mistress Heurodis's bony finger tapped peremptorily on her shoulder.

'You'll have to be quick, then, missy. Even one of the College should be able to feel what's happening here.'

The White Crow reached one hand back through the air towards the threshold. Blood tingled in her fingers, dropped to star the stone. The divine, immanent in this cell, receded from her touch as the long going-out of a tide; and for a second she leaned heavily on the rapier for support.

'What . . . ?' Candia, his back resting against the wall, slid down to a sitting position. The buff-and-scarlet jerkin rode up at the back, pulling his dirty shirt and lace ruffles loose from his breeches; one scuff-heeled boot lodged in the crack of a flagstone and arrested his slide. He gazed up at Heurodis. 'You're both crazy.'

'Far from it, boy.' The white-haired woman paced across the cell to peer out of the door, her voice coming back creakily. 'I believe I saw this done once before, about fifty years ago now. Worked, too. Mind you, it killed one of the two other people involved.'

The White Crow rested her chin on the backs of her hands. The metal of the rapier echoed faintly with the tread of god-daemons. Without moving her head, she shifted her eyes to the Reverend Master.

'Candia, why did you come back here?'

'Back?' His head resting against the masonry, the man

answered with closed eyes. 'We were seen entering, then? Yes. I was here before. We were here before. They let me go. After I saw what happened to Theo.'

Now his head fell forward, and he met her gaze.

'It took me time, lady, to find the courage to come back; and I found most of it in a bottle. Here I am. Useless. What did I think I could do? I don't know.'

The White Crow straightened, laying the rapier down on the flagstones. She held the blond man's gaze.

'Masons' Hall?' she said, too quiet for Heurodis's hearing. 'Could be, you came back out of guilt to be killed with Theodoret. I've known it happen among the College. Think that's true? Because, if it is, I can give you something to do that's almost guaranteed suicide.'

His bruised eyes blinked, startled. He unwillingly smiled. 'Lady, you're persuasive. What?'

A milky light began to seep through the joins of masonry, fogging the air in the cell. The White Crow put both hands to the flagstone floor. Strain tensed the stone. One of the paper talismans at the door snapped, a tiny *ppt!* in the silence.

'Paracelsus tells us . . . ' A tiny smile appeared on the White Crow's face. With a certain droll formality, she straightened up and inclined her head to the Reverend Master. 'Hear a lecture, Messire Candia. Paracelsus teaches that in every body there is one bone, a seed-bone, from which the body is grown again on the Boat as it passes the Night. We being in the Fane, in that same Night through which the Boat passes, it may . . . it may just be possible, by use of *magia*, to heal that way. The seed-bone is here.'

The White Crow reached across, pushing her fingers through Candia's hair, touching his warm neck and the hard knob of bone at the base of his skull. Arm's length, the stink of his soiled clothes filled the air; but he raised his head with an insouciant carelessness, caught her wrist and growled: 'Shame me into it, would you? What would you have me do? I'd do it anyway.'

The weak voice protested: 'Candia . . . my friend . . .'

She saw his eyes shift, at last rest without flinching on Theodoret's severed head. 'I'll do it!'

'This *magia* needs a third person to draw strength from.' The White Crow took her hand back. 'Mistress Heurodis isn't strong enough in body.'

The white-haired woman grunted ungraciously. The White Crow shifted her gaze to the severed head of Theodoret, and met a bright humour there.

'We're strong. Of course, the chances are that it'll kill Messire Candia and me, too. I've never done *magia* inside the Night of the Fane. The gods alone know what might happen.'

'It . . . may . . . even . . . work.'

Reverend Mistress Heurodis walked across to Candia, cotton dress rustling, and rested one veined hand on the wall above him.

'Better get ready, missy. I'll tell him what he has to do.'

The White Crow nodded. Under her bare knees and shins, the flagstones began to pulse almost imperceptibly: their rhythm the rhythm of particles and electrons in their universal dance. Practised enough from five years in the city called the heart of the world, she recognized, far off, an approaching tread.

'I will . . . help . . . if . . . I . . . can . . .'

The White Crow's nostrils flared at a sudden scent of woodsmoke. Melancholy, sharp: tears sprang into the corners of her eyes. Momentarily the stone gritting under her blood-slick palms became the creased bark of oak.

Boots rasped. Solid at her shoulder, Candia folded his long legs and sat cross-legged beside the wall. A sharp odour of sweat came off him. The White Crow glimpsed, through milky light, Heurodis's hand just touching his bowed head. She breathed slowly and deeply.

'My lord.' The White Crow shivered, reaching up with her left hand. Her bloody fingers rested lightly on the crusting blood and mucus on the iron spike. The Bishop's creased eyelids lifted, lines of his face shifting in pain.

Milky light softened raw flesh and shining bone; glowed in his pale hair. The White Crow brought her other hand up to rest on the spike below the severed head. 'I may hurt you worse than He did.'

'You . . . cannot . . . child.'

She let go of the spike. Sword and pack spread around her, rose-pricked palm bleeding, the White Crow knelt before the impaled and severed head. Her right hand sketched a hieroglyph on air, skeining pale light into a net.

'Now . . .'

Her left hand went up to touch her uncovered hair. A bee crawled over the dark red coils to her knuckles, skimmed into flight; drowsing a summer warmth into the dry air. The netted air paled, glowing, thinning to the gold of sunlight.

The white-haired woman nudged him. Candia wet his lips and, ignoring how they shook, raised his hands. The White Crow took them in her own. With infinite care she placed them to cup the severed head of the old man, supporting his corded chin.

'. . . Grotesque . . . !'

Seeing that same laughter in the old man's light eyes, the White Crow, her hands outside the blond man's and holding them tight to cool kept-living flesh, grinned and said: 'Now!'

The lintel of the cell cracked. Gunshot-sharp echoes rattled away into the nave. A heavy tread shook stone.

'Now, damn you!'

Eyes squeezed almost shut, the blond man closed his hands tight about the severed head and lifted it off the metal spike. Her hands felt the dragging resistance of flesh through his. Iron grated on bone. A wet, hollow, sucking noise made her gag.

The stink of decay choked the air. A breathless scream cut off.

Her right hand slid to cup the ripped liquescing verte-brae as Candia cradled the severed head in his arms. The

310

White Crow hesitated. A sweat-drop ran cold down the back of her own neck.

The *magia* light died. Imprinted on her vision, all three of them – old woman, young man and severed corrupting head – froze, caught in the stark whiteness of the cell.

'Now . . .'

This time only a breath, too soft for anyone but herself to hear it. The White Crow raised her left hand and slammed it palm-down on the point of the iron spike.

'Watch out! 'Way there! Coach coming through!'

A black-haired Katayan woman in a silk coat reined in the team of four horses, one boot planted up on the footboard. Beside her, gripping the corner of the roof, leaning down with tail outstretched for balance, Zar-bettu-zekigal brandished a torn white-and-gold banner and yelled enthusiastically.

'*That* way—' She stumbled and fell against the backboard, grabbing at the older Katayan's arm. 'Ei, *watch out!*'

Out of nowhere, men and women swarmed past the coach, running out through the dockyard entrance to Fourteenth's great square: fifty, a hundred, five hundred. One fell, lay kicked and beaten underfoot. Another pitched face down, and the lead brown gelding skittered in the shafts, half-rearing, refusing to trample the fallen boy.

'Whoa!' The older Katayan reined in again sharply. The coach jolted to a halt, wheezing back on its springs. Bodies thudded against the painted wooden doors. One of the geldings whickered, throwing its head up, eyes rolling. 'What the gods is this?'

Zar-bettu-zekigal jumped up. Balancing easily, dappled tail coiled back, she shaded her eyes against the black light and stared into the square. 'I see it! Keep us moving, Elish. Slowly!'

'Zar—'

'Trust me!'

She reached back, gripped the roof-rail, and swung down off the driver's seat; caught the wide open coach-window with one bare foot and let momentum push her over massing bodies of men and women streaming past. She plummeted into the coach's interior, landing sprawled across Charnay. The brown Rat hefted her off into the opposite seat, beside the Candovard Ambassador.

'We can't get through. No, wait!' She reached to grab the brown Rat's hand. 'One sword's not going to get us anywhere. There's a mob panic going on out there!'

She eased her rucked-up black dress down over her hips. Her eyes cleared, growing accustomed to the light shadow of the coach's interior. The Ambassador sat forward, peering through the opposite window, his grizzled face showing confusion. Charnay struggled with her half-drawn sword in the close confines. The silver-haired woman held up ringed hands upon which three sparrows perched.

'Ei! Clever,' Zar-bettu-zekigal appreciated. She leaned forward, hands locked, curving her tail up delicately to hold it invitingly before one bird. It cocked its head, stared at her with Night-dark eyes. 'Full-scale panic out there, Lady Luka. Shall we go back, try somewhere else – the palace maybe?'

'My dear girl!' The Ambassador, Andaluz, turned away from the window, his neat pepper-and-salt beard jutting. 'I would strongly suggest we . . . I would offer you the protection of the Embassy Compound, but as for what good that will be when *that* is happening I confess I don't know.'

Zar-bettu-zekigal looked at him in amazement. 'Oh, what! Haven't you ever seen a Night Sun before?'

She swivelled, resting her bare arms on the open window and her chin on her arms, eyes raised to the fiery blackness now at the sky's highest arc. Basking in the light shadows and cool beams, she said: 'Lady?'

Luka chuckled. 'Onwards, by all means, if we can. What is it you see?'

Zar-bettu-zekigal slid round in her seat, hooking one

312

foot up under her. The small woman transferred the sparrows to her shoulders, where they nestled in the white-spotted robes. She met Zar-bettu-zekigal's gaze with eyes of a guileless blue.

'One of those siege-engines the fa— That your son', she corrected herself, 'built for messire. It's here. Whoever's on it should know where both of them are.'

'Absolutely not. Most unlikely. We'll be overturned before we go much further.' Andaluz rested his stubby hand over the tanned hand of Luka. 'End this lunacy now, lady, I beg you.'

Zar-bettu-zekigal, about to sneer, ducked and slid back as the brown Rat finally hauled her sword from its sheath.

'Charnay!'

'They're only peasants.' Charnay smoothed her fur, translucent ears cocking; and grabbed the window-frame with one hand, pulling herself up to look out. 'They'll run when they're ordered—'

'They're running already and not from you!' Zari slipped back as the coach jolted. For a second all her view was sky through the window; deepest blue sky in which particles of darkness burned and danced.

Bright confetti colours dotted the sky.

'Stop the coach!' The Lady Luka trod heavily on Zar-bettu-zekigal's foot, leaning across the small coach to gaze out. Her feather-braided hair slapped Zari's mouth. Zar-bettu-zekigal scrambled up, glaring, opened her mouth, and the woman called:

'Elish-hakku-zekigal, stop the coach! Now!'

'Oh, what! See you, this isn't . . . '

The coach rocked on its springs, stopped dead. A horse whickered. Two bodies slammed against the door, running hard in the press of the crowd, then another: she glimpsed a white-and-yellow Harlequin face. Luka's hand slipped the catch and pushed the door open.

'Shit!' Zari scrambled across the seat, dropped a yard to the flagstones, and reached under the coach to release the steps. Grease smeared her hands.

313

Catching her foot, she stumbled.

Zar-bettu-zekigal looked down. A woman sprawled at her feet, eyes open and dead; the body of an older man fallen across her legs.

'It's a . . . battlefield.'

People still ran, away across the square. Where the coach halted men and women and children sprawled across the stained flagstones, the black tatters of plague racing across their flesh. Bright scraps of colour danced above their heads, crawled from between gaping lips. One veered towards her, and she jerked her head away, the garish red-and-blue of a peacock-butterfly filling all her vision.

'Souls . . . ' Wonder in her tone, the Lady Luka took the Candovard Ambassador's hand absently as she descended the steps, Charnay hard on her heels. 'Souls. Such flight! But – no preparation, no burial, no summoning of the Boat? They'll be lost.'

A Rat's hand fell heavily on Zar-bettu-zekigal's shoulder. She started, looked up into the face of Charnay. The brown Rat carried her sword in her free hand, and now lifted it and sighted along the blade at a wheeling butterfly.

'I don't understand. How will they find their way to the Boat?'

Zari lifted her head to their flight: moths and butterflies fluttering like leaves, dotting the air . . . and rising. Slowly but with purpose, spiralling up towards the Night Sun.

'They won't. Oh, Elish.'

She heard the older Katayan woman's boots hit the flagstones, and her light tread as she stepped between the tumbled bodies. A warm hand took her arm. She pitched round, throwing her arms about her sister, burying her face in the sweet-scented lace ruffles of her shirt. 'Elish!'

'Little one.' Work-hardened hands held her back and head, crushing her dress, pressing sun-cooled hair against her scalp. 'Hush.'

'Hard times deserve hard measures.'

Luka's tone, sharp now, roused her. Zar-bettu-zekigal raised her head. The small woman stood with her arms

314

outstretched, bamboo cane held up in one hand, head raised to the sky. Her feather-braided hair hung down over her breast, silver against the garish robes. The parakeet screeched, clinging to her shoulder.

Birds settled down.

Out of a clear sky, thrushes and starlings and hawks flew down, landing on the lady's outstretched arms. Sparrows, doves, pigeons, humming-birds – until her old arms bowed, and she flung them upwards, skywards. Zar-bettu-zekigal followed the gesture.

Dark under the Night Sun, birds circled. Great scarlet macaws, eagles, buzzards; peregrine falcons and merlins, mouse-owls and herring gulls, crows, ravens and vultures. Amazed, she hugged Elish tighter, deafened by the rush of great wings, wincing from the spatter of droppings that hit the flagstones; dizzied by the skirl of flight, hundreds upon thousands of birds flocking overhead.

'Follow! Follow-follow-follow!'

High as a jay's shriek, the old woman's voice pierced the air. She swept the bamboo cane high above her head.

A mottled black-and-white moth skittered across Zari's vision. A rush of cold wings sounded, whirring; and the scarlet parakeet seemed to halt in mid-air, beak snapping. The moth's body crunched. The bird flicked away on an updraught, beak pecking down the fragile wings.

'Elish . . .' Zari unknotted her fists from her sister's coat, knuckles white. A cold wind began to blow. 'Elish! What're they doing?'

Her heart thudded in her breast; Zar-bettu-zekigal felt it through her sister's flesh. The older Katayan said nothing, only stared upwards.

Swift, acute, cutting the sky: the great flock of birds circled and spread out, rising on dark wings, pursuing and catching and devouring the hundred thousand butterflies that spiralled up into the bright air.

Brick walls rose up about him. Lucas trotted to the end of

315

another alley, pacing himself, holding in tight frustration. The alley opened into a crossroads.

Five identical ways led off: indistinguishable from all the other alleys. He cocked his head, listened. At least no footsteps now, no pursuers.

'Gods damn it!' He slammed his fist against the wall. Brickdust and plaster sifted down. 'I don't believe it!'

Lucas stared up at the narrow strip of sky visible between roofs. The black glare of the sun blinded him, dead overhead, no use for directions.

He picked an alley that might lead away from the square and began to run down it, loping, muscles aching. Within minutes he hit a division of the ways, paused. Lost.

Lost.

'I can't believe I did this.' His voice bounced thinly back from the walls and shutters. He banged on peeling shutters. No sound, no answer.

Claws scratched on cobblestones, loud in the silence. A hard hairy body pushed under his right hand. Lucas froze as it brushed his leg, looked down. A white dog.

'*Lazarus?*'

Not a dog, a timber wolf; turning its thin muzzle up to gaze at him with ice-blue eyes. Dust clogged the pads of the animal's feet. It let its jaw gape for a moment, panting; then gave a quick high-pitched growl and trotted off down one of the two alleys.

'Hey!' Lucas hesitated. 'Where is she? Were you with her? What the fuck – you're an animal. What do you know?'

The wolf stopped, gazing back with feral eyes.

Lucas stepped forward. Heat rebounded back from the walls of the buildings, built up a thin film of sweat on his skin that the sunlight cooled. He began to walk. The wolf, as if satisfied at seeing him follow, turned and trotted on, loping easily down the dry central gutter.

Dust thickened thirst on his tongue. Now the wolf began running, the rocking pace that eats up miles outside city streets; and Lucas, one hand pressed over his breeches pocket and the letter, sprinted after, panting.

'Hey!'

A corner, a narrow alley, a flight of steps; another long alley, cut right, cut left; a short alley—

He caught a gutter-pipe to pull him round the next corner. The street shone dusty, dark, empty before him. Disbelieving, he slowed, panting; walking slowly along past a high wall.

'As if I *believed*—' Incredulity sharpened his voice; he hit his fist against his thigh.

A murmur of voices came from a high window.

Lucas stopped. He narrowed his eyes against the light shadows cast by the wall, staring up at the building's clustered chimneys and high peaked roofs. Still staring up, he walked along the wall to the massive iron-railing gates that stood open.

Chimneys cast light shadows across the paving. Cool reflected back from the walls on three sides, light glinting blackly from the windows. Great stone stairways went up at cater-corners of the courtyard, the wooden doors at the top of the left-hand flight standing open.

The murmur of voices from Big Hall echoed down through open windows into the courtyard of the University of Crime.

From gable and ridge and roof, from finial and spire, from pinnacle and gutter they rise up.

Great ribbed wings scour the sky.

Their shadows fall across the heart of the world, falling not light as all other shadows do, but still black: black as pits on the streets and houses and parks below.

The Night Sun bubbles their skins like tar. They shriek, rising up into the air, soaring.

The heart of the world stretches far out to the horizon, its thirty-six Districts and one hundred and eighty-one quarters; each District cut on its austerly sides by the darkness of the Fane, tentacles of stone building piecemeal across the earth. Houses, palaces, inns, temples;

317

courtyards and avenues, all empty now, no Rat-Lords, no humans, all lost or fleeing for refuge—

The acolytes of the Fane swarm, a hundred thousand.

Here they swoop low, bristle-tails beating the air, their thumb-hooked wings beating at the windowless Fane-in-the-Eighth-District. There they shriek, circling the buttresses of the Fane-in-the-Thirty-First-District.

They can no longer enter.

The Night Sun scorches their uncommon flesh, burning, burning.

Goaded they rise, blind with blood and fear. The Fane is closed to them. Over the city they swarm up, screaming.

Their Thirty-Six masters do not answer.

Clawed feet scrape the air: unflesh that can wither stone if it will. Wings beat: their breath can rip roofs from houses. Ears listen, hearing the beats of frightened hearts: the living who hide in their homes below and pray to the Fane's deafness.

Shrieking, they soar up into the burning black light. Gaining height to strike.

Plessiez clasped his onyx-ringed hands behind his back, gazing out over the building site of the House of Wisdom, Temple of the Two Pillars of Strength and Beauty, the Daughter of Salomon.

Abandoned barrows and diggers littered the earth, tarpaulins flapped loose over crates; drills, buckets, chisels and barrels lay on the ground and on the scaffolding platforms where they had been dropped. He stepped half a pace to one side as two black Rats, both in the lace and linen of minor gentry, carried the last of the dead men past by the hands and feet.

'The tents?' one queried. Plessiez inclined his head, glancing down at the body's heat-black and tattered skin.

'We need fear no infection . . . I believe.'

Dust still hung over the massive granite block by which he stood. From a blazing sky, dark light settled into the incised Word of Seshat, filling every carved channel. He rested his hand against the chill surface.

'As our great poet says, architecture is frozen music. A thaw would improve this greatly, I think. We'll have it demolished later.' He turned away from the site, now cleared of bodies, and walked down the broken steps. Without looking up, he added: 'How goes it?'

The Lord-Architect glanced up and winced. He wiped his face, smearing a white dropping across one dark copper eyebrow.

'Fewer butterflies,' he replied gravely. 'More birds.'

Plessiez nodded acknowledgement to a group of black Rats, merchants from one of the rich houses around the square; paused to exchange a word. To all sides now the square stretched away empty, but for the last of the impromptu squads carrying bodies to the abandoned Imperial tents. Careless, hard, cheerful: voices rang out. One ragged banner still flew, in the increasingly chill air.

'You have' – the Lord-Architect Casaubon drew on his voluminous blue satin frock-coat, and felt in his pockets – 'a monstrously tidy mind, Master Plessiez.'

Plessiez rubbed his hands together, restoring circulation. Giving a tug to his cardinal's green sash, he moved down from the last broken step to the paving, and into the bright shadow of the siege-engine. His scabbard jingled, harsh in the cold air.

'I see no reason these should not labour. Albeit minor gentry and merchants assume themselves too good for it.' A nod of his head to the velvet- and lace-clad Rats now milling in the square. 'I'll give orders later for some communal burial, some monument.'

'Later?'

Plessiez surveyed the crowds of his own kind, and smiled slightly. 'Oh, yes. After the present trouble.'

The Lord-Architect walked out a distance into the square and squatted down, studying the ground, blue silk breeches straining over his expanses of thigh and buttock. Rubbish still littered the paving about his feet:

319

feathers, masks, coloured ribbons, abandoned food and drink.

'Then let me tell you . . . '

A glass with an inch of stewed beer still in it stood by the Lord-Architect's foot. He absently picked it up, drank the dregs, and rose to his feet again.

' . . . just by way of a warning, since you're too gods-damned ignorant to perceive it for yourself . . . '

Casaubon felt in his deep pockets. He brought out, first, a stale chunk of bread smeared with something brown, which he bit into and then returned; and then a small sextant. Holding this up to the Night Sun with greasy fingers, he spoke through a spray of bread pellets.

' . . . that there's plague, and the black sun, but your troubles aren't half-over yet . . . '

Plessiez crossed the space between them in three strides, seizing the fat man's arm. 'What do you know? Is this your Art?'

' . . . therefore,' the Lord-Architect concluded as if he had not been interrupted, 'kindly stand aside, master priest, and let me get on with my work!'

'What work?' He loosed the satin sleeve.

'Plessiez!'

'Wait here,' Plessiez ordered, turning to face the voice. The noise of hoofs echoed across the square, the rider driving hard between the clear-up squads; reining in to a reckless halt by the siege-engine. She swung down from the mare's saddle, a plump black Rat in the scarlet jacket and *ankh* of the Order of Guiry.

'Fleury?'

'Man, are *you* in trouble!' She caught his arm, drew him aside, her naked tail lashing nervously. 'I rode from the palace. Fenelon told me you'd gone this way. Let me tell you—'

'Wait.'

Plessiez signalled to the King's Guard, sending them to stations a little distance from the siege-engine; glanced at the Lord-Architect (the fat man's attention fixed on the

Night Sun and his sextant); and drew the plump Rat into the shelter of the engine-platform.

'Now. And briefly.'

The black Rat priest blinked, her dark eyes wide. Specks of plaster clung to her fur; she smelt of horse-sweat and fear and cordite. Plessiez abruptly put his hands behind his back again, holding the one with the other, this time to prevent them shaking.

'Desaguliers holds the palace and the King.' She drew in a breath, began to relate in a machine-gun rattle.

Half-listening, half-absent, Plessiez narrowed his eyes against the cold wind skirling across the square. The shadows of birds, bright gold and fringed with light, fell thick across him, pelting like summer rain. Their cries diminished as they flocked higher, higher; drawn up after the swarm of brightly coloured insects seeking the sun.

'Your orders, messire?'

He reached out and ruffled Fleury's fur affectionately. 'My orders are to wait. We'll settle our discontented Captain-General, *and* St Cyr, when this is finished. Republic! What fools do they think we are?'

'Prodigious great ones?' The Lord-Architect Casaubon, padding back to the siege-engine, sat down by the heap of his belongings at the foot of the metal ladder. He beamed up at Plessiez, hooking on his heeled court-shoes, and pulling up one stocking that immediately slid back down around his ankle.

'I believe I can dispense with your services,' Plessiez murmured. 'The engine will do very well on-station here. Now, Fleury—'

'Gods rot your soul, I've half a mind to leave you to it!'

Bending, hitting his head on the under-carapace, the Lord-Architect moved under the siege-engine, twisting his head to peer up at the axle and gears. He reached up with delicate plump fingers, feeling among hard metal and grease. A sharp *clck!* sounded.

Plessiez stepped back. 'These men obey my orders,

321

Messire Casaubon. I wouldn't want to have to arrest you.'

The fat man backed out from under the machine, straightening; cracked the back of his head on the under-carriage again, and stared ruefully up into the bird-shadowed sky. At the blue empyrean, the rising dark dots and confetti-colours; and the cold blaze of black-ness at noon.

He sighed with something of a martyr's air: 'All in position?'

The bright shadow of the ballista fell across Plessiez, dazzling him momentarily. Courteous, while he raised a hand to call the Guard, he confirmed: 'Yes. One in each of the thirty-six Districts. Does aught else matter now? If you know of another danger, speak of it.'

The immensely fat man continued to stare upwards, while his ham-hands delved deeper into inner and outer pockets. 'Another danger!'

Casaubon, producing a lump of what appeared to be red wax from one pocket, and black chalk from another, took a last squint at the Night Sun and bent to inscribe curving lines on the paving-stones. Plessiez watched him backing away, rump in the air, periodically back-handing bottles or glasses out of his way. A laugh bubbled in his throat. He fought it down, fearing hysteria; drew his rapier and paced beside the pattern of hieroglyphs that curved around the Vitruvian siege-engine.

'What are you doing?'

At the simplicity of the question, the fat man tilted his head up for a second. 'Doesn't matter where the other thirty-five are, so long as they're in their Districts. Designed *this* one as the key. Activating it takes concen-tration, blast you!'

'But *why*? Is it what I feared?'

While Plessiez still fumed at the desperation he heard in his own voice, the Lord-Architect pointed with one filthy hand at the aust-westerly horizon.

'That's why.'

322

Whirling dark motes spun up from the spires and obelisks of the Fane. Plessiez automatically stepped back and raised his sword to guard position, staring as heads turned all across the square: Rats looking up from their talk and work to stare at the swarming sky.

The Lord-Architect Casaubon straightened up, and surveyed Plessiez over the swell of his chest and belly with arrogant authority.

'Master priest, you and I have scores to pay off. In future time, if there *is* future time, I'll make it my business to discover if you were workman or architect of this plan. Certainly you're one of the pox-damned fools who thought necromancy was a safe *magia* to loose on the world. It may be, even, that you're the cause of Valentine's danger.'

Plessiez, his gaze fixed on the sky, heard a tone in the fat man's voice that made him glance down.

'I'll make time for you.' Casaubon grunted, hefting the chalk lost in his massive hand. 'For the rest — acolytes. The acolytes of the Fane. Had it occurred to you, master priest, that at this hour of the Night Sun they are masterless, too?'

Over the noises of birds and voices, over the humming and chattering in the air, and his own voice calling orders, Plessiez heard behind him the rapid urgent strokes of chalk on stone.

Throat raw with screaming, the White Crow sobbed in a breath and muttered a charm against pain. Stone grated hard under her knees and shins; against the side of her face. The stench of ordure faded in her nostrils, replaced by the sweetness of honey.

Kneeling, slumped against masonry, a hard tension pulled against the muscles of her arm.

'Did we . . . ?'

She opened her eyes to rose-pale light.

A deep hollow, man-sized, pitted the stone floor of the cell beside her. New, but smooth; as if time or the sea had worn it down for aeons. And cradled in that absence

323

of stone she saw a foot, white and bony, a sharp shin, a knee . . . Her head jerked up.

A smell of honey, sweet and sleepy, sang in the air. The cell soared over their heads, white stone with a heart of rose burning softly in its masonry depths.

Candia knelt on the newly hollowed stone, bearded face gaunt now, his arm around the naked white shoulder of an old man.

'Gods! Oh, dear gods . . . '

The man's hands busy at his face touched flesh, white hair, nose, ears and lips; slid down to his Adam's apple and collar-bone and sharp-ribbed chest. Pale age-spotted skin all whole. Candia's buff-and-scarlet jacket swathed his hips; his thin legs and bare bony feet protruded from under it. His chest rose and fell smoothly. He broke into a sweet open smile.

All realization in a split second: pain slammed her vision black and bloody. She doubled up. A scream ripped from her throat. Tears ran down her face. Still kneeling supported against the cell wall, she stared at her outstretched arm and hand.

Her left hand impaled, four inches down on the jutting iron spike.

Solid metal poked up from torn skin and flesh. Blood and white liquid ran down her arm, streaking red, drying. Her flesh trembled: the bones in her hand grated against the impaling metal spike.

'God-shit-*damn*it . . . '

A hand covered her eyes; she smelt a fragrance of lilac. Heurodis's voice said: 'Don't look. Wait. *There.*'

Something gripped her left hand, pulled it up, free of the spike.

Pain ripped through her. She rolled foetally on the stone floor of the cell, screaming, left hand held out and away from her body. Warm trickles of blood ran over her wrist.

'Lady.' A new voice, hesitant, well spoken; light with age.

She opened her mouth, screaming. A cold numbness took her skin, sank into muscle and bone.

The White Crow pushed herself up on to her knees, supporting herself on her right hand, sweating and dizzy. The old man knelt at her side, shrugging Candia off, labile face creased into a triumphant smile. She looked down. Both his hands clasped hers, the light of summer leaves shining out between the Bishop's fingers.

Pain ebbed.

The light of forests faded.

She covered their hands with her free one, squeezed his for a second longer. His grip loosened. The White Crow took her hand back, examining the wound. Red muscle gleamed at the edges, and a white bone glinted. A skein of dermis glinted over raw flesh. Pain. No blood.

'I could do more . . . if I were stronger.'

The White Crow met his grey brilliant eyes. 'I could learn from your Church, I think. Honour to you, my lord Bishop.'

'Master-Physician. You'd better see this.'

Heurodis's voice came from the cell door. The White Crow stood, staggered in the hollowed floor, bare feet kicking the discarded rapier and pack, and lurched over to lean up against the door-jamb.

All the twenty or so strips of paper curled up from the step and jamb and lintel and snapped, bleached into blankness.

'We'd better move, if we can.' The White Crow, straightening up, took a step across the threshold of the cell. It opened now into the body of a vast high-vaulted hall.

She looked back. Framed in the cell door, Heurodis held the arm of the Bishop of the Trees, supporting him as he rose to his feet; Theodoret leaning part of his weight on the gaunt blond man's shoulder.

A voice, quieter than anything ever heard before but perfectly clear, spoke at her left hand.

'*Child of flesh, he was bait – for a healer.*'

Breath feathered her dark-red hair, pearled damp on her neck; a reek of carrion made her eyes sting and run over with tears. Her hand throbbed. Her legs weighed lead-heavy: she caught her breath, could not turn to where the voice came from.

Quiet as the rustling of electrons in the Dance, the voice spoke again.

'*You could not have healed him if I had desired him truly to die.*'

The woman has almost reached the sea again.

Andaluz hurries protectively after her, the coach abandoned. Her footprints, small and deep, wind across the sand of the airfield. His shadow pools in light around his feet. No matter how fast he walks, she is before him: her arms held up, the bamboo staff clasped in one hand, her bright-feathered silver braid penduluming across her back with her swift strides.

'Lady! Luka!'

Birds wheel above her head. Black-headed gulls, shrikes, cormorants: they swoop and skim the small woman's head or hands and rise, strong wings beating, in the wake of the flock that flies up to the Night Sun. Still they come, still they fly, still they pursue.

'Wait! Dear lady . . . '

Sweating, popping buttons as he pulls the neck of his doublet open, Andaluz comes to the marble balustrade and steps overlooking the lagoon. He leans against the balustrade, panting.

'Luka.'

A sea-wind blows, sharp with the cold of ocean depths.

Black light shines down upon the marble terraces, the promenade, and the tossing waters of the lagoon. Onyx gleams flash from the waves. No-one but Andaluz and the Lady of the Birds hears the rushing of that sea.

The docks stretch out, empty.

She stands on the marble steps that go down to the dock,

staring to where the Boat moored. Nothing is there. The Boat is gone.

Andaluz, sharp pains in his chest, sees her raise her head and open her mouth: her cry is forlorn as a gull's, desolate.

Timber sleepers, jammed between the surrounding railings and wired down, blocked the entrance to the underground station.

'Break it open.' Plessiez smiled sardonically. 'The strike is over, I think.'

He stepped back as Fleury beckoned and a squad of Rats with dirty velvet robes tucked up into their belts began levering away wood and cutting wire.

The scrolled railings and steps leading down to the railway stood on the corner of the square and First Avenue, outside porticoed town-houses. A few yards from where he stood, a dozen Rats furiously piled up paving-stones and planks, barricading the doors.

'Soon have it done.' Fleury nervously tugged the scarlet jacket down over her plump haunches. 'Plessiez, what are you thinking?'

The pavement thrummed under his clawed feet. Plessiez glanced across the square. A hundred yards away the siege-engine glittered darkly under the Night Sun. Blue-liveried King's Guard swarmed over the platform, rolling out barrels of Greek fire for the ballista.

Of the Lord-Architect Casaubon, there was no sign.

'These houses aren't defensible. I'm opening a means of retreat. If the siege-engines fail us, we can take refuge in the underground tunnels and defend the entrances.' Seeing Fleury's eyes widen, he added: 'Go round. Pass the word on.'

Wood screamed, splintering. A sleeper tipped up, crashed down. Two Rats gripped another slab of wood and lifted it aside. Plaster and cracked tile fell down into the stairwell. Plessiez's nose twitched, scenting for anything strange, detecting only coal and stale smoke.

A voice spoke behind him.

'Messire, you're coming with me now. To the Night Council.'

'What?' Plessiez turned, the cold wind blowing dust in his eyes.

Under the blazing blue sky and Night Sun, a burly brown Rat strode towards him between piles of debris. Her coat showed charred and scraped patches, but from somewhere she had found a bright blue sash to tie over her shoulder and between her two rows of furry dugs.

'Charnay? Good gods, Charnay!' He kicked rubbish aside, stepping to grip her arms and gaze up at her face. 'You made it at last. Late, of course; but not too late, one hopes.'

Plessiez's gaze travelled past the brown Rat. He smiled. A pale black-haired young woman stood a few paces behind Charnay, hugging herself with bare and goosepimpled arms, head bowed. A dappled black-and-white tail hung limp to her ankles.

'Or did you find her for me, Mistress Zari?'

The young Katayan in the black dress shivered, not looking up. In a low voice she said: 'You'll need a Kings' Memory. I'm here for that, remember?'

A third member of the group straightened up from a crouch by a pile of debris, brushing dust from a small hand-crossbow. A Katayan woman perhaps twenty-five: black tail and cropped black hair. She put her hand on Zar-bettu-zekigal's arm, the lace at the wrist of her silk coat falling over her hand.

Plessiez frowned. Momentarily putting aside the bustle of preparation, the stranger, Rats running past on errands, and the darkness seeping into the north-austerly horizon, he walked forward and put his hands on Zar-bettu-zekigal's shoulders.

'Why will I need a Memory now, little one?'

'The Night Council.'

'Don't be ridiculous. This is about to become a battle-field!"

He turned, opening his mouth to summon Fleury. Charnay blocked his way. Irritably he put one ring-fingered hand on her chest, pushing her aside.

Her strong hands gripped his sash and sword-harness, jerking him to a halt. Startled, swearing, Plessiez felt his feet leave the pavement as the brown Rat lifted him bodily, held him for a second six inches above ground, and dropped him. Stone jarred him from head to heels.

'*Listen to me, messire!*'

'You over-muscled oaf—!' He wrenched himself free. 'I have no time for your customary *stupidity*.'

'Listen.'

Cold hackles began to walk down Plessiez's spine. He looked up, meeting Charnay's eyes, seeing her blink slowly, slowly.

'They showed me how to get back to them. Down there.' She pointed at the newly opened station entrance. 'That will do. They want you, messire, and I'm bringing you to them. Either you can walk, or I'll knock you down, or wound you and carry you down there.'

Black sunlight beat down on her translucent tattered ears; on the grimy fur of her flanks. In her face shone memories of brick tunnels, of gibbets, of dangers passed and of whatever is unearthly in the city that lies under the city. She drew her long rapier.

'I can't leave. I'm needed. I can't abandon these people!'

Zar-bettu-zekigal refused to meet his eyes. The other woman had hunkered down again, sorting crossbow bolts from the debris on the marble flagstones.

The brown Rat said: '*Now*, messire.'

They do not see where a greasy-haired woman crawls on hands and knees through the bodies outside the tents, shedding armour at every move as if some insect abandoned its carapace.

She half-rises, grunts, slides down to lope painfully along in the shadow of the wall, supporting herself with one or sometimes both hands.

The Rats watch the darkening horizon, not the edges of the square. Her dark red clothes disguise her somewhat in bloody shadows. Unwatched, she limps towards the entrance of the station; pauses once to lift her head and bark a hysterical laugh at the sky.

She slides into the stairwell and shadow. Following.

Zar-bettu-zekigal clung to the brickwork either side of the arch, squatting in the niche, her knees almost up about her ears. She peered through the narrow slit at the back of the niche where a brick had been missed out.

'Just more tunnels.'

Without turning, she kicked back with her feet and let go, arms and tail wheeling, landing four-square on the cinder track. Moisture dripped down from the roof of the tunnel. She turned, looted black ankle-boots crunching on the cinders. Elish-hakku-zekigal walked light-footed from sleeper to sleeper, the lantern swinging in her hand.

Ahead, in shifting circles of lamplight on brick, the two Rats walked. Zar-bettu-zekigal shrugged, plodding to catch up with the older Katayan.

'The birds will take them to the Boat.'

'What?' Zar-bettu-zekigal looked up warily. The hard toes of her unfamiliar boots caught on the railway sleepers.

'Souls. That's what she's doing.' Elish-hakku-zekigal held the lantern higher. Its barred light swung over the curved brick walls. 'The Lady Luka. She calls the birds to eat the *psyche*, the butterflies, before they're drawn up into the Night Sun. So that the birds can fly to the Boat and the *psyche* be reborn.'

Zar-bettu-zekigal's shoulders lifted. She took a deep breath, mouth moving slightly. 'Oh, what! I knew *that*!'

The woman smiled, her gaze on the diminishing parallel rails.

'Of course you did.'

Zari skipped down from sleeper to sleeper, hands thrust in her black dress pockets, head coming up as she gazed around at the tunnel, bouncing on her heels. 'Elish, why did Father let you come here?'

The older Katayan momentarily shifted her gaze from the rails to her sister. 'He doesn't know I'm here.'

'Oh, what! See you, you told Messire Andaluz that you're an envoy.'

'I could hardly tell him that I'm a runaway.' Amusement made the Katayan's tone rich.

Zar-bettu-zekigal slowed to walk beside her, looking up at the pale face nested among lace ruffles, the cropped black hair combed forward. She took one hand from her pocket and slipped it into Elish-hakku-zekigal's free hand. A black tail curved up to cuff her ear lightly.

'Elish, I love you.'

'I know you do, buzzard. And I intend to see we both come out of this crazy place in one piece.'

'Back there . . . up there . . . *will* those things from the Fane attack?'

The hand tightened on hers. Elish-hakku-zekigal began walking at a faster pace. Her face in the shifting lantern-light might have shown a smile or a grimace.

'Why ask me, little buzzard? I don't know everything.'

She jerked the older woman's arm sharply. 'You *do*!'

Elish-hakku-zekigal's laughter echoed down the tunnel. The black and the brown Rat paused to look back. She shook her head, sobering. 'Well, then. Yes. I think they will. That isn't our fight.'

The big Rat stooped slightly, the pole of her lantern in one hand and her drawn sword in the other. Yellow light shone on her brown fur, on her naked tail and clawed feet. She raised her snout to stare at the roof, incisors glinting.

'Are we right?' Zar-bettu-zekigal called.

'Certainly! I just have to work out—'

' – where we are?' the black Rat completed, *sotto voce*, after a moment.

'It's going to be fine, messire,' Zar-bettu-zekigal said as she came up with them.

Plessiez sighed. He carried a bull's-eye lantern in one

hand, light glinting from the buckles of his harness, and his rings, and the slender drawn rapier in his other hand. The cardinal's sash glowed a brilliant green against his black fur.

'You had no right to drag me down here, away from . . . ' He stared at Charnay still, adding in a lower tone: 'I would be happier with myself if I could regret the leaving more sincerely.'

'This way,' Charnay announced.

The big Rat padded away, following a curve of the line. Zar-bettu-zekigal squatted down on a sleeper, pulling at the hard metal of the rails where another joined it; looked ahead to realize the line split. She hastily knotted a boot-lace and rose to her feet, following.

'Suppose a train came?'

'Suppose nothing of the kind!' Elish-hakku-zekigal reached out and ruffled her hair.

Zar-bettu-zekigal jumped from sleeper to sleeper, two-footed, grinning at the echoes coming back off the damp tunnel walls. 'How far down are we?'

'The lower levels.' Plessiez replied without turning.

Elish-hakku-zekigal lengthened her stride to catch up with the Cardinal-General. 'Two things you should perhaps be aware of, your Eminence. One is that we're being followed – No, Zar', be quiet!'

Zar-bettu-zekigal took her hands from her pockets and loped to walk between the black Rat and the Katayan woman.

'And the other is that your friend will have to take us off the track soon. You can't get there from here.'

The black Rat thrust the bull's-eye lantern at Zar-bettu-zekigal without acknowledgement, and she caught the handle just as he let go of it. Heat from the glass and metal warmed her hands. Holding it at arm's length, she saw a splinter of light: Plessiez now carried in his onyx-ringed left hand a triangular-bladed dagger.

Speaking across her head to Elish, the black Rat said: 'Who follows?'

'I can't tell who or what it is.'

'And the rest – you know about this "Night Council", I comprehend? And the ways to reach it? Oh, come – you've been in the heart of the world how long?'

Zar-bettu-zekigal muttered a protest, winced as the older Katayan woman's tail slapped her leg.

'She's a shaman,' she protested, ignoring Elish. 'Messire, you remember, when we came out from below last time, what we saw.'

Plessiez's upper lip wrinkled, showing white incisors. He quickened his pace.

A coil of mist brushed Zar-bettu-zekigal. She put her free hand up to her face, touching dampness. The metal surface of the lantern hissed gently, evaporating moisture.

'Look.' She held up the lantern.

The light cast Charnay's shadow ahead on to a bank of mist. Nitre-webbed brick walls vanished as mist thickened into fog. The brown Rat strode on, her lantern bobbing on its pole, becoming a globe of yellow light.

Plessiez's hand tightened on the hilt of his rapier. 'Well, we can't lose her now, I suppose.'

Zar-bettu-zekigal, conscious of her aching arm, held up the bull's-eye lantern, and took Elish's hand again. Her nostrils flared. Fog pearled on her dress, on the hairs on her arms; and she glanced up at the Katayan woman, seeing the sapphire at her throat dimmed by clinging moisture.

She stumbled, stared ahead. No tunnel walls. The clatter of her feet vanished into the fog, echoless. Three lanterns glowed, yellow in the mist.

'It smells strange.'

The black Rat briefly looked over his shoulder and murmured: 'Sewers.'

'No.'

'We're too far below ground-level for anything else, I assure you. Charnay, woman, slow down!'

Zar-bettu-zekigal shivered, chilled. She held the lamp and lifted her head to stare upwards, seeing nothing but fog, no tunnel roof. She pursed her lips to whistle for echoes; her mouth too dry. The lantern's muffled light could not even illuminate the cinders and sleepers underfoot.

'It smells . . . salt.'

Elish-hakku-zekigal's grip tightened.

Faint at first, on the edge of hearing, she felt the pulse and thunder of surf. A wind stirred the fog. She tasted seaweed and salt on her lips, pressing on faster to keep up with Charnay's lantern; brushing the black Rat's shoulder as she stumbled beside him.

'The sea!'

Wind roiled the fog, moving but not shifting it. The thunder of waves came from all quarters, the pounding of waves and the hiss of shingle sucked back. Zar-bettu-zekigal raised her head, neck prickling to the cold wind, searching for a lightness that would mark sky or sun. Wet air choked her. She loosed Elish's hand and stepped away.

'*No.*'

A black tail coiled around her wrist, pulled. She jerked to a halt.

'I want to see the sea!'

'No.'

Ahead, the bobbing lantern slowed. She caught a glimpse of Charnay, sword in hand, raising her snout to quest after a scent. Plessiez and the older Katayan woman hastened their steps.

'Oh, wait, will you!' Pebbles dragged at her feet and ankles, slid down her boots. Zar-bettu-zekigal stopped, bent, and put the lantern down on the beach; lifting her foot and reaching for the heel of her boot.

She froze. 'Elish! El!'

Brown pebbles crunched underfoot: friable, fragile. The lantern, standing tilted, shed illumination on the round shadow-pocked pebbles. All of a size: no larger than a walnut.

Tiny skulls.

Ragged eye-sockets caught shadow, lamp-light. Cranial sutures gleamed, black-thread thin; the articulate and precise joints of jaws shone. She stared, seeing some with lower jaws, some with only upper teeth; the ragged slits of noses. Thousand upon thousand, million upon million, stretching out under the fog in piled banks and valleys.

Underfoot, as far back as lamp-light shone, tiny crushed skulls marked their path. Zar-bettu-zekigal wavered, balanced on one leg, hand still gripping the back of her left boot.

'Elish!' She wailed. 'It doesn't matter where I put my feet, I'm going to break more of them . . .'

'I see it, little one. Keep walking.'

Zar-bettu-zekigal hooked off her boot, balancing one-legged, shook it and replaced it. She seized the lantern and lifted it. Fog swirled about her ankles, mellowing, concealing. The slope dragged at her feet as she ran after Elish-hakku-zekigal and the Rats.

'This place stinks,' she said bitterly. 'Ei, Charnay, aren't we there yet? How far now? Which way?'

She grabbed the brown Rat's sword-arm, fur slick and fog-dampened, shaking it. Charnay looked down at her.

'I forget,' she confessed.

'Oh, *what*—'

Plessiez, a yard or two ahead, interrupted. 'I think we've arrived.'

Lights shone through the fog. Zar-bettu-zekigal plodded on over the fragile beach, refusing to look down.

The fog thinned.

Ochre and red cliffs reared up before her and to either side; summits lost in distance. The sea echoed softly from wall to wall. A great amphitheatre of rock, in the flares of torches.

Warmth breathed from the stone, as if the sun had only just ceased to shine and it still gave back heat. Zar-bettu-zekigal stretched out her hands.

Hacked out of the bedrock brown granite, still part of the cliffs, great squared thrones formed a semicircle.

Zar-bettu-zekigal bent to place the bull's-eye lantern at her feet. Tiny skulls crunched under her boots. She reached back without looking, and Elish-hakku-zekigal gripped her hand. The older Katayan came to stand at her back, setting down her lantern, folding her arms about Zari's chest and resting her chin on the top of her head.

Charnay drove the pole of her lantern deep into the beach, brushing bone splinters from her fur. She straightened up.

Plessiez trod a few paces forward, past Zar-bettu-zekigal, until he stood at the focal point of those inward-facing thrones, lifting his head and resting his rapier back across the drying fur of his shoulder.

'Old . . .' Elish's chin jolted her skull as the woman whispered. Zar-bettu-zekigal gripped her sister's hand, pulling her arms tighter.

Silence breathed from the stone. Silence and a tension, the bedrock brown granite dense with aeons of geological compression.

The squared thrones jutted from living rock that continued above them into square pillars, soaring up. She tilted her head to follow; lost the sight in dim distance a quarter of a mile overhead. No sky. Nothing but foundation rock below the world.

Dizzy, she dropped her gaze to the empty thrones. Crude seats and arms and backs, smoothed not by artisans but by time.

'The carvings.' Elish's voice in her ear.

Lines marked the back of each brown granite throne, cut with no metal tools, cut with bone and wood and stone itself. She stared up at the human figures cut in stylized profile, the planes of muscle, the nakedness of bodies. She faced the central throne. Raising her eyes, Zar-bettu-zekigal followed the line of the giant figure's chest and shoulders. Scales marked the neck; the head not human but the head of a cobra.

She looked to the next throne, and the next. A man with the head of a viper, a woman whose black lidless

336

eyes shone in the head of a python, a young man with the blunt head of a boa, a woman whose shoulders supported the blue-and-crimson head of a coral snake . . .

Movement caught her peripheral vision; Elish's arms tightened; she heard Plessiez swear an oath, and Charnay grunt with satisfaction. Colour and movement. Each figure changing as her eye left it, changing from bas-relief to solidity . . .

They sat each one high upon their thrones, the light of torches sliding on their bronze human flesh. Giant figures, twice the height of a man. The torches flared and glinted from scales, from lidless black eyes, from pulses beating in the white soft scales under serpentine jaws.

Elish's arms loosened. She breathed: 'The Serpent-headed . . . '

Now each of the Thirteen arose, standing before their thrones, scales shimmering, forked tongues licking between blunt lips; old with the age of granite, of bone, of earth.

Plessiez sheathed his rapier with a tiny click that echoed back from the towering walls. The black Rat raised his head, gazing at the giant figures.

'You are the Night Council?'

A scent of musk and sand-hot deserts breathed from the beach, from the miniature human skulls tumbled to the foot of the thrones. From the centre throne the figure arose, standing with brown hands resting on the granite.

Light shone on his human body, brown, smooth-skinned and naked; and Zar-bettu-zekigal let her gaze rise to where skin transmuted into scale and his spine curved inhumanly. Rearing up, haloed by hooded skin, the eyes of a cobra surveyed them with bright anger.

He spoke.

'Yeth.'

She turned from the cell doorway, staring out into the Fane.

'*You could not have healed him, if I had desired him truly to die.*'

White stone walls shone in sourceless light. The White Crow looked out across a floor littered with broken glass, alembics, bains-marie and furnaces; eyes narrowing to witness the machinery of the alchemist. Flat glass bubbles, set in ranks into the wall, danced with moving pictures. She registered in peripheral vision outer views of the city. Past that . . .

This high vaulted hall opened into a nave, into a colonnade; into balconies, oratories, galleries . . .

So clear the air, no possible distance could make it blurred or diffuse. She saw into the heart of the Fane: all bright, all in focus. Colonnades of white arches hooped away, growing smaller in perspective; vaults shone and soared; galleries ran the walls, drawing zig-zag lines into the distance. All around: tower-stairs and loggias, porches and steps and halls starkly clear; white and intricate and shining as if carved from ivory and milk.

Glass rolled aside as she moved, ticking across the stone. She glanced down.

A rose-briar lay across the flagstones, jet-black, bristling with thorns. One withered leaf clung to the stem. Something had eaten away the petals of the remaining black rose. She raised her head, following it.

Insects crawled.

Cockroaches, locusts, scarab beetles, flies: a towering mass of bodies filled all the near end of the hall. Chittering, feelers waving, chitinous wings rasping; the insects crawled on a mountainous bulk that heaved although still.

The White Crow caught a glimpse of blackness under the mass, began to make out shapes. The circular rim of a great nostril, crusted with the bodies of locusts. Higher up the shapes of scales, cockroaches crawling under the rims. Tendrils of darkness sweeping back to where, through chitinous crawling bodies, an eye opens, disclosing a darkness greater than the Night Sun.

338

One-handed, she sheathed the rapier and beckoned the others to leave the cell.

He filled the whole space of the hall, so that she could hardly take in more than rising shoulders, basalt-feathered wings, tusked and toothed muzzle furred with insects. Cockroaches, locusts, black beetles; carrion-flies and scarabs; they clung, flew up a few inches, and fell to crawl again in worship over the body of The Spagyrus.

Dizzy with expense of power and sick with the receding tide of pain, the White Crow walked drunkenly across the flagstones until she stood before the Decan. A cockchafer burred past her face. Her head jerked back.

She held up her blood-stained and black-pitted left hand, and knelt to touch one knee to the stone floor.

'Divine One, Lord of the Elements, you healed him through me. I thank you for it.'

The shining basalt eyes closed.

The great body sprawled the length of the hall, flank up against curtain-tracery walls, head rising twenty-five feet into the air. Roses covered the massive paws and shoulders, clustered on the joint of a wing.

White light shone on living black basalt.

Clear now, unshadowed, she traced every lineament. Crusted nostrils, thick with hair and flies, in an upper muzzle that overhung the lower jaw by ten feet. Jutting tusks above the nostrils. Teeth spiking up from the lower jaw, digging into scaled cheeks; flowing tendrils around the head and tiny naked ears.

The White Crow got awkwardly to her feet. She heard someone kick glass as Candia, Heurodis and the Bishop came to stand beside her. The great eyes remained closed.

'Now . . . ' She tapped her closed right fist against her mouth. 'What do we do now?'

'What we do now is . . . ' Candia stepped forward, shaking out the stained lace of his cuffs, tugging his loose shirt into order. 'We play cards.'

'*What?*'

The blond man held out a filthy hand to Heurodis.

The white-haired woman felt in the pocket of her blue cotton dress and brought out a thick pack of cards. Candia grinned, boyish, and she tutted.

'Tarot cards.' Elegant, faintly comic, he stripped off the binding ribbon and held the pack up one-handed, cards fanned into a circle. The White Crow gazed at images stained-glass brilliant against the white walls and the wreckage, against the million insects crawling, worshipping, on the living stone skin of The Spagyrus.

'You're out of your mind, Messire Candia,' the White Crow remarked quite cheerfully. 'You know that, don't you?'

He ignored her, scooping the cards into a pack again. Automatically his feet took him a few paces one way, a few paces the other; glancing up at the silent Decan as he spoke.

'Divine One, you'll remember me. My name is Candia. Reverend tutor, University of Crime. Now, my talent is the use of the tarot pack. Four suits: Swords, Grails, Sceptres, Stones. Thirty trumps. Watch.'

The White Crow craned her neck to look up at the god-daemon's face. Briars and black roses tangled in the scaled and tendrilled head, coiled to ring a forearm; rustling with the living garment of worshipping insects. The basalt eyes remained closed.

The blond man gave Heurodis his hand as the small woman seated herself limberly cross-legged on the flagstones. Theodoret stood behind her. Candia very carefully lowered himself to sit opposite. His long-fingered and dirty hands shuffled the pack.

Bemused, the White Crow moved to look over his shoulder.

'A reading of all eighty-six cards,' he announced. His fingers quickened, the pasteboard images flashing past. 'To determine the immediate and near future. My own method. Now.'

The man laid out three cards swiftly, slapping them face-down on the stone floor. Another three, then five grouped in a diamond with one in the centre. He paused. More sets of three, five and six.

'Hey!' She grabbed at his wrist, missing it.

The strong thin fingers dealt two more cards off the bottom of the pack as she watched. Candia glanced up through flopping hair, eyes bright. He indicated the backs of eighty-six cards with a careless gesture.

'Broadest reading, three cards in the Sign of the Archer. What have we got?'

Heurodis leaned forward, grunting, and turned over the three cards. The White Crow saw a castle struck by lightning, *The House of Destruction*, the knot of a shroud, *Plague*, and a skull with blue periwinkle flowers set into the eyes, *Death*.

'I think . . . ' Candia's hand hovered over the cards. 'Probably not.'

He grinned at the White Crow, replacing the three cards face-down and then reaching out to them again. He paused, hand in mid-air, and gestured to her. 'You.'

She knelt cautiously and turned the three cards. The first, in bright colours, showed two children playing at noon in a garden, *The Sun*. The second, a man and a woman embracing, *The Lovers*. On the third, a hermaphrodite dancing among balanced alchemical symbols, *The World*.

'You can't do that!' Wide-eyed, she stared; aware of the distraction but not of when it had occurred.

Heurodis gave a long-toothed smile.

'I don't mean it won't work if you do, I mean that you can't do it!'

Candia fell to shuffling some of the lower cards, keeping *The Sun*, *The Lovers* and *The World* at the top of the reading. The White Crow stared intently, drew a deep breath and tried again.

'You can't sharp these cards. It isn't possible. They're constrained by the future. All the tarot's links are with what's going to happen; you can't cheat what's Fated!'

Fair hair fell across his eyes as he looked up. Practised,

he shook back the lace cuffs from his wrists; a deliberate staginess in his gestures.

'Readings influence what will come, as well as being influenced *by* it.'

The White Crow stood, rubbing her calf muscle with her right hand. The humming of insects made her dizzy. An incredulous laugh bubbled up. She stifled it.

'You're telling me the University of Crime can sharp *tarot* cards?'

Heurodis said: 'Not often, girlie. But when we need to we can.'

Candia turned over a Ten of Grails, Three of Sceptres and *The House of Destruction* in the position of the Sign of the Wilderness. He lifted his gaze to meet the White Crow's, one brow raised; and when she glanced down it was to see the Ten of Grails, Ace of Sceptres and *Fidelity*.

'Damn you, you just might exercise some influence. Here. You just might. Are you a good cheat, Messire Candia?'

'The best.'

A breath reached her: saline, musky. Black basalt eyes opened, twenty-five feet above her head. The great lips moved apart, and she stared up at a cockroach picking its way across the living basalt of the Decan's skin.

'Bait for a healer . . . which of my ten million souls here in the heart of the world, think you, is fated now truly to die? Can you tell, little magus? I tell you: they are already grievous sick.'

Insects buzzed. The White Crow gazed up at empty vaulting over the Decan's head.

'I don't think to outwit omnipotency, Divine One. That would be stupid.'

'My sister of the Ten Degrees of High Summer gave you a certain hour. You have not used it well.'

She grinned up at the Decan: a rictus of pain, fear and defiance. She held up her left hand. The wound in its palm gaped, raw but not bleeding. Her fingers, red and swollen, bore pin-prick marks from the briars of black roses.

'All the same, aren't you? All Thirty-Six. The hour isn't over yet.'

'*WE ARE NOT ALL THE SAME . . . !*'

Echoes shuddered. Quietly, beside her, the Bishop of the Trees said: 'He's sick. His Sign is occluded.'

He reached down to his side, more firmly knotting the sleeves of the buff-and-scarlet doublet around his hips. He wore the makeshift covering with an old man's slow dignity. A faint green light began to gather about his fingers.

'No. I agree. But even so . . . ' The White Crow shook her head warningly. 'This is the crucial hour. Plague outside, sickness in the Fane; and somewhere, somewhere . . . '

Great lips breathed carrion on the air.

'*They are far from here, and sick, and soon to die. Both the death of the body, and the death of a soul.*'

The White Crow cocked a jaundiced eye at the insect-ridden slopes of flank and shoulder rising, mountainous, before her.

'Yes? And will they die of the . . . same . . . sickness . . . ?'

She stopped. Her left hand burned, the pain connecting her to the substance of the Fane and the *magia* acted within it; and slowly, aloud, she followed the connection.

'You're the heart and centre of it,' the White Crow said. 'The truly dead, the plague, the death of souls, and the *magia* of necromancy. All of it begins here. Tell me, I know! I feel your power through the stone, I've spilled my blood here, I've healed a man with pain and your power channelled through me, and *I know!*'

She stopped to draw breath, grinning through tears that poured without volition down her face.

'One plague. Here and outside. *One* plague. Black alchemy . . . Oh, they will die of the same sickness, won't they! It doesn't have to be a human death, or the death of a Rat-Lord. Why didn't I think of it! What death would really uncreate the world? *One of the Thirty-Six!*'

Crowned with roses, worshipped by carrion-flies, his Sign occluded by his power still immanent in the Fane about her, the Decan of Noon and Midnight smiles.

'The most ancient question,' Theodoret murmured at her ear. '*Can* the omnipotent gods unmake themselves?'

She ignored him. Theodoret stepped back to where Candia and the white-haired woman bent over the spread of cards, their intensity of concentration aware but not admitting influence of even the Lord of Noon and Midnight.

'*I will let them play, little magus, until my Sign is past its occlusion. I will even let your bait keep his life, for as long as is left to him.*'

Insect-clouds swarmed as the great body shifted, one hind claw rasping at his basalt ribs. The great eyelids slid down, up; darkness glimmering in the depths of the eyes. The voice dropped to quietness.

'*We are not all of us alike: the Thirty-Six. We should not all hold equal powers. I give you a secret, little magus. When the Great Circle flies in pieces, then one of us will re-create it. And there will be not Thirty-Six, but One alone.*'

Carrion-breath stung her eyes. The rose-light smouldering in the masonry flared: all the debris and pillars and stones white as skin with blood beating a swift pulse under it.

'*I give you that secret, little Valentine. Tell whom you will. And what can you do, now that you know?*'

The White Crow looked down at one whole and one injured hand.

'If you're not afraid, Divine One, why stop me?'

'*Child of flesh, you speak of fear?*'

The White Crow laughed, water running from the corners of her eyes. She reached up with her right hand as if she would touch the Decan of Noon and Midnight.

'*Give* me my chance, then,' she challenged. 'What can it matter to you, you who know all, see all, are all? Give me the strength to search, and see if I find you out!'

Candia scratched at his overgrown blond beard and muttered: 'Shit!'

'Oh, I know.' The White Crow spoke to him without turning away from the Decan. 'The most unwise thing, to challenge God—'

Pain stabbed her fingers.

She brought her hands up in front of her face, trying to clench them against the fire burning under the skin. Her white nails shone – shone and lengthened, splitting. Whiteness ran back over her hands and wrists and forearms.

'Wh- whaa—?'

Faint down feathered the backs of her hands. She raised them closer to her face, knocking them against some obstruction. Her head twisting, she seemed to knock her nose against her hands: a nose that lengthened, darkened, pulled up her teeth into its growth as her mouth shrank . . .

The Spagyrus' laughter shook dust from the high vaulting of the Fane.

Stepping back, stumbling, she fell. As she fell, her body collapsed into itself, folding impossibly. Her feet still flat on the stone, she seemed to be crouching only a few inches above the floor.

She threw out her arms for balance. The Fane wheeled.

'Whaaack!'

Briefly, far below, she caught sight of human faces turned up to hers in fear and awe. Air pushed up under her arms, sleeked down her body. Pain threaded her arteries with hot wires. Double images blurred her vision.

'Crrr-aaark!'

She swooped at the floor and a black shadow rose to meet her. Wide-winged, the tail fanning to catch the air; no mistaking that blunt beak and body. She skimmed the stone, wheeling to rise again on wide-fingered pinions.

Divine laughter beat against her, abrasive as sand and splinters of glass.

'*Search, if you will! If you can!*'

The albino carrion crow wheels and flees into the heart of the Fane.

Anger shining in his lidless black eyes, the head of the Night Council spoke.

'I fail to thee what *exthactly* is tho amuthing.'

Zar-bettu-zekigal buried her face in her sister's lace ruffle, little whimpering noises escaping her. An open palm hit her sharply across the ear.

'Behave! Zar!'

She swung round, clasping her hands behind her back, kicking her heels in the bone beach. Her black ankle-boots crunched on fragile skulls no larger than walnuts. Fog touched her spine coldly. She gazed up at the thrones of the Serpent-headed, eyes bright.

'I didn't say anything!'

Dry heat radiated back from the endless cliffs, from the brown bedrock granite and the thrones of the foundation of the world. Twelve of the Serpent-headed seated themselves on their thrones; the last remained standing. Flaring torchlight gleamed on oiled human limbs, on naked hip and breast and muscular shoulders. On necks glittering with scales, serpent heads; blunt muzzles and the black lidless eyes of viper, coral snake, cobra.

'The, ah—' Plessiez coughed into his fist. Zar-bettu-zekigal tried to catch his gaze; he avoided her. 'The reason for this summons, messires?'

The head of the Council's sharp cobra jaw dipped, regarding the small group below. A black-bootlace tongue licked across his lipless mouth.

'We with to regithster a thtrong complaint. Grave thins have been committed againtht uth by the world above.'

'Excuth – *excuse* me.' Zar-bettu-zekigal rubbed her bare fog-dampened arms, digging in her short nails. By virtue of that she concentrated enough to call up across the intervening yards: 'Who are you, messires?'

The cobra head moved, lidless eyes fixing on her.

'Your thithster the thaman thould be able to tell you that. We are the Night Counthil. The mostht ancient godth of the world.'

Zari turned rapidly away, hugging herself; bumped against Plessiez and looked up as the black Rat glanced down. Their eyes met.

'"Thithster."'

Zar-bettu-zekigal spluttered.

'"Thaman"?'

She caught one glimpse of Charnay's puzzled face and elbowed the Cardinal-General in the ribs. Plessiez looked, drew himself up, snout quivering, observed, 'Messires, I apolo – apologize for my companion,' stuttered a few more broken syllables and threw his arm across Zari's shoulders and guffawed, head down, weak, snorting with laughter.

'I thuppoth . . . ' Unable to breathe, half-supporting his weight, she hugged his shaking body, nose pressed into the fur of the black Rat's chest. 'I thuppoth you think that'th funny!'

'Messire!' Charnay protested, outraged.

'Oh, he's gone.' Zar-bettu-zekigal struggled for breath, eyes brimming. She achieved poise long enough to add, '"Thithster"!', the black Rat's body quaked with another fit, and she snuffled and burst into raucous laughter.

'Messire Plessiez!'

The black Rat straightened up, one arm still resting across her shoulders, the other clasped tight to his own ribs; looking at Elish-hakku-zekigal. He shook his head.

'Lady, I don't *care* any more. I've spent my life being diplomatic under the most trying circumstances and this, *this* is the end of it. Frankly, it's ridiculous.' He showed his incisors in a sharp grin, staring up at the cobra-headed Lord of the Night Council. 'Quite ridiculouth.'

'For gods' sake be careful!'

The black Rat ruffled Zar-bettu-zekigal's hair. 'Oh, I don't underestimate the danger. You mistake me. This is too much. I no longer care.'

Torchlight flared on the mist behind Zar-bettu-zekigal. She gazed up at cold-eyed disapproving serpent heads. The heat of bedrock granite shone warm on her face. Unconsciously she held her hands out, warming them;

347

the breathlessness of laughter tight in her chest.

'See you, I'm a Kings' Memory. You have an auditor.'

A burly male with the head of a python spoke from the fifth throne.

'We know what you are, mortal. We requethted your prethenth.'

Plessiez snorted. He stood with his weight on one clawed hind foot, tail coiled out for balance behind him, smiling cynically.

'Charnay, for *this* you took me away from a battle? Well.' He reached up to his neck, pulled the *ankh* from his collar and threw it on to the beach of skulls. 'By the time we make our way back to the world, it will be one which we control. I may have the best of it after all.'

Zar-bettu-zekigal swung one-handed on the pole of the lantern where it stood jammed into the beach, scooping up a handful of skulls, the brown bone light in her fingers. She crunched forward, ankle-deep, tossing the tiny bones up into the warm air.

'So what is all this? And what's it got to do with us?'

The first steps of the throne jutted out of the beach before her, each a yard high. She craned her neck, staring up the cliff walls. Distance or fog hid the summits.

'You are here to witneth our complaint and judgement.'

The cobra-headed figure placed his hands on the crudely cut arms of the throne, lowering himself into a sitting position. His human skin shone red as clay. The skin about his head flared, white underscales pulsing rapidly.

'You have polluted uth!'

Charnay guffawed, her eyes brightening with realization. 'Oh! Plessiez, man, they all li—'

Plessiez trod down hard on the brown Rat's foot. She winced, puzzled, and fell silent.

'Mortalth, attend!'

'Whath'th the – I mean, what's the . . . ?' Plessiez shook his head and gave up.

'What'th the reathon for it? Thplit tongth, I thuppoth.'

348

Zar-bettu-zekigal's eyes danced. 'That's what you get for being one of the Therpent-headed!'

Elish's hands closed over her shoulder, fingers jabbing hard into the hollow under her clavicle. '*Will* you be quiet!'

Zar-bettu-zekigal rubbed her hand across her mouth, looked away; saw in peripheral vision the Cardinal-General straighten, his expression gravely sober. She shoved the remainder of a handful of skulls into her dress pocket.

'El, they're *won*derful. You didn't tell me about this! What are they?'

'What they say they are.' Pale, calm, Elish-hakku-zekigal spoke to include Plessiez. 'Chthonic idols – not gods, except by virtue of human worship. Exiled beneath the heart of the world when the Thirty-Six took up their incarnations here on our human earth. The most ancient idols never died, only took refuge below.'

Plessiez raised an ironic brow. 'Their powers?'

'Intact.'

Zar-bettu-zekigal moved closer to Elish.

'Hear uth, and lithten well.'

Now the heat radiating from the stone became humid, steam sliding in snail-tracks down the granite. Wisps of vapour coiled up. The Lord of the Night Council stood again, pacing the steps before the thrones; turning to fling out one human hand, pointing at the skull beach.

'Thith ith not made by our hand!'

Zar-bettu-zekigal swayed, wiping sweat from her forehead, amazed to be too hot. A thick musky smell crept into the air, unstirred by the wind from the unseen ocean; and the noise of the surf faded, muffled.

'You pollute the world below. Your nightmareth come among us. It ith *your* doing, Rat-Lord.'

The smell of green vegetation rasped in her throat, acrid and strong. She hiccuped, caught between the last paroxysm of a giggle and a sudden chill; reaching out for Elish-hakku-zekigal. Her sister's hand closed about hers.

Plessiez, not taking his eyes from the Night Council,

muttered: 'Charnay! What have you told them?'

'Oh, everything.' The big brown Rat tugged her sword-belt straight and set the feather in her head-band at a more jaunty angle. 'It was make a friend of them or find myself on one of your friend the Hyena's gibbets. Besides, they've been gods. What would you have me do, messire? I thought you probably wouldn't mind. You said don't tell anybody human and these people aren't human.'

The black Rat's face froze. He rested his long-fingered hand across his eyes, his shoulders momentarily heaving. 'You thought I probably wouldn't mind.' His eyes opened. 'Charnay, you are *unbelievably* stupid.'

Charnay shrugged massively muscled shoulders, brown fur rippling. 'Am I? *I* didn't plant necromancy under the heart of the world and then come back to admit it before the Night Council.'

'The Night Council doesn't care for the world above. What is there that I should admit to?'

Thirteen pairs of emotionless eyes looked down across the air. The cobra-headed god raised his hand.

'Very well, then. Behold.'

Tendrils of fog crept past Zar-bettu-zekigal and she rubbed her upper arms, feeling the skin damp and chill. A rustling filled the air.

The skull-pebbled slopes of beach *shifted* in the semi-circle of space between the thrones; rolling back from granite curved and hollowed by time and scored with chthonic marks of bone, horn and wood. From the far-end thrones, two of the Night Council paced down to stand in the cleared space. One with the body of an old woman and the head of a krait, one with a young woman's body and the glittering crest of an iguana.

They met and grasped hands.

A wind began to blow.

Zar-bettu-zekigal trod back, bumping her shoulder against the older Katayan's breast. Hair tangled in her eyes. The wind blew colder, scoring her skin. Plessiez and Charnay lowered their snouts against the gusts, the

350

brown Rat grabbing for the lantern as it fell.

A hurricane-wrench of air pulled the fog aside; light blazed in her eyes. She clawed hair from her face two-handed, shaded her eyes, opened her mouth to speak, and gaped.

The beach ran down to a black shore. Black water slopped thickly against the skull-pebbles. Debris tangled in the edges of the dark surf.

She put her fist to her mouth, staring. A corrosive vapour drifted, stinging her eyes.

All along the shore, as far as she could see, debris clogged the water-line. Broken wood and glass, the bodies of gigantic wasps; sodden entrails, a hand and arm rolling in the sea-drenched pebbles . . . The writhing bodies of ants, each as long as her forearm; a gouged-out eye; a basket-handled rapier rolling against the pebbles; a doll, and something dark-backed that broke the surface a little way offshore and vanished.

She stared offshore.

Ragged bedrock jutted up from the sea.

Giant tree-roots twisted up through the crags, splintering the ochre and vermilion stone. Glistening wet boles writhed across shattered blocks, stretching in island-ranges to the horizon. Zar-bettu-zekigal shuffled, turning, staring at the weed-covered stones, the masses of razor-edged shells clustering on ridges, the pods hanging down wetly from the giant tangles of roots.

Twenty feet away across the nearest strait, a man's body hung, head thrown back taut in agony. A thick root grew into his stomach under the navel, impaling him; his feet kicked against barnacle-covered rocks, razoring open his heels.

'Dear . . . *gods*.'

Zar-bettu-zekigal's hand moved to her mouth. She felt Elish tug at her shoulder; refused to turn away.

A figure hung over the screaming man, clawed feet gripping the wet bark, grinning with lengthened teeth. Its head turned as she watched. Subtly altered, strangely disfigured: the mirror-face of the impaled man stared at her. Pointed teeth smiled. The head continued to lift, to turn. It pivoted full-circle, neck cracking, until it stared down again at the pierced man: coughing quietly, laughing.

She looked just long enough to see how many human figures the root cages trapped, each accompanied by its distorted mirror-image tormentor; how far the islands stretched . . .

'I think I—' She faced about, spat bile on to the beach of tiny skulls.

'The pollution of nightmare. Dream-debris. Solid.' Elish-hakku-zekigal turned, embracing her, gazing back up at the semicircle of thrones. 'Solid. Real.'

The two of the Night Council paced back and climbed the steps to their thrones. Fog began to soften the horizon.

'You *infected* the world below.' The Lord of the Night Council pointed a red-nailed finger at Plessiez. 'Necromanthy. *Magia* of the dead, the truly dead . . . It ith your plague that kilth above, and in the Fane, and allowth the Night Thun to thine. You brought it below. Now you mutht dethtroy it.'

The black Rat's lip twitched, showing a gleam of incisor.

'"Kills above"?' Zar-bettu-zekigal asked.

Black serpent eyes turned upon her. Zar-bettu-zekigal shivered, hacked one booted heel into the miniature skulls and looked away. The voice echoed softly from the curving granite cliffs.

'We are not contherned with the above. Do what you will. We do not need you. But we will not have you corrupt uth! Your plague maketh their nightmareth real, here below.' The cobra-head dipped, unblinking eyes watching. 'Memory, tell what you have heard of pethtilenth.'

All laughter gone cold, she lifted her head and stared at Plessiez. 'Oh, I'd rather tell what I've *seen* – up there. Now. But you listen.'

She began speaking with the concentration of Memory.

'"Plagues may exist in flesh, in base matter, and bring bodies to death. And, we discover, there are other pestilences that may be achieved, plagues of the spirit and soul. And there are plagues that can be brought into existence only by acts of magia. They bring their own analogue of death to such as our masters—"'

'Not alone to such as those,' Elish interrupted. Zari saw the brown Rat catch the remark and shrug carelessly.

'"– such as our masters, the Thirty-Six Lords of Heaven and Hell, the Decans." Is that what you want? See you, there's more. The Hyena. "Memory, witness. Certain articles of corpse-relic necromancy to be placed at septagon points under the heart of the world, for the summoning of a pestilence—"' She broke off, lifting her chin, staring at the Cardinal-General. 'Did you know it would kill humans? Do this to them? Did you?'

Charnay turned a surprised and blandly supercilious face. 'What do you care? You're Katayan.'

'Messire!'

The Rat looked down over his shoulder. Fog dried on his black fur, leaving it dull. He reached to place his hands on her shoulders, long fingers warm through the fabric of her dress. She looked up at brilliant black eyes; his whiskers unmoving, the light shining through his ears.

She demanded: 'Did you?'

The black Rat removed his hands. He reached down to his haunch, ringed fingers unknotting the green silk sash, brought it up two-handed and looped it over her head. For a moment he still held the two ends of it.

'"How now . . . "' His incisors showed in a grin; his black eyes, feral, shone with a kind of fallen recklessness. Nothing to mark him as cardinal or priest now, all gone; he wore only silver head-band and black plume, sword-belt and harness. '"How now, two Rats! Dead, for a ducat, dead!"'

Charnay scowled. 'What!'

'I forget you're no follower of our great poets.' He reached to tug Zar-bettu-zekigal's short hair sharply, and swung round and strode back up the beach. Without lifting his head he called up to the Council: 'Messires, I'll do what I can. Charnay!'

'What?' The big brown Rat started, looked, and loped up the beach after him. 'Messire, I don't understand.'

Zar-bettu-zekigal stared after them, touching the still-warm sash. She slid one trailing end across her shoulder to fall scarf-like down her back. 'Messire . . . '

Muffled screams echoed from the ocean, invisible in the thickening fog. Granular mist rolled across the beach, glimmering. It swept across the departing figures of the brown and black Rats.

'What will you do?' she shouted. 'Messire! What will you do?'

Mist blurred distance; she glimpsed his hand perhaps raised in salute.

'Your plathe ith not with them,' the viper-headed god said. His slender body seemed a young man's; his black eyes unblinking and ageless. 'We have your tathk, thaman-woman. You mutht be a guide back to the world above. Take what ith not ours, what we will not keep, and what you mutht.'

Zar-bettu-zekigal followed Elish's gaze.

A few yards from the beach of skulls, resting low in the shifting debris and black water, an unmoored ship floated. Twenty feet long, clinker-built of wood and coated in black tar. No oars. No mast. One curve from prow to stern.

No reflection of that hull in the mirror-black water.

'What . . . ?' Zar-bettu-zekigal took a few crunching steps down the beach. Fog made the inhabited islands invisible.

Behind her, Elish-hakku-zekigal chuckled.

Zari raised her head, seeing the boat still floating just offshore, growing larger as she stepped closer: thirty feet long at least.

A sibilant voice echoed from the amphitheatre of thrones: the cobra-headed Lord of the Night Council.

'We warn you. Your way will not be unoppothed.'

Zar-bettu-zekigal stared. 'It's the *Boat*. See you, I swear it; I swear it is!'

'Only when the Night Sun shines. Only when all laws cease for that certain hour . . . ' Elish-hakku-zekigal's eyes showed a dazzled appalled wonder.

'Elish, don't!'

'Oh, you can *touch* it. Here, you can.' The Katayan woman strode past her, down the long skull-pebbled slope, splashing knee-deep into the black waves, ignoring her soaked breeches and the tails of her blue silk coat. Dark objects bobbed away on ripples, antennae feebly twitching. She gripped the edge of the Boat and expertly timed her leap so that it dipped, wallowed, but shipped hardly any water.

'Elish, I don't understand!'

The older Katayan woman stood up on the deck, gazing back over Zar-bettu-zekigal's head at the half-circle of thrones and the bedrock foundations of the world. Each of the Serpent-headed now stood, left or right hand up-raised. A smile broke out on her pale features.

'Lords, I came here because of a prophecy! It was foretold to me: "Your sister will travel on the Boat." I didn't want her to die and so I came to give what help I could. But I see she *will* travel on the Boat, and living!'

'Act thwiftly; your time ith almotht patht.'

The Katayan woman's eyes glowed. She laughed; a gamine-grin very like her younger sister's. 'Don't fear. I can guide the Boat back to the world above. Zar!'

Zar-bettu-zekigal padded down the slope to the edge of the sea. She slipped her boots off and slung them around her neck by the laces, wading out into black water icy about her ankles, her calves. She refused to look at what floated near her.

'The Boat?'

She reached out tentative fingers, laying them against the tarred wood of the hull. Elish braced a foot on the far side and reached down, grabbing her, pulling her up.

355

She staggered and sat on the rocking deck, and felt her shoulders taken in a tight grip; Elish's blue eyes fixed on her face.

'You must jump ship the *instant* we get back. Once we're in the world above, none but the . . . dead . . . sail this Boat . . .'

'The dead.' Zar-bettu-zekigal gripped her sister's wrist. 'See you, what you told me: Lady Luka, people's *souls* – what's happening to what she's doing if the Boat isn't there!'

Elish-hakku-zekigal looked down, blue eyes suddenly vague.

'Who is Luka?'

Nightmares knocked softly against the hull. Zar-bettu-zekigal felt the tarred planks rock under her. The Boat drifted. Fog shut out the skull beach now, the vanished thrones of the Serpent-headed; fog hid the islands of splintered rock and flesh.

Droplets of mist dampened her face, clung to her lashes. She shook her head sharply. 'Elish!'

The black-haired Katayan woman swayed as she stood on the deck of the Boat. Water pearled on her blue silk coat, her lace ruffle. Her left hand, up-raised in a shaman's gesture of power, hovered forgotten. She stared at Zar-bettu-zekigal.

'Who are you?'

'I'd be obliged if you'd stop scaring the first-year students,' Reverend Master Pharamond said. 'We set the exam up to keep them out of harm's way while all this is going on.'

Lucas gulped air, injected authority into his voice. 'A message for the university. Urgent.'

A Proctor swung the heavy wooden door of the hall to, cutting off Lucas's view of the students at their desks; Rafi of Adocentyn half on his feet. The door muffled their rising voices.

'You'd better come with me, Prince,' Pharamond said.

Lucas let the small man steer him away from the hall

door and down the sun-darkened corridor. The smell of wax polish and paper strong in his nostrils, he was abruptly aware of his clattering scabbard, torn breeches and shirtless state.

He reached up slowly, tugging the red kerchief from his head and undoing its knot. It smelt of sweat, of fear, of air made electric by the advent of the Night Sun.

'A message for the students and Board of Governors, from an Archemaster.'

Pharamond scratched his clipped beard with long strong fingers. A short sturdy man, he looked up at Lucas as he walked a half-pace ahead.

'Mmm. Thought as much. We're in emergency session; I can take you straight along with me. Assuming that there's some substance to this message, Prince?'

Lucas smiled crookedly. 'I'm the errand-boy, Reverend Master. But I can tell you what's going on out in the city *now*.'

'Oh, we know all about that. We've been subjecting it to some intensive research over the last month. I believe events are occurring much in the order that we predicted.'

Pharamond turned on his heel, boot squeaking on the polished boards, and threw open one of the carved wooden doors. He said over his shoulder, entering the large staff-room: 'But we can always use your help, boy. We need every hand here.'

An array of candles shivered in the door's draught. Dozens of them: jammed in pots and on bookshelves, on perpendicular-window ledges, wax-glued on the edges of tables and the backs of carved chairs. Fierce amber illumination banished the light shadows and the darkness of the sun. Two dozen faces glanced up as Pharamond entered.

'What's the news?' a freckled woman called from the table.

'All as predicted. We don't have much time.' Pharamond bustled across to where four long polished tables had been

357

set together and whole geological strata of city maps unrolled across them. Gold-headed map-pins impaled the papers at intervals.

Lucas followed, automatically nodding respectful greetings, caught between being a first-year student and Lucas of Candover; all the while staring at the panelled walls, whose painted crests had diagrams pinned up over them; at scattered paints and quills, and bookshelves in complete disarray.

'Has Candia showed up?' a dark-skinned man asked, as Pharamond arrived at the table around which the group sat.

Pharamond stepped back, avoiding an elderly woman who pounced on the bookshelves and seized a scroll. 'I don't foresee that happening, Shamar.'

The scent of hot candlewax drenched the room. Two dozen men and women, their ages between thirty and sixty, crowded the map table. University gowns abandoned, flung down in disorder over the room's chairs and sofas, they worked mostly in shirt-sleeves and light cotton dresses.

Lucas stepped back as another woman left the table to grab a volume from the shelves and riffle through it rapidly. The dark man, Reverend Master Shamar, leaned across to stick a pin in a particular house or street.

'Nor Heurodis?' an old woman asked.

Lucas saw Pharamond smile, rubbing his long fingers together. 'I suspect she's out playing dice somewhere.'

'*Dice?*' His question came out involuntarily.

'Or cards.' Pharamond folded his hands behind his back, leaning over the map-table. 'Prince Lucas, I suggest you read the message to us here. We have a full session. It can be debated.'

Lucas felt in his breeches pocket for the folded paper. The gold pin pricked his thumb. Movement flickered beyond the distorting glass of the Gothic windows. In the dark sky whirled a multitude of specks. Birds? The

Fane's acolytes? Both? He turned his back on the windows, unfolding the paper and holding it up to the light of a candle.

'"*Beneath Ninth Bank House, Moon Lane. Also beneath: The Clock & Candle at Brown Park. High Skidhill. North-aust side of Avenue Berenger. The Chapel of the Order of Fleurimond. Tannery Row. The Campanile at Saffron Dock. These being respectively in the 9th, 18th, 1st, 31st, 5th, 12th and 27th Districts.*"'

Lucas paused for breath, glanced up to see heads bent over the map-table, the men and women of the university muttering in suppressed excitement.

'Go on,' Pharamond said. 'Is there more?'

'Yes.' Lucas raised the paper again to the light, following the florid hasty script. 'He says: "*From Baltazar Casaubon, Archemaster, Scholar-Soldier of the Invisible College.*"'

Pharamond grunted, black brows rising. 'A respectable Archemaster mixed up with those vagabonds?'

'My dear Pharamond, that was discredited years ago. A completely fictitious organization. You'll recall Dollimore's excellent article in *Mage and Magia*. However . . . ' The elderly woman who had asked about Heurodis rested her chins on her hand, staring down at the map-table. She pointed with a plump finger. 'This person *has* named all seven locations of the necromantic *magia*, and in two cases more accurately than we could. I believe we should listen to what else he has to tell us.'

'You know about the necromancy?' Lucas blurted.

Shamar glanced up, remarked, 'Discovered and monitored this past two weeks,' and went back to rustling the maps, dragging out a second set from under the first.

'It's come at *just* the wrong time. First term's always a bitch.' The freckled Reverend Mistress at the far end of the table looked up, her dark eyes meeting Lucas's. 'Your own attendance-record's pretty bad, Prince Candover.'

'Regis, this isn't the time for that!' Pharamond tugged at

359

his black beard, made to lean down the length of the table, and had to move around to the side to stretch across and grab a chart. He reached back without looking, snapped his fingers, and took the golden pin that the elderly woman handed him.

'*Archeius-arcanum-elementum-hal-hadid-aurum-neboch!*'

His beard jutted as he raised his chin, gabbling through the incantation. Lucas saw him pass the pin through the nearest candle-flame and stab it into the map-paper.

A tall man on the far side of the table hitched himself up, looked, frowned, then nodded. 'That should hold it for now.'

'If we'd known the university was investigating . . . ' Lucas scratched through the hair of his bare chest, gazing at the room from under dark meeting brows. His loosely buckled belt and stolen sword jingled as he shifted position, shoulders straightening. 'We might need what you know!'

'Candover couldn't *afford* us.' The dark man, Shamar, made a small gesture at the paper in Lucas's hand. 'Well? Read the rest of the *message*, lad.'

'"We . . . "' The image in his head not Candover, the White Mountain, Gerima or any other, but red hair streaked with silver, and narrow shoulders in a white cotton shirt. He squinted at the Lord-Architect's scrawling hand:

'"*From B. Casaubon, Etc., to the Reverend tutors:*

'"*What I do now with the Archemaster's Art is against immediate danger. Time leaves me time for nothing else, until that's done. You are not above this battle, masters. Therefore this appeal to you.*"'

Pharamond snorted. The freckled Reverend Mistress held a map of Nineteenth District up to the darkness of the windows, impaling a point with a silver pin.

'"*You will realize, or I am mistaken in your Arts, how one single cause brings about epidemic in the city, powerlessness in the Fane, and the demonium meridianum, the Night Sun. Therefore this appeal . . .*"'

Lucas read with difficulty, hearing his own voice falling flat into the air.

'"*Masters, you are students of knowledge and wisdom. I put this to you plainly therefore.*

'"*It hath oft been writ, nothing can be done in magia without knowledge of that branch of Mathematics which is mystical and spiritual, that is, Mathesis.*"'

Lucas held the paper up, letting his gaze sneak past it. Heads around the table lifted, paying attention.

'"*To wit, Pico della Mirandola his eleventh conclusion: 'By numbers, a way is had, to the searching out, and understanding of everything able to be known.'*"'

'A mathematical analysis is the basis of a sound understanding, very true.' The dark Reverend Master Shamar nodded thoughtfully, resting his chin on his hand, his gaze still on the piled maps. 'A man of learning, your Archemaster.'

'Not to say craft.' Lucas lowered his gaze and hastily read on:

'"*And to our immediate crisis this:*

'"*Doctor Johannes Dee his Book, writes how the gods, through their divine Numbering, produce orderly and distinct all things. For Their Numbering, then, was their Creating of all things. And Their continuall numbering, of all things, is the conservation of them in being. And, where and when They shall lack an unit, there and then, that particular thing shall be Discreated.*"'

'We're already facing a consensus reality breakdown.' Pharamond stroked his beard. 'What would he have us do – pray to the gods to keep numbering the formulae of our existence?'

'Don't be ingenuous.' Regis snapped her fingers impatiently. 'What does your Archemaster say? What does he want us to do?'

Lucas cleared his throat and read into the attentive silence:

'"*You have amongst you natural philosophers, professors of Mathesis, physicists. You must set about numbering the formulae of the world; add your support to Those Who number All, in this hour when They begin to fail us.*

'"*Do this. Hold fast to the measurements and proportion of macrocosm and microcosm, as they become discreated – as it is the law that spatial, temporal, diurnal things be discreated when They cease to hold them in existence.*

'"*Break that law, masters.*

'"*Not merely the criminal law, but the laws of nature. Cheat physics, matter, energy, and form.* Break the laws of Mathesis. *No hope to counteract the equal and opposite reaction to the use of true necromancy now, no hope – but this.*"'

All through the vast network under the heart of the world, lanterns and candles bob circles of light on brickwork. Rats and humans crowd the platforms and the train-tunnels where nitre spiders across curved walls.

Here and there, they fight.

Refugees: some sleep in an exhausted daze; some stare into nothing; some calm their children; some cry themselves into hysteria.

Even in the train-tunnels it is possible to hear the crashing collapse of buildings in the city above.

Refugees.

A female Rat in a torn scarlet jacket, the priest Fleury, crouches with her hand to the cinder-floor of a tunnel. Far, far below the heart of the world. Below (although she has lost all direction) Ninth Bank House, Moon Lane. Through long dark fingers resting on the earth, she senses something.

Silver gleams.

A substanceless petal brushes her snout, and she springs up, hand going to the *ankh* at her throat. Black petals drift down from the tunnel ceiling. Voices behind her shriek.

Now even an untrained priest can tell that necromantic *magia* flowers beneath the city. Growing, still. Growing into its full power. Transmuted from its first design and purpose until, now, it is nothing its creator would recognize.

QVI NON INTELLIGIT, AVT TACEAT, AVT DISCAT.

MONAS HIEROGLYPHICA
IOANNIS DEE, LONDINENSIS,
AD
MAXIMILIANVM, DEI GRATIA
ROMANORVM, BOHEMIÆ ET HVNGARIÆ
REGEM SAPIENTISSIMVM.

IGNIS

AËR

DE RORE CÆLI, ET PINGVEDINE TERRÆ, DET TIBI DEVS. Gen.27.

Guliel. Silvius Typog. Régius, Excud. Antuerpiæ, 1564

'*It hath oft been writ, nothing can be done in* magia *without knowledge of that branch of Mathematics which is mystical and spiritual, that is, Mathesis.*'

Title page of *Monas Hieroglyphica*, John Dee, Antwerp, 1564

Black and silver, unbearably sweet: the haunting of roses throws out tendril and bramble and runner, choking the tunnel ahead, spreading rapidly towards her.

She has no desire to begin a panic stampede in the crowded tunnel.

Not until she sees the tide of nightmare flooding up in the wake of the haunting does Fleury break, scream and run.

Ribbed wings curdled the sky. Dust puffed out from between the masonry blocks of the wall. Desaguliers shouted a warning and leaped.

The wall of the palace's aust wing slid out, almost slowly, gathered momentum and collapsed into the court-yard with a roar and a whirlwind of dust. Flying glass and splintered beams battered the side of the commandeered siege-engine.

'Fire!' Desaguliers clawed his way back along the plat-form to the Cadets loading the ballista. One tripped the lever as he got there. The catapult shot up, slammed against the upper beam and halted, the machine quivering.

A scoop of Greek fire sprayed skyward, lashing the bodies of the swarming acolytes. The burning gelatine clung.

'It's not affecting them! They don't even feel it!'

Desaguliers slid into cover beside St Cyr at the back of the machine. Masonry dust drifted by, shadowing them with light. Screams echoed from Rats trapped in the collapsed building. St Cyr pointed.

'The Chapel! It's their next target.'

Black wings beat, falling from the sky. One acolyte gripped the roof with claws that sank into the blue tiles, bristle-tail whipping up to curve about a spire. Down, down: ten, fifteen, twenty of the Fane's acolytes covered the roof and walls, digging in with their fangs and clawed feet and the claws at their ribbed wing-joints.

Desaguliers touched his hand to his lean snout, brought it away bloody. His other hand ached. Dully surprised, he

realized it gripped the stump of a sword. He prised his
fingers open and let it fall, reaching across the slumped
body of a brown Rat to take her rapier. He shoved a fallen
pistol through his belt.

'Try to shift them from there?'

'We've taken thirty per cent losses, at least.' St Cyr
flinched as the siege-engine shook, another bolt of fire
catapulted skyward. 'We can't do anything else. Retreat,
for gods' sakes.'

Desaguliers stared out across the great courtyard. The
Night Sun glinted from shards of glass, from buckles and
rings on fallen bodies. At least a dozen Cadets lay in plain
view: most dead, one moving still, another screeching. The
gutted palace cast shadows of light across split-open halls
and chambers and kitchens.

Black shadows fell only from the daemons, shrinking as
they soared, growing immense as they struck.

Over the crackling of fire and screams of the injured, he
heard a roar. The roof of the chapel fell in, rafters jutting
up like broken ribs. A scarlet-jacketed priest ran outside,
his black fur burning. An acolyte swooped, beak dipping.
Across the intervening yards Desaguliers clearly heard the
snap of the priest's spine.

'Down into the lower tunnels?' Tired, he heard a
question in his voice that a while ago would have been
an order. 'St Cyr?'

'We can defend the train-tunnels. They'd be at a dis-
advantage if they followed.'

He looked at the other black Rat, smiling wearily.

'Give the orders, then. Retreat. Take whoever you can
with you, civilian or military. Close the tunnels after
you.'

Desaguliers knelt up, one hand on the hot metal of the
engine-platform.

'"You"?' St Cyr demanded.

Desaguliers rubbed his eyes, wincing at sandpaper
vision. Burned patches charred his fur; a lean black
Rat, febrile, running on nervous courage and little else.

One shoulder lifted in a shrug, and he winced as his sword-harness chafed a patch of raw flesh.

'I'm taking a squad of the Cadets.' He jerked his head towards the last unfallen roofs of the palace, the shattered windows of the cloverleaf-vaulted audience hall. 'His Majesty. They can't be moved, not now. But defended – possibly.'

'No!'

'No, I know,' Desaguliers said softly, 'but loyalty's a hard habit to break. In the end.'

Before St Cyr could protest again he leaped from the metal ladder to the ground, running at full tilt across the wreckage-strewn courtyard, yelling hoarsely to the Cadets as he ran.

Warmth struck. Lucas glanced up to see heating-pipes running along the vaulted arches of the Long Gallery; stopped, his breathing suddenly shallow.

Machines towered to either side. A narrow space ran down the centre of the hall, diminishing into distance all of a quarter of a mile away. Bars of light-shadow fell from clerestory windows to a polished parquet floor. Lucas held up the five-branched candelabrum. The smell of hot wax dizzied him.

'Analytical engines!'

He strode forward, barefoot, the candles held high, sword and sword-belt clashing at his hip. His kerchief, knotted about his dirty neck, tangled with carved stone talismans hanging on chains.

Ranked to either side, cogs and shafts gleaming with darkness where the Night Sun's light shafted in, the great analytical engines rose twice his height and more. He walked staring at banks of dials, levers, ornamented iron handles; moved a step closer and held up the candles to peer at the interlocking network of large and small cogwheels, springs, iron shafts and notched gearwheels.

A small iron plate shone, dye-stamped with a factory's mark. *White Mountains: Candover.*

Hot wax spattered his hand.

He winced and set the candelabrum down, absently peeling the white discs of cooling wax from his skin. They left clean marks. He unknotted his red kerchief and wiped his hands and arms, conscious of dust, oil, bloody scratches; wiped his face. He smiled wryly, scratching through his hair, now grown long enough to catch in the chains of the talismans hung about his neck.

'Gerima would call me a base mechanic. And Uncle Andaluz—!'

He turned, decisive, and strode back across the floor to the Reverend tutors. Shamar waved his arms excitedly; Pharamond rubbed at his clipped beard, and gestured for quiet; Reverend Mistress Regis tucked her blond-red hair back behind her ears and glared severely at Lucas.

'I suggest we send this young man back to the Archemaster with a message of some description. His class-record is not such that I think we'll find him useful in an emergency. You know how irresponsible these outland princes are.'

Heat touched his ears and cheeks. Lucas pressed on doggedly. 'The message said, cheat *mathesis*—'

Pharamond put his hands behind his back.

'There are certain numbers that control the Form of the world. The formulae of force, attraction, gravitation, celestial and terrestial mechanics. These the Decans number and keep in existence. As well as those formulae that create the shapes and souls of men and beasts; formulae written deep in our cells—'

'Oh, if we *could* cheat, yes!' Shamar interrupted the easy fluency of the lecture hall. His dark eyes glowed as he looked at the ranked analytical machines.

Lucas frowned. 'I don't understand—'

'Why should you think you could understand?' Regis snapped. 'You're a first-year student, and a mostly absent one at that.'

Shamar chuckled. A lightening of the tension went through the group. Lucas, for that reason, bit back a protest.

Regis added kindly: 'You wouldn't understand. And this is an emergency.'

Light caught in the corners of Lucas's eyes, blurring his vision with silver and blue. The levers and gear-wheels of the analytical engines stood out black against the windows.

'I study to be wise, but I'm not ignorant to begin with!'

He drew himself up; all the bearing of Candover's princes coming back to him now: one hand resting on the hilt of his sword, his shoulders straight as he stared at the six or eight tutors of the University of Crime.

'Do you know who I am? The Emperor of the East and the Emperor of the West meet at my father's court! Do you think his wisest tutors failed to teach me how it is *mathesis* that holds the Great Wheel of the heavens in place? It's our serfs in Candover that build these mathematical engines! Now I'll tell *you* something.'

Regis's freckles stood out darkly. She opened her mouth.

'A magus told me,' Lucas said. 'A woman who isn't sitting here safe in the university! Do you know where she is, now, this minute? She's inside the Fane . . .'

He shook his head. 'Sorry. *None* of us is safe. But I'll tell you this. Yes, you can get these machines producing the Form-numbers of all things – stars, stones, roses, bricks, butterflies. You can run the formulae. What *good* will it do us? The White Crow told me what a Decan told her. All these formulae are going to be uncreated, finally, and for good. Now.'

Breath caught in his throat.

The scent of candlewax drenched the air. Muffled by glass, the shrieks of acolytes echoed across the university's courtyards. The silence in the hall pressed on his ears. Anger drained out of him; the last of court training reasserting itself.

'I apologize, masters. I *am* hindering you; I crave your pardon. Excuse me.'

He bowed shortly. 'What shall I tell Lord Casaubon when he asks why you don't act?'

Pharamond glanced away from the group of tutors: the elderly Reverend Mistress buttonholing Shamar, haranguing him; Regis stabbing a finger at both as she interrupted; four or five others clustered down the gallery by the ranked handles of the analytical engines.

The bearded man touched the handle nearest to him, cranking it thoughtfully. Cogs shifted; numbers rolled in the dial. 'Tell him we don't, imprimis, have the manpower—'

Lucas grinned. Air bubbled in his chest; he suddenly seized the smaller man by the shoulders.

'You do,' he said. 'You do! Just wait!'

'*Prince—*'

'Believe me, you do!'

He hit the door-jamb with his shoulder, racing out into the hall; feet hitting every third step down the great polished flight of stairs. Black light shone in from perpendicular windows; a scent of burning crept in through the creaking joins of the leaded glass. Lucas skidded across polished marble tiles and hit double-doors with both hands extended.

A burst of voices quietened; he gazed out at alarmed faces in Big Hall.

'Rafi!'

'What in hell is happening?' Rafi of Adocentyn demanded. He rapidly strode towards Lucas, who shut the door behind him and seized his arm.

'Get up to Long Gallery.'

'Oh, *what*? What are you on about, Candover?'

Lucas grabbed a chair from the nearest desk, climbed on it, yelled across the heads of the assembled students. The noise-level fell a little: fifty or sixty heads turning.

'*Listen!* Get yourselves up to the Long Gallery. Do it *now*. You're going to be running the analytical engines. If we do it right, we've got a chance of clearing up this mess!'

A flurry in one corner of Big Hall: the Proctor shoved into a corner and shouted down. Almost all faces turned towards Lucas. Students he recognized shouted questions, others yelled. As if by unspoken consent they began moving closer.

'I haven't got time to explain; it doesn't *matter* if you don't know what you're doing—'

'Nor you, Prince?' one voice yelled. Lucas laughed.

'Nor me, neither. *Listen*. There's a dozen Reverend tutors up in Long Gallery and they're wetting themselves because they can't run the machines on their own. Now, I'm going back up there. Come with me if you want. If you don't, then sod you!'

He kicked the chair aside as he leaped down; it skittered across the doorway. He ran out ahead of the crowd, Rafi of Adocentyn the only one close enough to catch up as he sprinted back up the stairs.

'Candover, what the fuck are you doing?'

Lucas's steps slowed. He heard feet pounding the stairs behind, and glanced back to see the Night Sun glint from fair and dark hair, students running, yelling, laughing with the relief of action. Caught up in action, only a few spared a glance for the world outside the windows.

'I don't know.' Lucas, dizzy with shouting, grinned at Rafi's narrow puzzled face. '*I* don't know. I'm trusting these idiots who teach us to know what they're doing. I'm trusting White Crow when she says Lord Casaubon knows what he's doing.'

The dark young man frowned. 'Those two that were at Carver Street? Gods, Lucas! You're crazy.'

Lucas grabbed the back of Rafi's neck, turning the young man to look across the top of the stairwell and out of a window that overlooked the heart of the world. '*Go outside and then tell me I'm crazy!*'

He swung the doors of the Long Gallery open, holding back the heavy oak. Rafi frowned, strode through. A girl followed, two more; a fair-haired Katayan; then a rabble of a dozen, then more. He stared at their excited shouting faces, searching for something, some conception of what had occurred outside the university in this hour of the Night Sun.

'I suppose', Pharamond's voice came from behind Lucas, 'that they don't have to know what they're doing here to do it. *You, Hilaire, walk!* Shamar, get them sorted out, will you?'

Shamar raised his hand. The warm light gallery flooded with voices, with students who ran, shouting to each other; the Reverend tutor directing each to set a dial or crank a handle.

'Lucas, listen.' Pharamond sighed, resting his arm up against the door-jamb. 'Go and tell your Archemaster we'll do what we can, but probably it's not much. Yes, now we can run the numbers. But we can't cheat to prevent the discreation.'

Lucas froze. Half-suspecting, half-speculating, he looked across at the tutor. 'What would you have to do, for that?'

'Pattern compels,' Reverend Master Pharamond said. 'As above, so below. But the influence runs both ways. Our ciphering of the numbers of the cosmos is compelled by the divine numbering of the Decans, yes. But if we could cheat, and make Their numbering dependent on *our* results, here?'

Lucas stared.

'We don't do it often, boy, but when we need to we can – usually. We cheat with our results, and that cheats the world to comply with us.'

The dark Reverend Master, Shamar, approached the door and paused as he came up with them. 'Pharamond, we've always said we could do it, but could we? Really?'

'Not without the mechanical skills!' Pharamond nodded his head sharply at the ranked lines of levers.

'Mechanical skills.' Lucas paused, breath tight in his throat.

'We'd have to gear the machines for the results we want, not the results it'll give us now, considering what's

371

going on out there in the city. But . . . ' Pharamond shrugged. 'The faculty's mechanics aren't resident in the university.'

'Where will we find them?'

Regis's deep laughter echoed back from the Long Gallery. 'Find them? *Find* them? In that chaos out there?'

'She's right,' the bearded man said. 'She's right.'

Lucas reached out and rested his dirty hand against the stamped plate of Candover on the nearest engine. A quietness had fallen in the Long Gallery, most of the young men and women over the immediate excitement of their arrival. He heard their voices, saw how they watched him speaking with the Reverend tutors.

'I – it wouldn't be any use – well, it might—'

Regis snorted. Pharamond held up a hand, arresting what she might have said; moved it to tap Shamar's shoulder for the dark man's attention.

Heat coloured his face; Lucas shifted his feet, stared at the floor.

'I don't want my father ever to know this! That I've been mixing with serfs, or with the trade of *thaumaturgike*, or— The truth of it is, I know how these machines are put together. I think the Lord Casaubon must know that: we've talked. I used to . . . to sneak away and spend a lot of time in the workshops.'

The silence bit into him like acid. Somewhere down the hall, a richly amused voice that sounded like the Prince of Adocentyn said: ' "Trade"!'

Raising his head, and with an odd dignity that belonged neither to the past nor to Candover, Lucas said: 'Master Pharamond, I can probably get these machines to do whatever you want them to. I was in the workshops when the Mark Four was being designed. But if you don't have any other mechanics here, and there's only me—'

Voices shattered the quiet hall: Regis protesting, Shamar protesting, and the bearded Reverend Master's voice drowning them both out: 'Yes! We'll do it! We can argue afterwards if it was worthwhile, if there is an afterwards.

Masters, we stand in such a place that *any* help we give is worthwhile. Regis love, go and get the students organized – Shamar, you, too. Good!'

He swung round, speaking over the clatter as they ran down the Gallery: 'Candover. Tools down there; if you need anything, ask for it. Take a look, then I'll tell you what you've got to do.'

'Yes . . .'

Lucas, Prince of Candover, unbuckled his sword and hung it by the belt on the back of the door. He walked across to squat, sit and finally slide himself down into the concrete sump under the first engine.

He picked up and adjusted a wrench, fingers black with oil; paused, looking up through the interlocking rods and gears.

'If this happens to help you, it's more than I have a right to ask.' Prayer not seeming relevant now, he contented himself with breathing her names: 'White Crow. Valentine.'

Loud footsteps clattered down the hall, each student going to set a dial or heave on a lever; shouting, voices edged half with fear and half with a wild excitement. Returning, Pharamond's voice vibrated with the same emotion: 'Do *exactly* what I tell you.'

Lucas, listening, reached up with the wrench to adjust the first gear.

Footsteps pounded past. Out among the debris and rubble of Fourteenth District's square, the last unwary Rats ran towards barricaded doors and tunnel-entrances. The undercarriage of the siege-engine shook deafeningly: liquid fire hissed up into the air.

'Ei, *you!*'

A torn edge of blue and yellow satin whisked past the Lord-Architect Casaubon's vision. A sharp and very solid finger poked him in the rump.

'Where's my bloody rent, you oversized fraud?'

Casaubon, straightening, clipped one ear-lobe painfully

against the underside of the engine as his heel skidded in leaked oil. He grunted, backing out without turning until he could stand up.

'I *beg* your pardon?'

A woman of perhaps forty folded her arms under her ample bodice. Yellow coils of hair fell across her ripped satin dress. Oblivious of the now-deserted New Temple site, the other buildings' neo-classical doors barricaded with torn-up marble paving-slabs, ignoring the Guards up on the siege-engine platform, and the broken windows from which musket-muzzles jutted, Evelian stared up at the Lord-Architect with glassy determination.

'You heard me! You owe me a month's back rent! *Where is it?*'

'I – that is – unavoidably absent—'

Casaubon picked up his blue satin frock-coat, drawing it on over his filthy shirt. He drew himself up to his full six foot five, looked down over his swelling chest and belly, and shrugged magnificently. He spoke over the thunder of approaching wings.

'Mistress Evelian, I was, and *am*, busy. Now, if you don't mind—'

'That brat Lucas landed you on me, but the university's never heard of you; *they* won't pay me! If I can't get coin from them, I intend bartering those crates you left behind for whatever I can get for them!'

Casaubon absently retrieved a half-eaten lamb chop from an inner pocket, and paused in the act of biting into it.

'Are you mad? Absolutely *not*.'

'Calling yourself a Lord-Architect; I don't believe that for a minute.'

'Aw, *Mother!*'

A straggle-haired fifteen-year-old ran around from the other side of the siege-engine. She glanced up once at the brown Rats loading Greek fire into the ballista. A torn yellow-and-white sash had been tied over her plasterer's silk overalls.

374

'Get down!' She pushed the older blonde woman towards the side of the engine, her face upturned to the Night Sun.

'Don't *interrupt*, Sharlevian.'

The Lord-Architect Casaubon wiped grease off his chin with the back of his hand, smearing machine oil across his fair skin. He replaced the half-eaten chop in a deep outer pocket of his coat. 'Get under cover somewhere, rot you! I don't have time for this pox-damned nonsense!'

'Wanna go home,' the blonde girl said pugnaciously.

Evelian put her fists on her hips. 'I'm going nowhere until I get this account settled!'

'*Ah*.' A new, male voice cut in. 'Messire, do you have any authority here? Can you tell me who does? I wish to register the strongest-possible complaint—'

A *thunk!* and hiss from the ballista drowned his words. The Lord-Architect nestled his chin into three several layers of fat, looking down at a middle-aged, rotund and sweating man. A verdigrised chain hung about the man's neck.

'Tannakin Spatchet. Mayor of Nineteenth District east quarter.'

The Lord-Architect Casaubon rested his weight back on his right heel, planted his ham-fist on his hip, and raised his chin. He surveyed the woman, the girl and the middle-aged man; let his gaze travel past them to the battered façades of buildings surrounding the square, and the azure sky dark with acolytes and the Night Sun.

'A lesser man would be confused by this,' he rumbled plaintively.

'My *rent*—'

'We can't stand out here in the open—!'

'Severe damage to life and p-property—'

The Lord-Architect, ignoring the man's stutter, reached down with plump delicate fingers. A dark glint shone among the links of the Mayor's chain. He lifted a carved stone hanging on a separate chain.

'You hired a Scholar-Soldier! Damn me if that isn't Valentine's work.'

Tannakin Spatchet frowned, bemused.

'White Crow.' Seeing him nod, Casaubon let the talis-man fall back. Another glyptic pendant rested in the division of Evelian's breasts; and a third, the chain lapping round several times, hung from Sharlevian's left wrist.

A crackle of musket-fire echoed from the engine-platform above their heads. Casaubon winced. Clouds of dust skirred up.

The Lord-Architect rubbed his stinging eyes, swore; grabbed Evelian's elbow and pulled her into the shelter of his bolster-arm as a daemon tail, a bristling thick cable, whiplashed down and cracked across the marble paving.

Stone chippings spanged off the side of the siege-engine.

Evelian glared. 'My—'

'*Rent*, yes, I know,' the Lord-Architect muttered testily. 'Rot you, get up on the machine. *All* of you. Safer. Move!'

He caught Sharlevian by the scruff of her overalls and pushed; looked round for Spatchet and saw him already halfway up the ladder to the platform. Following mother and daughter, the Lord-Architect swung himself ponder-ously up the metal rungs.

'And stop that!' He batted one hand irritably towards the ballista. A brown Rat in Guard uniform yelled for a temporary cease-fire.

Above, the wings of acolytes cracked the air. Bristle-tails lashed down. The portico of a nearby house frag-mented: stone splinters shrapnelled. A balcony collapsed and spilled six Rats and two men down into the rubble of the square.

The Lord-Architect Casaubon pushed through the Guards to the back of the platform and knelt down. He folded back the deep cuffs of his satin coat, and scratched thoughtfully in the hair over his ear, peering down at the back axle.

Wheel-tracks and spilled oil marked their arrival, the

tracks diminishing back down the avenue by which they had entered the square.

The Night Sun's black light gleamed on the marble frontages of temples, palaces, banks and offices on the surrounding hills; glinting from the horizons of the cityscape, from the very top of the Fane-in-the-Twelfth-District.

His china-blue eyes vague for a moment, he touched a filthy hand to his mouth, frowning. His lips moved, framed a word that might have been a woman's name. Inaudible in the roar of falling masonry, the shrieking and beat of wings.

'What are you *doing*?' Sharlevian demanded.

She collapsed into a sitting position beside him, silver-chain ear-rings dangling, narrow face pale. Remnants of yellow and white paint clung to her jaw and ears and hair-line. She clutched his arm, the bitten fingernails on her hand pulling threads from the satin.

'Hey!'

Casaubon's free hand went to one of his pockets. He dug in it, brought out a roast chicken-wing, absently offering it to Sharlevian. She sat back, disgust on her face. The Lord-Architect shoved the chicken-wing back; dug again, and his hand emerged clutching the small sextant. Still kneeling, he sighted up at the Night Sun.

He beamed.

'At *last*,' he said.

He prised his fat fingers under one of the iron plates on the platform, opening it up. The ends of two thickly plaited cables of bare copper wire shone in the Night Sun's light. Wrapping each of his hands in the tails of his frock-coat, he carefully twisted the cables together and slammed the hatch shut.

Sparks leaped.

He sat back, grabbing Sharlevian's shoulder. The girl fell against him. Heads turned at the searing actinic light.

For a split second it clung to the siege-engine: St Elmo's fire. Rat Guards cursed, swore, beating sparks from their uniforms. Mistress Evelian's gaze abruptly focused: she seized the Mayor's arm.

Searing blue-white light ran to the ground, to the spilled trail of oil staining the flagstones. Tiny blue flames licked up; then a thin rippling aurora-curtain of light. It sprang up from the spilled-oil trail, running powder-train swift back down the engine's tracks, down the avenue away from the square.

Wildfire-fast, spreading, running, the aurora-curtain of blue light sped up towards the distant hills, cornered, curved, divided and divided again: a brilliant track across the streets the siege-engine had followed.

The Lord-Architect Casaubon grasped one of the ballista struts. It creaked as he pulled himself up, foot scrabbling for a hold, until he saw the hills surrounding the docks and the airfield, the great city stretching away to every compass-point to the horizon.

Far in the distance other light-curtains began to spring up, thin as the spilled trail of oils from other siege-engines.

The electric-blue aurora tracery wavered, rising into the air, hovered at roof-level here, grew taller further off, shorter in other Districts. The Lord-Architect raised one great fist, punched the air; seams straining and at last popping under the arm of his frock-coat.

'Aw, I don't . . . ' Sharlevian's puzzlement trailed off.

The light-threads of the labyrinth threaded the city streets, spreading far, far out of sight, following the oil-trails from specially constructed cisterns in each engine. Out through avenues and streets and alleys to all thirty-six Districts and all hundred and eighty-one quarters; netting the city that is called the heart of the world in a bright maze.

Sharlevian, at his elbow, wiped her nose on the back of her hand and sniffed. 'So you *are* an architect. They taught us the Chymicall Labyrinth in Masons' Hall. We build that pattern into our homes sometimes. But what *good* is it?'

One fat finger raised, the Lord-Architect Casaubon

paused. His head cocked sideways as if he listened for faint music. The black shadows of the Fane's acolytes fell across him, across the square, thousand upon thousand.

Wheeling. Turning.

Thousands, tens of thousands wheeling and turning as one.

Unwilling, constrained, they wheeled in their flights: gliding on burning wings to fly the pattern of the labyrinth. And *only* the pattern of the labyrinth.

Casaubon lowered his hand. Breath touched his oil-stained cheek, a remembrance of the heat in the Garden of the Eleventh Hour: the roses, and the black extinct bees that fly the knot garden's subtle geometries.

'Don't they teach you apprentices anything in your pox-rotted Masons' Halls?' he rumbled. 'Patterns compel, structures compel. Will you *look* at that? Rot her, why can't Valentine be with me to see this?'

The acolytes of the Fane flocked, falling to fly the pattern of the burning labyrinth. Great ribbed wings spread under the Night Sun, blistering with its heat; bristle-tails flicked the air. Beaks and jaws opened to cry, cry agony.

Sparing no glance from blind black eyes for human or for Rat-Lord; tearing no stone from stone; uprooting no roofs now. Only gliding upon hot thermals, rising and falling; flurried wings lashing and falling again to a glide, compelled by the maze-pattern drawn in city streets that now they gaze on. Sightless gaze and are trapped, under the black scorching sun.

Across the city that is called the heart of the world, the labyrinth burns.

Pain hollowed each air-filled bone.

Cold air pressed every planing pinion as the white crow wheeled again, rising to glide down vaulted hills. A bird's side-set eyes reflected perpendicular arches, stone tracery, fan vaulting: a white desert of shaped stone.

'Crraaa-aak!'

Frosted air sleeked the feathers of her breast. She tilted

aching wings, pain catching her in joints whose muscles still, at cell-level, remember being human. The scents of rotting hay, of weed left behind at equinoctial tides impinged sharply on her bird-senses.

'Craaa-akk-k!'

The white crow wheeled again and skimmed a long gallery. Age-polished stone flashed back her fragmented image, an albino hooded bird. She flew wearily from the gallery, wings beating deep strokes.

What use *is it to search for the dying . . . ?*

She lifted a wing-tip and soared. Pain flashed down nerve and sinew. She welcomed it. When her body no longer remembers that it was other and ceases to pain, she will have become what she is shaped to.

No-one tell me that the Decan of Noon and Midnight has no sense of humour . . .

The internal voice seemed hers, forcing its way through avian synapses. Double images curved across the surface of her bright bird's eyes: the great pillars of the Fane seeming spears, soon to tumble into confusion as after a battle. The air resisted her wings so that they beat slowly, slowly; Time itself slowing.

The great depths of the Fane opened around her. Masonry crumbling with age; floors worn down into hollows by aeons of divine tread. Lost ages built in stone: the Fanes that are one Fane, the inhabitation of god on earth. Built out as a tree grows, ring upon ring, hall and gallery and tower, nave and crypt and chapel. Growing, encrusting as a coral reef.

And as for what Rat-Lord and human empires rose and fell while this gallery was building, or what lovers and children died while these columns were cutting . . .

She stretched wide wings and lay herself on the air, letting it bear her; the voice in her head that is still Valentine and White Crow less frenetic now, slowing with the depths of millennia opening out.

They're not idols, magia or oracles. They're the Thirty-Six, the principles that structure the world. Why did we think we could go up against them? Why did we think that anything we did would not be what they ordained, even to the Uncreation?

'Craaaa-akk!'

She flew into the Fane of the Third Decan.

Into a hall in which cathedrals might have been lost, colours blotting her sight. Bright images burned in what should be perpendicular windows, but no light is needed to illuminate these shafts of colour. To either side they shine, fiery as the hearts of suns, scarlets and blues and golds: depicting dunes, lizards, beasts of the desert; ragged stars, comets and constellations long pushed apart by Time.

Depths swung sickeningly below her wings as she dived. Her instincts human, flight is precarious. She cawed, hard and harsh, the sound recognizable as a bird's copy of human speech.

'Xereful! Akeru! Lord of Yesterday and Tomorrow!'

An ornate marble tomb towered in the centre of the nave, gleaming white and gold and onyx-black. Her wings held the air as she curved in flight around the pomegranate-ornamented pillars, the scarabs cut into the great base and pedestal.

A great scorpion shape crowned the tomb, thrice the height of a church spire.

White stone articulated the carapace of the scorpion: its high-curving tail and sting, great moon-arced claws. The segmented body gleamed hollow. Chill air drifted between the joints of the shell, caressing angular legs, clustered eyes. A scent of old dust haunts the air.

'Xereful! Akeru!'

Time frosted the stone exoskeleton beneath her wings, shimmering as if ice runs over the fabric that, after aeons of divine incarnation, is no longer stone.

'We do not fear.'

Air whispers between the carapace-joints. The jointed tail quivers, a point of light sparkling at the tip of the hollow sting.

'We do not fear, as you do. We may choose now to incarnate Ourselves in the celestial world and not here on earth. Or

381

We may raze this world and begin again. The game does not weary Us.'

The white crow wheeled across the cliff-face of the image, time stretching as she skimmed the distance between moon-curved claw and claw. Her heart pounded more rapidly than a watch, ticking away her slight bird's lifespan.

'Sick! Sick! You have! Plague here!'

Her travesty of human voice cawed, echoing from hollow shells. One serrated claw shifts. A shining globe-eye dulled as she flew past, and crumbling stone dust drifted down on the air.

'Xerefu! Akeru!'

The whispering air lies silent.

The hollow stone that incarnates the Decan of Beginnings and Endings, the Lord of the Night of Time, two-aspected and of two separate speeches, begins to crumble into fragments.

'Craa-akk-kk!'

Wing-tips beat down against unyielding air. The white crow folded wings to body and dived, feathers out-thrust to brake and sending her whirling into the passage and stairs to a crypt. Her wings clipped the corner of the wall. Falling stone misses her by a heartbeat.

Out of the crypt: now great rounded pillars rose up to either side of her. She flew on a level with their carved tops: human faces tall as ship's masts, with lilies growing from their mouths and eye-sockets. The corded stone columns sheered down into the depths of the Fane below. She flew too hard and too high to see what lies there.

The white crow flew under ribbed vaults, and into the Fane of the Twenty-Sixth Decan.

A ledge reared up.

One wing-tip flicked up in shock; she skidded to land, claws scrabbling, on an ancient surface. The white crow folded her wings. She raised her head, jerking her beak from side to side, rawly disgusted at ridiculousness no human eye can see.

Hard as mountains under aeons of permafrost, the ledge chilled her.

'Chnoumen! Destroyer of Hearts!'

The ledge ran around the inside of a domed round hall, the colour of old blood. Gold veined the red walls. Arched, huge; too vast even for echoes. Her bird's vision brought her sight of black line paintings on the dull red: thirty-six images colouring the walls around the three-hundred-and-sixty-degree circle. Too distant for their subjects to be deciphered.

'Chnachoumen! Opener of Hundreds and Thousands of Years!'

The floor of this round hall, blood red and blood dark, ripples: stone becoming liquid. She tilted her head, staring down. The stink of rotting weed dizzied her. Under the surface of the water, dark shapes moved.

'*You have no business here.*'

Translucent suddenly: glowing transparently scarlet as arterial blood, the interior sea ripples with white and gold light. Carved in planes of diamond, the coils of a great kraken fill up the pool. Tentacles curve, sinuous. The Decan of Judgements and Passing incarnate in adamant.

'Divine One!'

The white crow paces the ledge jerkily; cocking her head to one side to clearly see ahead. Scales shine on the beaked head of the kraken. But a dim film covers the golden eyes. She steels her voice to discipline.

'Divine One, if you created us you owe us something. You at least owe us the acknowledgement that we have universes inside *us*!'

The arterial scarlet of the inland sea lightened, becoming rose. The living diamond of the Decan's limbs coiled into rose-petal patterns. Liquid tones hissed from the domed ceiling and walls, amused.

'*Why else should We take on flesh, but that for flesh has such universes within it?*'

Her harsh crow's laughter lost itself in the spaces of immensity.

'To hurt? To be cold, to be hot? To bleed, kiss, fuck, shit? To eat? To love?'

'*Child of flesh, We have loved Our creation, but nothing lasts, not even love.*'

Her clawed feet slipped. A flake of red stone crumbled from the ledge.

She flicked into flight without thought, skimming down to follow it: this substance that should not be subject to time and decay. Her pinions spread, the wide-fingered wings of a crow. From the red water, rose light shone up through her feathers.

Heat scalded.

The stench of a butcher's shambles choked her. She flung herself up into suddenly blazing air, wings thrashing, blindly flying: one glimpse of water turned thickly bloody and the threshing of diamond limbs left imprinted double behind her eyes.

'Craa-akk!'

Gravity pulled her: not down, but onwards. The white crow spread her wings to their widest. The changing stone spun past below her feathered body. The names of Decans beat in the confines of her brain and blood: *Chnoumen, Chnachoumen, Knat, Biou, Erou, Erebiou, Rhamanoor, Rheianoor* . . .

A faint echo came down one high hall, a whisper caught out of time:

' "*I also know how difficult it is to get thirty-six of anybody to agree on anything and act as one.*" '

She cawed a crow's harsh bitter laughter.

A wall reared up before her. Her wing-tips brushed an arch of brick. Small smooth ochre bricks; the ghost of sun's warmth in their depth. The touch against her feathers froze her through to her hollowed bones.

Her feathered shadow skipped across a courtyard.

Black roses lay worm-eaten, tangled, dead in the Garden of the Eleventh Hour. The gravels of the knot garden lay smeared, patternless.

The crow's wings flapped slowly, curving into a descent.

A brown blight covered the brickwork eaten away by lichen. Grubs gnawed the leaves of black roses. Tiny curled dots showed on the earth, black bees lying dead.

The sky above shone brown, yellow, the colour of paper about to burst into flame.

'Divine One! Lady! Of the Eleventh Hour!'

The white crow wheeled, feathers cutting the air, gliding to land among ivy and lichen at the base of the great brick paw. The sand-bright sphinx bulked above her, mortar crumbling from between ochre bricks: the Decan of the Eleventh Hour, of Ten Degrees of High Summer, the Lady of Shining Force.

A crow is a large bird, some eighteen inches from beak to tail, and unwieldy: she landed heavily in a skirr of feathers. She raised her head, double vision shining with the ivy-bitten forepaws and breasts and head of the god-daemon.

'Divine One, you see all. Know all. Are all. The Decan of Noon and Midnight sends me. To tell you the Great Circle of the world breaks now.'

A sand-blast of heat breathes from Her curving lips.

'*It is so.*'

'To tell you. If it can be re-created from chaos. There won't be Thirty-Six, but One. I begin to see – why he wishes it. What other change – can omnipotence *desire*? What else could be impossible?'

The brick-curved linen draperies of Her head drift dust into the air. The lids of Her slanting eyes slide up. A gaze as pitiless as deserts impaled the crow.

'*I am omnipotent, child of flesh, and I do not desire non-being. If I tire of this world, I will make more. If I tire of the cosmos, I will make things other than universes. It has been long and long that I have guided the Great Wheel, long and long that I have created and changed it; it shall be longer still before I weary of all that is and all that can be.*'

Gravel chilled her bird-claws. Silence shimmered in the Garden. The white crow strutted on the earth, making a movement of wings and body oddly like a human shrug.

She stabbed a hard carrion-tearer's beak at the air.

'He's weary. The Spagyrus.'

'*Flesh corrupts him. We do not weary unless we choose. It is not beyond us to forget, when we weary. Each springtime is the first of the world. Each winter the ending of an aeon. We need not weary of it.*'

'You can't let him!'

The Decan's head tilts, facing down to the earth; to the bird strutting among dead rose briars and the curled bodies of black bees. Aeons of deserts under noon fire and arctic cold burn in Her eyes, burn with the pain of fissure, dissolution, decay.

The white crow's wings open slightly, on the verge of panic flight.

'*Gods are not permitted, or hindered. If He can uncreate, then that is well. If He can uncreate us all, then that is well. All things done by the Divine are well.*'

'Naw!' The bird's croak sawed the air: comic, ludicrous before the Decan of the Eleventh Hour. 'No! You're wrong!'

'*The Divine are not wrong, child of flesh, for whatever we do is right, because it is We who act.*'

'You sent! Me! To heal!'

'*For then it would have been I who was right, and not the Lord of Noon and Midnight. Child of flesh, heal if you will. If you can. Until now, the hour had not yet quite come – but it has come, now.*

'*Now.*

'*It is time and the Hour is striking!*'

The white crow's feathers flurried as she strutted across the gravel, the earth that smelt faintly of mould, of rot, of corruption. Black bird-eyes glimmered, piercing. Her heavy beak stabbed the ground before great brick claws that, closing around her, could have cracked her like a flea.

Human speech cracked out of her as a thrush cracks a snail: shattering, raw.

'Who! Dies! Now! *Who?*'

The Decan weeps.

Lids slide down over Her eyes that hold deserts, rise to show the diamond-dust of tears. A shadow begins to cover Her breasts. Her head is raised as if she listens to the striking of some inaudible hour.

'Cannot you tell, child of earth?

'It is he, the Decan of Noon and Midnight. How else may he hope to be One, who is one of Thirty-Six, unless he can uncreate and self-create himself? He must die, truly, to create himself again out of non-being, and if he cannot – why, then. Nothing. For Us all.'

'How! Can! You! Allow!'

'We foresee it will be so. Create it will be so. Past his death we cannot see nor create.'

The corruption of plague shines in the desert eyes of the god-daemon.

Past speech, past debate, past miracle; the weight of aeons waits for the moment in which this may exist: true death.

'No! Hrrrakk-kk! No!'

Battered by a Divine suffering that no mortal flesh can behold, avian or human, the white crow flees, flying out into the Fane.

'You're a fool! Hrrrrakk! I won't! Let you! Do this!'

Wings beat, her frail heart pulsing urgency, sensing how in the air it trembles now: the striking of the noon of the Night Sun.

8

Becalmed.

Black water slopped. Fog coiled across its cold surface. The one lantern's yellow light made no reflection
in the water.

The forgetfulness of the Boat pulled at Zar-bettu-
zekigal, at every cell in her body. Her eyes darkened
with Memory.

'You always *call* me buzzard because I used to sound
like one. When I was a baby. *Mee-oo*,' Zar-bettu-zekigal
called. '*Mee-oo*.'

The harsh sound echoed back flatly from fog and darkness. She walked across the deck, the untied laces of her
black ankle-boots ticking on the wood, arms wrapped
about herself. 'See you, El, you remember that.'

The older Katayan woman sat cross-legged at the stern,
by the lantern, one hand resting on the tiller of the Boat,
lace ruffles falling over her wrist. A frown of intense
concentration twisted her face.

'More.'

'Oh, what! See you, I'll tell you about the first time
I ever met Messire . . . It was in an austquarter crypt.
He said, *Students, Charnay, but of a particular talent. The
young woman is a Kings' Memory*. And then: *You're young,
all but trained, as I take it, and without a patron. My name
is Plessiez. In the next few hours I – we – will badly need a
trusted record of events. Trusted by both parties. If I put that
proposition to you?*'

She squatted down in front of Elish-hakku-zekigal.

'Trust me, El?'

Sweat plastered the woman's black curls to her forehead;

388

her pallid face seemed stained, under the eyes, with brown. Elish's lips moved silently, concentrating on the voice, following Memory's bright thread.

'I remember what you said to me when I left South Katay. *Learn hard, little buzzard, it opens all the world to you, and you're a wanderer. I'll be here to hear your tales.* I love you, Elish. I'll always come back and see you.'

Zar-bettu-zekigal knelt, hands on her knees, tail coiled up about her hips. She leaned forward to study the compass rose set into the deck before the shaman woman. The needle moved ceaselessly, swinging in five ninety-degree arcs around the circle, in turn to all five points of the compass. She sat back, willing Elish the power to steer through the amnesia of the Boat, stronger now with night and nightmares haunting its drifting.

'Listen, there's more—'

Outside her circle of Memory's voice, fleering mirror faces begin to gather.

The torch pitched forward, flaring soot across the floor.

His vision cleared.

Plessiez climbed to his feet, rubbing his haunch. Mist hung above him, choking the brick shaft they descended. He made to pick up the torch, and stopped.

The guttering torches on the stairwell shone down on a distorted curving brick floor that crested up, curved down in hollows, rippled out in frozen curves. The last of these steps had not been the last, once. It lay embedded in a tide of brick paving that had *flowed*, like water. His torch rocked in a deep hollow.

Brushwood rustled. Sound hissed back from the walls, with the drip of water. Nitre spidered white patterns. Plessiez stepped down into the hollow, bending to pick up his torch. Flames glimmered blackly along the pitch. The fingers of his other hand cramped on his rapier's hilt; the point circling, alert.

On the steps above a voice Charnay's and not Charnay's hissed: '*Go back little animal go back go die go away!*'

He spun, sword raised. 'What?'

Her blunt snout lowered, regarding him. She frowned. 'I said, this is strangely altered since the last time we ventured down here.'

'You – heard nothing?'

'Heard?' Charnay stared past him. A constricted passage some six feet high remained between roof and floor. This tunnel, lightless now, hissed unidentifiable echoes back.

'Bring another torch.'

The brown Rat trod heavily. Her scaly tail lashed debris on the steps: brick rubble, desiccated wood, the brown knobs of animal vertebrae. She tugged her stained blue sash across her chest, scratching at her furred dugs.

Brick gave way underfoot to earth and gravel.

He held up his torch, blinking. The yellow light and black smoke of burning pitch faded into a wider open space.

Twin gibbets now stood by the entrance to the catacombs. Outlined in a pale silver glow, their nests of chains hung down, wound about bones, ragged flesh, cerements.

'*Those* weren't here before.'

Gravel crunched under the brown Rat's clawed feet. Charnay rested a hand against one of the white marble obelisks that flanked the opening, staring up at the inscription. She snorted.

' "*Halt! Here begins the Empire of the Dead* . . ." You always did have odd humours, messire.'

'*Magia* indicated this one of the septagon sites, not I.'

All perspective vanished in darkness. No torches burned inside the catacombs. Cold struck up from the gravelled earth beneath his clawed feet. A smell of nitre and dank mud sank into his fur.

'Charnay . . .'

Sound whispered back from the galleries.

' . . . you would do me a greater favour, I think, to go back up the shaft and guard the way against our over-enthusiastic follower.'

A hand clamped on his shoulder. The brown Rat stared him in the face, lowering her head to do it.

'I'm not in the business of doing you favours, Plessiez, man. I don't trust you. You see your own advantage in matters very clearly. I don't trust you not to work out some even more clever plot, and make things even worse.' She cut him off before he could interrupt. 'I don't *like* all of this. I want things back to normal. You're going in to put an end to this, and I'm going to be at your back every step of the way!'

She drew a deep breath. Plessiez, shaken, turned his gaze pointedly to where she gripped his shoulder. After a long minute her fingers loosened.

'You were compliant enough when it was a matter of a little sickness among the human servants, and the Decans our masters being persuaded to remove further off—'

'Ahh!' The Lieutenant spat. She held up the torch, shadows leaping violently in the gibbets' chains. 'You and his Majesty are a pair of fools, all of you. Now this dangerous nonsense with black suns and acolytes out of control – and you call *me* stupid, messire priest!'

A knob of bone rattled across the earth, rolling to rest at Plessiez's feet. 'I think . . . I think we should go back.'

Muted light dazzled his eyes as she lowered the torch, peering at him.

'Obviously we can do no good here; it was idiocy to suggest so.' Plessiez faced about, putting his back to the catacomb-entrance. One-handed and with some difficulty he sheathed his rapier. 'I don't have the knowledge, I don't have the equipment for *magia*; we should retreat and reconsider this. Perhaps return later, better equipped. You as a soldier will recognize the sense in this.'

His tail twitched an inch one way, an inch back; he fell to grooming the fur of his shoulder for a moment.

'*What*?' Charnay demanded.

'I've told you. We're leaving. We'll return here in due course.'

The brown Rat said: 'You're going in there.'

Plessiez leaned his hand up against the brown brick wall. Nitre sweated under his long-fingered hands. He lowered his head for a second, then lifted it, staring up at the rusting gibbet-chains, and the white-painted inscription across the entrance.

'No,' he said. 'No.'

'Plessiez, man—'

'*I won't do it!*'

Echoes hissed off the low walls. Cold and damp struck deeper, chilling blood and bone. A soft chuckle rustled through the chains of the gibbets. The black Rat leaned dizzily against the brickwork.

'Now I envy you. Charnay, I would to gods I had your thick skull and your ability not to foresee.'

The brown Rat lugged out her long sword, leaning the point on the earth. She cocked her head to one side, a frown on her blunt muzzle. 'Messire, *I* don't know what to do in there.'

'Neither do I!'

The black Rat rubbed his hand across his face, smoothing fur that slicked up in tufts. His eyes glinted darkly, meeting Charnay's.

'Now, listen to me, Lieutenant Charnay. I suspect that when we emerge on the surface it will be to find the servants, humans and all, in confusion. H'm? Their temple destroyed, their ranks thinned by pestilence.'

Plessiez picked at his incisors with one broken claw.

'His Majesty, gods preserve them, I fear to be dead, if what young Fleury said is true. And the Lords of the Celestial Sphere, one might prophesy, *returned* to that plane and only overlooking our earth with their Divine providence. All which, if I am right, leaves clear room for one determined in his aims. He – he and his friends, Charnay – might do much, now, in the government of the heart of the world.'

'*You're going in there.*'

The black Rat knelt, driving the shaft of the torch into the soft earth and gravel. He got to his feet slowly. Black eyes bright, he said: 'No. Not for my life. No.'

Silver glinted on the onyx rings on his fingers, on the head-band that looped over one translucent pink ear and under the other; shimmered on the black feather plume that moved with his breathing. Nothing of the priest about him now: more gone than *ankh* and insignia. Charnay took in his febrile tension.

'I'm not a fool.' She shrugged. 'I know enough to be afraid. Leave *magia* alone and working for weeks, and the gods alone know what it's become now! But we don't have any choice. I told the Night Council that if you destroyed one of the seven points it would stop the necromancy working. Get in there and *do* it. You promised the little Kings' Memory.'

The black Rat turned his head, staring into the depths of the catacombs. He scratched at the back of his head, sliding a dark palm round to rub his snout as he lowered his arm.

'So I did.'

He shuddered: cold drifting out from the low arch of the catacombs. A visible pulse beat in the soft fur of his throat. His sword-harness clinked.

'What will you do now, my friend?'

The brown Rat, torch and long rapier in her hands, blocked the way back to the stairs. Her eyes narrowed. She thrust her torch at him so suddenly that he must grasp it or be singed; swung the sword up two-handed, and cut at the rusty chains.

Bones and cloth hit the earth; Plessiez skittered back. Charnay, backhanding, cut at the other gibbet. The rusty chains resisted; the rotten wood of the support cracked loud as musket-shot, teetered, and fell forward into darkness.

'Now you're equipped, messire. Now *move*.'

A hard knot of tension under his breastbone, Plessiez knelt, holding high the torch, swiftly and distastefully fumbling through the heaps of bones. What seemed most useful he wrapped in cerements; after a moment's hesitation tucking the bundle securely under his sword-belt.

'Well, then,' he said. 'Well.'

Damp cold prickled his spine, and he stepped forward with his tail carried fastidiously high. Smoke from the pitch made his eyes run with water. He raised the torch as he walked through the catacomb-entrance. Shadows of rib and pelvic bones danced on the cavern walls.

At his right hand rose the beginning of a wall of bones.

Forearm and thigh bones, laid crosswise like kindling and as brown, built up a retaining wall a head taller than himself. Into the space between the arm and leg bones and the cavern wall, ribs and vertebrae, carpals and metacarpals, pelvic bones and all else had been carelessly thrown. Along the top of the wall, jammed jowl to jowl, lay skulls. Rows of skulls jutting their eyeless long snouts into darkness, yellow incisors impossibly long.

The brown bone glowed, sprinkled with nitre as with frost.

Skulls, set into the walls of knobbed bone joints, made patterns of chevrons and *ankhs*; and long intact skeins of tail-vertebrae snaked around them, jammed in tight.

'We can be followed in here.' Charnay rescued the other torch, waving it to cast light down the curving passages and cross-passages of the royal catacombs. Another wall rose beside her; unencumbered with torch and rapier she could have stood in the centre of the passage and touched a hand to both.

'And outdistanced . . . '

Plessiez paced forward, torch high. Black shadows darted in the hollow rings of eye-sockets, in the channels of snouts, and over incisors still clinging to bony jaws. The brown Rat held her torch close to the white marble plaque, one of a number set into the wall at intervals.

' "*Behold these bones, the . . . the nest . . .* " '

Plessiez completed, rapidly and accurately enough to put down some of his terror, ' " . . . *the nest of each fledgling soul*." Poor poetry, I fear, but his Majesty's taste was always less than highbrow—'

He broke off as the hilt of the brown Rat's sword nudged him. Without looking back, he walked into the catacombs and silence.

'And if it were only true, now, further in!'

The interior of the plague-tent shone, full of light-shadows.

Shock chilled her back to reality. Evelian stepped outside and let the canvas flap fall to behind her. She rubbed a work-roughened hand across her face.

'I've . . . found Falke for you.'

Her skin sweated, despite the Night Sun's chill. Slanting bars of light-shadow fell from the Imperial pavilions down into Fourteenth District's square. Gold-and-white banners hung limp, the canvas cloth now thickened with ice. Frost glimmered on shattered masonry, on abandoned muskets and greaves and shoes thrown together in a pile by the Rat-Lords' clear-up details.

'The master builder? Here?'

Through blazing black light, the Lord-Architect came towards her from the construction site, moving with a frighteningly rapid stride.

'He's . . . *Falke* . . . When he was a boy, we used to talk about all this. About House of Salomon and how we should build . . . I swore I'd never get mixed up in it again after it failed the first time, but what would you? Poor bastard.'

She drew a noisy breath, huffed it out; dizzy with shock.

'*All* those poor bastards.'

The fat man's tread shook the paving-stones. She automatically stepped out of his way. She smelt machine oil and sweaty linen. The Lord-Architect Casaubon threw the tent-flap open, staring past her, to where the plague-dead lay stacked like winter wood.

'Rot him, I *needed* him!'

Casaubon pushed past her into the tent, the bulk of his body brushing aside her and the canvas with equal impatience. Evelian stared. Outrage flared in her, old temper reasserting itself.

'Damn you, man, what right do you have to say that? What right do you have not to care that he's dead?'

'Oh, I care!'

She turned her eyes away from the laid-out rows of men and women. Some wrapped in blankets or cloaks; some in summer clothing, still with the traces of lead-and-ochre paint on their faces. Afraid of how many she might recognize under the black disfigurement of plague.

'You *can't*—' Evelian stopped. The Lord-Architect Casaubon knelt down by Falke's body, one fat hand knotting surcoat and mail-shirt both at the shoulder, pulling him up into a half-sitting position, while his other hand searched the recesses of the man's clothes.

'Rot him, he knows things I need to know. Damn him for dying now of all times!'

White hair fell back from the plague-tattered flesh of the dead man; his mouth gaped slightly. A thin line of white showed under his eyelids. One hand flopped, too recently dead for rigidity. Casaubon handled the weight effortlessly, fat-sheathed muscles tensing. Evelian grunted.

'Not the joker you were in Carver Street now, are you, my *lord*?'

'Get out!'

Her heart pounded. She tasted blood, coppery and cold, on her breath; suddenly certain she had stayed too long away from her daughter. She stepped back.

Black air fogged vision, hiding the barricaded buildings around the square and the distant reaches of the construction site. Hiding the sky, beyond which distant wings moved; casting a veil of black across the streets, and the aurora-geometries of the labyrinth . . .

'Sharlevian!'

High above in darkness, the Fane's acolytes still screamed. Fisting the blue-and-yellow satin dress, she tugged up the hem and stalked across the square. She strode through abandoned debris, guns and tankards, ribbons and trowels and flowers, kicking aside a broken marionette; running past where, head in hands, Tannakin Spatchet sat on the marble steps, to Sharlevian leaning back and kicking one heel against the foundation-stone carved with the Word of Seshat.

'*Mo*ther . . .' The yellow-haired girl didn't move out of Evelian's embrace; if anything, tightened her arms around her mother's waist. Evelian ruffled the girl's hair, then buried her face in it.

Footsteps clicked across the empty square, echoing back from distant buildings. A weighty tread.

'Archemaster, what will happen now?' Tannakin Spatchet's voice sounded flatly.

She rubbed her cheek against her daughter's warm hair and head, aware of the muscles tense in the child's back. Hiding her own fear, she put the girl back to arm's length and gave her a shake.

'There's my Sharl, eh.'

'Aw, leave off.'

The girl tugged her silk overall sleeves up to show her wrists, bracelets jangling. She shrugged Evelian's hands away.

'I heard something today.'

Caught by his tone, Evelian looked at the Mayor and found Tannakin staring at Casaubon.

'A prophecy, Lord Archemaster. This. *In one hour, the circle of the living and the dying shall be broken. In one hour, the Wheel of Three Hundred and Sixty Degrees will fly apart into chaos: stone from stone, flesh from bone, earth from sun, star from star. There shall not be one mote of matter left clinging to another, nor light enough to kindle a spark, nor soul left living in the universe.* Is this the hour?'

Evelian saw the fat man's blue eyes widen. 'Where did you hear that!'

'They say it has its origins in the Fane, messire.'

'Aw, yeah.' Sharlevian sniffed, resting her hands back

against the Word of Seshat carved into the abandoned foundation-stone. 'That's been going round. Been lots of stuff like that.'

The luminescent shadow of the foundation-stone seemed to hold a little warmth. Her hands behind her back, wrapped in the folds of her skirt, Evelian drew courage enough to look up at blazing darkness.

'I never thought to see that come in my time. The Night Sun . . . Now will they leave us, the Thirty-Six? And wipe the world away and start a new one? Is the prophecy true?'

She looked down. A step or two below, his back to the square, the big man stood at eye-to-eye level with her. Anger tautened his massive shoulders.

'Are there other master builders here? Answer me, rot you! Who else would have the plans for the Temple? And workers, construction workers. I need them. I can't act without them!'

A cold wind blew. Tangled spars of light-shadow slanted from the scaffolding. Numbness bit at her feet and fingers. Evelian stared out at the glittering darkness of the Night Sun, eyes watering.

'You see where we are? You see what's happening to us?' She smiled, shook her head, one hand extending out to the deserted square. 'Those that aren't dead have run, messire. Now I've helped you search for Falke, I'm taking Sharlevian out of here. If it wasn't for *that*—'

She stabbed a finger at the distant siege-engine. Away from the stone of Seshat's warmth, black light clustered, hiding the aurora of the labyrinth, the trapped daemons.

'We shouldn't have listened to you anyway. We should have run when we had the chance!'

Tannakin Spatchet rose to his feet, pulling his greasy grey doublet straight. He gazed up at the fat man.

'Archemaster, I may say that I admire your skills in protecting us from the acolytes. We thank you for that. Now I feel it might be wise if we attempted to take cover, all of us. Ultimately it may make no difference, but then again . . .'

'Oh, Tan, for gods' sakes!' Exasperated, Evelian rubbed the corners of her eyes as she walked down the steps, as if the darkness might be in her vision and not in the air. Shock numbed her, left her whole seconds of calm normality before the chill reasserted itself.

'We used to hold a market . . . ' She looked out towards the littered stone flags. Now faint metallic sparkles precipitated out of the air, falling to shine on porticoes and balconies. 'In Nineteenth's square, of course. Not here. Fourteenth is a Rat district . . . I don't suppose that matters at all now.'

She fisted her hand and touched it gently to Casaubon's arm, as she passed.

'That's what Falke wanted. But it's too late to think about that now, isn't it?'

The Lord-Architect sat, both hands palm-down on the frost-cracked steps, his head tipped back and leaning against the foundation-stone. Folds of satin coat blotted up moisture from the stone, that darkened his blue silk breeches. One of his court shoes lacked a heel now, and both stockings slid down his tremendous calves to his ankles.

'Falke could have given me the designs of the New Temple.'

He spoke so quietly that the silence almost drowned him.

'Mistress Evelian, deep structures have a power on the universe, witness what power the labyrinth has to compel the Fane's servants. The structure of building has that power, also; and I might have used it, if he had lived to tell me.'

The radiance of the Night Sun began to pulse: to tick, the time of some great heart or clock beating in it.

'I told the lady White Crow.' Tannakin Spatchet turned, hands fussing with his cuffs. The strands of hair combed across his balding head fell across his eyes now; and he jabbed an accusatory finger at the Lord-Architect. 'When she made us talismans, I told her that young Falke was a fool, and engaged in plague *magia* and bone *magia* and the Thirty-Six know what else! You had a month to act in. Why didn't you? Why wait until *now*? Until the Night Sun's here, and it's too late?'

'Ask the pox-rotted Bitch who denied us a month to work in—!'

The air vibrated to a striking that might have been inside the ear-canal or over the distant horizon in another District. Casaubon's head came up. Copper hair fell over his forehead, straggling down to his eyes, and he gazed up through it. A liquidity swam in his eyes. The fine lines of his features, fat-blurred and buried, lost all good nature and humour.

' "When that hour strikes, then act—" '

His rounded delicate lips quivered with some emotion: anger or misery.

'Damn Her, the bitch! Treat an Archemaster like this!'

He reared to his feet, as if he would actually shake his fist towards the Fane-in-the-Twelfth-District. Some rigidity left his spine.

'Damned Divine mother of all bitches. Give me thirty days to prepare and I might have done something, but no! No! What's it to Her? Pick people up and put them down where it suits Her, no thought about what we can or can't do; Valentine to the Fane, me to this farce—'

Evelian, in a sharp voice that Sharlevian automatically winced at, snapped: '*Lord Casaubon!*'

To her surprise the large man's tantrum halted. He stared down at her, a faint pink colouring his cheeks.

'Damned Decans think they can play god-games.'

'Is that where Crow vanished to? The *Fane*? With you? You fool! That woman was a friend of mine, as well as a lodger; if you were stupid enough to drag her into the *Fane*, of all places in earth and heaven, then—'

'She's there now, woman! Willingly. Searching out ways to avert your prophecy, Master Mayor.'

The Mayor reached to his throat, fingering a malachite talisman carved with symbols.

Evelian reached behind and sat down on the steps without looking, the muscles of her legs turned liquid. Stone jolted her. She looked at her daughter, who shied pebbles idly across the construction site and paused to hook up one coil of her hair with a flashy pin.

'Sharlevian . . .'

The Lord-Architect stood as if he felt danger through the earth beneath his feet. His gaze travelled through the abandoned chaos of the construction site, staring towards the north-austerly horizon and the black pyramids of the Fane-in-the-Twelfth-District.

Evelian looked up at him.

'What were you going to do? I think you had better try it, Messire Lord-Architect.'

He shook his head ponderously. 'How? Given plans, given workers . . . I could have at least built out the *ground-plan* of Salomon's Temple. There were people enough here, before the pestilence, for me to do it; but time ran out for us.'

Shuddering through bone and flesh and blood, Evelian felt the striking of an hour. She reached up a hand as her daughter picked a way back across the broken steps. The girl took it, staring at the fat man.

'See you, Master Falke isn't the only builder. I'm an Entered Apprentice.'

'Ah, love . . .'

Sharlevian pulled free of her hand, reaching up to twist her fair hair into a worker's knot, pinning it securely, ear-rings jingling. Plaster-dust stained the knees of her pink silk overalls. She smiled, sly; excluding everything that lay outside her expression of pleasure at her own intelligence.

'Why don't we build the Temple anyway?'

The Lord-Architect Casaubon looked at her in silenced disbelief.

'*No*,' the girl said. 'A *model*. There's enough stuff here. It's all pattern, like you said. Oh gods, the lectures I've had in Masons' Hall about *structures*.'

401

She sighed self-consciously. Evelian, gathering her blue-and-yellow skirts and getting to her feet, said 'Do you want a slap, missy?' and then laughed at incongruous reflexes. 'Love, tell us.'

Abashed, the fair-haired girl mumbled: 'Doesn't matter what size it is, then, does it? Doesn't have to be full size. Still got structure, hasn't it?'

Casaubon's plump hands seized her by the shoulders. 'A model!'

Evelian walked past his padded torso, taking her daughter's arm. A long exasperation faded. She gripped both of Sharlevian's nail-bitten hands.

'Shall we do this? Or shall we try to take shelter?'

'Aw, Mother, *c'mon*. Might as well. Why not?'

'Right. Tan and I will help. Let's do it. Collect bricks – wood – nails – what you can. *Move!*'

She strode up the steps. Behind her Casaubon protested, 'There's no plans! No blueprints. I don't know what rituals he planned to use!'

'We'll build it how *we'd* want it to be. Who would it be for, after all?'

The fat man reached into an inside pocket and extracted a rule, a plumb-line and a notepad; the last of which he began to figure on rapidly.

Evelian climbed the steps to the site rapidly, and stopped with her hand on her stomach. Black sparkles fringed her vision. The smell of cold flared her nostrils; her breath fogged the air. She bent to seize the handles of an abandoned barrow.

Enthusiasm or desperation beat in her head with her pulse. Conscious of the Mayor at her side, unearthing bricks, tiles, bags of plaster, and stone fragments, she abruptly straightened up and began to laugh.

'Evelian.' Tannakin Spatchet stopped, hands deep in a toolbox, peering up at her over his much-darned doublet-shoulder.

It wheezed out of her, tears cold in the corners of her eyes. 'Tan, didn't you always want to be a hero? I did, when I was Sharl's age. This *isn't* what I had in mind.'

He straightened his back and threw a handful of chisels and knives into the barrow. A wind from somewhere began to tug at his doublet and patched breeches, and blow strands of thinning hair across his eyes.

'Evvie, I've never known you satisfied with anything.'

Her shoes lodged in the mud. She bent to free them, and to heave the barrow back towards the edge of the site.

'Look.'

Tannakin lurched through the soft earth and grabbed the barrow's other handle. As he pulled, he looked, and she saw him frown.

All else darkening, now, as if storms approached; some faint light yet remained. The abandoned foundation-stone of the New Temple glowed with a flickering warmth like firelight. It beat against her skin as they plodded back, the barrow jolting over the rubble. In its light, the immensely fat man sat with legs sprawled wide apart, reading from his notepad, directing Sharlevian and sketching with chalk on the paving-stones in front of the carved Word of Seshat.

'Let's have an open courtyard, too!' Sharlevian sprawled on her stomach, elbows outspread, careless of her silk overall. She reached over and planted two bricks, and a third, to form a plain arch.

'Main gates,' she announced. 'Build it in a rectangle or square, you can have a gate each side, people can walk in.'

The Lord-Architect reached across with the hand that enfolded his pencil and moved the bricks closer together, making the arch smaller. 'No coaches.'

'Oh, sure. Just so people can walk and the kids can play out of the way.'

Evelian heaved the barrow to a halt and left the Mayor to sort around in its contents. She gathered her skirts and knelt down on the broken marble.

'What are you doing?'

The Lord-Architect Casaubon measured a lath with his rule, snapped it expertly to length, and fitted it along the chalk lines of the model Temple.

'The proportions of great buildings should rightly be made the same as the proportions of the body, as Vitruvius writes.'

He knelt up, knees wide apart, silk straining to encase his huge thighs and calves. The top two buttons of his breeches had come undone, she saw, unequal to holding in his belly. His crumpled fleshy face wrinkled up with innocent concentration.

'Symmetry's the relations of the proportions of the part to the whole. As, the face – always the same distance from the bottom of the chin to the underside of the nose, as from nose to eyebrows, and eyebrows to hairline.'

He reached across, one fat finger tapping Sharlevian's chin, nose and forehead. The fifteen-year-old giggled, vaguely flattered; and Evelian's heart suddenly lurched for the normality of Masons' Halls and building instruction.

'Likewise, the length of the foot is one sixth the height of the whole body; the length of the forearm one fourth . . . And since man's a microcosm, and thus like the larger macrocosm, so the proportions and symmetry of the Temple, matching the body, can mirror the proportions and order of the cosmos.'

'The cosmos isn't as ordered as all *that*.' Evelian smiled grimly. 'Allow for it being flamboyant and disordered from time to time, Archemaster.'

'Well . . . yes.'

'I'd build the place with room for people.' Sharlevian looked up, face smeared with chalk, totally unself-conscious. 'You go up to the avenues round the royal palace and *boom*! – it just hits you. You feel about *this*

'I'd build a garden. In the centre of the Temple. Laid out in pattern and proportion, but built of growing things . . .'

Heidelberg Castle and Gardens, engraved by Matthieu Merian from *Hortus Palatinus*, Salomon de Caus, pub. Johann Theodore De Bry, Frankfurt, 1620

high. All those blocks, so massive – and you have to get up on the pavement or the coaches just knock you down. I'd build our Temple so people could sit around and just meet in the evenings, and there'd be places you could buy food, and the temple would look as though it wanted you to come in . . . '

'I . . . ah' – Tannakin Spatchet emerged from the depths of the barrow – 'I'd have the courtyard big enough to hold a regular market, and a place for the Market Court to meet, and somewhere to have a drink with colleagues when business is over . . . '

'And what a time you'd have with university students!' Evelian laughed. The sound startled her. 'Well, and why not? I'd like a place I could go to meet my old friends, a place that we'd helped build and was ours. No Lords! *And* I'd allow Temple coins, so that we could buy and sell in the Temple precinct, not barter. Even if that only happened there, it'd be a beginning. Say you – build your Temple and I'll run the bank for you!'

Her daughter giggled. Casaubon rubbed a cement-covered hand across his lapel, staining his coat.

'I'd build a garden. In the centre of the Temple. Laid out in pattern and proportion, but built of growing things: flowers, mosses, trees. A microcosm laid out in concentric circles, with the plants of each Celestial Sign growing in their proper places. I built gardens in my city . . . '

He raised his head, meeting Evelian's eyes.

'No Architect-Lords in that city now. Not any more. Oh, Parry's good enough to me. She's a senator in the Republic; she sees projects are put my way. But . . . '

'It should have a dome!' Sharlevian rolled over and grabbed the edge of the stone of Seshat to pull herself to her feet. She scrambled, careless of a rip in her overalls, to exhume an old leather bucket from a rubbish-pile.

'With the Celestial Signs,' she added, scratching with a nail on the interior surface. 'Or . . . Archemaster, will the Decans still be here on earth?'

Her tone had increased in respect since she saw the

Chymicall Labyrinth function. She now eyed the Lord-Architect with expectation. Evelian smiled slightly, and caught the fat man's eye, and imperceptibly shook her head.

'Mistress Sharlevian, who knows?' He placed the makeshift dome on the central circular walls.

Tannakin Spatchet, peering down, said: 'Steps up to the main building – the flower- and fruit-sellers use them.'

'And fountains, to drink.'

'And let people draw on the pavements . . . '

Evelian shivered, ignored the coldness that bit at her fingers, and twisted wire in the proportions of golden mean and rule; watching it begin to take shape. Tiles propped up to form walls, bricks standing for outbuildings, the carefully measured wooden frame of the main building topped by its ridiculous bucket-dome – Casaubon and Sharlevian sprawling by it like children on a rug. Tannakin Spatchet unearthed a hose-nozzle, and ceremoniously set it in the tile-marked-out 'courtyard' as a fountain.

Evelian said: 'I thought you were a fraud when you arrived. I see I was wrong. I never did believe Crow's stories of her Invisible College – I see I was wrong in that, too.'

Casaubon's fingers, surprisingly delicate in their movements, wired lath to lath in parts of a growing framework. The skeleton hinted at outflung quirky grandeur: classical proportions extended into pleasing irregularity – towers, balconies, buttresses; comfortable small rooms, colonnades, courtyards.

'Not a fraud.' He placed another part of the framework on the chalked stone. It rocked. 'Just out of my depth, Mistress Evelian.'

Sharlevian, mixing mud in her hands, began to plaster the courtyard's outer walls smooth. Ignoring a broken fingernail, she sketched *trompe l'œil* designs, so that her mother (closing an eye, squinting, forgetting scale) could see how the designs would lead one to perceive longer galleries and an apotheosis of images on the ceiling.

'I was hoping that at least *one* of the four of us knew what we're about.'

The Lord-Architect's gaze lifted first to her and then to the enclosing black light. His breath misted the air. He said nothing.

Four sets of hands built the model, in the warm shadow of the foundation-stone. The wooden-lath frame and hessian-and-plaster walls took on solidity. Rickety, makeshift, it none the less began to body out a shape.

The air shook again like a tolling bell.

Higher above the city that is called the heart of the world, birds soar.

The air is chill now, and thin. Below them the city curves with the curvature of the world. Eagles, wild hawks, cormorants and finches; bright parakeets and humming-birds: all frail feathers beat against the troposphere. Beaks snap. Butterfly-bodies crunch.

And still, higher and further, the bright blobs of moths and butterflies fly upwards. Drawn up by the black fires that sear the sky, hot and bitter as a plague-sore. Souls drawn up by the Night Sun that scars the sky as black tattered flesh scars the plague-dead.

Air thins in the frail bones of birds, but still they strive for height, striking at the bright insects, devouring.

A black-and-white death's-head moth bobs in the air, feeling on dusty fragile wings the cold of the Night Sun. The chill that will crisp the *psyche* into nothingness.

The death's-head moth flies up towards that oblivion, away from the beating wings of a dusty brown sparrow.

The black fire that does not give life but takes it: that can create only the death of a soul.

The white crow flew through the hollow body of the dying god.

A stone rib-cage soared above her. All hollow, hollow and white, that had been ebony: the Decan of Noon and Midnight.

The crow soared up, her wing-tips bending to the pressure of the air. Ice glinted on the pale stone ribs curving up to rise above her head,

'Hhrrraaa-kk!'

She flew through the void of it, vast as cathedrals: a gutted empty carcass. If stone can rot, this stone flesh rotted. It curved like a vast wall at her right side. Ribs, muscles, tendons clearly delineated.

On each lump of tendon and muscle, and lodged in the splintered crevices of bone, white wax candles burned. The yellow flames leaped in the draught of her wings. She felt their heat. Fire palely reflected in the stone flesh, warming no thaw in the frost.

Receding ranks of candles burned on each hillock and lump of petrified gut. The sweet smell of beeswax dizzied her. So far away that only avian sight detects it, the great ribs curved down again.

She beat frantic wings to soar up. The great spine of the Decan of Noon and Midnight jutted infinitely far above her head, vertebrae an avenue of spiked pillars hanging down into void. Light blazed back from the blade of a shoulder, vast as a salt-plain. Stone guts hung from stone ribs in profuse lace drapery.

Dust brushed her wing. She side-slipped in the cold air. A great slew of stone flesh avalanched down, raising dust and chill. Decaying, the rib-cage opened to the air beyond, a mist of gold and rose-colour that her bird's vision could not penetrate. From candle-starred heights another chunk of stone fell, alabaster-white, turning slowly in the air. She glided, caught in fascination; it roiled the air, falling past, tumbling her end over end; shattered in thunderous fragments below.

Weary, she skimmed the air, gliding down to flick her shadow (pale as ice) across the rounded joint of a limb, domed as great buildings are; rose again, straining, avian heartbeat ticking fast as a watch. The hollow between clavicle and jaw opened up ahead, flesh rotted away into stone-dust.

She beat her wings, straining to reach the gap. The great jaw-bones shed scales, marble slabs that might have stood for walls in the Temple of Salomon. An ache bit into what would have been her shoulders and the muscles of her breast. Cramp twinged. She wheeled and spun down – down – down; the floor of the body so great a distance below that she feared her strength would fail, and she fall despite her shape.

A colour: scarlet.

Far below, a man climbed slowly and painfully over the uneven surface between rib and stone rib, his bare feet slipping on the icy marble among the candles. One splash of colour: he wore, still, its arms knotted around his waist, Candia's buff-and-scarlet doublet.

Naked, his ribs showed bony as the Decan's.

'*Dies irae!*'

White silence shattered at her caw. She spread crow's wings, gliding down the pale air. Double images from her wide-set eyes merged as she focused on the man below.

'I take it to be that hour.' Theodoret raised his head. Grey eyes brimmed with a mutable brilliance, following the curve of her flight. He shook the hair back from his eyes, smiling. 'Well, child? Young Candia believed help to be found in the Invisible College. You should have come before.'

'I did. The Decan. The Eleventh Decan. She moved me.'

'To this crucial hour . . . '

The white crow spread pinions to cup air, stalled, and gripped a splintered rib between her claws. She hopped from one jutting splinter of bone to the next. Warmth of candle-fire singed her breast-feathers, the stone under her claws icy.

'Oh, the world – is *always* saved. Always. In some form. Or another. What matters—' She forced breath from minute lungs in a toneless parody of speech. 'What matters – is what happens – to people. Individuals. They're not. Always saved.'

She tilted her head to look from one eye and gain a clear image.

Theodoret smiled, genuine amusement on his lined face. 'You're a very cynical crow, lady.'

She spluttered a caw that began in indignation and ended in something unrecognizable.

'But it *is* time.' Theodoret tugged the knotted sleeves tighter about his waist. He picked up a fallen bone spar or splinter from the floor, bracing his steps across the uneven flesh.

The white crow flapped into the air, landed scrabbling on the smooth side of a rib, and skidded down into the hollow between in a flurry of feathers. The Bishop of the Trees laughed. He trod onwards, bare feet unsteady on the icy stone.

'Craa-aak!'

She recovered herself, flapping up, curving in long glides back and forth across his path as he clambered over neck-bones, knee-deep in decaying stone-dust.

In the void ahead of her, a paler light shone down from empty eye-sockets vast as rose-windows, into the interior of the skull. The great head of The Spagyrus lay tilted, fangs wide as pillars crossing his half-open jaw. Wax stalactited the ledges of jaw and palate, and the curving roots of broken teeth: white candles burning with a pure flame. She flew wearily in the cold air, soaring up.

An old woman and a young man sat on the floor of the jaw.

Between them they scattered small cubes. The white crow skimmed the air above their heads, catching double visions of dice as she passed. Heurodis's smoky-blue gaze never wavered as she drew the dice towards herself and cast. The bearded blond man sprawled back on one hip, a finger tapping at his mouth; and as she passed he reached out and scooped up four of the six dice and tossed them down.

A feather falling – or is it rising? – against a blue sky: *Flight*. Meshing cogs and gearwheels: *Craft*. In a

411

field of corn and poppies, two lovers embrace: *The Sun*. And – escaping its weighted cast towards the androgyne that dances masked, *The World* – the flower-eyed skull of *Death*.

An intensity of light burned about the bone-cubes, images bright with colour in that white desert. She felt through the tips of spread pinions how air and probability strained there; the edge of the field catching her, and she wheeled, gliding back towards the Bishop of the Trees.

'Not cards, now. Dice.'

She strained to fly a few yards further, stalled, and slid to nestle in a hollow part of the great jaw's hinge.

Theodoret paused, lifting his head.

'Can birds smell?' he asked softly. 'This is the way it would smell before snow, I remember when I was a child . . . '

'The world is not always saved.'

Tendoned, articulated, the machinery of the jaw rose complicated above her tiny niche. Stone chilled: she fluffed out breast-feathers. Her heart hammered. Candles dazzled. She cocked her head to one side, gazing out across the alabaster spaces. Candia and Heurodis at this distance two spots of colour, no more.

The vast curves of the god's skull rose, ledged with candles. Infinitely far above she glimpsed rose-light as another suture crumbled away into dust.

The whisper echoed again along the walls in fossilized flesh, vibrating in her hollow bones: *'Are you not gone from here?'*

Theodoret lifted his head. The crow, perched at eye-level, looked across at him. The candle-light shone on his silver-grey hair, finger-combed clean and curling to frame his lined face. His eyes shone, his lips parted slightly. The flesh of his shoulders and bony throat shone yellow against the Decan's alabaster ruin.

'No, nor likely to, my lord.'

He smoothed the doublet under his narrow buttocks and seated himself, with some effort, on the knotted marble.

'*I have succeeded.*'

The white crow opened her beak and cawed softly, the manipulation of the bird's larynx coming too easily.

'Divine One, think. Think. What you do. What you are. This sickness is – not necessary.'

'*I know. It is my choice.*'

Theodoret's gaze searched for some source of the disembodied whisper. Movement rustled. The crow shifted her stabbing beak, jerking her head around and her other eye to focus.

Whiteness moved.

A feeler vibrated on the air. Carapaces rustled. Carved as if from milk and ivory, moving blindly across the palate and teeth and jaw, white cockroaches crawled. Now that they moved, she saw them: marble scarabs clinging to splintered fangs, burrowing through deep and glittering alabaster dust. Intricately carved stone blowflies, and ants, swarming across the ridged floor of the vast skull-pan.

They approached the bare legs of Theodoret, where he sat calmly. She flicked into flight, curved down to skim the floor, and then reared up. Lack of her own human size had deceived her. Insects crawled, large as dogs or small ponies.

Stone feelers and legs rustled. Candle-flames glimmered on carapaces bright with frost. The rustling modulated, taking on a chorus-voice: '*I am the Thirty-Six. You cannot compel me. You cannot move me by pleading. Will you complain that I have done this, who am a god?*'

Her wings rose and fell, beating wearily. She fanned her tail-feathers, gliding on a long curve to take her back to where Theodoret sat.

'Divine One, you forget—'

'*I do not forget. I know all that you know. I made the world and you.*'

The whiteness of stone blinded her. Aware to each side of her vision of pinions bending, forcing down cold air, beating hollow-boned, she cawed: 'I could tell you – hrraaa-ak! But I forget. I forget. I become. What I seem.'

413

Air roiled. From below and all around, the rustling of stone insects formed a voice: *'Will you require me to play by my rules? I am not so constrained. You desire your own shape, you bargain for it. But I perceive you, bone and blood and soul, down to the particles that dance below sense's awareness: I know what you know – and it is nothing.'*

The crow cried out.

Stone fractures, falling to splinters among the columns of limbs: far off, far off. Like thunder the echo resounds.

'I am above your choices and desires.'

She skimmed the old man's shoulder, curving in flight, dazzled by the light of candles on frosted marble.

'For no reason, but my whim.'

Pain slammed through her.

Every vein threaded with glowing wires, every bone weighed solid and fracturable; she whirled, flinching from the smooth marble that slammed into her body. Her head jerked up and back, neck cracking.

Gravity slammed her down. Her ribs burst wide, skin stretching, losing the goosepimple-lodging of quills. Claws uncurled, bones of feet stretching, stabbing. A sheer weight of body threw her down, wings spread out: spreading still although she couldn't move, knocked breathless, skin pushing out from beneath white feathers, skin and shaped bone—

Heaviness weighed her pelvis, her back. Fire coursed through her, cramp released from a cellular level; tears burst from her eyes, and she jerked her arms, moving them from the shoulders, to bury her face across her callused hands.

The woman lay face down on ridged marble.

'I do not need reasons.'

Loose feathers surrounded her hands.

She knelt back on her heels, staring at the white pinions and down that scattered the stone. Frost chilled her. She reached out hands palm-forward to the heat of candles on the ledge above her, and stared at short nails and skin.

414

Not young: sallow skin with a minuscule incised diamond-pattern, healing from a cut here, marked (she turned the palms to her) with the calluses of pen and sword.

'Thank . . . you . . . ' She spoke blindly, to the air. 'Thank you!'

A hot tear chilled down her cheek. She wiped it with the heel of her hand, wrapped her arms around her naked body and staggered to her feet. Her foot curled, clawing for purchase. She slipped, automatically throwing her arms out to the sides, not forward to break her fall; and other hands gripped her and pulled her to kneel by the stone on which he sat.

'Rest.'

'I don't have time—'

She raised her head and focused her single gaze on the old man. The Bishop of the Trees smiled. Her voice in her ears sounded like song. A smile moved her mouth.

' – but I don't suppose this matters now. Except to me.' She shivered, arms tight across her body. 'Except to me!'

Theodoret reached down, took one of her hands and unfolded it, and placed her fingertips against her temple.

Unfamiliar softness brushed her fingers. She leaned forward, staring into the smooth reflecting surface of the nearest marble, the skin about her eyes creasing as she squinted. Dark-red hair fell about her face and shoulders, curling finely, streaked with white.

In the hollow of each temple, just where the white hair began to grow out, a patch no larger than her thumbprint grew. White down, the feathers soft as fur.

'He doesn't need reasons.'

Before she could become fascinated, staring at her face in the shine of marble, she leaned her hands against the stone and pushed herself to her feet. Unsteady, she gazed down at Theodoret.

'I'm sorry, my lord. Scholar-Soldiers . . . I don't have *magia* now for this; all *magia* derives from the Thirty-Six powers of the universe, and they so weakened now—'

A grin stretched her face. Drunk on speech, she

415

stretched up her arms: body stretching, shoulders, breasts, stomach, legs. Feeling the cold of ice upon her skin and the fretful warmth of candles, and she shook her hair back and laughed.

' – *Won*derful!'

The Bishop of the Trees burst into laughter, rich and resonant. A wistfulness chilled the air. The rustling bodies of insects swarmed over the nearer stone.

With a crack that split air and sound together, the cathedral-skull split from tooth to eye. Intolerably bright, the rose-light glared in.

Stone poured down. Shards of marble rumbled down the slope of the inner mouth, bounding as boulders do in avalanches, resistless. The White Crow tilted her head and stared up at the falling rock, shafting through the air towards her. Breath made a hard knot in her gut.

'My lord Bishop, you are laughing at me, I think.'

She put both hands up to her head, fingers brushing the down at her temples. One knuckle nudged a gold bee-pin. All muscles tensed to take wing – pain threaded her human shape. She rose on the balls of her feet to run. Stone ripped down out of the air.

Unconsciously her hand tightened around the gold bee, loosened at a sensation of fur and whirring wings. She touched her fist to her mouth, breathing a name; threw out her hand. As the bee flew she stared up into hollow whiteness. Into mortal and divine substance fast decaying.

Taking his hand away from placing a piece of plaster, his fingers shook. Cold bit into his skin, blotching it white and blue. Casaubon stood awkwardly and tucked his fat hands up into his coat-armpits, squinting at the sky.

'Is it finished?'

Evelian grabbed his arm. Her hands didn't close about the width of his wrist. She jerked furiously at his satin sleeve.

'Is this finished? What's happening? What can we do?'

He took his arm away without noticing her grip. He felt

in his left-hand pocket, then his right, one inside pocket and then the other; and finally from a pocket in the tail of the frock-coat unearthed a large brown handkerchief. He blew his nose.

'It . . .'

The white still-wet plaster model shone. Low buildings surrounded a courtyard, some entrances reached by cellar-steps, some by risers; all within a long wire-framed colonnade. Arches opened into the yard, too small to permit coaches, wide enough for walking. Steps and seats littered the yard at irregular geometric intervals.

Over it, the dome of the Temple rose, swelling up from the body of the complex: a dome to stand stunningly white and gold against summer skies, to be surrounded by doves, to be surrounded also by gardens – sketched in with chalk and a few uprooted weeds from the building site – growing with the brightness of roses. Open arches led from temple to gardens, from gardens to temple . . .

A model rocking on chalk-marked broken paving. Wired laths. Hessian. Plaster.

All precisely measured: to proportion, in symmetry, to scale.

'Given what it is, it's the best thing I've ever done.'

Casaubon reached up and scrubbed a hand through his copper-gold hair, leaving it in greasy spikes.

'Damn the whole lot of you. Your city, the Scholar-Soldiers, Decans, and me above all.'

His arm fell to his side. The black light glinted on oil and grease-stains on his satin frock-coat and breeches. His cravat hung unfolded over his open shirt. With no preparation, he sat down heavily on the top step; the marble vibrating under his bulk. He rested one cushioned elbow on his thigh, and the heel of that hand ground into his eye-socket.

'You all can rot, for all I care. I sent her into that place, promised her help I can't perform. I . . .'

He lumbered back up on to his feet.

'Of all the pox-rotten fools. She's good with *magia* and

better with a sword, and I, *I* had to make her into a Master-Physician! Of all the stupid, *stupid*—'

Something brushed his cheek.

Startled, he raised a hand, lowered it.

A bee crept across his dirty knuckles, faceted eyes gleaming. Mica-bright wings quivered; its legs feather-touched his skin. Casaubon held his breath. The banded furry body pulsed, lifted into flight.

For one second he heard the hum of summer, of clear days, and the smell (too sweet, too rich) of rose gardens.

Metal clinked.

He knelt down ponderously, sweeping aside one of the skirts of his frock-coat, and felt on the paving until his fingers contacted metal. He straightened, opened his palm. Heavy, glinting with the black light, a golden bee lay in his hand.

'Lord Casaubon?'

The Mayor's voice.

Black light moved with the viscosity of honey. It thickened, rolled across the construction site, sliding down from the sky and the Night Sun. A hard metallic taste invaded his mouth. He spat, wiped his mouth on his satin sleeve.

'She needs me . . . '

The fading warmth from the stone of Seshat illuminated their faces. Shadowed eye-sockets, noses; glinting hair and bright eyes. The straggle-haired girl knelt by her mother, one hand gripping the woman's, intent on the model. Evelian leaned forward, yellow hair spilling across her breasts.

'I forget her for whole minutes at a time.' He smeared one plaster-wet hand down his shirt to clean it; weight resting back on one massive heel; brushing blindly at the grease-stains on the coat's embroidered lapels.

'So many years to find her, and then by *accident* . . . '

Water brimmed in his eyes and overran. Tears spilled down his cheeks, acid-hot and then cold in the cold air; running down cheeks and chins, runnelling wet marks down his stained linen shirt.

418

'I never heard her speak of you.' Evelian's voice held wonder. 'I knew there had to be *somebody* the cause of it.'

He covered his face with his hand. As loud as a child, he snuffled, and wiped his leaking eyes and nose on his sleeve. He sucked in a breath and looked down at her with the total bewilderment of pain.

'What's happening to her? I thought' – his voice wavered, thinned, began to ululate – 'that I'd *help* her, gods rot her. Now. That I'd be able to . . . to *get* there, and . . . '

He rubbed his face with soaking hands. Tears and snot soaked the cuffs of his coat. He hiccuped, gasping in air; muffling a sob in the palm of one hand.

'I brought her into this!'

The chill on his wet hands burned in the Night Sun's enveloping cold. Arctic, a wind blew grit across the construction site. Sand tacked against his cheek.

His left hand tightened on the metal bee, and he opened it and looked down, watching beads of blood ooze out onto the plaster-stained lines of his palm. Cold numbed the pain. He folded his hand over the sharp wings and antennae, clenching hard.

'Valentine. *White Crow*!'

Cold blossomed.

As swiftly as if it were the light of some dawn, cold air fractured the world. Thick spikes of ice jolted down from the scaffolding. Marble paving crackled underfoot. He scrambled to his feet and stumbled, falling awkwardly, sprawling on his back with a heel caught in the skirts of his coat. The metal bee fell from his hand.

The Word of Seshat faded from the foundation-stone, remaining for a long moment imprinted on his vision.

In the dark he called out: 'White Crow!'

Broken marble littered the stone.

As far as her human eyes could see, ruined stone lay. From fragments small as a finger-bone to blocks the size of houses: all tumbled, splintered into a landscape of rubble. Occasional crags jutted up, white slopes yet covered with burning candles. A mist of light curled across the stone.

The White Crow stood with the Bishop of the Trees in a clear circle some thirty yards across.

A marble cricket, large as her hand and carved intricately, squatted on a ledge of the broken jaw. Its hind legs rasped together. The small voice sounded clear and perfect after the thunder of stone: *'Little animal, you are laughing at me, I think.'*

The stone under her bare feet crumbled, becoming friable and then dust. She sifted it between her toes. The White Crow smiled, not able to stop; sensuous in the new awareness of her self. She stood naked with no embarrassment.

Theodoret laughed.

'Why, what do you think I was doing, my lord Decan, while I lived in death here? I learned. There's much to be learned in the Fane, when only a miracle stands between you and death, and', the old man said tartly, 'you wish that it didn't.'

'You have learned to wish to die.'

'No, my lord. *You* learned that of *us*. My young friend Candia always swore you pried too closely into mortal concerns and mortality.'

The White Crow squatted, running her hands through the dust of the Lord of Noon and Midnight. It sparkled on her fingers. Only the tiny voice remained now, guttering as a candle . . .

She sat back, bumping her bruised buttocks, grinning. The alabaster dust sparkled white and silver on her shins, in the red-gold curls of her pubic hair. She rubbed her hands against her nose, smelling sweat and frost and fire.

'The Eleventh Decan told me, Divine One. The Lady of the Ten Degrees of High Summer. You can forget, you can change your nature; it's only Rats and humans that have to live with limitation.' She stretched out a leg, examining bruises already yellow and purple. Fierce unreasonable joy fired her. 'Forget, change, become a miracle.'

'*I have made true death.*'

'Black miracles. Black miracles.'

'*And I will become One.*'

The White Crow gripped fistfuls of stone dust, sifting them out into the cold air. Abruptly she folded her legs under her buttocks, dug her feet in, pushed; and stood up without using her hands: every muscle electric with energy. She turned, arms outstretched, letting the last of the dust fall.

Theodoret, his hands folded primly on his knees, said: 'I learned that I am a fool, for thinking to instruct one of the Thirty-Six. I learned that when the Decan of Noon and Midnight pretends ignorance of human conspiracy it may be because he is using that conspiracy; letting us place your true-death necromancy under the heart of the world; bringing the plague and the Night Sun and your sickness—'

All the joy of the Scholar-Soldier in her, the White Crow put in: 'Or else, being clouded by base Matter, only taking advantage of what conspiracies mortals had already put into action—'

'– and I learned, my lord Decan, that foolishness is not a province of humanity. But that', Theodoret said, 'I always knew.'

The cricket's fretted hind legs ceased moving. White stone gleamed. No voice formed.

The White Crow gazed up at the old man. She touched his warm shoulder with a faintly proprietorial air and smiled. The air about them crackled, temperature falling towards sub-zero.

'I should despair.' She shook her head, grinning ruefully. 'It's this, I think. When you were healed, did you feel . . . ?'

'Master-Physician, yes.'

'As if it were impossible to be hurt, ever again?'

He put both hands on her bare shoulders, the touch of his fingers warm. Light gleamed in his grey eyes

421

like water; silver and silky as his flowing hair. Briefly he kissed her, on the dark-red hair above her temples. The White Crow startled. His breath, warm and damp, smelt of cut grass.

'Now,' he said.

He turned, kneeling, burying his hands in the dust.

The last outcrops of rounded marble slumped into dust, white light blazing hard enough to bring tears to her eyes. She raised her head. Her heart beat in her ears and groin.

'I have learned,' Theodoret said.

A dank smell of leaf-mould penetrated her nostrils. The sole of her foot moved in some slick substance, and the White Crow looked down. Ankle-deep in stone dust, her skin sensed a moment's texture of river mud.

A faint light the colour of sun through beech leaves burns around the Bishop's hands – fades, fails and dies.

The Thirty-Six feel the great wheel of the world hesitate in its turning: pause, poise. Wait.

Some fractional movement above, where iron flood-doors hung suspended in grooves in the tunnel roof, warned Plessiez. He leaped forward as the chains and shutter crashed down.

'Plessiez!'

'Charnay, is all well?'

Her voice came, muffled, from behind the iron door. He picked himself up off his knees, realized that he stood in a brighter light than the fallen torch could account for.

The brown Rat's voice faded. His ears rang with the noise of the shutter's falling. After a moment she appeared at one of the close-barred window-openings where the tunnel doubled back on itself. 'I'll get round to you another way. Press on, messire. Courage!'

Under his breath, the black Rat murmured: 'And if what I find now is some way of slipping past you, regaining the surface?'

422

Sound scuttered at the edge of hearing. He snatched up the fallen rapier, the leather-wound hilt warm and worn under his palm. Here brown bones stacked the walls, racked up in barriers eight or nine feet tall; the close-packed knobs of bone broken only by jutting inset skulls. Plessiez moved cautiously down the wet slope. Ahead, the floor of the tunnel ran steeply down and the ceiling rose, until both widened out into the central cavern of the ossuary.

'A little short of omens and nightmares,' he whispered, sardonic, shaking.

The sound ran down ahead of him, hissing into echoes, not fading but growing; increasing in volume until it yawped up the scale into laughter.

'Charnay?'

Steep flights of steps angled down into the great cavern from other, higher entrances. Marble altars stood to each side, among the bones and obelisks. Light glowed on the smooth walls, rounded almost into bosses, brown strata hooping up with the curve of aeons. Black candles towered in ornate stands, each one lit. His shadow on the passage wall and the cave roof leaped, agile, frantic, despite his even pacing.

'Fool,' said the Hyena.

She swung lithely down from an entrance whose tunnel must cross above his. A basket-hilted rapier balanced in her right hand. Greasy hair fell down over her slanting brows, over the shoulders of her red shirt that hung torn to her waist. Her filthy red breeches were cut off at the knee; her bruised and cut feet moved without hesitation across the gravel as she ran towards him.

'Lady, you follow me fast enough to outdistance me.'

She yawped a laugh that made his pelt shiver.

Quickly he knelt and took the bundle of bones from his belt, tucking them under the nearest protruding wall. Skulls brushed his hand, friable and warm. He tightened his grip on his rapier. Without further speech he ran forward, seeking the flat cavern floor.

'Gods—'

Her blade leaped fire and light in the corner of his vision. He parried; scrabbling back to look wildly at what lay in the centre of the ossuary cavern.

On the far side, the catafalque of the Rat-Kings stood on a raised dais, on a dozen marble steps: a fragile lacy thing of white stone, engraved with the symbols of each of the Thirty-Six, with the insignia of the Churches – including Plessiez's own Guiry – of which the Rat-Kings would be titular head. Friezes of ancient nobles in procession circled the body of the catafalque, upon which, in equally execrable taste, a circle of seven robed Rats lay in a King. Under their bier, carved in precise mirror-detail, seven Rat corpses, their bony vertebrae intertwined, lay in various stages of stony decomposition: this one a skeleton, snout crumbling, incisors gone; the next a shrunken fleshly body, with tiny carved marble worms emerging from it; the next a petrified mummy . . .

Plessiez ignored the floridly baroque bad taste, staring past the dark-haired woman, past the blade that shot highlights from the candles.

'That—' Some bright sanity burned in the woman's eyes. For a moment she straightened from her sloping crouch, the animal gaze gone. 'Is *that* what they all were? What we took from you, what we placed under the heart of the world?'

They lay on the gravelled earth before the catafalque – the femur and tail-vertebrae and skull of a Rat, scarcely large enough to be adult. A scarlet ribbon tied them in curious knots. One long knobbed femur, a rib, a rib with vertebrae attached: the long decreasing series of tail-bones. They made a kind of irregular septagon shape, the skull and lower jaw-bone crowning it. Now Plessiez realized where the light came from. These, that had been new and scrubbed bones – boiled down for cleanliness – now glowed as white as roses in morning sunlight.

Fear shocked it out of him.

'Lady . . . four times the Divine upon this earth and

by some black miracle caused a soul to die. We made our necromancy from their mortal remains.'

The Hyena's whisper hardly broke his trance: 'There's nothing there. *Nothing*.'

Red ribbon tied the bones in angled geometries. Red ribbon threaded the eye-sockets, attaching the skull to the bone framework upon which it rested. Ribbon, and the gravel on which it rested: all solid, all bodied into form and existence . . .

The whiteness of the bones, now, the whiteness of absolute negation.

'I saw them with butterflies all in their mouths,' she sang, 'seeking the Boat, and born again. But this . . . ' The woman's tone dropped to growling speech. 'This isn't death, but *nothing*.'

Plessiez raised his eyes. The woman, unarmoured, stood as if she still wore the Sun's ragged banners; brows come down over her slanting dark eyes. Yellow shadows moved at her feet, mottled and smelling of heat and dust. She met his gaze. Her eyes dulled: flat, cunning, bestial.

White light shone from behind her. The arctic negation of that light chilled him: so small, so bright.

'They are the bones of the truly dead.' He stared around. At the whiteness sifting down upon the catafalque, upon the stacked bones of the royal dead: each with the seed-bone removed, each long since boarded the Boat and travelled the Night and returned again.

The chill of the earth faded under his clawed feet. Numbness replaced it, radiating out from the tiny pile of bones in the centre of the cavern.

'You may not blame me, lady! Blame the Decan of Noon and Midnight, who thought fit that Guiry should share his alchemical work—'

Bare feet scuffed gravel. Her sword swung up. He knocked it aside, metal clashing harshly, echoing up into the cavern's dry heights.

'It didn't shock you.' Her breath sawed. She flung her free hand out, pointing at him. 'I saw. Falke died. I saw

425

your face. They all started to die. It didn't – even – *surprise* you. You *knew* the plague would hit us—'

On the walls of the ossuary cavern the shadows of the woman and the black Rat danced: sword-blades engaging, darting, each movement exaggerated, each swirl of the Rat's plume, each stoop-shouldered dash of the woman. Laughter yammered, drowning the hiss of bare feet on the earth.

' – ours and the Decan's, the same pestilence—'

'*Wait!*'

His long wrist pivoted. He beat her blade back, wrenching his shoulder. Gravel bit his heels. His panting breath echoed back off the walls with the clang of metal. Habit took him to guard position; found him the snap in her concentration and lunged – parried, beat her blade down and jumped back.

' – *you* the same cause—'

The woman crabbed sideways three steps and scooped up a brown thigh-bone from the ossuary heap nearest, weighing it in her left hand. The bone-wall groaned, teetered.

'You're by far a better demagogue than fighter.' Plessiez trod forward, his eyes meeting her dulled flat gaze. Anger burned him breathless. And fear. 'You're a fool, get out.'

'Yes, a fool. Yes, a fool to listen, ever, to you. I am the last now: the last of Sun and Roses. If I *am* a hyena, I can make you carrion!'

Highlights glinted in the woman's eyes, the eyes of a woman no more than adequate, he would guess, with a blade; but now flat and hard and cunning, echoing the yellow shadows that moved with her, mimicked her movements, padded in shadows, laughed inhuman laughter.

White light burned.

Now multiple shadows danced on the cavern walls. Brightness scarred his vision. He risked a lunge, continued it on into a run: dashing for the flight of stone steps leading up to another exit. In one loping jump the woman made the lower step: rapier darting up at his breast, he

426

parried, skidded to one knee, staggered up, breath hot in his mouth.

He grabbed at his belt, finding the main-gauche lost somewhere; lunged again, one foot on the bottom step, drove her up three steps; brought a heel down half off the edge of the sheer flight; leaped backwards and landed on the earth, left hand and tail out for balance. She half-loped and half-fell down the steps towards him.

The point took his gaze away. He only sensed her hand move.

Reflex brought his left hand up. The thrown femur jarred his wrist, clattered away on the floor. She lunged, leaping from the steps; and he bound her blade and kicked, crouched, whipped his scaled tail hard across her ankles. She fell.

She pitched past him, into the ossuary wall that she had loosened the bone from: in a rush and shatter of femurs and skulls and ribs and pelvises the mass of dry brown bones avalanched down on her. She sprawled face-down, greasy hair flying, one bare foot scrabbling for purchase. In the same second he fell forward into the furthest extent of his lunge and felt the penetration of flesh clear up the blade.

Through his grip on the hilt he felt his own pulse or the last fibrillation of her heart.

A Rat skull bounced across the floor. Vertebrae scattered like dice. The bone-pile slid to an unsteady halt, balanced up like kindling. The woman sprawled, partly covered in splintered brown bone, the half-inch-wide blade jammed up through her stomach and under the lowest rib. Blood rivuleted, staining her shirt; a dark stain marked her breeches as bowel and bladder relaxed. Her bubbling, blood-filled breath echoed into silence.

The rapier blade scraped a rib as he withdrew it, bracing his clawed foot against her shoulder.

Light tore. In the whiteness of the bones of the truly dead, a rip appeared.

*   *   *

Tumblers click, numbers roll.

In the university building Lucas scrambles from under the meshing gears of an analytical engine. There is no noise, no smoking oil, no ripping metal. Only an intolerable strain that holds the fabric of the air taut, taut.

Away across the heart of the world, a makeshift lath-and-plaster model of a building glows, moon-bright. A fifteen-year-old girl on her knees beside it, ear-rings jangling, breaks into tears at something she cannot explain: perhaps simply the extravagant order and complexity of its proportions.

Enamel-imaged dice, scattered and chipped, lie among the discarded Thirty Trionfi cards, in a hollow of whiteness where a man and an old woman fall, fall endlessly.

Breaking strain. As if in the weak forces that glue the universe together, some sudden slippage could be felt. Strings pulling apart, order losing its probability.

Plessiez staggered back, sitting down on the bottom step of the nearest flight of stairs.

Blood pooled from the rapier's point to the earth. He sat staring at it, how it glistened in the white light. His chest heaved. He brushed his wrist across his mouth, touched matted fur; touched it again and took his hand away.

One cut ripped his lip, just over the left incisor. He tasted blood, not knowing until he felt the slick matted fur on his right haunch that she had wounded him twice. Numbness began to fill the cavern, hiding the pain. Feeling the weakness of her deep wound, he with shaking fingers unbuckled his sword-belt and rebelted it tightly around his haunch as a tourniquet.

'Well, now . . .'

His voice, even at a whisper, sounded loud as gunfire in a cathedral. He wiped the rapier, fumbling it; leaned the point on the gravelled earth and pushed himself upright.

With a sharp snap, the blade broke.

The black Rat staggered. His naked bristling tail whipped out for balance. He stood, eyes half-shut, peering at the clouded air before his face. The white light leached colour from the fallen bones, from the great catafalque and the ossuary cavern itself. He gazed up at the dark tunnel-entrance to which the stairs led.

Plessiez looked back.

The great Wheel falters, loosens and forgets the unheard cadences of the Dance of all things; particles of earth and stone and bone dissolve upon air.

He let the broken sword fall.

One hand clenched hard enough to drive rings into his flesh.

Not a light, but a leaching-away of substance.

The earth beneath his numb feet not lost in brilliance, but dissolving into air, and air itself dissolving into nothingness . . .

Plessiez squatted down awkwardly, one arm resting across his unwounded knee, staring at the bones.

Moments ticked past, marked by the slow spreading of blood from the murdered woman. A tension thrummed deep in the stone. On the edge of audibility, Plessiez sensed the loosing of bonds in the heart of the earth. The bones and their red ribbon imprisoned his gaze, nested in the warm whiteness of oblivion.

He spoke softly.

'Now we are the same, you and I . . . Myself stripped gradually and willingly of all I've earned: cardinal's rank, priesthood, power, and friends and skills. And you stripping the heart of the world until nothing remains. True death. Your portent in the sky: the Night Sun – there by a god's conjuring, and mine. Well, we are the same.'

He lifted his snout, looking up at one of the stairs and exits.

'No matter how fast, I would be very close, still, when it happens. So where is the point of running?'

One translucent ear twitched. He heard no sound of Charnay, lost in the ossuary labyrinth; and the rattle in the dead woman's throat would not be repeated.

'Believe that I did not know you would be like this –

but, then, one is seldom sure of outcomes, dealing in matters pertaining to the Divine. Does The Spagyrus regret you, I wonder?'

Above his head, the stone roof of the cavern creaked.

'And I am like you in this: I admit of no possibility of victory. Even though I think I perceive – I *think* – a method towards it. But you could not expect it of me.'

Talking to the bones as if they were his mirror image, the black Rat slid down to sit on the gravel: the nearer stones leached of colour and substance.

'Well, and if it were fire I might manage that, and if it were flesh and blood there's *her*—' One slender dark finger pointed to the corpse of the Hyena. 'But hardly of use, I fear, with the life departed from it. Death's no cure for entropy.'

A large chunk of stone dislodged itself from the roof and fell, cracking the corner from the catafalque of the Rat-Kings. Part of a carved rose rattled down the steps. The smell of blood and ordure began to lessen, and even the chill in the air became mild.

'*But*—' The black Rat argued obsessively, leaning forward. 'You could not expect it of me. Even if I willed it, even if I saw nothing else to be done, even if – and it is possible, oh, I grant you it is possible – I *desired* it, well, still the flesh would not let me. That has its own desire for survival.'

He lay down now, on his side, tail coiled up to his flank, and one arm cradling his head. His black eyes glowed. With his free hand he reached out, testing the limits of absolute numbness near the bones: the milk-white bones glowing in brilliance.

Expecting a pulse of tension, it brought fear hot into his throat to feel, through fingertips, the sensation of fracturing thin ice, of falling suddenly from the step that is not there—

The knowledge of how short a time before the world split and rolled up like cloth burned in him. His eyes half-closed. White light split into rainbows.

'Well,' he said.

Plessiez, *ankh* and priesthood discarded both, all conspiracies broken and bloody, lying on one elbow now, as if to read, or by the side of some lover, reached out and with a gentle touch took hold of the infinite whiteness of bone.

The ceiling of the cavern cracked and fell.

High above darkness, high above where the labyrinth in city streets gutters and dies; high above the straining wings of eagles, and soaring into the face of darkness, flies a moth with death's-head markings on its wings.

Airbreathed wings of dark fire reach out.

The Night Sun's blackness burns, a beacon. In the thin air, thinning with height of atmosphere, and with the loosening charges of electrons, the moth beats black-dusted wings furiously, rising, reaching up—

A sparrow stalls in the air, snaps, crunches the moth's soft body. Its gullet jerks twice, swallowing.

The wind thins.

Caught in dissolution, in air dissolving; the strangeness of matter that is its body fading, the bird begins to fall.

And suddenly the sky is gold.

'*Messire!*'

Through rock that tumbled down, immense and slow, great boulders bounding and crushing heaps of bones, Lieutenant Charnay dodged and lumbered down the longest flight of steps, sword-rapier in hand.

She ran across the floor of the ossuary cavern, moving fast, sparing one glance for the dead woman; heading for the slumped black figure before the catafalque. Shouting, voice lost in the roar of splintering rock.

She flung herself to her knees beside Plessiez and turned him over.

And stared into a face so changed she might never have recognized it if she had not, once, met his grandfather.

His black fur was now faded grey; white about the jaw. His shrunken body moaned as she held it, light as sacking.

431

Under his loose pelt, his ribs and collar-bone jutted in stark angles; slim fingers reduced to thin bony sticks.

His head fell back. The flesh of his ears had turned translucently grey; and, as he blinked slowly, she took one look at his eyes – milky with cataracts – and turned her head aside to vomit.

One of Plessiez's age-withered hands grasped a skull's lower jaw: brown and old and fragile. A coil of red ribbon ringed his wrist. All the nails of his hand were cracked, yellow, waxen.

His other hand moved feebly. She dropped her sword and clasped it.

'Plessiez, man.'

The black Rat, whiskers quivering, raised a hand that trembled. His head bobbed on his thin corded neck. He peered at her.

'And I had always wagered' – his thin voice shook – 'that I would not live to die old.'

A roar from above warned her. She had one second to look up at the falling rock, to see how many layers of the catacombs now fell in towards their foundations. Plessiez groaned. The brown Rat tightened her grip on his hand. She threw her body protectively across his, at the last reaching out for her sword.

Stone soughs into dust.

A weakness as of internal bleeding hamstrings her. The White Crow presses both fists into her stomach under the arch of her ribs. Body shaking with sudden cold, teeth grinding, she sits down hard in the alabaster whiteness.

Maggots boil up like milk.

Their soft bodies slide against her skin. Revolted, too weak to stand, she reaches out a hand to sketch a hieroglyph on the air. Her hand drops to her side, the powerless shape left unfinished.

'He's dying—'

Waves of maggots belly up, silky and cool about her

shins and ankles. The solidity of what stone remains under her begins to soften.

Quietly, the White Crow laughs.

'Theo, my lord, you did say "corrupted". The divine and demonic souls of the universe don't decay into *maggots* when they die! Oh, he learned this of us.'

The absence that weakens her grows now, as if her heartblood leaks away through weakened aorta and ventricle at every pulse. At some deep level of cells, still resounding from the miracle of shape-changing, the White Crow shivers into dissolution.

She shouts: 'You didn't have to do this! You're a god; even these rules don't bind you!'

'He chooses that they do.'

Theodoret stands, Candia's doublet still kilting his waist. Age-spotted skin gleams sallow in the growing intensity of light breaking down. His red lips part, he frowns; his head high, grey hair flowing.

'Young woman, the Thirty-Six were fool enough to choose to exile the Church of the Trees and degrade their worshippers. I've suffered from that all my life. Don't tell me about Divine capriciousness and stupidity!'

She twists around on her knees, smearing the crawling maggots to a paste. Effort burns her lungs. As if the cells behind her eyes dissolve also, her vision whitens.

'Ahhh—'

Not her vision, it is the world that whitens. She perceives with preternatural clarity this last moment; her voice hissing in her ears like static: 'He's dead!'

Weakness grows, pressing against her skin from inside. A void too large to contain. Her numb fingers no longer feel each other, nor her arms pressed to her sides; thighs drawn up tight to her belly and breasts.

Her fingers, touching her flesh, feel the decaying voices of the Thirty-Six. Scholar-Soldier, student of *magia*, Master-Physician: she has the skill to hear their last cry, fading in the wake of dissolution—

And something else.

'Listen! *Feel*! Something's happening.'

The old man looks sharply down at her. 'What is it?'

Far across the city that is called the heart of the world, echoes of destroyed *magia* vibrate. She, in the wasteland of ruined marble and maggots, points up at his hands. A faint luminescence clings to them, the colour of green shadows and sunlight.

Above the city, the sky is suddenly gold.

Dusty wings beating, the sparrow falls. In the bird's bead-black eyes, reflected clearly, the Night Sun is over-spotted with a leprous golden light.

Flat as an illustrated manuscript, the sky over the heart of the world sears yellow as fever.

Voices thundered in her head. Visions blurred her eyes. The smell of corruption choked her, sickly sweet. The White Crow retched, dry heaves that twisted her gut.

'Don't hesitate!' The White Crow lifted her head and shouted. '*Now*, my lord Bishop, now!'

Wood-sunlight limned his bony fingers. The old man's eyes narrowed, wincing. 'He hurt me, hurt me unbeliev-ably. I can't find in me the charity to forgive him.'

Acerbic fear tugged her smile crooked. 'You don't forgive gods, Theo, my lord, the day for *that* isn't in the calendar. And what can you expect from a Decan who's had entirely too much contact with humans?'

'"Too much"?'

His beaked nose jutted as the corners of his mouth came up, deepening the folds of his skin. His brows contracted, and the skin around his eyes wrinkled. Sudden laughter spluttered in his voice.

'What can I *expect*—?'

She fell forward on both hands.

The sweet smell changed.

Her hands slid in the cool flesh of maggots, and it changed. On hands and knees she stared down. White rose-petals covered her hands, buried them to the wrists;

she knelt on them. The thick heavy sweetness of roses breathed up from crushed flowers.

She knelt up, head lowered, staring at the wave-front of whiteness travelling away from her among crumbled marble: the heaving bodies of grubs transmuting to flowers. She bent and pushed her hands forward into the mass.

Thorns snagged her skin.

Her skin, tanned, gold by contrast with these white petals and green spiked stems; her skin that smelt of sweat and dirt, now stitched across each arm with the dotted scars of rose-thorns. A bead of blood swelled. She lifted her arm to her mouth and licked.

'Oh, but *what*—?'

She began to laugh.

'Above, beneath: branch and root . . . '

His voice from behind her resonated with a calm casual expectancy. She, magus, Master-Physician, echoed him joyously; feeding the power of the words into the world: 'Above, beneath: branch and root—'

'Pillar of the world . . .'

A bramble coiled her ankle, the spikes too young and soft to do more than tickle. Roses fingered their way across her thighs where she sat; coiled up an arm; spread into the masses of her dark-red hair. She shook her head, white petals fluttering down, the corners of her eyes wet with laughter.

'Oh, hey—'

Ten yards away, he stood with his back to her. The old man, the Bishop; his hands folded calmly behind him, his chin a little raised. The wave-front of generation pulsed out from where he stood. 'Leaf in bud: shelter and protection.'

'Light of the forest . . . '

She stood up, naked, the white roses hanging heavy in her hair. A scent of them breathed on the suddenly blowing breeze. Heat fell down across her shoulders, unknotting the muscles there, relaxing her spine; so that

435

she stood with her weight back on one heel and reached up with both arms, stretching up to light that glowed gold and green.

Spikes pushed up through the drifts of white roses.

She took one step forward and then another, unsteady on her feet; and twigs poked up, growing, sprouting into the air, knitting the air together about them – great clumps of blackthorn and may, elder and wild roses: sparkling with green shoots, pale in the light.

'Protection of the branches that support the sky . . . ' Saplings jutted from the earth around his feet. Brown twigs, one looped leaf spiking up from each.

'Heart of the wood . . . '

'Oldest of all, deepest of all—'

Blackthorn grew, tough wood spearing higher than her head now. She felt how it knitted earth together within its roots, beneath the roses; how it knitted together, too, at microcosmic levels, binding energy, possibility, structure.

'Rooted in the soul of earth—'

'Who dies not, but is disguised; who sleeps only.'

'Heart of the wood!'

On the nearest branch a tiny leaf uncoiled, bright green beside the thorn-spikes and white flower. So close that she crossed her eyes to focus on it, giggled and stepped back. Leaf and flower together, spidered now with flowering creeper, the horns of morning glory, columbine, old man's beard, and ivy: green and white and dappling the light with new shade.

The White Crow spread her arms wide.

She traced through her fingertips the divine and demonic in the structure.

'Theodoret! Theo!'

Heady: oxygen and excitement filled her lungs. The light of her inner vision blazed green and gold, filling her veins. Beech saplings sprouted from the earth all around her.

She walked barefoot, wincing as a sharpness dug into the sole of her foot; stopping to balance and pull out a

thorn, and on impulse kiss her finger and press it to the
infinitesimal wound and smile, smile as if her face would
never lose that expression.

Warmth shone down.

Warmth bloomed up from the earth beneath Theodoret's
feet. Runners of ivy criss-crossed the ground, the leaves
of other plants poking up between. And between one step
and another the coiled heads of a myriad shoots unfurled,
unwinding into flowers, and she walked knee-deep in
bluebells with the old man.

A dappled light shone on him, silvering and greying his
hair by turns: a light of trees only yet potential.

'You're doing it!' Joy filled her; she shouted to the
growing trees.

'I can reach him, child – *just*.'

Wind creaked through the branches of trees grown tall,
skittered over a ground clear of undergrowth in this newly
mature wood.

As far as she could see, the perspectives of the wood
stretched. New leaves shimmered on trees, bluebells
misted the distance. Far off, far away, in the heart of
the wood . . .

The White Crow let her arms fall to her sides. Aching,
she stared; keeping the long sight down into the centre as
a part of her; hidden, dangerous, glorious.

She turned.

This way the trees were not so thick, and she glimpsed
past them a light of rose and gold: swirling, granular,
hot.

'You . . .'

'Me.' Theodoret rasped.

He pressed back against the smooth bole of a grown
beech tree behind him. Sunlight and shadow spotted his
bony chest, dappled his legs and thighs. He pressed his
hands and spine against the bark.

The waves of generation sank back.

Unsteady, the White Crow staggered towards him.

A tendril of ivy crept around the bole of the tree, looping

the old man's wrist. His skin darkened, silvered. Before she could draw breath his skin cracked and fissured, merging so swiftly into the lumps and curves of the beech-trunk that she had no time to turn away her gaze.

The tree grew.

He grew with it, embedded into the wood. His long mobile features darkened to green, to silver-brown; his hair flowed out across the bark, rooting down into it.

He opened his mouth and called a word of healing.

She fell down, the leaves and fragments of bark imprinting her flesh.

The call echoed into the heart of the wood.

His jaw strained open, strained further open, and she thought it must surely crack; his head tipped back and growing into the heartwood of the beech.

Two sprouting pale-green leaves poked from the corners of his mouth.

Swift, swift as thought they grew; jutting out like tusks and coiling back, growing into the trunk of the beech.

'Theo! My lord Bishop!'

She pulled herself to her feet, craning her neck to see the tree. Already the trunk was too vast for her to perceive all of it, and its leaves and branches shadowed the world. The coolness of forests shivered across her skin.

'*I have found him.*'

A cool heartbreaking wind blew around her, out of the heart of the wood. Awe dried her throat. Sweat slicked the skin of her elbows, behind her ears, her thighs: blood and cells burning, warm with a knowledge of solidity. She shook her hair back and craned her neck to look up through shedding petals.

The sense of an old story rose in her, unbelieved, unconquerable; and she gazed up into the heights of branches and green leaves.

'*Now* . . .'

Her spine shuddered, prickled the hairs at the back of her neck. She touched her fingers to her mouth. Vibrating at cell- and DNA-level, voices sang in her flesh: thirty-five of them. Voices of the Decans of Hell and Heaven.

Something tickled her hand. She lifted it. Blood-heat, imperceptible, red liquid trickled from her palm and dripped to the earth. Blood smeared the sweating flesh of her knee, her ankle. The black bee-stings of the Decan's maze throbbed, her left hand raw and swollen.

'*Act*—'

'*Act now*—'

'*Channel us*—'

'*We will inform you*—'

'*Breathe in you*—'

'*Speak in you*—'

'*Open our Selves to you*—'

A sand-bright voice, clearer than all others, thrummed in her human flesh: '*We made you in Our image and with Our power. You are all star-daemons. My child, my lover, my bride of the sun and widow of the moon, call down the universe now. Heal!*'

Sprawling naked, without sword or book, her suntanned flesh scratched with the thorns of impossible roses, the White Crow reached out. With her left hand she drew hieroglyphs, skeining down the bright air to twist in *magia* patterns. Watching how the light shifted, as leaves shift in a high wind; feeling for the moment and sensing it—

At some level above or below perception, binding took place.

A sapling birch brushed her arm, white bark peeling like paper. Transparent green leaves sprinkled the branches. Heat burned into her back.

The dappled light of beech shade fell cool across her skin.

She reached up, holding her hand in the sign of protection. The feedback of power between microcosm and macrocosm, Scholar-Soldier and the elementals, filled her with an electric energy; drawing power down the chains of the world from the Thirty-Six houses of the heavens.

She sprang up, barefooted, stamped a foot down into new grass. Beeches surrounded her, growing up to the invisible sky. Their great boles towered like pillars, soaring up a hundred feet to where they arched together, new green leaves rustling, and a bird sang.

Divine and demonic: demonic and divine.

Tall slender branches rose as pillars to the sky, meeting overhead in arches of new foliage. Birds sang in the branches, caterpillars and woodlice crawled among the roots.

A mass of broken marble lay embedded in the earth. Walking closer, she gazed up at it. Solid, some fifteen or twenty feet high; cracked and fissured and gold, still, with the light of extinguished candles. The last of the ruined mortal matter that had hosted a god-daemon. The White Crow walked close enough to touch, to feel the cold radiating from it.

She drew rapidly, smearing blood from her hand in complex astrological and cabbalistic signs on the broken surface of the marble. A frown indented the dark-red eyebrows, and she rested her free hand against the stone as support, leaning her forehead on that arm. The scrawled signs covered a half, two-thirds of the rock. The symbols grew cramped, smaller as the surface became more crowded; and the White Crow frowned in concentration, muttering the remembered first prayers of training.

'O thou who are the four elements of our nature, and the hundred elements of nature itself; Powers; star-daemons; rulers of the Thirty-Six Houses of the Sky and Earth . . . '

'*Draw down power. As above, so below. You are Our creation and We created you kin to Us. Draw power down the linkages of the world and heal!*'

The stone split under her fingers.

Cracking like a shell: sliding, splitting; stone fragments falling to splinter on the floor of the wood. She stumbled back. Her hand dropped, lifted again to draw with blood-stains on the air. Rubble fell away, echoing like gunshots, from the massive shape disclosed.

In a shaft of sunlight, great wings unfurled.

Ribbed wings opened, glowing first pearl and then pale rose and then gold. The wind from their beating knocked her from her feet. Earth hit her. She grunted, breath jolted from her body. Grass and twigs imprinted her bare stomach. She raised herself up and rested on her forearms.

A great muzzle dipped, vast dark-gold eyes opening. Scales glinted on monstrous cheek-bones. Tiny naked ears flicked alertly. Tendrils floated upon the air, anchored across the head and around the eyes. Tusks jutted up alongside the pit-nostrils, crusted with deposits of adamant crystal. The overhanging upper lip wrinkled.

She hardly breathed. 'Lord of Noon and Midnight.'

The leonine body unfolded, rising from marble fragments to stand forty feet high: spotted yellow as a leopard, brown-gold as a hyena. Great wings sheathed. Lids slid up to narrow the eyes watching her. The full closed lips curved.

'I had forgotten how it is, to become so young . . . I had forgotten how it is to forget . . . '

Miracle beat in her blood, staggered her feet, so that she stumbled to her feet, head fizzing as with wine. She held out one hand empty of sword, the other empty of scroll; grinning up into the newborn face so hard that it hurt her jaws.

The overhanging muzzle dipped. She flinched. Closed lips touched her. She smelt fire, comet-dust, the green breath of trees.

'Where's Theo? Divine One . . . '

The massive head lifted. Ivy coiled, ringing the tusks with white and green. Insects crept in the folds of the upper lip; woodlice and wild bees and lizards. She stared up into eyes liquid with golden blackness; smelt from the delicate-lipped mouth a scent of cut grass. A shiver walked up her spine, exploded between her shoulder-blades.

'Forget, change, become a miracle.'

The voice sounded like the rustle of leaves, like the echo of sound in great spaces of stone.

'*I had forgotten what it is to change! Each spring is the world's first; each winter the ending of an aeon; each summer the high and changeless meridian of pleasure. Now is the millennium. Now I see!*'

The great long-muzzled head lifted. Wide nostrils and mouth encompassed a speckled darkness, the yellow darkness of sun in shadowed cavities of wood. The god-daemon shifted, haunches sinking, wings curving up to frame the high shoulders. It sat immovably in the cathedral of trees.

She shook.

The tension of green hung in the air; paused, poised, hesitated; hung in balance.

The Decan, The Spagyrus, Lord of Noon and Midnight, reached out one clawed limb and touched the bark of the great beech tree. White flesh and bone tumbled into shape: the old man sprawled in the grass. The White Crow held out her right hand, and the Bishop of the Trees seized it and pulled himself to his feet.

'We . . . did it.' He laughed, dazed, face creasing.

The White Crow gazed up through shifting beech leaves, the brightness of the green tingling in her blood and vision.

'Yeah. We did it and here's the end of it . . . '

The voice of the Twelfth Decan rang through the aisles of the trees, deep and new. His sandstone-and-gold pelt rippled.

'*End? No. I perceive . . . We perceive . . . that We have erred. No, this is not the end. You have scarcely been admitted across the threshold of miracle. It is the beginning, now.*'

The ancient voice burned with energy and new fire. In the Scholar-Soldier's head it echoed with the voices of the Thirty-Six who make up the circle of the sky.

'*Now We see that We should not for so many aeons have concealed Ourselves in stone. Now We throw down the Fane. And now . . . We will walk amongst you.*'

The White Crow craned her neck, staring upwards.

All the flat gold of the sky softened, turning to great

towering masses of brilliance that paled: here to rose, there to pink and gold . . .

The sky shredded; stretching and pulling apart. The depths beyond glowed blue.

Clouds parted, the sun's beams turning them gold and pink. Parted, pulled aside, no trace of the flat gold sky now; only a heat and a brightness that dazzled her.

A white-yellow disc brought water to her eyes.

She stared up into the infinity of a blue summer sky.

'Captain-General, something's happening!'

Desaguliers straightened, leaning his musket and rest back against his haunch. He stared up at the top of the barricade where the Cadet crouched. 'Did no-one ever train you to make an exact report? *What* is "happening"?'

The young Cadet – a slim black Rat, hardly more than a Ratling – clung with tail and one gloved hand to the shattered joists of the palace wall. Powder-burns scarred his livery and smooth-furred snout.

'I don't know!'

Desaguliers, hearing battle-fatigue in the young Rat's voice, leaned his musket against the barricade's bricks, joists and jewel-studded furniture; drew his pistol, and loped along to scramble up the slope.

A stray shot spanged off a corner of the demolished wall. Desaguliers ducked, glancing back. Nothing new – the main palace hall broken open to the sky, slashed with the light-shadows of the Night Sun, and barricaded from the courtyard where human refugees hid behind rubble and risked shots with captured weapons.

Darkness clung to masonry, illuminated only by powder-flashes. The blue light that mazed the streets sank into dimness. Desaguliers rubbed his sore eyes. The wings of acolytes overlapped the sky, flying down to cling to broken walls, precariously leaning roofs.

'They're . . . not attacking.'

Desaguliers, hand poised to give the signal to fire, hesitated. 'Not yet, I think.'

Ribbed wings folded, obsidian claws clutching coign and balcony and gutter, bristle-tails coiling: by tens and dozens the acolytes settled on the besieged palace.

He turned his lean snout, staring down from the barricade into the body of the hall. Shattered glass and treadmills, torn drapes, the inlaid floor splintered with soldiers' running feet; here and there the black smears of extinguished fires. Blue-jacketed Cadets lined the barricades, steadying muskets on rests or cleaning swords black with daemon blood.

Clustered in the centre, under the last remaining arch of that clover-leaf roof, away from attack and falling walls, eight Rats clung together. One brown Rat nursed a bloody arm, resting back in the arms of two black Rats. A silver Rat trod down a scarlet robe under one hind claw, clutching at a bony black Rat. They clung. The fattest black Rat lay on broken marquetry flooring, curled around the clump of intergrown tails that he clutched to his furred stomach.

'They're *not* attacking, messire.'

Desaguliers narrowed his eyes, stroking his scarred cheek. 'They're going to come right over us next time they try, that's obvious. Messire Jannac, is your blade dull yet?'

'Er, no, messire.'

'We're going to move down into the nearest train-tunnels while this lull lasts.'

'But his Majesty?'

'We're going to cut his Majesty free; it's the only way we'll move them.'

'Messire!'

He turned his head, swearing at the Rat daring to protest; stopped dead, staring at the Cadet. A pale light glinted on his black fur, shone from the young Rat's broken nails and sword-hilt. Desaguliers raised his head.

The light-shadows blurred and vanished. Above, the world lightened to yellow, to gold, to brilliance.

He raised his eyes, staring up to where the Night Sun

had blotted the sky, and looked directly into the white-hot disc of the noon sun.

Desaguliers scrambled up on to the highest point of the barricade, careless of fire; eyes running tears in the brilliance of daylight, the summer sun's heat like fire on his pelt.

He grabbed a metal rod projecting from the rubble, blotted his eyes with the fur of his arm, and stared out across the city. Across the courtyard, where men and women walked out wondering into sunlight; across the city roofs black with clustering acolytes, to the great darkness in the north-aust.

Walls and buttresses tumbled, falling slow into clear air.

Desaguliers beckoned wildly, aware of Jannac climbing to his side. 'Do you see, messire? Do you *see* that?'

'The Fane!'

Black walls splintered, shifting, falling. Arched roofs crashed down into naves. Desaguliers felt through clawed feet the rumble of the impact; sound twitched at his ragged ears. Dust billowed up from the Fane-in-the-Seventh-District, spires crumpling, falling like rows of dominoes. The breath of a smell came to him in the summer air: dank stone, opened crypts, and something that choked his throat with unshed tears.

'The Fane . . . '

He sheathed his sword, loping up to cling to the edge of the broken wall and lean outwards. Shadow skirred across him. He jerked his snout up. The daemon-acolytes beat their wings, spiked tails clutching the palace masonry, beaked jaws open and screeching.

Dust and haze thundered up in the north-aust sky.

Captain-General Desaguliers shaded his eyes with a callused shaking hand. Gripping brick with his other hand, he leaned out and squinted to the aust-west. Far distant, down in Eleventh District, the midnight silhouettes of black masonry collapsed . . .

'It is . . . it *is* destroyed.'

445

About to call down in triumph to the Cadets, Desaguliers choked on wonder.

He had swivelled round to climb down, and now faced the Fane again. Colour danced: scarlet, green, blue, white and purple.

From out of the Fane's black rubble and ruin, from tilted pillars and crumbling buttresses, from ogive windows and broken spires, plants began to flower. Roses, hawthorn, forget-me-nots, apple blossom; orchids and cowslips, blackberries and alyssum; out of season and out of time, growing, spilling out of the ruins like a lava-tide . . .

Below him, the Cadets rested muskets and sheathed swords, climbing the barricades to walk among bewildered men and women in temporary truce. The Rat-King milled in confusion. Desaguliers stepped, slipped, slid a yard down a tilted limestone slab, grazing his haunch; grabbed the torn stone edge and stared, wordless, at the Fane.

Among the ruins of millennially old stone, miraculous flowers opened petals to the summer sky, spilling down into the city streets.

The wings of acolytes rustled agitatedly on the roof above. Desaguliers looked up to see each beaked muzzle pointing at the Fane's ruins in dumb expectancy.

Grey heat burned her bare shoulders.

She threw her head back, muscles unknotting from tension; feeling her rose-tangled hair hot under the sun. A granular grey summer's heat burned in her, fogging her vision; pricking her skin with ultraviolet, loosing all strains.

She stared up into a blue sky.

Open, blue: the sun an unbearable white hole into heat and light. One glance upwards blinded her, tears pouring down her cheeks; she saw, smeared, to each horizon: north, south, aust, west and east, the city that is called the heart of the world.

At every horizon, the Fane is tumbled into ruin: obelisks

jutting like broken teeth, buttresses fracturing into stone lace, roofs falling, walls split, open to the summer air.

'*We have chosen Our new way. We have hidden Ourselves for too long. Now We choose to walk amongst you.*'

All Fanes are one Fane.

Her feet are conscious of hardness, that she walks now on brick paving, and she stares up – in a courtyard where pottery brick walls collapse – at the stone-warm image of a sphinx.

Black bees swarmed frantically, the air full of buzzing black dots. The White Crow walked forward, hands gently brushing bees aside, their furred feet tickling as they crawled across her bare shoulders. She lifts her head.

'*The Wheel turns. The Dance begins again.*'

'You'll . . . build again?'

Terracotta full lips smile, anciently and with warmth. The Decan of High Summer, the Lady of the Eleventh Hour: a sphinx-shape that towers high above the woman; heat radiating back from sun-warmed brick flanks and head-dress and heavy-lidded eyes.

'*We have confined Ourselves to the Fane too long,*' the Decan's voice repeats, attendant with echoes, until it seems that all the Thirty-Six are speaking in a confusion of voices. '*My Master-Physician, all that the Divine does is right, because it is We who do it. Come.*'

The White Crow's feet stung with the reverberation of a brick paw falling to the ground. She swayed, staring up. Moss-crusted flanks stretch, great shoulders arch; the vast body of the god-daemon rises from the earth. Impossible, articulated, the incarnate stone flesh moves; shining in the noon sun with the brilliance of deserts.

The footfall's reverberation shook her flesh. The White Crow stumbled, half-walking and half-running. The shadow of ancient stone fell across her, and she, legs turned rubbery, staggered to walk beside the god-daemon as the Decan slowly paced forward.

'*Come. We will walk out into the world.*'

*   *   *

Parquet flooring, hot with impossible sun, burned his palms.

Lucas slid out from the pit under the last analytical engine in the Long Gallery and stood up. Other students crowded the doors, the high windows, clamouring. Black grease smeared his hands and arms. He reached to grab his discarded doublet with filthy fingers.

'It's the sun!' Rafi slapped his bare shoulder, running past. 'It's daylight out there! *We did it!*'

Bodies jostled. Lucas floated in their movement, hardly conscious of it; aching with weariness from wrench and gear and rod, eyes stinging with tiredness. He let himself be carried down the grand stairway into the university's entrance-hall.

'Outside!' A blonde girl hammered the door-beam out of its socket with the heel of her hand.

Above his head, the carved applewood beams shimmered. He raised his head. Summer heat and light flooded in through the opening door. A sharp sweet smell drifted in.

One pale green spot appeared on the wood. It swelled, bubbled up, unscrolled into the air – a leaf. A veined green leaf. Lucas pushed his head-band further up his brow, shifting the hair from his eyes, gaping.

All the beams supporting the roof burst into leaf. A tide of green swept through the hall, leaves unfolding, rustling; springing from the wood of beams and panelling and doors, darkening the sunlit hall to a green shadow.

Lucas pushed into the throng of students and Reverend tutors, finding himself carried towards the door. Pink blossom burst out on the now-knotted beams.

'The sun—!'

A silence fell. Lucas stepped out into the courtyard, the other students slowing as they pushed out into that wide paved space. Briars wreathed the great sandstone staircases rising up at cater-corners of the yard. Glass windows shimmered, river-bright. Acolytes clung to the towering chimneys, bristle-tails writhing down among flowering wooden window-frames.

Pharamond caught his gaze across the heads of other students: the bearded man with his hair dishevelled, his face dazed. 'We did it. We cheated the laws of nature!'

Lucas brushed his arms, the faint dew and wind raising the small hairs down his forearms. Black machine-oil glistened. Over the courtyard and the open gates, an early-summer sky clung to roofs and streets and spires. A sky hot and soft and pale with heat.

A Katayan student clapped his hands rhythmically, broke off, caught a dark-haired woman's hands and pulled her into a dance-step. Lucas, to his own astonishment, picked up the clapping rhythm. Two girls snatched up soft-thorned briars, weaving them into garlands. Processional, ragged, yelling, the students burst open the university's iron gates.

Lucas stifled fear under fatigue, triumph and sheer blinded brilliance. With each step the sun shone more brightly, until he had to turn his face away from the blaze and look down at his black shadow on the paving. He passed under the main gate, and a shower of green leaves flew about him, brushing his shoulders; white and pink apple blossom whirling into the air, petals clinging damply to his skin.

The heat reflected from alley walls and bright windows, smelling of dust and dirt, of manure, of bird's feathers and fruit-stalls and drying washing. Fragments of song burst up into the air, one student beginning a catch, someone else drowning it. A shatter of glass made him stumble. He turned to see Regis, the sun bright on her freckled face, standing ankle-deep in an arcade window and passing out bottles of wine.

The yellow-haired Katayan male knocked against Lucas as he stumbled past, chanting an unrecognizable song:

'Now we shall walk—
'Now we shall walk—
'Now we shall walk amongst you—'

449

A flash of white caught Lucas's eye.

He staggered into a run, breaking for an alley-entrance, panting, legs spiked with pain as he turned and ran up the hill. The bleached sky burned above.

Its shadow dark on the cobbles, the silver timber-wolf trotted quickly around corner and corner.

Heart hammering, lungs burning, Lucas caught up. He ran from the last houses, out on to the abandoned building site surrounding the Fane-in-the-Nineteenth-District. A confused impression of abandoned scaffolding and stone, of black marble and jungles of flowers blurred his vision.

Like lava it ran down the hill into the city, a resistless tide. Daisies sprouted from guttering, ivy from door-posts; wild roses threshed up into great banks of scent and colour. Sparkling mosses thrust up from roof-tiles. The wind filled his mouth with the scent of cherry and roses and stocks, slowing his steps until he paced, resting his oil-grimed fingers on the ruff at the wolf's neck.

Exposed under the pitiless noon sky, he momentarily shut his eyes. His palms sweated. Anticipation pulsed under his ribs, in his guts. His hand closed hard over the wolf's rough pelt. Lazarus whined.

'Lazarus! Hey, boy!'

Lucas's eyes flew open.

She trod the chalky ground of the site, dust whitening her bare feet and ankles, her face tilted up to the summer sky. A warm wind tugged the masses of dark red hair that fell about her shoulders, hair whitened at the temples, and wound with white roses that shed petals as she walked. Brown smears of dried blood marked her left hand.

She walked naked in the summer's heat.

He mouthed her name. He heard the skitter of gravel as she kicked it, walking across the site; saw her head come down, eyes sky- and sun-dazzled, and a wide smile spread across her face. Now, closer, the young man saw how dirt creased in the folds of skin at her elbows and jaw; how sweat shone on her forehead and breasts. Dust paled her dark aureoles, glimmered in the dark-red curls of her pubic hair.

'Lucas.'

He reached out with both hands, cupping her bare shoulders. Oil smudged her skin. She smiled, the skin crinkling around her tawny eyes; tilted her head a little to the side. Flowers spiralled across the chalky earth, coiling up about her ankles. He smelt her warm sweat, tasted salt as he kissed her mouth and licked her cheek. Energy sang in her skin, pulsed in her blood; the backwash of some tide not yet gone from her consciousness.

'Lucas . . .'

Her arms came up under his, tightening around his ribs and across his back. Her breasts pressed against his skin. He grabbed her to him, probing her mouth with his tongue, suddenly and appallingly inexpert. Some tremor shook the body he held: laughter or disgust? He gripped her more tightly.

He felt her hands slide down and unhook his belt, smoothing his breeches down his hips, guiding him to sheath his aching and too-ready flesh in her transformed body.

The sparrow soars down from the heights.

This is the same midday heat that would drive it to shelter under eaves, or seek out a dust-bath to flutter feathers cool. Now, dropping to earth, the bird's unblinking eyes take in the heart of the world.

White stone wings extend, hissing in the clear air. The sparrow stalls, flicks to perch on a vast extended finger. It cocks its head, taking in the naked and narrow-hipped body that lounges upon the wind. An eagle-head dips, golden eyes blinking. A dream of feathers blows about the god-daemon's stone skin.

The Decan of Daybreak, Lord of Air and Gathering, lifts his finger and touches – so delicately – his colossal carved beak to the bird's head.

'See . . .'

All the austerly horizons burst into flame with flowers.

451

Air shimmered over the model, over the single bricks that formed a makeshift wall around its five-metre-square plan. Walled and gated by bricks, interior gardens sketched with chalk, domes and halls slapped together from hessian and wet plaster on a wired lath frame. A model rocking on chalk-marked broken paving.

'Ah.' The Lord-Architect Casaubon looked up as a shadow fell across the scaffolding and bricks and masonry of Fourteenth District's square where he sat. 'I thought you'd be along, sooner or later.'

A vast sphinx-shadow covered the broken paving and the granite block engraved with the Word of Seshat; darkening the shabby makeshift model of the New Temple.

The Decan of the Eleventh Hour stands against the sun, the warm and glowing substance of Her incarnation wreathed with trailing wild roses. Black bees swarm about Her face, nest in the crevices of brickwork drapery. The summer breeze blows from behind Her, scented with desert dawn and arctic night.

'Well done, little lord.'

The Lord-Architect climbed ponderously to his feet, rump momentarily skyward; tugged his blue silk breeches up and brushed with one ham-hand at the dirt on his shirt and frock-coat.

'I know what you've come to do.' His china-blue eyes blinked against the new sunlight. He rubbed his stomach and gently belched. 'Hadn't you – I beg your pardon, Divine One – hadn't you better get *on* with it?'

'Hurry is for mortals.'

One copper eyebrow lifted. The fat man opened his mouth, hesitated, and shook his head. He began to feel through each of his deep coat-pockets in turn. At last he unearthed a tiny notebook and pencil.

The Lord-Architect stripped off his voluminous blue coat, spread it over an expanse of step, and eased himself down to sit on it. He balanced the notebook on his immense thigh, and licked the pencil thoughtfully.

'There is something yet to do, little lord.'

The Lord-Architect Casaubon lifted his head from his writing. He pushed up his shirt-sleeves with the pencil still folded in his plump fingers. A line of tiny neat letters marked the notebook's page.

'I said, there is—'

A grin creased its way across the fat man's oil- and plaster-stained face. He spread one open palm. 'Divine One. *Do* it. I always had a taste for a good miracle myself.'

Radiant and stinging as the sunlight, divine amusement beat against his skin. He rested his chins on his hand, and his elbow on one vast up-raised knee, and held the tiny notebook up.

'I see . . .'

Heavy-lidded eyes close, open, with leonine slowness. Sun gleams on high cheek-bones and nose, shines back from tiny ochre bricks and the white dots of roses. The salt-pan whiteness of Her gaze fixes upon him.

'Knowing all, then, you will not need Me to tell you that she lives.'

A shudder passed through his flesh, shaking his chins and belly. He wiped a sweat-drenched forehead, smearing plaster-dust in clumps into his hair, and breathed in sharply. For a moment he sagged in relief. Then he tapped the notebook against his delicate lips, hiding a broad smile.

'No – but I thank you for the thought.'

'If you are not damned, little architect, it will not be the fault of the Thirty-Six. Very well, then. Your expected miracle. See now what I conceive it necessary to do!'

Light blazed.

In that second he saw no lath-and-plaster domes, no brick colonnades or chalk-drawn gardens, only the deep structure of order and proportion and extravagant flamboyance that lies in particles, cells, souls.

Breath knocked out of him, the Lord-Architect sprawled on his back. He grunted, getting himself up on to his elbows.

453

'Madam, I congratulate . . . you . . . '

The stone of Seshat lay embedded now in a wall, mortared in with a cement that seemed to bear the weathering of many seasons. Beside it, before the Lord-Architect's startled gaze, mellow red brick soared up into a foliate gate. He stared through the opening, too small to admit a carriage, across lawns flanked by comfortable low colonnades. A fountain shot thin jets into the sunlight.

'Oh, I do,' he said. 'I do.'

Beyond the fountain, wide steps suitable for traders' booths or just for resting rose to a rotunda and tiled dome; its arches open and without doors to close them.

Somewhere beyond the main body of the temple, a campanile put delicate brick tracery into the summer sky. He stared at the ledges, balconies and open belvedere. His gaze fell to gardens, and clear through the gateway came the sound of river-water.

'*Look* at it . . . ' A woman's husky voice sounded above him. Casaubon pushed himself up to a sitting position beside Mistress Evelian.

'It was bound to happen.' Pride crept into the fat man's voice. 'Such acute construction ought never to be wasted—'

'Sharlevian!'

With eyes for nothing else, not even the presence of a god-daemon, the yellow-haired woman ran through the gate, catching up the hem of her dirty blue satin dress. She flung her arms around a figure in pink overalls, swinging her daughter's feet off the ground.

Tannakin Spatchet, hovering on the edge of their joy in embarrassment, caught the Lord-Architect's eye. The Mayor drank from a pottery jar, lifting it in salute.

Behind him, spreading out through the grounds that now seemed to fill all the site-space lying behind the square, black and brown Rats, and humans still in the remnants of carnival dress, wandered wide-eyed up from the underground tunnels. Talk sounded gradually louder on the air.

Casaubon stood and walked under the arch of the gateway. He rested one brick-grazed hand against the wall. Flesh curved, creasing his face into a ridiculous and ineradicable smile; he swept his gaze across the Temple grounds – cool passageways, wide steps, seats, fountains; the glimmer of mosaics in the ceiling of the great dome; distant tree-tops, and the explosion of blossom, and the growing crowds – and finally swung back, arms wide.

'Didn't I say, the best thing I'd ever done! Oh, not as magnificent as many, not as *grand* – but for the *form* of it! That structure all but compels them to rest, to walk slowly, to talk peaceably—'

'*Compelled? Invited, rather. And was it your conception, little lord? I think it was also the woman's, and the child's, and the other man's there.*'

'Well . . . Yes. I admit it. Baltazar Casaubon doesn't need to fear sharing credit, Divine One.'

Her head rises against the blue summer sky, incarnate, ancient and young. Black bees hum around her shoulders and flanks. The Decan of the Eleventh Hour raises Her head and gazes into the heart of the sun itself. The full curved lips move.

'*So . . . but yes. Yes. Haste is for mortals – but there is still one thing to be done.*'

The deck slewed.

The Boat, gripped in a midnight current, raced into noise and darkness. Clawed hands tore at the hull, wood shrieking as it ripped. Zar-bettu-zekigal staggered back and forth across the deck, boot-laces flapping, hacking her heel down on nine-clawed hands, spitting at catfish-mouthed human faces. She swallowed, saliva wetting her sore throat.

'I can keep this up all night if it helps. Isn't *anything* I don't remember.'

Far up, in the vaults of darkness, a line of white glimmered. Zari narrowed her eyes. In her moment's inattention, the humming chant behind her faded into vagueness.

'Elish!'

'I hear you, Zar. What happened then?'

'Oh, she told me to get out of the tent. I had it *just* where I planned and she – all *she* cared about was that I shouldn't talk to the press!'

Zar-bettu-zekigal let the stream of words come. She balanced on the moving deck, knees aching at the shifts of balance. Water curved up – *up* – in a great hill: obsidian-black, sharp with rills and knot-hole eddies. Above and ahead, at the crest of the rising water, whiteness foamed. Zari's hand shot out and grabbed a thwart.

'And why *shouldn't* I talk to Vanringham? I'm a Kings' Memory! I can talk to anyone I like!'

A chuckle. 'But can you stop?'

A whisk-ended tail whipped about Zari's ankle. She glanced back. Elish-hakku-zekigal sat cross-legged at the tiller, one elbow hooked about the black wood; her free hand tapping a shaman drum-rhythm on the deck. Her cornflower-blue eyes gleamed in the guttering light of the one lamp.

'Need you, little one. Who else could keep my memory stirred?'

She began to hum, deep in her throat: a shaman chant. The hairs rose down Zar-bettu-zekigal's spine, and the familiarity of it stirred a reckless joy in her. She jerked her head, hair flying.

'And that? Up ahead?'

'I think, for good or ill, the end of us. Hold on!'

The roar of the impossibly-rising hill of water deafened her. Zar-bettu-zekigal whiplashed moisture from her tail and tottered back across the deck.

'Steer us away from it – across the current!'

'Trying, little one. Come help.'

Zari set her narrow hip against the wooden tiller. It shook against her hands. The lantern on the stern-pole swung wildly, sending faint light across the water.

456

Filament-mouthed faces shone in the blackness. Crustacean claws lifted. Something with fleer-eyed malice swam frog-like at the bows. She braced herself hard against the tiller, turning to stare ahead.

'Hey!'

Fish-eyes gleamed in nebula-clusters, burning green and gold in sudden brilliance. A ripple of gold ran through the hill of water, spider-threading infinite depths.

'El, what is it!'

'Baby, I'm here; it's all right—'

A wave rushed down the hill-slope, battering the prow of the Boat. Spray soaked Zar-bettu-zekigal. She shook wet hair from her eyes, swearing. The Boat dipped, wallowed; she dug heels into the deck and heaved the tiller hard over, looked up into darkness, and her heel skidded. She clung to the wooden spar.

The darkness curdled, cracked. She rubbed salt water from her streaming eyes, staring up. Overhead the blackness flaked, crumbled . . .

The god-daemon lay calm among waters.

Light shone between granite horns.

He lay between rows of cracked grey pillars, sea-washed, carved over with hieroglyphs; and incised in the flagstones around the plinth she saw, sea-worn, the signs of the Thirty-Six. Black water threshed and foamed against living stone.

Zar-bettu-zekigal looked up from vast webbed black hands gripping the plinth, to capriped forearms, to shaggy throat and shoulders. The great horned goat's head towered above into darkness: cracked grey granite, informed with the presence of the Decan.

'Divine One.' Elish-hakku-zekigal bowed her head, not losing her grip on the tiller.

Tor-weathered, the shaggy granite flanks shed sea-foam and beating water. The mountain-range of shoulder and spine and haunch stretched away into darkness to where, far off, his scale-crusted tail lashed black waters to storm.

A rich smell dizzied Zar-bettu-zekigal. Rich enough to

drown out the oil, fish, ooze and excrement that composed
it; rich with the energies of generation and corruption and
growth. She sneezed and wiped the back of her wrist across
her face, leaning out over the hull of the Boat to stare up
at the god-daemon.

'Oh, hey . . . ' Utter contentment in her voice. 'Elish,
I've *seen* one!'

The older Katayan spluttered into brief laughter.

'Say you, you have. And if it's not the last thing we ever
see, then doubtless I'll never hear the end of it!'

Between the coiled sky-reaching horns a white disc
burned, burning with the blotched stains of lunar seas.
Light fell across the deck of the Boat, shining on her,
and on the older Katayan's face, turning it stark black
and silver.

Stone flaked: the eyes of the god-daemon among the
waters opened.

Zari kicked a heel against the deck of the Boat, tilting
her head to judge their speed as they rushed up to where
the hill of water crested: to where, head lowered, the
Decan of the Waters Below the Earth watched seas pour
away into infinity. The roar of the waters falling all but
drowned her shout: 'If he doesn't do something, El,
we're finished!'

Great slanting eyes opened, liquid darkness staring
down from under stone lids. The moon's light sent hard
shadows across the horns and ears and muzzle, across the
vast lips curving in an ancient slow smile. Far, far above
her head, the coiled horns shone red with strings of roses:
minute as blood-drops against the disc of the moon.

The dark of the Decan's eyes glimmered on foam and
sea-fret. She felt her mouth go dry. As if it swung into dock
between pilot and tugs, the Boat curved across the rising
hills of water and slowed, slowed and stopped before the
web-fingered hands of the god-daemon.

Her neck hurt, craning to look up. Raw throat, drenched
and dripping coat, chilled to the bone: all became, for that
instant, unimportant. Zar-bettu-zekigal gazed up at the

long caprine face, the stone goat's muzzle whose beard jutted forked bone and forked wood; sea-serpents and crustaceans infesting the crevices.

Crumbled to bone at elbow and shoulder, none the less, green leaves sprouted to cover the great mountain-range spine. Moss spidered across the stone, fresh green. Seaweed sprouted bright yellows and ochres between the vast webs of fingers.

Nightmares swarmed about the distant flanks, small as pismires, that were large enough to swallow the Boat complete.

'Lord Decan!'

With a peculiar pride in courtesy, she looked into the stone-lidded eyes and bowed her head. She couldn't keep from grinning widely, excited.

'Zar.' The older woman stood and stepped away from the tiller, her black-furred tail whipping around Zar-bettu-zekigal's wrist and tugging her aside.

'Oh, what!' She pulled herself free.

A cluster of red roses sprouted on the Boat's black-tarred thwart. A green runner coiled the length of the tiller. Barbed green thorns shot out of it, serrated leaves unfolded; a whole hedge-tangle of pink dog-roses weighed the tiller into stillness.

Serrated fins scraped the hull. Water slopped. She wiped her wet hair off her forehead and licked her lips; tasted the faint sweetness of ordure and gagged.

Moon-crested, lying between the Pillars of the Waters Under the Earth, the Decan bent its horned goat-head. The great-fingered hands shifted.

The waters boiled.

A heavy weight dipped down one side of the Boat. Zari stepped back, bumping her shoulder against Elish-hakku-zekigal where the shaman woman stood quietly at the prow. The Boat rocked again.

'Oh, hey . . .'

Only a breath, almost silence. She squatted on her haunches, leaning to stare at the wet footprints tracking the empty deck. She smiled in wonder. Shifting and shifting again, the Boat rocked and settled deeper into the waters. She stared up at the stone upon which the Decan lay, seeking for footprints wet among the carved flagstones of the plinth, but it towered above her head.

Crowding, overlapping: sourceless shadows of men and Rats stained the deck.

'Elish.' She touched one finger to a swift-drying mark (the print of a small Rat, by the size), feeling no substance by it. She stood. The air across the deck curdled, somehow full. She tugged Elish's satin sleeve and grinned. 'Passengers!'

'I thought it would never . . . Something's changed.' Elish-hakku-zekigal raised her eyes to the god-daemon. 'Again, the Boat carries the dead.'

Stone lips curved in an ancient uncanny smile; pursed very slightly and blew. The Boat rocked. The curve of the falls shot back gold light from black water. The lantern, guttering, tipped to the deck and smashed. She grabbed at the side of the Boat, Elish's hand catching her shoulder.

'We're going to go over!'

The shaman Elish-hakku-zekigal lifted her head and began to hum in the back of her throat. The chant for finding homecomings sounded, soft and quiet under the roar of waves. The current grabbed the Boat suddenly enough that it jolted Zari off her feet. She scrambled up with skinned knees.

Elish sang.

Zar-bettu-zekigal kicked off her black ankle-boots. She ran forward and leaped up, one foot either side of the sharp prow; knelt for a second and then stood, tail coiled out on the air for balance, wind lashing short wet hair back from her face.

'Hey!'

She pushed down on the balls of her feet as the prow dipped, rode the push upwards; yelling in unmusical concert the shaman chant, kicking out at a webbed hand grabbing her foot. A filamented mouth gaped,

460

teeth gleaming. The crest of the hill of black water rushed closer.

'*Go, little ones.*'

A breath on the waters, warm as spring; a glimmer of fire, sea-green; and the voice of the Decan: '*Go back to the world.*'

She turned her head, sketched a bow, coat-tails flying. The prow fell away from under her feet; she slipped, banged her knee, and knelt to stare ahead at the beating crest of waters now all white fire and lace about the Boat—

'Look!' Elish broke her chant for a second, rushing forward beside her and pointing down. 'Look, the stars!'

Monstrous forms clung to thwarts and prow, fish-mouths wide, gaping for water; screeching. A clawed finger raked wood into splinters beside Zari's foot. She bent and grabbed a boat-hook from its ledge under the rail, scrambled up the prow, stabbed down among masses of green flesh and scale thick enough now to slow the Boat.

The rising wave crested.

Below, above, all around: she stared up dazzled at the stars in their Houses, burning in the Three Hundred and Sixty Degrees. Elish's warm hands gripped her shoulders. Dark and day spun across her sight, wheeling, turning . . .

Sunlight dazzled.

Zari heaved herself up to stand on the prow, one arm flung up against the sudden light. So all the later, famous pictures show her: a young black-haired Katayan, coat flying, arm raised as she beats down the swarming nightmare-monsters under the Boat's prow. She balances there, beneath her the tumbling bodies of nightmares, all framed by the great onyx-and-marble Arch of Days where the canal flows from the grounds of Salomon's Temple.

The older Katayan woman stands by a rose-shrouded tiller; her head back, her mouth open, chanting to the sun that shines full on her face.

Sun dazzles.

461

Canal-water boiled in motion, light shafting up and blinding her: the clawed and tendril-mouthed horrors diving for the depths. Zar-bettu-zekigal straightened, shaking out her wet greatcoat.

'*Ei!*'

'Now, Zar!'

A tail coiled around her wrist and jerked. She staggered to the deck, avoiding the mast – the mast? – and glared at Elish-hakku-zekigal. A crowd of people jostled them.

Women, children, Rats, men, Ratlings. The deck shone, shadowless.

'*Off*, now. Move!'

Strong hands gripped the shoulders of her coat, pushing her across deck towards the gangplank – the gangplank? – and her heels skidded as she dug them in and staggered, clutching at a splinter.

'Say you, yes – but we both—'

'I came this way; I can go this way: I have to guide the Boat: now will you *leave*?'

Zar-bettu-zekigal staggered onto the gangplank. She let her shoulders slump in acquiescence. The heavily laden vessel wallowed. She folded her hand back and grabbed the solid vertebrae of the older Katayan's tail, and let her full weight swing them both to fall across plank and canal-water and tow-path.

The canal walkway whacked her between the shoulders. Dimly she heard shouting, cheering; sensed the movement of the great vessel on the waters. Pounding footsteps approached; dozens, hundreds.

She hitched herself up on to her wet elbows, raising one knee, her own tail twitching. The older woman sprawled, rubbing the base of her wrenched tail.

'Don't want you dead. Want you here. With me.'

'You shave-tailed little idiot!'

Twin masts shone black against a blue summer sky, the rigging bare. The Boat drifted in the canal, between gardens, people running up from far away, joining the growing crowd. Elish-hakku-zekigal stared.

She began to hum absently in her throat.

The vessel straightened, swinging to point away from the Arch of Days. It began to glide, weighted down by passengers who cast no shadows; to glide away in the sun . . .

Elish shot her one broad grin and staggered to her feet, shaking out her coat-tails and lace ruffle. She walked unsteadily down the canal path, lifting her head, singing the guiding chant, her eyes all on the Boat and not on the front runners of the crowd who fell back, cheering, to give her passage.

Sun blazed.

Zar-bettu-zekigal felt a hand at her shoulder, at her elbow; and grabbed wildly as they swung her up on to her feet. A man shook her hand, another wrung her other hand; a woman threw her arms around her and kissed her.

Over the heads of the crowd the shaman chant sounded, high and clear.

She laughed, shook hands, kissed back; began to walk shoulder-by-shoulder with men and women in rags, recognizing no faces; walking with small red-faced children, and brown Rats in the rags of King's Guard livery.

'Oh, hey, I know *you*.'

She elbowed herself a space as a small man fought through the crowd to her side, falling back a few yards from the people that flocked around Elish as she sang.

The small man, his white hair standing up like owl's feathers, grabbed her hand and wrung it. With his other hand he felt in the pockets of his greasy cotton coat and unearthed a broadsheet which he thrust at her. She dropped it.

'Nineteenth District broadsheet—'

Cornelius Vanringham dabbed at his sweating forehead. Two men at his heels raised cameras, flashbulbs popping. From another pocket he rummaged out a notepad and a pen, waving them at her in an explanatory manner.

'We were interrupted before. I wonder if I could talk to you now. Please.'

She shoved her hands deep in her greatcoat-pockets, swirling the hems, which steamed a little now in the drying sun. A great swath of the crowd slowed, staying with her rather than with Elish. Her head came up, and she walked with a kick-heeled strut, feeling the dust of the canal walk hot under her bare feet. She smelt sweat and wine and roses. Heat blazed out of a hazed blue-grey sky.

'Oh, see you . . . '

Voices at her shoulder fell silent, others further back hissed for quiet. Attentive silence spread out like ripples in water. The crowd jostled her, human and Rat, as she sauntered in the wake of her sister.

A grin quirked up the corners of her mouth. Hands in pockets, she shrugged, superbly casual.

' . . . Just *ask* me. I can tell you! I'm a Kings' Memory. What do you want to know?'

Candia, sprawling down on a stone horse-block, scratched at thick blond stubble and spread out stained pasteboard cards. A dazed child's wonder blanked his expression.

Brilliant image succeeds brilliant image, no tarot card what it has been before, all new and strange and altering again even as he turns them: lions coupling in a desert, a river flowing uphill, a steel-and-granite bird circling a star, a throned empress giving her child suck . . .

Acolytes clung to every projection of stone above him, gripping gutters, façades, strapwork and chimneys; staring down into the overgrown university quadrangle.

The black gelding grazing loose by the block raised its head and whinnied, sweat creaming its haunches, eyes white and wild. Candia glanced up. He sprang to his feet, the cards scattered.

'My lord! Theo!'

He put his arms carefully around Theodoret's shoulders, embracing him. The Bishop returned the grip, careless of the younger man's sweat-stained and filthy shirt.

'My friend, I haven't thanked you—'

464

'Don't. It took me long enough to come back, and I had to be pig-drunk to do it—'

A shadow halted him in mid-word. Behind the white-haired man, bright in the sun, a sandstone-and-gold shape paced between tall university buildings that only shadowed His flanks.

'Lord Spagyrus.' He swallowed, mouth dry. 'You live, still?'

'*Yes, little Candia, I live. I live again!*'

The great head lowered, tusks gold against the sky, tiny scaled ears pricked forward. The scales of the Decan's muzzle glinted. The Bishop of the Trees reached up and laid a veined hand on the tip of one down-jutting fang, just below the vast nostril. Breath stirred Candia's hair. An almost-mischievous smile creased Theodoret's face.

'*I am the elixir, I am the prima materia, I am the stone that touches all, the marriage of heaven and hell. I had forgotten,*' the Decan's soft voice boomed, echoing in sandstone courtyards where the slim leaves of bamboo sprout from shattered windows, '*and I perceive that I have erred, the while that matter clouded me.*'

Candia shoved his straggling hair back under its sweat-band, put his fists on his hips, and glared up at the Decan of Noon and Midnight.

' "Erred." ' He eyed the Decan with an exasperation long since past the point of caution. 'Erred! Would you like me to tell you about it!'

'*The error is not one that concerns you.*'

Candia rubbed the back of his wrist across his mouth. The horse whinnied again. His breath came back to him, rich with the scent of the dusty yard: sweet, salt, rose- and dung-odoured. Clamour continued to sound outside. Through the archway, across the District to the harbour's marble piers and aqueducts, to the far south-aust horizon where tides of flowers flowed.

'Who, then?'

'*These.*'

To each roof-ridge, chimney, gable and gutter, the

dispossessed Fane's acolytes clung. They roosted restlessly, membraned wings furling and unfurling in the
new sun, obsidian claws gripping stone and metal. Candia
tilted his head back, staring up into slit-eyed beaked
faces.

Malice and pain stared back.

'*They suffer.*'

Candia grunted. 'Good. They made us suffer for centuries.'

Daemon-wings flared open, beating the bright day into
dust-storms. One beast clung head down on lead guttering,
picking with its beak at new vegetation, spitting dumb
hatred down at him.

'*They are Our just instruments. They have no minds to
recall, else they would remember how you sought to betray
fellow-humans to them.*'

The Decan's scented breath skirred dust about Candia's
feet. He sank to one knee in the courtyard, head high; his
mouth opening and closing several times.

'*I have always been able to rely on mortals for treachery.*'

Stubbornly suppliant, Candia remained kneeling, a ragged blond man squinting against the light. A resonance of
his swagger and competence of a Sign ago haunted him,
now, much as he haunted this deserted university. The
Decan's shadow fell across his flopping hair, his filthy
shirt and breeches.

'*These are only animals. Death is death to them; their
generations do not return. Except in the darkness behind the
eye and in the Fane, they have no voice. We must make some
end of these servants of Ours, now that We walk out into the
world. What would you have Me do? Tell Me what you would
do, little Candia.*'

The Fane's acolytes raised restless muzzles to all five
points of the compass, sniffing the blossom-scented wind,
searching for the Fane.

His face heating, Candia muttered: 'Why ask me? I'll
answer for Masons' Hall. It was my choice. As for these
butchers, they were your instruments!'

'*Tree-priest, you suffered most. What would you?*'

'Lord Decan, it's you I can't forgive.' Theodoret's veined hands spread in a Sign of the Branches, faint sparks of green and gold flowing under the skin. 'I'm an old man, therefore familiar with discomfort. You and they gave me pain that should have killed—'

'*Forget.*'

'You haven't yet paid for that!'

'*God does not pay. We do not incur debts. Whatever We do is well and right, because it is We who do it. Who can deny that?*'

Candia muttered: 'Bollocks!'

A raw tone echoed back from the courtyard's walls. Candia only knew it much later for a Decan's laughter.

'*It is true that much is different now, but that does not change. But give an answer. What shall be done with these?*'

Candia stared up at the misshapen bodies. 'Freeze them into stone for all I care, and let them stick there until the city's demolished!'

Prescience gave an image of how it would be, clear as a tarot card: each massive building lined with rows of stone guardians, bodies frozen in a rictus, rain streaming from their open beaks . . .

The Decan's full lips parted. One gold fang dulled with his summer breath, birthing the beginning of a word.

'No!' The day's heat dappled on Theodoret; he seemed to move in shade and the shifting of leaves. 'Lord Spagyrus, no.'

'*Why not so?*'

'Animals are innocent murderers, Divine One.' The Bishop's ascetic mouth wrinkled, distaste mingling with resignation and a certain sly justice. 'You should pay something, Lord Spagyrus. What penalty one asks of the Divine, I don't know. Perhaps you should pay by taking responsibility. They are yours, these daemons.'

'*We have no use for these servants now. What they did, We will do Ourselves.*'

Spitting temper, Candia pushed the hair back that flopped into his eyes. 'Call *that* taking responsibility!'

'*I perceive that I have erred. See how I will pay.*' Grave humour echoes; like the Bishop's, young beyond its years, and fully cognizant of dubious moral standpoints. '*Let them have speech and souls. I create them so. I create them free of Us!*'

'Speech and souls—'

Candia grabbed the Bishop's arm, pulling himself to his feet. The old man's lips opened, anticipating, awed.

'Praise the Lord Decan!' a gargoyle-figure shrilled, hanging head-down from a high gutter.

'Praise be buggered!' A raucous cry. Bristle-tail lashing, a daemon uncurled black wings and flew up to hover over the roof. His eyes gleamed amber. 'He's thrown us to our enemies, that's all He's done! They'll take revenge for what He made us do!'

Beaked muzzles rose, opening, and harsh voices cawed in competition with one another.

'We're different now; Rats and men won't hate us—'

'*Won't* they!'

'I have a right to be here; it's our city, too!'

'No home, here; no place for us—'

'All ours! Sky and roofscape, all ours.'

'But I want more than that—'

'The Lord Decan will tell us what to do!'

'Not me, he won't tell!'

Wings rattled in the heat, circling; shadows falling to dazzle Candia as he gazed upwards. Apprehensive of the copper taste of blood, he waited for that ancient warning of their presence. Nothing came. Black ribbed wings, moth-eaten brown furred bodies, spiked long tails – mortal gargoyle-daemons swarmed above the university quadrangle.

Theodoret's elbow dug his ribs. Through the archway, black specks began to rise in confusion across the whole district. Dumbfounded, Candia scratched at his blond stubble.

'The Rat-Lords aren't going to like this. His Majesty *really* isn't going to like this.'

'Choice. Knowledge and choice. I think I *am* revenged. Let these have all our problems! Let them deal with us, and his Majesty – *and* the Thirty-Six in the world, and—' The Bishop suddenly guffawed. 'My friend, no one's going to like it!'

An elderly gargoyle-daemon on a gutter linked clawed thumbs across her flaking breast. Her ribbed wings, drawn down, furled about her shoulders, gleaming tar-black and smelling of old buried stone. One finger moved to scratch under a drooping dug. She stared down at Candia and Theodoret with a light in her eye.

'Who *asked* you to like it?'

Andaluz rolled down one black woollen stocking, folded it neatly on the canal steps beside its twin, and lowered his lean feet into the water.

Early-afternoon sun shimmered, light webbing his pale skin. He flexed his toes in the cold water.

'I assure you, Lady Luka, this canal is real enough. Although to my knowledge it's never been here before—'

He broke off, spreading his hands to acknowledge the city of wonders; shook his head, smiling.

'One says that of so much. What's one canal!'

The plump silver-braided woman walked in a swirl of bright robes to where he sat. She shaded her eyes with her hands. 'In a city of wonders . . . !'

Andaluz slid his heavy doublet off his arms and shoulders, letting it fall carelessly on the steps. He unfastened a button-toggle of his shirt. Sweat dampened the cloth between his narrow shoulder-blades; heat drove sixty years' chill from his bones. He lifted one foot from the canal and hooked his arm around his knee.

'Luka?'

She gazed at the sky: at the heat-hazed, soft grey-blue, empty of all birds. Past her profile, the new wide waterway here opened out into the harbour. Heat and summer's brightest light glared back from the marble palaces that lined the great canal. Andaluz left wet splashes on the marble as he drew his feet from the water and stood up.

'Lady, what is it?'

Marble-and-gold steps and walkways paralleled the canal, running down to where the light flashed from the sea-harbour. Hot on the air came the smell of the sea. Miles of city fronting the harbour shone now in the sun, bright with apple and cherry and blackthorn flower.

She turned to face inland. 'Listen!'

The buzz of the approaching crowd grew louder. The Candovard Ambassador stood barefoot, in shirt and breeches, scratching at his grizzled hair. He reached down towards his discarded doublet. The movement arrested itself midway: he straightened, resting his hand on the woman's arm.

'Luka, dear lady, tell me—'

'There!'

A sudden black spar reared over the heads of the crowd. Appearing between the frontages of palaces, where the canal curved back into the city, the prow of a black ship glided into sight.

The smell of tar came to him in the hot sun, sparkling on the planks. Great black masts towered, white sails belling from them. A sweet rich scent set Andaluz to rubbing his eyes; he frowned, focusing.

Sails hung in tangles against the sky, great curtains and draperies of roses depending from the rigging. The flower-sailed ship glided deep and steady in the water, no hand at the wheel. Figures lined the rails. Ripples lapped the marble steps at Andaluz's feet.

'It's the Boat! Dear lady—' He turned to her, eyes bright with a sudden comprehension.

One of her slender fingers pointed. 'And it's young Elish!'

Crowds of people walked the canal paths. Noisy, hand-in-hand or arms about each other's shoulders, sweating in the heat and calling to their neighbours on the far canal bank, the people of the city crowded out into the sun.

Between a stocky brown Rat and an elderly Fellowcraft,

the Katayan walked. Her pale face raised, she moved her mouth; he could hear nothing of what she chanted. The power and joy of it beat against his skin, as hot as the sun's light.

'Madame Elish!'

He pushed his way forward between people and embraced the thin woman. She shifted her gaze from the Boat, the wall of the hull towering beside them as it glided slowly towards the sea.

'Ambassador!' She caught his hand and swung him to walk on with her to where Luka stood waiting. 'You must know, messire, I lied to you. I'm no envoy.'

'My dear girl, I don't care whether you are or not; you're infinitely welcome.'

The great vessel began to slow. The Katayan woman, licking her lips and drawing in breath, chanted a few soft syllables. She ran forward to grip Luka's hands, laughing down at the middle-aged woman. Andaluz caught his bare foot on a stone, staggered against someone in the crowd. A tall bearded man smiled and handed him a wine-flask.

Andaluz began to shake his head, stopped, took the wine and drank. 'My thanks to you, messire.'

'Welcome. Welcome!'

'Oh, see you—' A hand gripped his bare elbow. 'Messire Ambassador! Isn't it *won*derful?'

Andaluz ran his finger down the younger Katayan's palely freckled jaw-line. He smiled. 'Mistress Zari. My nephew, if he yet lives, wishes you found. Do you know this?'

'Nephew – oh, *Lucas*.' Zar-bettu-zekigal chuckled. 'Oh, *he'll* be all right. He's a good kid. Ask him from me what's he going to be when he grows up.'

Andaluz roared with laughter, pushed a way for them between men and Rats to Luka's side. The older Katayan knelt, bending to drink from the canal's clean cold water. The Lady Luka stared out across the great canal at the heavily laden vessel.

She held up a hand, gripping her bamboo cane. She

471

nodded, once, the motion folding the soft skin at her throat. Andaluz stepped to her side. Her head moved on bird-delicate shoulders; she looked up at him.

'They're here.' She spoke barely above a whisper.

Andaluz strained to hear over the crowd's babble: voices and sudden laughter, a dropped bottle, a Ratling's squeak. He frowned, hearing only a gull's cry and the creak of rose-laden masts.

'I don't—'

The gull cried again: sharp, desolate, joyful. Andaluz stared at Luka. He lifted one hand, touching the feathers wound into her single braid.

Shadows of bird's wings fell across her, across her silver hair and orange-and-purple robes; across his blunt-fingered hand.

'Oh, lady.' Sudden tears constricted his throat.

The woman lifted both arms. Rings glittered in the sunlight. Her orange scarves swirled. Tiny bells on her leather belt jingled, soft as hawks' jesses. Bright-eyed, she laughed; raised her voice and called out an answering gull's shriek.

Dots flocked in the high haze.

Silence spread out into the crowd, Luka's voice soaring over theirs. Andaluz stood quite still, arms hanging at his sides, mouth slightly open; openly relaxed into his own amazement.

They fell down from the sky – soaring in great squadrons, clouds, flocks: hawks and eagles, gulls, thrushes, humming-birds; owls and cormorants and wild geese; chaffinches and peregrine falcons and sparrows . . . All the air full of wings, whirring, full of dusty feathers and bird-calls and droppings; thousands of birds circling in a great wheel that had, in its eye, the silver-braided bird-woman.

Andaluz softly said: 'Oh, my dear lady . . . '

Luka's raised hands shot forward. The cane reached up towards the black vessel riding the canal. A great herring-gull caught the hot still air under its wings, curved in flight to skim across the water and land on the rail of the Boat.

A thrush flicked to land on a coil of rope.

Luka reached her hands out across the water. Hard concentration furrowed her face. Bird after bird flew down, soaring towards the high invisible deck.

Andaluz stared at figures crowding the rails, figures with no shadows. He felt his own heart beat in his throat.

'So many dead . . . '

The Boat settled into the water. Flocks of gulls and starlings circled the flower-draped sails. They dipped, curving flights to cross the deck.

He moved as close to her as he dared, eyes still fixed on the Boat. Ripples ran across the canal from its hull, dazzling in the summer heat. He took a great breath of humid air. 'Is that what I think?'

The small woman gazed up, plump face beaming. She fumbled her cane; pulled the orange-and-purple robes looser at her neck, and rubbed sweat from her forehead with the heel of her hand. She rocked back and forth on her sandalled heels.

'Yes, my birds carry them back to the Boat, and, yes, the Boat will carry them through the Day and back to birth again . . . '

Andaluz stared up. A hawk clung to the Boat's nearer rail. It raised half-open wings, head down, hacking a harsh call. It choked.

The bright body and wings of a butterfly unfolded from the bird's beak, hacked into the air by its strangulated call. Andaluz laughed. Drunkenly, the bright *psyche* flew up to cling to the bottom of a rose-woven sail.

Elish-hakku-zekigal chanted, her voice croaking quiet as a whisper. The Boat moved out, no faster than walking pace, flanked by crowds on either side of the canal now; gliding on towards the lagoon.

A vast crowd of bright moths and butterflies clung to the Boat, almost hiding the black wood with gold, scarlet, green, purple, azure. Bird after bird swooped down to the deck, then soared up to fly off across the city . . .

Figures at the rail glided past Andaluz. A black woman in a faded green gown, who stretched her fists up to the sun and laughed, silently, as if she couldn't have too much of the light. A man pushing between two brown Rats to lean on the rail, milk-white hair blowing in the summer wind; gazing down at the crowd with wide pit-black pupils. A slender black Rat in a scarlet priest's jacket, who touched a white rose to her furred cheek and held her other hand close by the rail, admiring how no shadow marked the wood . . .

More, more: too many to see and note.

'I—' Andaluz abruptly turned to Luka. The woman rubbed at her wet eyes with plump fingers, smiling up at him. His own eyes ran water. He folded his arm in hers, patting her hand, and lifted it to his lips and kissed it.

She smiled with a brilliance that outshone the sky.

Elish-hakku-zegikal touched his arm and pointed. Her chant croaked on, breathless, unfaltering. Freckles stood out on Zar-bettu-zekigal's pale skin. The Candovard Ambassador stared upwards, following her gaze.

Six yards above, at the black rail, a shadowless woman leaned her chin on her arms and frowned as if memory troubled her. Slanting black brows dipped over reddish-brown eyes webbed around with faint lines. Broken butterfly-wings tangled in her short greasy hair.

'Lady!' Zar-bettu-zekigal's hand jerked up, stopped, fell to her side. 'Lady Hyena!'

Warm wind brushed the woman's face, smoothing away the frown. A ragged Sun-banner sashed her red shirt; and she fisted the cloth in one hand and rubbed it against her cheek, her glance sliding away from the Katayan girl.

Andaluz rested his arm across her shoulders. 'She'll come back, Mistress Zari. If not to you, then to others.'

Zar-bettu-zekigal broke from his embrace. 'Oh, what! I know *that*—'

Her greatcoat swirled about her pale calves. Loping strides took her ahead, paralleling the woman at the rail.

474

Her hands fisted at her sides, black against dazzling light and water, as she came to the carved steps where the canal opened out into the lagoon.

A frown dented the woman's slanting brows.

Suddenly the woman grabbed at her hip, as if she expected to find a sword there. She thrust her way down the rail, limping, pushing her way between men and Rats; walking level with Zar-bettu-zekigal.

No shadow marked the deck.

A sweet smile broke over her face, relaxed and content. She stopped, standing still; and – as no other on the Boat – lifted her hand in farewell. Andaluz glanced down. Zar-bettu-zekigal's eyes glowed.

'Did you see that! She said goodbye. To *me*!'

The Boat moved out into the lagoon, prow turning towards the open sea. A humid wind shifted the masses of roses, and the rose-leaves sprouting from rail and bow and spar. Limpid water rushed against the curving tarred planks of the hull.

Andaluz shaded his eyes with his hand. Sweat slicked the grizzled hairs on his skin. The Lady Luka gripped Elish's arm for support and lowered herself to sit on a step, easing her sweat-pink feet into the cool water. He stepped down beside her, resting one hand on her rumpled robes.

'Andaluz, look!'

The harbour water flows, a net of diamonds; and in lucid depths adamant limbs now stir: Chnoumen, Chachnoumen, Opener of Hundreds and Thousands of Years, implicit in the lines of sun on water.'

'Things can't be the same after this . . . '

A tread behind warns him, that and the sudden silence of the crowd.

Towering over the marble-and-gold palaces, Her ancient terracotta smile secret and triumphant, the Decan of the Eleventh Hour walks amongst Rats and humans that scurry like ants about Her feet. Bees hum among the roses that chain her, sweet and white in the afternoon sun.

Andaluz tastes salt and sand in his mouth.

'I wish I knew my son were here and safe.' Luka raised her head, surveying all; bird-bright glance softening with dreamy reminiscence. 'He was always so delicate as a child, my Baltazar. His chest, you know. He never did take *care* of himself.'

Andaluz bit the inside of his cheek firmly. 'Ah . . . yes. Mistress Zari's described Lord Casaubon to me so well that I feel I already know him.'

The younger Katayan woman gurgled. She caught a light-standard and pulled herself up on to its marble base, gazing over the heads of the crowd, searching.

Luka patted her silver braid, twisting a feather more tightly in it. 'I know he's never been too proud to ask his mother for help; that's why I came at once. I'd never *say* that to Baltazar, of course. He'd be dreadfully embarrassed. Did he look well when you last saw him?'

'"Well"?' Zar-bettu-zekigal grinned and pointed. 'See for yourself, Lady. Ei! *Lord-Architect!*'

'Baltazar!'

Luka elbowed her way between people, Andaluz at her heels. Andaluz glimpsed copper hair as a head turned.

An immensely tall and fat man walked beside the Decan of the Eleventh Hour, stately and beaming. His shirt hung out of his breeches, unbuttoned, stained black with machine-oil. The two top buttons of his breeches had gone missing, and both stockings were unrolled to his ankles. He moved massively, the crowd parting in front of him.

Luka hallooed: 'My little baby *boy!*'

The Lord-Architect Casaubon stopped, sat heavily and abruptly down on the top step of the quay, put his padded elbows on his vast knees, and sank his face into his hands.

' . . . Mother.'

Slowly the Boat moves into distance, hazed in the afternoon heat; gliding down the path of sun-dazzles on the water.

Still from the sky they pour down to follow it, the

birds that fly from thin-aired heights; and, high above, white stone wings curve on air: Erou, the Ninth Decan, Lord of the Triumph of Time, soaring in the changing brilliance of the sky.

'We will never be the same again.'

Into the silence of gathered tens of thousands, a clear voice sounds: the Decan of the Eleventh Hour, Lady of the Ten Degrees of High Summer, whose gaze now scatters miracles over the god-haunted heart of the world.

'Death is not final—'

From the Fifth Point of the Compass they come, walking out from the ruins of the Fane into the world. In the great Districts that stretch across a continent, bells ring in abbey towers, ships' masts burst into flower, women and children and Rats and men clasp hands and dance, in chains and pairs, through streets, and through the midnight-marble ruins.

Stone-bodied, immense, beast-headed: god-daemons stalk streets and parks and avenues, squares and palaces.

' – only change is final; and now it changes again!'

After millennia of construction, thrown down now and laid waste, the Thirty-Six Decans walk out of the Fane's ruins and into the world.

9

White heat-haze lies over the full-leafed summer trees, shadowing their green canopies blue.

Where she lies, in tall cow-parsley between field and formal gardens, damp grass and shadow imprint her body. Borrowed shirt and breeches shade her from sunburn.

Up on the hill-slope, past garden fountain-jets ten metres tall and impromptu open-air feasting, the rotunda of the New Temple curves across the sky. Warm brick, pennants and flags, tiny dots of faces where people walk in wonder along its outer balconies . . .

Time enough to go back to crowds and questions in a few minutes. The woman lies in the grass, hearing birds sing; now gazing down past where the Arch of Days lies invisible under the foot of the hill, past the new canal, to distant hills hollowed with blue shadow.

A large figure approaches, down in the valley, walking along the canal path. Frock-coated: copper hair glinting a clear quarter-mile.

The White Crow rolled over on her back, staring up through the dust of meadowsweet, reaching up with scarred hands to play with the swarming black-dot haze of bees. And abruptly shifted, sprang to her feet, and began to run back up the hill towards the Temple.

A distant clock chimes.

Blazing white light reflected from pale gravel and a pale sky. Zar-bettu-zekigal sprawled on the fountain's marble rim, knees and black dress spread apart, nostrils flaring to smell the day's heat.

'I know the answers to every question now.'

'Every question?' Lucas pulled at the neck of his shirt. He lifted a wine-bottle to his mouth and drank. The young Katayan woman sat sideways on the fountain's rim, one foot up on the marble, her black dress falling down between her knees and over her tail.

'I'm a Kings' Memory: I know.' She snorted. 'Which is more than *they* do.'

Sheaves of paper lay scattered on the gravel about her feet. Blackletter, with illustrative grey-and-black photographic images, and narrow columns of print. The fountain's odorous spray speckled them with water.

'Vanringham got *this* out fast enough! Listen.' She hauled a sheet of paper out from under her other heel. *The Moderate Intelligencer*'s still-damp ink marked her fingers.

' "Visiting student Prince Lucas of our far-flung colony of Candover played a curious part in events. It is creditably reported that he authorized the students of the University of Crime to go on a spree of looting, they only being discouraged at the last by the disclosure of his background in the mechanic trade—" '

'What!' Lucas, choking on a swallow of wine, sat up and grabbed the paper. 'I'll sue!'

She shuffled paper-clippings, dropping a small pair of silver scissors on the gravel. 'Here's another one. "Rumour speaks of the late Master of the Hall in Nineteenth Eastquarter, Falke, being instrumental in preventing the late outbreak of plague from worsening." Ei! *Won't* I talk to Vanringham! I told him everything true, and he's just distorted it all!'

Lucas turned the page of Thirtieth District's *Starry Messenger* over, reading aloud.

' "Accusations against Reverend tutor Candia of the University of Crime have been dropped. It was reported that Master Candia had dealt with persons unbecoming to the reputation of the University of Crime, and was to be dismissed from his place on the Faculty, but after representations from the Church of the Trees—" ' Astonishment edged Lucas's tone. ' " – from the Church

479

of the Trees all charges have been dropped." '

'Oh, say you, that's because of this.'

Zar-bettu-zekigal proffered Eighth District's *Mercurius Politicus*.

' "Bishop Theodoret instrumental in dismissing Black Sun; makes overtures to the Thirty-Six; intervention of this *gaia*-church successful; The Spagyrus ratifies new status for the Church of the Trees; see pictures page six." '

'Pictures?' Lucas took the clipping, peering at silver-and-grey images of the Cathedral of the Trees and that square's gallows, a tiny figure in the foreground recognizable as Theodoret. The cameraman had, quite sensibly, made no attempt to include the Decan, but a vast shadow lay across the foreground of the square.

At Theodoret's side, small and bright, stood the White Crow.

Breath stopped in Lucas's throat, left a lump past which he could not swallow. Zari's voice faded from his consciousness for a minute. Lucas gazed across the gardens to the canal. Small boats bobbed on the water, where music and laughter sounded. He smiled, almost hugging himself.

His fingers remember the touch of skin.

'If we'd known how it would end . . . ' He scanned her narrow face, searching for differences from the young Katayan in the university's courtyard, and in Austquarter's crypt and the palace throne-room. Memory nagged. With sudden discovery, he said: 'Plessiez? I heard that . . . I haven't seen him. Is he . . . ?'

Zar-bettu-zekigal looked up, her lively features still.

'Elish – my sister Elish-hakku-zekigal, she's a shaman – she did a vision. She told me. She sees true. She saw Messire Plessiez at the end, underground, somewhere where there were bones . . . '

Her fingers slid to the sash about her waist, a length of green silk casually knotted around her black dress.

'You can say what you like about the university. And

480

about your old White Crow. It was Messire who went in to break the *magia*. Elish saw – and then her vision couldn't see through the dust: the whole cavern-roof caved in and came down on him. Him and Charnay, too.'

Her eyes, sepia with Memory, shifted.

'I wish I could have seen him on the Boat.'

Lucas took the *Tractatus Democritus* broadsheet between finger and thumb, staring at the print without reading it. He grunted cynically.

'Cardinal Plessiez? He had no more conscience than a fish has feathers! If you ask me, it's a good thing he didn't make it.'

The paper tore, snatched out of his hands.

'Mistress Zari? I didn't mean . . . '

The Katayan hunched her shoulders, bent over the heap of broadsheets, and began with frightening care to scissor out clippings from the remaining papers.

Passing humans and Rats brushed by him; Lucas stood and stepped back with automatic courteous apology. He backed further away from the fountain. Bright silks shone on the far side of falling screens of water.

Up on the terrace, in front of the open pillared rotunda where many danced, a crowd blocked the path. Men and Rats pressed in on the White Crow, shouting questions. She laughed; her hand resting on the green-and-gold sleeve of the Bishop of the Trees.

'Damn. Why does he have to be there? Or any of them? Well . . . Well.'

He shrugged and began to walk up towards the terrace.

Abandoning press cuttings, Zar-bettu-zekigal dipped the tuft of her black-and-white furred tail into the fountain, lifted it above her head, and shook a fine spray over herself. Cool water spotted the shoulders of her black dress. She crossed her ankles and leaned back, supported precariously by her arms on the marble fountain's wide rim. Her face up-turned, eyes ecstatically shut, she dipped her tail again – stopped, sniffed, opened her eyes, and turned a disgusted glance on the green fountain-basin.

'Ei! What a stink.'

'Low-quality lead piping,' a voice rumbled, its owner invisible through the falling fountain-spray. 'My dear child, ought you really to do that?'

The Lord-Architect Casaubon strode magisterially around the fountain-basin, mud-stained satin coat over one bolster-arm, his shirt unlaced and his sleeves rolled up. Black oil and grease smeared his blue silk breeches and braces. The rag with which he wiped his face looked as if it might have been an embroidered silk waistcoat.

'Very inferior work, all of this.'

'You just can't trust miracles any more, messire architect!'

Zar-bettu-zekigal flicked her tail in greeting. Water-drops cartwheeled in the sun.

He beamed. 'Trust miracles? From now on you can!'

The distant clock sounded again. On its last stroke, the sound of trumpets clashed out. Jets shot up fifteen or twenty feet from twelve surrounding fountains. Zar-bettu-zekigal put both hands up to push suddenly wet hair out of her eyes, nose wrinkling at the stronger low-tide-mud stink. A burst of complicated music blasted from sound horns in the statuary.

'Ei!' Zari cocked one black eyebrow.

The Lord-Architect looked down his nose, chins and the considerable expanse of his belly at the fountain. A pained expression crossed his features at the sight of carved nereids spurting water from their breasts, and ragged sea-monsters jetting water from nostrils and every other orifice.

'Florid.'

He slung the blue satin frock-coat on the marble rim, careless of one sleeve trailing in the water, searched the pockets, and brought out a metal hip-flask.

She rolled over on to her stomach on the marble. 'I want to talk to the Bishop of the Trees and Master Candia.

About inside the Fane. And Lady Luka, how she got here. Have the whole story.'

Startled, the Lord-Architect met Zari's eye.

'I'm . . . ah . . . not certain where Mother is.'

'I told her *you* were up in the rotunda.' The Katayan stretched, water-spotted dress already drying in the heat, and grinned at his evident relief.

The music ceased abruptly, with a mechanical squeak. The jets died. Shadows, precise-edged, blackened the steps and the flagstones and lawn around the fountains. Her own elbow-and-knee-joint shadow, tail up, coiled into a florid curve worthy of the fountain's statues.

'*Hei*! Master Casaubon!'

A blonde girl in pink satin overalls swaggered up, silver chains jingling about her neck and wrists. She threw herself down on the marble rim between Zari and Casaubon, sparing no glance for anyone but the Lord-Architect.

'Mistress Sharlevian.' He kissed her bitten-nailed fingers and waved a casual hand. 'You two aren't acquainted, I believe. Entered Apprentice; Kings' Memory . . . Mistress Zari, I was about to ask – have you seen young Lucas of late?'

Zar-bettu-zekigal shifted from her elbows to lie on her side, opening her mouth to answer. A sharp voice cut in: 'Oh, Lucas. *I've* seen him. He went off looking for that red-headed cow who's one of my mother's lodgers.' The girl pushed tangled yellow hair back out of her eyes. Her silver-chain ear-rings glinted. 'Always mooning after her, dozy old bag. Well, she's welcome to what she gets, that's all I can say!'

The Lord-Architect raised both copper eyebrows.

'Kids!' The girl sniffed, wiping the back of her wrist across her nose. She leaned her arms back on the marble, weight on hip and heel. Under the remnants of paint, her complexion had a child's clearness. 'I don't know why I go around with kids. I mean, that boy – poke-poke-bang and it's all over, y'know? I wanna go with men who are worth the time.'

Zar-bettu-zekigal smothered an exhalation of breath, for once without useful comment. The Lord-Architect opened his mouth to speak, rubbed his chins bewilderedly and shook his head. Sharlevian leaned to one side, her breast pressed against his shoulder, her breath warm and moist against his ear.

'What I say is, why go out with a kid when you can go out with someone . . . mature?'

Zar-bettu-zekigal coiled her dapple-furred tail sensuously across the girl's thigh and, when she had her attention, grinned. 'Maybe Lucas feels the same way.'

'Of all the—!'

Sharlevian stared from Zar-bettu-zekigal to the Lord-Architect and, as it became apparent that he would make no response, reddened, stood, and stalked off.

'It's true, he's looking for White Crow.' Zar-bettu-zekigal stared up at the rotunda's terrace, seeing the Prince of Candover and a dozen House of Salomon officers, and no Bishop Theodoret. No White Crow.

'Anyone would think', the Lord-Architect rumbled, 'that that woman is avoiding me.'

Zar-bettu-zekigal crossed her ankles, rested her chin on the backs of her hands, and directed her gaze to Casaubon. 'No! Go on!'

Horn and harpsichord ring out, lazing down the late afternoon. Human and Rats take refuge under trees' shade. Water-automata play. Hot scents of wine, dust and roses fill the air, spreading out across the miles of the New Temple's gardens.

Lazy under that same heat, the air and the cells of flesh vibrate with the voices of Decans: more speech between the Thirty-Six in this one day than in the past century.

The black Rat St Cyr stood with the Bishop of the Trees, watching a play.

A few planks rocked on top of barrels, with the canal and the nearest wall of the Temple for a backdrop. On

the impromptu stage, a ragged grey-furred Rat brandished a banner:

> *'Not sun of pitch, nor brightest burning shadow*
> *Daunted our noble King – they lay*
> *A-quiver, pissing in their satin bed,*
> *Whether the threat came from a friend or foe.*
> *Twice-turned, a traitor saved them. (Saved myself*
> *A life of luxury in the world to come!)*
> *Witness, you renegades, what is gained by such*
> *Devotion as I showed my lord the King!'*

Both humans and Rats in the crowd cheered.

'I perceive', the Bishop of the Trees observed, 'that that
is intended for Messire Desaguliers.'

'You're right.' St Cyr chuckled. He paced elegantly forward through the mixed crowd. 'Well acted, messires!'

A woman appeared at the old man's elbow. The paleness
of the Fane marked her. Sun brightened her dark-red
silver-streaked hair, caught up at the sides and shining with roses that tumbled down on to her shoulders.
Minuscule down-feathers grew at her temples. St Cyr, a
little awed, bowed.

She grinned at Theodoret. 'Let's get out of here before
they get on to the Fane again. Mind you, I think they do
you very well . . . '

Theodoret's beak-nose jutted. He swept the green robe
up from his bare feet, snorting back laughter. 'Say you
so?'

Behind them, from the stage, the harsh *caw*! of a
crow rang out.

'Much better than they do me. I don't know what
that Vanringham's been telling people, but I regret his
source of news caught me when I was in shock enough
to be honest!'

'Zar-bettu-zekigal is an engaging child.'

'She's a plain nuisance. I remember thinking *that* when
she arrived at Carver Street.'

485

St Cyr followed the direction of her gaze, seeing the woman spot the young Prince of Candover and frown. About to comment, he found his arm seized; she walked between himself and the Bishop of the Trees, away down towards the gardens.

'Hey!' The White Crow gave a loud hail as they came under the shadow of beeches. 'Reverend Mistress! Heurodis!'

Sun and shadow dappled the old lady and her companions. St Cyr made his bow to the representatives of the University of Crime.

'Feasting and rejoicing is all very well.' Reverend Mistress Heurodis's face wrinkled into a smile that showed her long white teeth. 'However, we ought not to miss our opportunities.'

She leaned on her cane, regarding with satisfaction the procession of students, largely first-year Kings' Thieves and Kings' Assassins, passing with jewel-boxes, candlesticks, portraits, gemmed books, rings and *ankhs* from the earthquake-tumbled ruins of the Abbey of Guiry.

St Cyr raised furry brows; thought better of it.

'Zu-Harruk!' The old woman snapped a yellow flower sprouting from the head of her cane and tucked the blossom behind her ear. Her smoky-blue gaze rested unimpressed on miracle. 'Come here!'

A tall yellow-haired Katayan student staggering under a box of altar regalia stopped, grunting, while she clucked and, with a jeweller's eye, abstracted a number of the smaller and more perfect diamonds.

'Don't dawdle!' she advised. 'When you've transferred this to the university, I trust I've trained you well enough to go on to the other Abbeys and the royal palace?'

'Yes, ma'am!'

The old lady ignored St Cyr, and rapped her cane against the White Crow's elbow. 'We have a reputation to keep up.'

'Er. Mmm. Doubtless. Yes.'

'Now that's *his* trouble.'

THEATRVM
VITÆ HVMANÆ

'Well acted, messires!'

From *Rituale Aegypticae Nova*, Vitruvius, ed. Johann Valentin
Andreae, Antwerp, 1610 (now lost – supposed burned
at Alexandria)

She pointed between sun-soaked trees to where Reverend Master Candia sprawled, asleep.

'No sense of duty. With all due respect to you and Theodoret and the Rat here, the man hangs out with Tree-priests and Scholar-Soldiers; he just isn't *respectable* enough for the University of Crime.'

St Cyr sees the White Crow laugh; glance anxiously back over her shoulder.

Heat beats back from the courtyard's brick paving.

In shadowed colonnades, they shelter; eating and drinking, weeping, searching for known faces. Rat-Lords in their lace and velvet elbow women in factory overalls. Quarrels break out in corners.

A silence.

Shrouded in dark wings, stooped, casting a shadow purple as plum-bloom, a gargoyle-daemon paces across the New Temple's courtyard and stoops to pet a child.

Inside the rotunda of the New Temple, the Mayor of the eastern quarter of Nineteenth District, a little dizzy from the afternoon heat, accepts another drink from a man in Master Builder's overalls.

The man fingered the chained talismans about Tannakin Spatchet's neck.

'Our consortium is naturally interested in the – shall we say? – the mass production of these talismans that warn of daemons' presences.'

Tannakin Spatchet glanced past the man. Under the great arch, between two of the great sandstone pillars that opened to the courtyards, old blankets and cushions had been thrown in a heap. Eight or nine draggled Rats clustered there, talking, preening, snarling for pages to groom them. No courtiers flocked to them.

Their co-joined tails were lost in the cushions. He saw the eyes of a silver-furred Rats-King fix on him.

Beyond, in the courtyard, a gargoyle-daemon leaves a human child, and fixes its amber gaze on the Rats.

'Sir.' He bowed stiffly to the man, noting the House of Salomon's ribbons on his overalls. 'You may find such talismans don't function now. All things change.'

The man protested. 'But you know her! The Master-Physician, White Crow. You *know* her.'

'I flatter myself that I have some influence in that quarter, it's true. Yes. Excuse me.' The Mayor put the Master Builder aside gently, weaving through the crowds towards the Rat-King. 'In case things don't *all* change, I have to discuss the repeal of a few local by-laws.'

Lucas walked by the food-booths in the Temple grounds, letting his feet carry him without direction except that necessary to walk through the crowds. He knocked the elbow of a brown Rat, who turned with a curse and then shrugged her shoulders.

The White Crow walked with strangers and friends. He dogged her, at a distance. On one terrace he stopped, between great lead figures of sea-monsters spouting a fine spray of jets.

'Young Lucas.' A voice rumbled at his elbow.

'Piss off.' He looked sourly up at Casaubon.

'Is that any way for my page to speak to me?'

The fat man seated himself with his legs apart on a stone bench, mopping at his brow with a lace handkerchief. Sun glinted on his copper hair. One garter had come unravelled, and his silk stocking sagged down his immense calf.

'If I *were* your page . . . ' The Prince of Candover sighed, crossing to the bench and kneeling down. He tugged the fat man's stocking up and tied the garter in a flamboyant bow below the knee. 'I'd quit. You're impossible!'

Casaubon rested his elbows on his knees, and his chins on his hands; face peering out from among the froth of white lace cuffs. 'Is *that* any way to speak to your prospective cousin-in-law?'

'What?'

489

Without lifting his head, the fat man nodded. Lucas stared down past the nereid fountains to the lawns.

A small man in Candovard formal doublet, his hair grizzled black and white, stood holding both a woman's hands in his. The woman, plump and swathed in orange robes, was recognizable from Vanringham's broadsheet photographs: the bird magus, Lady Luka. She said something, her face shining; and the Candovard Ambassador flung his arms around her, burying his face in her neck.

Lucas breathed: 'Andaluz . . . ?'

'He may not have any *magia*; but, then, my lady mother has all the political sense of a sparrow. They suit extremely. So. Your uncle, my mother; I'm her son, that makes us cousins *de facto*—'

'Oh no!' Lucas groaned.

In tones of great hurt, the Lord-Architect remarked: '*I* think they make a very nice couple.'

'I . . . you . . . ' He turned back to the terrace. The White Crow moved among velvet-clad Rat-Lords, and masons in silk overalls. 'It's just . . . it's just too much!'

The Lord-Architect patted Lucas carefully on the shoulder. For once he said nothing at all.

White sea-mist cools the flanks of the Thirty-Sixth Decan, wading in the heat-haze between city and garden.

Sun blasts Her ochre bricks pale, dazzles from roses that trail in Her wake; is dimmed only by the brilliance of Her eyes. Her cowled head lifts.

In the heat-soaked summer sky, Erou, Ninth Decan, Lord of Time and Gathering, shadows Her with white marble wings. His muscled body slides the air, angel-wings feathering horizon to horizon, and He smiles, meeting Her gaze.

Particles, electrons, strings, weak forces: Their pulse beats with the Dance.

In the middle air, a small and sharp *crack*! sounds.

Pale in the sun, a premature celebratory firework scatters green sparks across the sky.

*   ★   ★

Lucas craned his neck, watching through the garden's trees the thin trail of smoke over the rotunda. No further explosions sounded.

A tall man in dockside gear called: 'You the Prince?'

He left Rafi of Adocentyn and the other students to impressing young Entered Apprentices, and loped across the grass.

'I'm Lucas.'

'Met a woman. She lookin' for you.'

A hard pulse hit him under the ribs. Lucas nodded.

'She say her ship just got into Fourteenth District harbour,' the man observed. 'Calls herself Princess Gerima of the White Mountains, Gerima of Candover?'

Outside the rotunda, the White Crow paces a colonnade between tiny mirror screens, set in vast ornate metal frameworks. Like the congeries of bubbles in the demolished Fane-in-the-Twelfth-District, the screens glowed pale blue.

She pauses to stare into them, seeing scenes of revelry in other Districts. Down by the factories, and in the docks. Across the estuary, up in the high hills, and far across the continent to all points of the compass . . .

The White Crow looks into an oval screen. Swirling iron petals cup it. The image shows humans and Rats together at a banquet on Seventeenth District's beach, so far to the east that the sun's light has faded, and they revel by torches and pastel light-spheres and the rising glow of the moon.

She fists her hands, stretching her arms up in the afternoon heat; bones and muscles creaking. The sun dazzles in her red-brown eyes.

Her mouth moves in a quiet smile, feeling a gaze resting on her back.

The black-browed woman caught up her formal gown, lifting the hem as she raced up the terrace steps to Lucas and hugged him.

491

'I didn't know what was happening when we arrived; three days out from land the portents started, and such sudden miracles seen at sea! But you're safe. You're safe.' Gerima drew breath, pale face flushed under dark curls. 'Tell me. Which is she?'

'Over there. In white.'

'Her? I thought she'd be . . . younger.'

Lucas moved out of his sister's embrace, rubbing the back of his sweating neck. He looked from Gerima to the Scholar-Soldier further down the terrace. 'I don't care if you don't like her!'

Gerima smiled at the red-haired woman.

'Like her? But I met her while I was looking for you; she's the magus who was in the Fane! But that's wonderful! When you (gods forbid) inherit the throne from father, what better to have as a queen than a woman with *magia*?'

She put her short curls back from her face, features sharpening with concentration.

'If you're serious, we can have the wedding later this year. Father will take you out of the university. You ought to give him at least one grandchild before you leave White Mountains again. Don't you think? And she could teach at the University of the White Mountain while we train her in statecraft . . . What's the matter, Lu?'

The Prince of Candover pulled down his knotted handkerchief and wiped his forehead, his head turning uneasily between his sister and the White Crow. He opened and shut his mouth several times.

'Maybe', he said at last, 'we should think about this.'

The Princess Gerima of Candover, passing by the Master-Physician White Crow, concluded their earlier and longer conversation with a short wink.

Mid-afternoon drowses; long, lingering, with somewhere the scent of fresh-cut grass.

'It's a climate of miracles now . . .' Theodoret touched

a blunt finger to the White Crow's temple, and the chick-soft down growing there. 'All these people are thinking that tonight is for rejoicing and tomorrow for putting the world back together. But it'll be a different world when they do.'

'They know it.'

The White Crow reached down and scratched in the ruff of a silver timber wolf. The wolf scrabbled in the soft earth at the edge of the flower-bed, nosing a bone to the surface, and trotted off with it in its jaws.

'Scholar-Soldier, are you waiting for the moon?' Bishop Theodoret asked. 'To see what might be written on it?'

She opened her mouth to reply and stayed silent.

The Decan of Noon and Midnight, afternoon sunlight soft on sandstone and gold flanks, paced between flower-beds and fountains. The tusked and fanged muzzle lowered, moving in the ancient smile. Where He passed, people stopped their talk and knelt on the cool grass. The White Crow smelt stone-dust, and the distant burning of candles.

Theodoret's face creased into a smile. 'The man will catch up with you sooner or later. Heart of the Woods! Talk to him, lady, and then I can stop avoiding him in your company. I have somewhat of a desire to speak with your architect-magus.'

A gargoyle-daemon whirled leathery wings, roosting on a balustrade; cawing something softly to a man who stood beside her and did not kneel to the Decan of Noon and Midnight. One Rat in red satin folded his arms insouciantly and stared at the sky. A little distance away, young Entered Apprentices continued their dancing.

The Spagyrus touched His lips to the fountain, raised His head, passing on. The White Crow scooped her hand in and tasted, lips numbed with heavy red wine.

'Who knows *what* may happen?' She grinned. 'My lord Bishop, I think we should have another drink, before they dispose of the lot.'

'Not much chance of that, I would have thought.'

The White Crow gazed down into the gardens, at men and women and Rats. 'Don't bet on it. Some of this lot could out-drink a miracle, no problem.'

In a further garden, Captain-General Desaguliers swept his plush cloak back with ringed fingers. Medal-ribbons fluttered. The white ostrich plumes in his silver head-band curved up in a fan, one dipping to brush his lean jaw, almost blinding him. The jewelled harness of his sword clanked as he walked.

'Well, now . . .'

He gestured expansively. Four Cadets walked with him, each similarly overdressed; the tallest – a sleek black Rat – stumbling over the hem of her cloak from time to time. Desaguliers belched. He leaned heavily on the shoulder of the gargoyle-daemon.

'I think we should serioushly talk . . .'

'I agree.' The harsh caw, muted now, didn't carry further than this corner of the garden. The elderly acolyte-daemon waddled on clawed feet across the grass, her shabby wings pulled cloak-like around her shoulders. Her claw-tipped fingers clasped each other across her flaking breast as if she prayed. 'Messire Captain-General, I offer no apologies for what we were before—'

'No, no. 'Course not. Victims of circumstances. Superior orders,' he said owlishly, bead-black eyes widening.

'Had we been otherwise then . . .'

Desaguliers pushed himself upright, halting the gargoyle-daemon with a pressure of his furred arm. He laid his snout across her shoulder, crumpling his ear against her beaked head, and pointed with his free hand.

'See them? Tha's his Majesty the *King*. Just needs a little looking after, is all. Going to call a meeting, me and the Lords Magi 'n' others, form a Senate.' He stopped, puzzled. 'That isn't what I was going to tell you. What was I going to tell you?'

The gargoyle-daemon's body shifted under his arm as he felt her draw in a long breath.

'What *was* it, messire?'

In a rather less slurred tone than he had been affecting for the past few minutes, the Captain-General put his mouth so close to her that his incisors rubbed her small round ear, and said: 'Lot to worry us now. These rabble peasants will want things their own way. 'N' your people, too. Got to make sure we can come to arrangements. Sensible arrangements.'

'Exempli gratia?'

The black Rat's whiskers quivered. He blinked. 'Oh. Yes. For example, we – the new Senate – we keep his Majesty in order. And you, you tell us about *your* masters.'

'Who are no longer our masters.' The gargoyle head turned to follow the passing of a Decan's shadow in the sunlit air. Desaguliers prodded the air with one dark finger.

' 'Zactly! We got the King sewn up. *You* keep us posted on the Divine Ones. Well, then! Elbow-room for everybody. Then we'll set about the peasants.'

He snatched a goblet of wine from the tall black Rat. The gargoyle-daemon's clawed wing unfurled, and her fingers reached out and gripped the metal, indenting it. Desaguliers stood, arms hanging at his sides, amazement on his lean scarred face. The daemon, wine spilling, none the less got most of the goblet's contents into her beaked mouth.

'Urp!' She scratched at her flaking brown-furred dugs. 'Outwit the Divine Ones? While they dwell amongst us, out in the world? Well . . . *urp* . . . who knows? We might do it at that . . . '

The cover of the sewer stood open.

Zar-bettu-zekigal picked the petals from an ox-eye daisy and let them fall, one at a time, into the darkness.

She listens: hears no yawping laughter, that hyena-hysteria quieted now. Hears no rush of waves upon hot and mist-drenched shores. No immensurate wings.

Now she is still, only the dappled-furred tail twitching; straining to hear in the foundations of the world the Serpent-headed Night Council. Below her bare feet is silence and a hot pregnant blackness.

For lack of a grave to put it on, she throws the ravaged flower down into the dark.

Lights hovered in the air, globes of pale fire, unsupported. They dotted the gardens, transparent against the long evening light. Now that the sun sat on the aust-westerly horizon, their pastel colours began to glow.

The lights clung to the pillars and dome of the open rotunda, shining down on a chequerboard floor of ash and ebony. Couples moved in wild measures, coats and robes rustling; music chimed.

Surrounded by questioners, the White Crow stood at the edge of the open-air dance-floor. With one hand she gestured, answering a tall brown Rat's question; the other held a spray of cherries that she bit into, nodding and listening.

Zar-bettu-zekigal elbowed through the crowd until she got to the Lord-Architect.

'Ei, you!'

The Lord-Architect turned on one two-inch heel, the satin skirts of his frock-coat swirling. Dirty silk breeches strained over his thighs and belly, failing to button; and leaving some inches' gap between themselves and a shirt black with machine-oil.

'There you are!' A delighted smile spread over his face. He took her hand in gloved fingers and bowed over it. His copper-red hair had been scraped together at the back, and a tiny tuft tied with a black velvet string. 'Honour to you, Kings' Memory.'

'Care to dance?' she said.

'My honour, lady.'

Zar-bettu-zekigal touched the fingers of her left hand to the Lord-Architect's arm, resting them on the twelve-inch turned-back cuff's silver braid; rested her other hand in

496

his; hooked her tufted tail over her elbow, and stepped out into a waltz. Someone called her name, and she grinned, hearing a scatter of applause.

'I heard about the Chemicall Labyrinth. So that's what those machines were for! Damn, I wish I'd seen it!'

The Lord-Architect lumbered gracefully into a turn, narrowly missing a Rat in mauve silk. 'I adapted the little priest's design.'

'If not for him and his Majesty, there wouldn't have been a plague. But then, if not for him, it wouldn't have stopped. I *wish* he could have been here.'

They swung close to a pillar. Looming by it, some eight feet high and with night wings furled about his shoulders, an acolyte-daemon gazed with yellow eyes at the dancing. She smelt his cold breath.

'H'm. A little uncouth, perhaps,' the Lord-Architect admitted. 'But, then, they'll have had little experience of this sort of thing . . .'

Zar-bettu-zekigal nodded to Elish-hakku-zekigal in the crowd as she danced by; and lifted her head again to the Lord-Architect.

'I've been talking to your lady. She's not bad, y'know? I should have got to know her while she was in Carver Street. Don't suppose I'll get the chance now.'

China-blue eyes looked down at her.

'You suspect her on her way to Candover?'

'Oh, what! Don't you?'

The gentle pressure of his fingers steered her towards the edge of the dance-floor. Sunset put the long shadows of the pillars across the dancers.

'I'm going to take steps,' he announced.

Somewhere between affection and cynicism, Zar-bettu-zekigal demanded: '*What* steps?'

The fat man looked puzzled for a few seconds. 'Perhaps . . . Yes! Perhaps I should finish my poem?'

'What p—?'

Zar-bettu-zekigal stared after him as he walked away. '*Poem?*'

A hand tapped her shoulder. She glanced back. Resplendent in sky-blue and iris-yellow satin, Mistress Evelian of Carver Street smiled down at her.

'You left owing me rent— *Oof!*'

'I'm so glad to see you!' Zar-bettu-zekigal hugged the woman harder.

Evelian settled her puffed ribbon-decorated sleeves, tugging her bodice down over her full breasts.

'And I you. Zaribeth, don't be heartsore for too long.' She flicked the Katayan girl's cheek with her finger. 'I want to see you happy.'

Away from the dancing-floor, the Lord-Architect Casaubon felt absently through the outside left-hand pocket of his stained blue satin frock-coat, then the right-hand pocket; and finally abandoned them both and investigated an inside breast-pocket. From this, he brought out a large speckled goose-egg.

'For a member of the Invisible College,' he remarked, 'you seem to be remarkably visible.'

The White Crow, sitting at the end of the abandoned banqueting-tablet, shrugged. 'I wasn't planning on staying here anyway.'

He tapped the goose-egg against the marble buttock of a *putti* on the nearest balustrade, a delicate and economical movement that knocked off the top of the shell. Egg-white ran down his plump fingers.

'*I'll* cheer you up . . .'

He lifted the shell to his mouth, tipping it as he threw his head back. She watched in awed fascination as his throat moved, swallowing.

'I have a present for you!'

He belched, wiping his mouth with the back of his fat hand, and dropped the now-empty egg-shell. He looked down over his swelling chest and belly at the rose-haired woman.

The White Crow folded her arms and glared up at him in exasperation.

'A present. OK, I'll buy it. What present?'

The Lord-Architect, satisfied, leaned back against the marble balustrade. She heard a quiet but distinct pop. The Lord-Architect heaved himself off the stone, and put his hand into the satin coat's tail-pocket.

He brought out a handful of crushed shell, his fingers dripping egg-white and egg-yolk.

'*Knew* I had another one somewhere,' he observed, picking off the shell and licking his fingers. 'Now . . .'

The White Crow put her head in her hands and groaned.

With his moderately clean hand, the Lord-Architect Casaubon reached into his buttoned-back cuff and pulled out a folded sheet of paper.

'It's a poem. For you. I wrote it.'

He swept the skirts of his coat back in a magnificent formal bow, beamed vaguely, and wandered away down the terrace. The White Crow rested the folded sweat-stained paper against her lips. Dark red brows dipped.

'You don't fool *me* . . .'

She stared at his departing back.

' . . . not for a minute.'

The carved limestone balustrade pressed hard against her hip-bones. Zar-bettu-zekigal leaned over, shading her eyes against the level sun. Day's heat beat up from the stone. She shrugged the black greatcoat more firmly about her thin shoulders, wrapping it across her chest.

She watched the red-headed woman walk away down the lower terraces towards the fountains and flower-beds, a paper clutched in her left hand.

A voice spoke acidly behind Zar-bettu-zekigal: 'Yes: the eminent Master-Physician. I perceive, as our poet says, that there is an upstart crow amongst us – "a player's heart, wrapped in a tiger's hide" . . .'

'Tiger's heart wrapped in a woman's hide!' Zari corrected automatically.

And spun on her heel fast enough to stumble.

A very large brown Rat wheeled a chair to a halt on

the gravelled terrace. In the wheelchair sat a stooped and frail black Rat, his fur grizzled to grey, and white about his muzzle. A healed scar marked his upper lip above the incisor.

His body reclined half-drowned in the emerald silk and white lace of the Cardinal-General of Guiry's robes. He lifted yellow-cataracted alert eyes to her face.

'Messire . . . ?' Her voice cracked. 'Charnay! Messire Plessiez, you . . . Oh, messire, it *is* you!'

She flung herself down beside the chair, throwing her arms around him, burying her face in the warm silk and fur. Gravel scarred her knees. His shaking hand stroked the back of her head. Long fingers unsteady, chill. She sat back on her heels, feeling his fragility; her eyes wide.

'Messire, how . . . ? *Is* it you?'

'Charnay, you may go and gladden your heart by getting drunk.'

'Yes, messire!'

'While I talk with Mistress Zari. Apparently I have things to tell her.'

Charnay grinned and slapped Zar-bettu-zekigal's shoulder as she passed. Long-shadowed, she loped down the steps to the lower terrace, scarlet cloak flying; swaggering towards a group of Cadets, lithe young male Rats. Within a few seconds she sprawled at one of their benches, bottle in one hand, and with the other pulling the most drunken of the male Rats onto her knee, her tail waving cheerfully in the air.

'Zari.'

The black Rat gripped the chair's arms and, with effort, stood. His gown rustled against her cheek. She stared up. Age left him sharp, fragile, acute. Abruptly she scrambled to her feet and offered her arm.

He rested weight on it as he walked along the terrace, favouring his right leg. She breathed, dizzy, the warmth of his body, the odour of his fur; all the fragile lilac scents of age. She glanced back. Beside hers, his shadow ran stoop-shouldered and long on the gravel path.

'You will be told all, Kings' Memory, never fear. Somehow one never seems to keep anything from you.'

Awed, she looked up into his gaunt face. Of the sleek duellist, the sharp priest, only echoes remain in that flesh. She wound her dapple-furred tail anxiously about her ankle as she walked.

'You *died*, messire. Elish saw you.'

'Such an accusatory tone!' His sardonic marvelling broke in a shallow cough. The Cardinal-General lowered his lean muzzle. She followed his gaze. To the green sash that, under the open greatcoat, she wore as a scarf.

'But how!'

'You ask me that, in this world of Divinity run riot?'

As if some wing brushes between him and the sunset, Plessiez is dazed with a momentary awe.

'The past later. Other matters first, I think; concerning the future, whatever shape that may or now may not hold—'

He broke off.

'I am asking you this very badly.'

'So far, messire, you're not asking me anything at all.'

A wheezy chuckle escaped him. He looked back to the interior of the New Temple, where a table composed of Lords Magi, the District's master builders, and two former acolyte daemons settled down to banquet. Zarbettu-zekigal paused as he did.

He spoke without looking at her.

'I ask you to leave your university training. Oh, continue it if it pleases you, but you scarcely need it; Memories like you come once in a generation. Leave. Leave and be my Memory now, for what years of work are left to me.'

Her thin lips quivered. A little hoarsely, she said: 'I like the plea for sympathy, messire.'

Plessiez's delicate fingers closed over her arm. She opened her mouth hurriedly, falling over syllables, and he halted her with a smile.

'Walk with me. Don't answer yet. I'll answer your questions, and tell you what use I put my lost years to

501

'– and whether I had sooner died than lost them.'

Zar-bettu-zekigal frowned.

Plessiez continued his slow pacing; a thin and fragile black Rat in silk robes and lace, an emerald-studded *ankh* nestling at his collar. His clouded dark eyes blinked.

'I could lie to you. No other lives who knows the truth except myself. And the Decans, one supposes, who know all. I would sooner tell you now than have you discover it later. I must tell you how the Lady Hyena came to die – came to be murdered. And then make your answer to my request, if you will.'

The young Katayan woman loosed his arm and moved a pace ahead.

Hot and level sun blazed in her eyes. In the arch of the sky, the first stars showed. Scents of roses and cooking-oil drifted up from the gardens and courtyards.

His voice finished:

' . . . and that is what happened. I can tell you no more.'

He waited. She turned.

'Messire!'

All condemnation, all solemnity burned out of her by a fierce joy; grinning widely, fists on her hips, greatcoat swinging open as she moved. The sunset light blazes her shadow long across the terrace, as in future years their influence will cast a bright shadow on the city.

Gracefully and with dignity, she dipped one knee to the gravel terrace, taking the black Rat's hand and kissing the ring of the Cardinal-General of Guiry.

Plessiez snatched her to her feet, holding both her hands tight in his; long jaw tight with repressed emotion.

'Oh, see you, messire; and I thought age was supposed to make people reform!'

The black Rat recovered himself enough to smile sardonically. The Katayan woman linked her arm in his, walking slowly, giving him all of her strength that he needed for support.

*   *   *

Black bees throng, swarming in the flowers that weigh down the city's gutters, blossom from ships' masts in the harbour. Their noise is all heat, all summer, all dusty sunset days.

The Decan of Noon and Midnight, Lord of the Spagyric Art, turns His face to the setting sun. The ancient smile widens. At His feet, children play in the Temple's spouting fountains, shrill cries undaunted, not yet called in to bed.

Sunset glared from ivory-and-gold statues, from the rippling water of the ornamental lake, and from the bright flowers of the formal gardens.

'Damn.' The White Crow leaned forward and bit into the hot vegetable-roll she carried. She spilled grease on to the gravel and her borrowed shirt and breeches. 'Ah, I'm still not used to this. Arms and legs and things . . . '

'That's what you get', the Bishop of the Trees observed, 'for being given the bird.'

She shied a lump of pastry past Theodoret. It ricocheted off the back of his marble bench, fragmenting. Ducks from the ornamental lake squarked and pecked it up.

'But, you see . . . '

Candia, insouciant in buff leather and scarlet silk, arranged empty wine-bottles along the edge of the lake. His blond hair flopped forward. As he set the first of a handful of long-stemmed rockets in the bottles, he completed: ' . . . I know why that happened to her.'

The red-headed woman's eyes narrowed.

'Go on.'

'Obviously, because it's always quicker as the crow flies.'

'*Can*dia!'

Unrepentant, the Reverend Master grinned at the Bishop. Theodoret, on the bench, linked his hands across his stomach. 'Therefore, as you might say, she decided to wing it . . . '

'One of you is a man of the cloth,' the woman observed,

503

'and the other doubtless recovering from the shock of recent events, *otherwise*—'

'At least', Theodoret added, 'she got me off the hook.'

The White Crow bit into her vegetable-roll again, glared at the Bishop, and observed through a mouthful of pastry: 'That's what you get for being stuck up!'

Candia squatted, removing a tinder-box from his breeches-pocket. 'Who says you can't play dice with the universe?'

'Aaw!'

Candia chuckled. 'Something the matter with her?'

The White Crow licked grease from her fingers. She stood up. Inside the breast of her shirt, a folded paper rustled, scratching the skin as memory scratches at peace of mind.

'You two deserve each other,' she said. 'I might come back when you're being sensible.'

Candia struck flint. Theodoret inclined his head graciously at the White Crow's departing back, and then jumped as the rocket hissed skyward.

Softly explosive, pale against the still-bright sky, the first of Reverend Master Candia's fireworks exploded in a shower of red sparks.

Gas-lamps gleamed. The sky above glowed almost a pale mauve, the sun sitting on the horizon, heat still soaking from the stones. Stars shone in the top of the sky.

The White Crow walked by the canal, and the Arch of Days, holding the stained paper up to the level sunset light.

Her lips moved as she read, silently testing the words:

> 'You are a banquet for a starving man,
>   All sweet savouries in your flesh presented.
> Of this food I offer you the plan
>   Anatomized and elemented:
>   Freckle-sugar-dusted thighs
>   Cool and cream-smooth: enterprise
>   The drinking of these syllabub sighs;

This table laid out in the candle's flicker
Garnished with sweat's tang and the body's liquor.

'Lady, your dish delights the tongue:
    Hot crevices and subtle flavours.
I taste your breasts, your skin: undone,
    Abandoned, gluttonous, to your savours.
        Such intricate conceits demand
        A Paradox. You understand:
        I sit to feast, and yet I stand.
Save that, for me, for this one time at least,
I would not come unbidden to the feast.

'Such banquets, self-consumed in mutual pleasure,
    Display a goddess' skill in their erection:
Giving, receiving; both in equal measure
    Of which I'm expert to detect perfection.
        But this feast her own guest invites,
        None may enjoy without those rights,
        So I go hungry from delights.
Lady, I love you: I leave love behind me:
Or, if you love me, follow me, and find me.'

Elish-hakku-zekigal, finding her silk coat knotted in the
red-headed woman's fist, pointed away from the New
Temple in bewilderment.

'The Lord-Architect that Zar keeps talking about? He
left. No, I don't know where. If you look, Scholar-Soldier,
you'll see the moon is marked in blood. A signal.'

The woman let go of her coat, scowling.

'Damn, the Invisible College can be *any*where!'

'I remember once he spoke to Zar of a city he built as
Lord-Architect. Would he return there?'

The White Crow abruptly grinned.

'No . . . Thank you; but I've just worked it out. It
doesn't matter where he's planning to go from here – I
know where he'll be *before* he leaves.'

      ★   ★   ★

Clock-mill strikes the hour in Carver Street. Wheezing metal machinery clangs.

She does not even pause to see how sun, moon and star-constellations on the dial are different now.

She kicked the door without knocking and entered his room.

The Lord-Architect Casaubon sat in the iron claw-footed bath. She saw very little water: his bare knees, elbows and stomach jammed together to take up almost all the room. He looked up as she came in, eased himself a little, and brought the soap up from a lap invisible beneath bubbles.

'Yes?' Innocent blue eyes, under a draggled mop of copper-gold hair.

'I want to talk to you.'

The White Crow pushed the door shut behind her without looking, and slid the lock-bar across.

'I'm hardly at my best,' the Lord-Architect complained.

Amusement tugged up the corners of her mouth. 'It's how I remember you.'

She padded across the floorboards. Patches of sun falling in at the window made the wood painfully hot under the bare soles of her feet. A scent of herbs came from the stacked crates, and the less identifiable scents of wax and perfume and badly cured parchments.

The Lord-Architect gripped both sides of the bath, hoisted himself up an inch, and slipped back. Water slopped up, splattered on the floorboards. The White Crow stepped back, laughing. Casaubon folded his massive arms across his pink stomach, with an air of injured dignity. The soap slid down his chest and plopped into the water between his legs.

'Talk to me about *what*?' he demanded, irritable.

'Poetry!'

She covered her mouth with one fisted hand, looking at him for a minute over her knuckles.

'Too easy,' she said. 'You're the same and I'm the same

– we're *not*, but somehow we've grown in the same way. It's as if I'd never left.'

The Lord-Architect Casaubon looked up at her loftily. He flicked water from cushioned fingers and held out a demanding hand. The White Crow grabbed his hand, heaving to help him from the bath.

Her heels skidded on the floorboards, his hand wrapped around her wrist and pulled. The White Crow swore, startled, sprawled face down across his chest, and slid to sit in his lap and six inches of soapy water. The Lord-Architect let go of her hand, and bent a painful inch forward to kiss her, bird-delicate, on the lips.

'Shit-damned-cretinous-moronic—!'

She slumped back against his thighs and knees: padded as pillows. One of her heels skidded for purchase on the boards, but obtained no balance. She sat back in the hot soapy water.

'You might as well', Casaubon said, 'have a bath while you're here?'

'*Cas*aubon . . . !'

The White Crow pushed flattened fingers through the tiny copper curls on his chest. She shook her head. Reaching his cheek, she patted twice, hard enough to sting. He sat very still, arms hanging out of the sides of the bath.

'I can't be here any longer' – he made a sideways movement of the head that took in the city called the heart of the world – 'and not touch you.'

His large hands came up, moving delicately as watch-maker's fingers to unbutton her wet shirt.

The White Crow drew his head forward to her breasts.

THE END

Short Bibliography

ACKERMAN, James S., *Palladio* (Penguin, 1966).

ANDERSON, William, *The Rise of the Gothic* (Hutchinson, 1985).

BARTON, Anne, *Ben Jonson, Dramatist* (Cambridge University Press, 1984).

BUDGE, Wallis, *Egyptian Magic* (Kegan Paul, Trench, Trübner, 1899).

DAVIES, Natalie Zemon, *Society and Culture in Early Modern France*, Polity Press edn (1975).

EVANS, E. P., *The Criminal Prosecution and Capital Punishment of Animals* (William Heinemann, 1906).

FRENCH, John, *John Dee* (Routledge & Kegan Paul, 1972).

GARSTIN , E. J. Langford (ed.), *The Rosicrucian Secrets: Dr John Dee* (Aquarian Press, 1985).

HONOUR, Hugh, *Neo-Classicism* (Penguin, 1977).

HORNE, Alexander, *King Solomon's Temple in the Masonic Tradition* (Aquarian Press, 1972).

McINTOSH, Christopher, *The Rosicrucians*.

—, *The Rosy Cross Unveiled* (Aquarian Press, 1980).

McNEILL, William H., *Plagues and Peoples* (Penguin, 1976).

MUMFORD, Lewis, *The City in History* (Penguin, 1961).

SCOTT, Walter, *Hermetica*, Vol. 1 (Boston, Mass.: Shambala, 1985).

SEZNEC, Jean, *The Survival of the Pagan Gods* (Princeton, NJ: Princeton University Press, 1940).

SHEARMAN, John, *Mannerism* (Penguin, 1967).

STRONG, Roy, *The Renaissance Garden in England* (Thames & Hudson, 1979).

VITRUVIUS, *The Ten Books on Architecture,* trans. Morris Hicky Morgan (New York: Dover Publications, 1914).

YATES, Frances, *Giordano Bruno and the Hermetic Tradition* (Routledge & Kegan Paul, 1964).

—, *The Occult Philosophy in the Elizabethan Age* (Routledge & Kegan Paul, 1979).

—, *The Rosicrucian Enlightenment* (Routledge & Kegan Paul, 1972).

—, *Theatre of the World* (Routledge & Kegan Paul, 1969).

THE ARCHITECTURE OF DESIRE
by Mary Gentle

They have come home now: Lord-Architect Casaubon, and
Valentine, called White Crow. Home for Valentine is the
rambling manor house she abandoned fifteen years ago to
pursue the ways of *magia*. But home – as she and her family are
about to discover – home is not safe. Mercenaries in lace and
steel roam the countryside. Valentine has more than the
necessary *magia* to defend Roseveare House from their swords
and muskets – but not from the news that their captain,
Pollexfen Clamady, brings to his old friend Baltazar Casaubon.
Casaubon is needed to solve the mystery of why the eye of the
sun – the new domed temple being built in the City of London
– is cursed and unbuildable.

To London, then. Above the bridge, the impaled heads of
criminals whisper a recitation of their crimes. In city cellars the
astrologers of Royalist and Protectorate factions meet. In
Queen Carola's poverty-stricken palace of Westminster, and
the Protector-General Olivia's garrison Tower of London,
conspiracies and coups begin.

And into all of their lives now comes the catalyst: the Puritan
girl Desire-of-the-Lord Guillaime, bringing a private message
from the Protector-General to Valentine. Desire will travel with
them; Desire will haunt Valentine's steps wherever she goes.
Against the background of a winter amnesty, under the shadow
of the hangman's rope, the shifting relationships of these people
play themselves out.

From the highly acclaimed author of *Rats and Gargoyles*, *The
Architecture of Desire* is comedy and tragedy both; a story about
love, and rape, and the price of everything.

Available now in Bantam Press hardback.

0593 01952 0

A SELECTED LIST OF FANTASY TITLES FROM CORGI BOOKS

THE PRICES SHOWN BELOW WERE CORRECT AT THE TIME OF GOING TO PRESS. HOWEVER TRANSWORLD PUBLISHERS RESERVE THE RIGHT TO SHOW NEW RETAIL PRICES ON COVERS WHICH MAY DIFFER FROM THOSE PREVIOUSLY ADVERTISED IN THE TEXT OR ELSEWHERE.

☐	12566 0	**THE WIZARDS AND THE WARRIORS**	*Hugh Cook*	£3.99
☐	13130 X	**THE WORDSMITHS AND THE WARGUILD**		£3.99
☐	05930 19520	**THE ARCHITECTURE OF DESIRE** (hardback)		
			Mary Gentle	£12.99
☐	13661 1	**THE DOOR INTO FIRE**	*Diane Duane*	£3.99
☐	12679 9	**MASTER OF THE FIVE MAGICS**	*Lyndon Hardy*	£3.99
☐	12680 2	**SECRET OF THE SIXTH MAGIC**		£2.95
☐	13440 6	**RIDDLE OF THE SEVEN REALMS**		£3.99
☐	13400 7	**THE STORY OF THE STONE**	*Barry Hughart*	£2.99
☐	12646 2	**BRIDGE OF BIRDS**		£2.99
☐	13295 0	**THE AWAKENERS**	*Sheri S Tepper*	£3.99
☐	13419 8	**THE GATE TO WOMEN'S COUNTRY**		£3.99
☐	13540 2	**GRASS**		£4.99
☐	12620 9	**THE TRUE GAME**		£3.99
☐	13221 7	**THE COMING OF THE KING**	*Nikolai Tolstoy*	£4.99
☐	13101 6	**SERVANTS OF ARK I: THE FIRST NAMED**		
			Jonathan Wylie	£3.99
☐	13134 2	**SERVANTS OF ARK II: THE CENTRE OF THE CIRCLE**		£3.50
☐	13161 X	**SERVANTS OF ARK III: THE MAGE-BORN CHILD**		£3.50
☐	13416 3	**THE UNBALANCED EARTH 1: DREAMS OF STONE**		£3.50
☐	13417 1	**THE UNBALANCED EARTH 2: THE LIGHTLESS KINGDOM**		£2.99
☐	13418 X	**THE UNBALANCED EARTH 3: THE AGE OF CHAOS**		£3.50

All Corgi/Bantam books are available at your bookshops or newsagents, or can be ordered from the following address:

Corgi/Bantam Books,
Cash Sales Department,
P.O. Box 11, Falmouth, Cornwall TR10 9EN

Please send a cheque or postal order, (no currency) and allow 80p for postage and packing for the first book plus 20p for each additional book ordered up to a maximum charge of £2.00 in UK.

B.F.P.O. customers please allow 80p for the first book and 20p for each additional book.

Overseas customers, including Eire, please allow £1.50 for postage and packing for the first book, £1.00 for the second, and 30p for each subsequent title ordered.

NAME (Block Letters) ....

ADDRESS ....

....